ALLEN STROUD

FEARLESS

This is a **FLAME TREE PRESS** book

Text copyright © 2020 Allen Stroud

FLAME TREE PRESS
6 Melbray Mews, London, SW6 3NS, UK
flametreepress.com

US sales, distribution and warehouse:
Simon & Schuster
simonandschuster.biz

UK distribution and warehouse:
Marston Book Services Ltd
marston.co.uk

Publisher's Note: This is a work of fiction. Names, characters, places, and
incidents are a product of the author's imagination. Locales and public names
are sometimes used for atmospheric purposes. Any resemblance to actual
people, living or dead, or to businesses, companies, events, institutions, or
locales is completely coincidental.

Thanks to the Flame Tree Press team, including:
Taylor Bentley, Frances Bodiam, Federica Ciaravella, Don D'Auria,
Chris Herbert, Josie Karani, Molly Rosevear, Will Rough, Mike Spender,
Cat Taylor, Maria Tissot, Nick Wells, Gillian Whitaker.

The cover is created by Flame Tree Studio with
thanks to Nik Keevil and Shutterstock.com.
The font families used are Avenir and Bembo.

Flame Tree Press is an imprint of Flame Tree Publishing Ltd
flametreepublishing.com

A copy of the CIP data for this book is available from the British Library
and the Library of Congress.

HB ISBN: 978-1-78758-542-3
US PB ISBN: 978-1-78758-540-9
UK PB ISBN: 978-1-78758-541-6
ebook ISBN: 978-1-78758-544-7

Printed and bound in Great Britain by Clays Ltd, Elcograf S.p.A.

ALLEN STROUD

FEARLESS

FLAME TREE PRESS
London & New York

PROLOGUE

1969

Here follows a restricted memoir extract from an unnamed mission controller of the Apollo 10 mission during its journey around the Moon. This document remains classified, despite the maximum information embargo (one hundred years) being exceeded. Any inquiry I have made about the reason for this has been stonewalled. Even now, I am only able to forward you this partial transcription. The redacted elements have been restored with a little guesswork.

All efforts to attribute the writing lead nowhere. None of the registered controllers on duty that day published stories of their experiences, and this document contradicts the official accounts of the astronauts and NASA at the time. The only thing that makes me consider that there's some sort of truth to it is that it remains restricted and the identity of the author is still classified. If there was nothing to this, why would the authorities continue to keep it back? Why not publish and call it out as lies?

★   ★   ★

The transmission occurred one hundred and two hours, twelve minutes into the mission. At this point, Apollo 10 was out of communication range on the far side of the Moon.

According to the debrief information, Commander Tom Stafford and lunar module pilot Gene Cernan were in the lunar module, callsign 'Snoopy', while command module pilot John Young was in the main spacecraft, 'Charlie Brown'. At that point, the two spacecraft were separated in a simulation of lunar liftoff. Each craft had its own transmitter.

Dialogue between the astronauts involved their operational tasks and a discussion about food. The communications were over a radio link between the two transmitters. On the recording, which was subsequently published, all three men complain of hearing a strange musical sound in the background of their radio comms. This matter was also raised when Apollo 10 returned to Earth and the team was debriefed.

A detailed spectrum analysis of the recorded conversation does reveal the sound as being present. However, it appears to be much quieter than the astronauts claimed in their interviews. After forty-eight hours, Stafford, Cernan and Young were all told that the noise was due to feedback between the two transmitters. Astronaut Young had, in fact, guessed that this was the cause and the explanation confirmed his theory. However, the three were reminded that the information remained classified and they should not discuss it when they were allowed to leave the base.

After they were gone, radio specialists continued to work on the recording. It had already been established that the frequency range for the signal did not match what would be expected for radio transmitter interference. Some speculative allowance was made for the lack of atmosphere and the effect of this on the 'waves', but simulations still did not match what had been recorded.

After this, further simulations were attempted, looking at the possibility of the transmitters being misaligned before the mission left Earth. However, this answer was also discounted as the signal only occurred during a short period while the spacecraft were on the dark side.

Six days later, copies of the recordings were requisitioned by several different military departments, and NASA's analysis team was instructed to abandon any further work on the matter. The 'interference' explanation was confirmed as being the official answer on the matter, and the case file closed.

I can't help but think that—

*   *   *

The classified extract ends here. The transcript of the Apollo 10 conversation was released thirty-nine years later in 2008, but the audio recording did not resurface until 2016, when it was published as part of a retrospective documentary. Subsequent interviews with other surviving Apollo mission astronauts revealed there were other incidents of similar noises being heard at different times during lunar missions. However, journalists collating these incidents were dismissed as pedalling alien conspiracy theories. There was a popular mythology being bandied around at the time that the Moon landings were faked. Both stories found audiences among the same counterculture online communities.

The retainer you put me on is now spent. If you want me to follow any of this up, you'll need to get in touch.

You have my number.

CHAPTER ONE
Shann

I was born in 2080, with no legs.

Perhaps that gives you an image of me? An image that defines who I am to you as a person? Maybe you get a sense of who someone is by their limitations? Do you think who we are is determined by what we look like? What we can't do? Or what we don't have?

The world doesn't work that way anymore.

"Captain to the bridge."

"On my way."

I open my eyes and reach up, grasping the steel bar above my bed. The straps holding me to the mattress fall away, and I float across the room to the door, which slides back with a faint hydraulic hiss as I reach it.

In the corridor, I'm gliding, pushing off with my hands and adjusting my momentum as and when I need to. Zero gravity is like flying, but it's easy to forget there's not a lot to slow you down before you crash into a wall or a person.

I love it.

My earliest memories as a child were being taken to a municipal swimming pool. I must have been four or five. For the first time, I could move freely, as fast or faster than anyone else. I can remember laughing and smiling constantly until my face hurt.

"Captain Ellisa Shann to the bridge, priority one. Captain Ellisa Shann…"

"I'm coming!"

The wall speakers won't quit repeating the call until I get there. There's good reason. The ship's crew will know I'm taking this route, that it's urgent, and they'll stay out of my way.

I reach the far end, slowing myself by running my hand along the wall rails. There's a ladder to the upper deck, and I propel myself that way, grabbing the rungs and pulling myself upward.

Although in space, it isn't really *up*; it's just a change of direction.

AD 2118. Humanity has colonised the Moon, Mars, Ceres and Europa. Asteroid mining is big business and the new joint venture of nations, corporations and entrepreneurs. No government can afford the investment alone, so private public partnerships are the route to the stars.

Out here, people are commodities, just like water, hydrogen fuel, oxygen and everything else that isn't vacuum. Humans in space are expensive. Everyone who gets up here has to earn their keep. In Fleet, we're all specialists, exceptionally skilled and committed to the work. There's plenty of downsides to this life, but I wouldn't want to be anywhere else.

Another panel slides back, and I've reached my destination.

"Captain on the bridge!"

This is my office. A wide room, with a wall of DuraGlas that slopes away to reveal the cold, dark vacuum outside. The ship's command crew are all here, at their posts, strapped into their chairs.

You never get used to that view. It's not like the old films, with a vista of stars and cloudlike nebulas. Those twinkling pinpricks of light disappear under the glare of the sun. Instead, you're looking at a deep, endless empty, unless something gets in the way of our star's dictatorial scrutiny.

In those moments, the stars come out to play and looking out the window is a real treat. The ribbon-like quality of the Milky Way, like a churning line of clouds in the night sky, is something you can only see from space. One for the tourists.

But not for us.

I've learned to love the emptiness. There's something serene and permanent about it. Occasionally, when we're at the farthest end of our run, the two views mix, and you might catch glimpses of silver powder, a little like seeing the moon on a cold winter's morning.

Jacobson is looking at me; he's turned his chair and he's half out of the straps, his hand raised in salute. He's big-boned, Swedish, in his midtwenties and on his first run. According to his Astro-Mathematics score, we lucked out in getting him, but he's still wet behind the ears.

"At ease, Ensign; just tell me what we've got."

"Automated distress signal from a freighter just outside our navigation plot. It's the *Hercules*. She's three days out of Phobos Station."

"Any details?"

"Not at the moment, but we're the nearest ship equipped to assist."

"Okay, have you calculated a course correction?"

"Looking at it now."

"Good. When you're done, signal them that we're on our way."

This is how we work. Most of our time is spent moving between spaces, operating computer systems, making decisions. Each time we choose, we're balancing the limited resources we have against a new need. In this case, a course alteration means a burn, using up fuel. A delay in making port at Ceres means breathing more oxygen, consuming more water and food.

But that's part of the job, part of the reason there's a solar system transit service.

The whole reason we're out here – to help.

In the maritime age, there were wars on the high seas. Merchant ships would struggle across the Atlantic with their wares, evading pirates, storms and all manner of hazards. Traders would invest in their cargo, gambling everything on the chance of making a fortune.

Out here, it's the same, but different. The dangers have changed, our technology has improved to cope, but we're no less vulnerable.

"Computation is done, Captain."

"Send the message."

"Aye, aye."

Our ship, the *Khidr*, was commissioned by the United Fleet Consortium of Earth – or Fleet to everyone who didn't design the plaque. There're six vessels like ours, patrolling the trade lanes, too few to make space safe, but enough to make a difference. On board, we have twenty-five skilled crew, including the command team. We can operate the ship in two shifts, with some redundancy in personnel and capacity. If we need to help someone, we may have to leave people on their ship, or rescue a stranded crew onto ours. Our job means we carry extra, just in case.

We're also armed. Personal firearms are kept in two arms lockers, while guided rockets and gas-powered projectile weapons are available for our use if necessary. There's even a close-range six-gigawatt laser. All the ship's weapons are the responsibility of Keiyho, our master-at-arms, who is currently sitting on the far side of the bridge.

Duggins and Le Garre make up the rest of the team on shift in here. Four manned consoles for navigation/communication, weapons/sensors, pilot and engineering.

The fifth seat is empty; that's mine. I push myself off from the doorframe and glide toward it.

"What else you got for me?" I ask. "You wouldn't have called me up just for a distress call and course correction."

Le Garre turns around in her chair. Her smile is a challenge. She's French, old-school Eurospace and a major in her country's air force – Major Angel Le Garre. Technically, that's a higher rank than mine, but she doesn't have the same time out of Earth's atmosphere. Could be she's after my job, but for now, she's our pilot. "Captain, we've requested the *Hercules*'s cargo. Her registered inventory has just come through."

"What's the issue?"

"I think you should take a look for yourself."

"Send it to my console with flags."

I pull myself into the vacant chair. I pluck the comms bead from my ear and tuck it into a pocket. The command screen on the tray table activates and strapping snakes out, enveloping me as I lower myself into the seat.

Every workstation is constructed to hold people in place, to protect our bodies against acceleration and deceleration, but we aren't solid objects; we're fleshy bags of liquid that rushes and slops around. The forces need to be absorbed. That's why there's give in the straps, pressure-sensitive cushioning on the seats and more. There are trays for limbs and torso that lock down when we're pulling high g's.

The only difference with me is that I have fewer limbs than some other people.

I could have legs. There are cybernetic units on board the ship for me to use when I need to be in a gravity environment. Medical technology on Earth can even grow matched DNA transplant limbs and organs should anyone need them. But there's a catch; the instability threshold that they discovered back in the twentieth century hasn't been conquered. Legs for five years that slowly degrade and create a whole new set of disease risks?

No thanks.

I mean, I can see why other people might want that, but up here there's no practical need. Going through all the surgical stress and post-op stuff for something that has no ambulatory benefit in my day-to-day life up here isn't something that appeals to me.

The file is in front of me now on the portable screen, as I settle into the seat. Le Garre has highlighted the relevant sections. I scroll through them, making a mental note of each anomaly.

"Why is so much of this blanked out?"

"That's what I wanted to discuss with you," Le Garre says in her soft accented voice. Her face appears on my screen alongside the report. Dark hair, dark eyes, a little half smile and a microphone bead just under her lip. I clip in my headphones and hear her words live and over the feed. "It's unusual."

"Yes, very unusual."

Freighters like the *Hercules* are run by corporate government partnerships. Many stations and colonies rely on water and oxygen restock, with the freighters shipping raw materials back the other way. That's normal business. Cargoes have to be registered, approved and made public, but certain items can get clearance above our grade. When that happens, the itinerary fills up with 'Consortium Sanction Granted' labels, which generally make our life difficult.

"Jacobson, notify Phobos Station that we'll need a full manifest, not this piece of shit. If anything on that ship is a possible hazard, I need to know about it."

"That'll take more than an hour, Captain," Jacobson says. "Should we hold off making the course correction?"

"No, we signal the crew and make the maneuver. We'll do the job either way, but any more information we can get will help."

"Aye, aye."

Jacobson's calculated course is streaming onto my console. The auto-navigation system has verified his numbers, so we're ready for the burn. Le Garre will initiate the maneuver, firing our thrusters in sequence. "What's the damage on our reserves?" I ask.

"Eight per cent of total fuel," Duggins replies. His first name is Ethan, and he's a gruff Texan, a fifth-generation driller, born in oil field country after the oil ran out. Eighty years of dry wells and no jobs broke the United States back in the 2080s. Now, there's three countries, one of them based in his home state. "We'll add four days to our journey, provided we're still making for port at Ceres."

"We are," I reply. That's what Jacobson's calculation states. "We're stocked for the extra time?"

"Yes, we'll cope," Duggins says. "According to the schematic, the *Hercules* has eight crew. We can accommodate them, too, if we have to."

"I hope it won't come to that."

"Yeah, me too."

Jacobson activates the ship-wide comms. "Attention, all hands. Prepare for course correction burn in three minutes. Calculated force is five gravities. Strap yourselves in."

The automated voice takes up the message, repeating Jacobson's request. I pull up the desk cameras and sweep through the different rooms. Keiyho and Duggins will be doing the same while Le Garre and Jacobson concentrate on the maneuver. We have to make sure everyone is secure before we initiate the burn.

"Bring down the shutters."

"Yes, ma'am," Jacobson replies.

The blackness disappears behind metallic plates. I can feel the engines spinning up, ready to initiate the maneuver. I tense instinctively and have to consciously relax, taking a breath or two before placing my arms in the runners. More force-sensitive straps and magnets deploy, fixing me in place.

"All decks clear, Captain." Keiyho's Japanese voice has a singsong quality to it that contrasts with the building hum of the ship. "All crew checked in."

"Initiate burn," I order.

"Aye, aye."

There's a rumble and I'm pressed into my seat. We're on the move.

*　　*　　*

The *Khidr* has been in service six years. I've been in command of her for three.

Our run is a repeated patrol. Repair and refit at Earth's ageing International Space Station, then push out to Apollo, the Luna orbital platform. A couple of days resupply, then on to Mars and Phobos, before heading out to Ceres and the belt. Our belt course varies, as the mining stations are mobile, so we plot a different route every time.

Every run takes just over six months.

Each time we visit an outpost, things have changed. It's great to see the progress people make. Out here, there's a unified sense of purpose to make things work, to tame the harsh environments we've chosen to live in. The investment to set all this up has been enormous, but necessary. All Earthers should see what being up here is like. Maybe that'd stop them squabbling.

There's a price to pay for living in space. Your body changes. You have to take care of what you can and manage what you can't. Muscle mass quickly goes if you don't exercise, and your eyesight degrades with protracted time in zero gravity.

The *Khidr* has a rotational section that's locked down when we're accelerating. It's a vertical torus that surrounds the middle of the ship. Access is through a central shaft elevator in which you gradually start to feel the weight of your body. For me, that's a gathering sense of disappointment. Once you're out of the elevator, the torus is divided into four spaces – gym, lounge, meeting room and science/medical. The generated gravity in there is about point seven of Earth's. We all spend time in there. I don't like it, but the others do; it's a regular social space, the nearest many of them have to a home away from home.

The only other time we feel an equivalent gravitational force is at times like this, during a burn.

Five g's is about the same stress as one of those roller coasters people used to ride. People would go on them for fun, shouting and screaming as they flew around loops and bends.

Out here, our softer bodies don't take the same stress so easily. Living without the constant presence of the gravity that shaped us causes them to change. We have to exercise to maintain our resilience, or otherwise we can't endure the gravitational force when we need to maneuver. Our bodies shut down and we black out.

As the ship changes position, the chair rotates. A human being can withstand more horizontal force than vertical, so I'm pivoted to best cope. It doesn't stop everything going grey and blurry. I'm grinding my teeth under the strain. I can barely breathe. I want to move my arms, hug myself into a ball, but I can't. I know the reaction is instinctive and wouldn't help, but it doesn't stop—

"Burn complete," the ship's automated voice announces, and I feel the press on my body ease. The course correction and acceleration are done. We're aiming for the last recorded position of the *Hercules*. There'll be further adjustments, but those won't require the same exertion, until we need to slow down.

There's a red light flashing on my screen. I blink a few times, my vision clears, and I read the warning. The words make me cold inside. "We've got organic contamination in corridor six. Looks like something wasn't locked down. Cameras are out."

"It'll take a few minutes for a team to check," Duggins says. "We've still got systems offline on all decks."

"Soon as you can, please."

It takes time for everyone to recover from the aftermath of five gravities. Jacobson's doing better than me; his recent time on Earth means he's still got the resistance. Now he's double-checking his math and recalibrating our position. "Course correction checks out, Captain. We're exactly where we wanted to be."

"Good." I'm unstrapping myself from the chair. When that's done, I push off toward the door. "Dug, get a team to meet me in corridor six."

"Aye, aye."

CHAPTER TWO

Shann

There's blood, shit, piss and brains floating around in corridor six.

In the corner by the door next to me, there's a chair. The straps are torn or cut. About twenty metres away, a cloud of organic bits floats around a body, drifting near the far exit.

I'm as far away as I can get without being in another room. I'm wearing a respirator and protective clothing. Next to me is Doc Bogdanovic, who's completed his visual assessment.

"Looks like he secured the lab and strapped in out here," Bogdanovic says. "The acceleration made him fall. Would have been like tumbling off a roof, only five times as fast."

"Poor guy. Was it quick?"

"Can't tell at the moment. There's an impact wound in his chest. I can't see if something punctured his heart, but we should know once we've sealed everything up."

"How many people do you need?"

"Two plus me."

"Who do you want?"

Bogdanovic frowns behind his plastic mask. "Keiyho has some medical experience, Johansson too. They'd probably be best."

"You'll have them. Get to it."

"Aye, aye."

Accidents are difficult in space. Right from the beginning, you have to get used to the fact that you're going to be breathing recycled air and drinking recycled water. However, organic contamination is on another level. If someone cuts themselves, the blood goes everywhere. You have to have a means of collecting it. Localised vacuums help, but this is on a whole different scale.

Specialist Drake from hydroponics weighed a hundred and forty pounds in Earth numbers. That's a lot of liquid wrapped up in skin. The longer it drifts around the corridor, the more likely some of it will get into the filtration system, and that means we'll be breathing him in.

Not something I want to think about.

I'm backing out of the door, but I tap the doctor on the shoulder. "How long before you'll have a full picture?"

Bogdanovic shrugs. "About an hour. Then another hour or so for cleanup."

I nod. "We've time. Until then, this passage is off-limits to anyone else. Bring your report to the briefing."

"Will do."

I'm out at the intersection and breathing more easily. The panel slides up, locking the doctor inside. When the other two arrive, they'll seal the room airtight and work from tanks and respirators. Once the scrubbing's done, we can use the corridor again.

"Shann to bridge?"

"Bridge receiving. What's up, Captain?"

"Le Garre, I'm on my way to you. Get going on some projections on the *Hercules*. I'll have to start writing up what happened to Drake."

"Want me to pull the regs?"

"Yes, that'd be a plan."

I think about the torn strap, floating away from the chair. Had it been cut, or did it give out? Either way, the magnetic locks should have been enough to keep him in his seat. The restraint system has a whole list of redundancies and backups, just like everything up here.

In all my years in space, I've never had an incident like this.

Jonathan Drake was serving on this ship before I signed on. He was from Scotland and served on board for five or six years, supervising the hydroponics bay. He was in his midthirties and one of the highest performers in our physical examinations. Certainly not a candidate for some kind of panic attack or blackout, but I guess you never know.

Drake was also a really nice guy – quiet, seriously into his plants and a regular member of the board-game club in the recreation lounge. He had an exemplary record. We weren't close, but I can't remember us ever disagreeing on anything.

What happened here?

I'm back on the bridge, returning to my seat. Le Garre's turned around, watching me. "What's the protocol, Major?" I ask.

She shrugs. "The regulations are circumstance dependent. I think some of the scientists who wrote them were in a dark place at the time."

"What do you mean?"

"Well...there are a lot of references to 'organic mass' and 'reconstitution processing'." Le Garre frowns. "However, 'Captain's Discretion' is at the top of the page."

There's bile in my mouth. I swallow it back, but it leaves an aftertaste. "We're not some lost expeditionary mission desperately trying to conserve resources, so there's no need for that here. Once Bogdanovic is done, we bag up Drake and seal him in a container with the cargo. When we make port at Ceres, they can work out what needs to happen next."

Le Garre nods. "Is the cause of death known?"

"He fell out of his chair and smashed into the ship wall while we were accelerating." I'm floating over my seat, my hand resting on the chair back. I scoop up one of the loose straps. "His harness gave way."

"Those straps don't fall apart," Duggins drawls. "Sabotage?"

"We don't know. The corridor's on lockdown. The doctor's got two people helping him." I look at Le Garre. "I'm pretty sure the regs require an executive officer to lead an inquiry."

"They do," she says. "That means you, me or Travers."

Travers. My thoughts turn to the sleeping lieutenant who is due to take shift in about four hours. My executive officer is a reliable man. We've worked together ever since I got the commission. He'd been on the *Khidr* under the previous captain. "Travers hasn't been part of any of this so far. Best it be you or me."

"Then it's me," Le Garre replies.

"Done."

*   *   *

The next hour is filled with minor course corrections and a damage assessment.

Duggins and his team go over the ship, checking all the interior compartments. There are no further issues. The techs even check the strapping on the acceleration seats. None of them show any sign of ripping or giving out.

When he's done, he returns to the bridge and I help him brief the others on where we are.

"We'll have to contact the Fleet. We stick to what we know for now. Jonathan Drake died during a course correction. We're investigating the circumstances. Not much more we can say."

"What about family?" Jacobson asks. "Do we want to say something to them?"

"It's unlikely they'll be informed until we provide more information," I explain. "Our notification of what's happened should just be the facts for now. We can send condolences later."

Jacobson frowns but doesn't say anything else, so I press on. "Keiyho is still down in corridor six, and Le Garre's going to be busy over the next few hours. I need you to play pilot and comms until the duty shift change. Can you do that?"

His frown fades but doesn't completely disappear. "Sure, Captain, I can patch both systems through to my screen," he replies. "So long as we don't get into trouble, things should be fine."

"Good. Keep trying to get hold of the *Hercules*. I want an update. Anything you can get on her full manifest and new position." Giving the new ensign responsibility is a good tactic. It'll keep his mind on the mission while we manage other matters. "If you need to make any significant adjustments, you alert me. Got it?"

"Aye, Captain."

"Get someone else in here if you need them too."

"Aye, aye."

I turn to Duggins and Le Garre. "Wake up Travers and meet me in the briefing room. We need to fill him in and work out our next steps. Spin up the gravity deck. We'll talk there."

Duggins grunts an acknowledgment, and Le Garre nods. I'm planning for the worst-case scenario here. Someone may have murdered Drake. That means there's a killer loose on my ship.

We move out of the room.

★   ★   ★

Generated gravity isn't the same as the real thing. You can feel the difference, the subtle shifting as the ship's torus spins. I guess some people can ignore it.

I can't.

Spending time on the gravity deck isn't something I enjoy. I'm strapped into a set of lightweight cybernetic limbs that jack straight into the nerve endings on my spine. They have some anticipatory software to supplement my control of them, and I can walk just as easily as anyone else. Under a one-piece work suit, anyone who didn't know would be hard-pressed to tell the difference between me and anyone else.

But I know, and I never forget.

There are seven individuals in the crew who use prosthetic limbs. Much as we share the experience, we've all got different takes. It's an occasional discussion point, but not one that makes us some kind of community or group. We're people, not factions. Space has that effect on most of us, improving our international perspective.

We keep the windows blacked out up here; the motion makes some feel sick when they look out. That means the meeting room is like being in a dingy office, cut off from the rest of the crew.

"You wanted to see me, Captain?"

Travers looks like he hasn't slept well. He's a bearded African American thirty-something from Boston with more years as a bridge officer out here than both me and Le Garre combined. He's not due on shift for another four hours, but given the circumstances, I need to make sure he's fully briefed.

"How much have you been told?"

"I spoke to Bogdanovic before coming here. His people are just finishing up."

"So, you know about Drake and the *Hercules*?"

"I've got the basics, yes."

"Okay." I'm standing and leaning over a table. A quick touch of the surface and it fades into black, punctuated by stars. Circles appear, coloured to represent planets and other objects. The *Khidr* is a blue dot, travelling along a red line toward another blue dot.

The *Hercules*.

"This is the updated tracking position based on calculations from after the course correction. We're just waiting on a new transponder ping from them and we'll make adjustments."

"I see." Travers leans over the other side of the table. "Was there any additional information in the distress signal to give us an idea of what to expect?"

I glance at Le Garre. She gives me that smile again. "Not much; it was from the automated system, relaying position, distress and mentioned drive trouble."

"That could mean a shutdown or lockout," Duggins says. "If it's the former, we can probably help with a quick repair. If it's the latter, we may have to park the ship and evacuate the crew."

"I take it you're preparing for either scenario?" I ask Duggins.

He snorts. "Of course, but we'll know more when we get the next transponder reading."

Drive lockout isn't a common malfunction. When a ship performs a burn, commands are sent to the engines from the bridge. The drives spin up, and hydrogen fuel is ignited to push the ship in the direction required. The requirements for course corrections are very carefully calculated, so each use of directional thrust is measured in the amount of fuel to be used and the necessary duration.

After activation, sometimes a drive won't shut down; it remains open – locked out and burning until the fuel tank exhausts itself.

If that happened to the *Hercules*, she might be locked in some sort of spin or fast course that she can't correct. Either will make docking with her very difficult.

Le Garre taps on the blue dot we're heading for. "I wonder why the crew haven't messaged? I wonder what's happened to them?"

"Won't know till we're there," Duggins replies with the obvious.

"How many personnel are you going to need?" I ask.

"Six if we're lucky and it's a shutdown," he says. "Just a case of finding out what's wrong with the engines and repairing them. If the situation's more complicated, it could take all of us."

"Who do you want to brief?"

"The selected rescue team first. Then we'll do two briefing shifts, provided that's okay with you?"

"It is."

"Great."

"We shouldn't rule out other possibilities," Le Garre says. "It'll be a while until we're there. The situation could have worsened by the time we arrive."

"We plan with the data we've got," I say. "Let's save the speculation for item two on the agenda."

"You mean Drake?"

"Yes."

There's an awkward silence between us all. I chew my lip and look at each of them, but no one wants to meet my eye. "The worst case needs to be planned for."

"And that is?" Travers asks.

"That we have a murderer on board."

The words defy generated gravity and hang in the air between us. Eventually, Le Garre clears her throat.

"You gave me responsibility for the investigation," she says. "How do you want it done?"

"Start with the scene. Get everything you can from Bogdanovic and then report back to us here. If there's any evidence to suggest this wasn't an accident, we'll move on to interviewing all crew members, one by one."

"And we do this in the middle of a rescue operation?"

"We have to. If there's a murderer, we can't leave them running around the ship. The longer we delay, the more chance they have to hide their tracks or the more damage they might do."

"Fair point."

"At this stage, who can we trust?" Duggins asks.

I smile at him. "You know where I was; I know where you were. Same with Le Garre, Keiyho and Jacobson." I turn to Travers. "Where did you secure yourself?"

"In my room. I was sleeping when the call came in."

"Anyone able to verify that?"

"No. Is that a problem, Captain?"

"We're getting ahead of ourselves," Le Garre says. "First step is to find out what happened."

"Yes," Travers says, his tone neutral and his gaze flicking over each of us. "I'm sure a few other people will find themselves in the same situation as me."

"You're not being accused of anything, Bill," I say.

"I know," he replies, giving me a thin-lipped smile.

"What about camera footage?" Duggins asks.

I sigh and run a hand through my hair. Personal surveillance is classified on board a Fleet ship. Crew members are entitled to privacy in their rooms unless there is a good reason to breach that privacy. The ship has cameras and records continuously in all locations, but only the captain can authorise a viewing of footage from someone's room.

"Stick with public access for now," I tell Le Garre. "If we complete the interviews and you need to view anything else, I'll make a judgement."

"That might compromise your position as judge," Travers says.

"If it does, you'll have to step up," I tell him.

Travers smiles, but the expression doesn't reach his eyes. He's still pissed about the verification question. "I wasn't volunteering."

"Too bad."

Duggins pulls something out of his pocket and drops it onto the table, making the stars, planets and course track vanish. It's an acceleration-seat strap.

"When I heard the strap had failed, I pulled this from corridor five for a comparison to the broken one," he says. "Replaced it with one from stores. Take a look."

Travers picks it up. "What am I looking for?" he asks.

"Exactly that," Duggins replies. "Nothing. There's nothing wrong with it."

"How's that helpful?"

"This is a multi-woven plastic polymer." Duggins's slow Texan drawl makes the words more palatable. "It's really strong. You can't cut it or tear it by any conventional means. You might use a laser to burn through it, or some kind of acid, but if either of those were in corridor six, they'd have triggered an alarm."

"Could it have been weakened?" Travers suggests.

"Possibly," Duggins replies. "Or it was subject to a massive force, exceeding the tolerance limits."

"What about the active locks?" Le Garre asks.

"The active locking works as soon as you're in proximity of the seat. The straps are programmed and powered from a local computer unit in the chair. The two ends seek each other out, embracing the detected person. It's possible they could have been reprogrammed."

"So, what you're saying is…"

"This wasn't an accident, or if it was, I've no idea how it happened." He drops three black circular discs onto the table as well. "These are the mag sensors sewn into the chair. They are powerful enough to hold a person in place at five g's without straps and with thirty per cent failure. There's massive redundancy in these units."

"These from stores as well?" I ask.

"Of course."

They're all looking at me again, waiting for my call, which is good. We're in this together. I trust these three. I *have* to trust them.

"Speculation starts and stops in this room," I say. "The crew will talk, come up with ideas of all sorts, and we can't stop that, but we can discourage it and remind them of procedures. You want to voice something, you bring it here, with all of us together."

"That go for you too, Captain?" Travers queries.

"Absolutely," I reply.

CHAPTER THREE

Shann

Four hours have passed. My shift is over and I'm back in my room.

After the briefing, Le Garre went to check in with Bogdanovic, Duggins started calling up his team for the *Hercules* intercept, and I went back to the bridge to help Jacobson.

Being in command is a blessing and a curse out here. We are all part of an interplanetary mission, and Fleet is a huge organisation, but you don't feel that when you spend six months with the same people every day.

Some of the officer training manuals talk about 'maintaining objective distance' from the crew, but that never takes into account how being out here brings people together or drives them apart. As captain, I get to make that call – to be as close or far away as I want. I'm not a great people person, but I know I need to try, and I do try, every day.

I have friends, but I could do with making a few more.

While I was on the bridge, we received an update on the freighter's position from the transponder and made some small adjustments. Then, just before I went off shift, Phobos Station came through with a more detailed cargo manifest.

That's what I'm looking at now on my personal screen, scrolling through the listings. It looks like we've been sent a scan of the customs document. There's information written all over it in scrawled notes.

I'm trying to decipher them. I can make out the occasional word – *live organic material, toxic compound, radioactive material detected…*

Phobos Station is a fairly new addition to Earth's space colonisation outreach. Originally, the Mars colonies relied on an old orbital waystation platform called Gateway. This was one of the first colonial arks to reach the planet back in the 2030s, and for decades after, it acted as a transition point for new visitors, allowing ships to dock, reconfigure, repair or fuel up as needed before their crews made the trip planetside. It's still there, working as a communications relay point, and gets an occasional visit from technicians or history buffs.

Phobos Station was built to take over the day-to-day management of space traffic around Mars. It's a purpose-built rotating torus and maintains its position in a geostationary orbit around Phobos itself. The whole place has been operating for less than a decade, and the people who work there tend to be keen on their rules and regulations.

The scrawled notes are clearly the results of the inspection. I can only imagine the arguments that happened when the notes writer insisted the classified containers were opened or scanned. Whether they were or not, I can't tell from what I have here. I'm not a mining expert, but my knowledge of the export regulations is pretty good. Sure, there's a reason why small amounts of any of the above might be needed on a mining outpost in the asteroid belt, but crate after crate?

Something is very wrong with all this...

I open a comms line to the bridge. Travers's face appears on my screen.

"Bridge here. What can I do you for, Captain?"

"Travers, have we sent Drake's death notification?"

"It went twenty minutes ago."

"Good. Lodge an official request with Earth for the full unredacted manifest of the *Hercules*. Tell them we're on a rescue operation and we've reason to believe some of the classified cargo is dangerous."

"You think we'll get anywhere?"

"We have to try."

"Okay." Travers glances down. "We've had a mail call come in. I wasn't going to wake you, but if you're up, do you want your messages?"

"Sure, send them over."

"Will do."

"Thanks."

When you're this far out, communications from anywhere take time. The *Khidr* receives data packages regularly from colonies, ships and outposts that lock on to its transponder and broadcast a tight data stream. If we change course, this process becomes harder, as we become difficult to locate. So, there are also relay points – space buoys – that are continually looking for everyone and hold transmitted messages for us until we pass by.

In the old days, signals between distant spacecraft and mission control on Earth would be sets of piloting instructions jammed into the tiniest data packages possible. There's less need for remote commands now, but more need for human contact beyond the ship. A reminder that life goes on outside our steel box.

The screen pings as my messages upload. I can tell straightaway who they're from. Five are work-related queries, one is a programme subscription, and the last one is a video message from Earth.

That'll be from my dad.

I stare at the screen for several moments. I need to steel myself to watch that message. Dad and I don't get on, but I respect the fact that he stays in touch. He still lives in Edmonton. He knows I'm never coming back. For some reason, he takes that personally, as if he's failed as a father.

I select the message and bring it up. "Hi, Dad," I mutter.

"Hello, Ellie, I… We miss you."

His recording stares at me in silence, as if he can see me through time and space. I suppose he was imagining my face as he spoke. He looks old and tired. I haven't seen him in a year or more, I guess. I'm blinking and wiping my eyes.

"Jethry's not well, Ellie. I thought you should know." Dad looks over his shoulder. There's clearly someone with him, but I don't know who it is. Mom died seven years ago. Jethry is my younger brother; he lives with his wife and two children. We don't speak to each other.

Dad looks at me again. "Jethry's been taken in for surgery. The cancer's back. It's in his lungs. I thought you'd want to know, wherever you are. I hope this reaches you in time, so you can pray for him."

The message ends. I flick it off.

You bastard, Dad. I'm helpless out here. He's hoping I'll come back, forgive and forget all that's been said. I can't, even if I wanted to. I'm too far away. All this does is make me feel guilty, like I'm somehow to blame.

Maybe he thinks I am.

I don't believe some higher universal power will reach down and save people if you make a wish. Sure, the universe is beautiful, there has to be something that made it, but we're an insignificant part of all that. Life is fleeting and unfair. You make your own path with what you've got. I certainly have.

Maybe Dad doesn't realise what he's done here. He's got no one else to tell, I guess. Something else for me to shoulder, along with all the rest.

The other messages will wait. The programme subscription is for *Celerity* – a period drama I watch when I get the chance to switch off. Doctors recommend we have an escape, something totally different from our work environment. Most of the crew enjoy those full immersion simulations, but we're a long way out and that means data restrictions, so books, films and audio are best. I prefer them anyway. A Japanese programme about the fourteenth century shogunate period is pretty far away from what I do. The characters, situations and vistas are nothing like life on the ship. It's subtitled, but I'm starting to pick up the language.

Some people find watching these things a reminder of what they're missing, and it gives them something to look forward to when they get back from a tour. For me, they're just a distraction and a way to slow down so I can relax.

That's not happening now.

I boost myself off the seat and over to my bed. I grab the straps and pull myself down. They begin to wind themselves around me. The programme is automatic, adapted from a system first installed in secure psychiatric wards. I can feel the magnets in the mattress and my clothing too. The same must have happened to Drake when he moved into the chair.

Maybe that's the weak link, like Duggins said. The computer system in the chair. If it had been reprogrammed, the straps wouldn't activate.

Surely Drake would have noticed, though. If he'd seen the straps fail to engage, he would have activated his comms and reported the fault.

I close my eyes. For once, my mind drifts away quickly.

★   ★   ★

When I was a child, I could doze whenever and wherever I wanted. The world of dreams could be a better place than reality, an escape from the sidelong glances and whispers behind my back.

Restful sleep has always been harder to find. If there's something on my mind, I'll be thinking about it right into my dreams and nightmares.

Medical advances make life better for people with problems, but it takes time for attitudes to change. Growing up, I was surrounded by a well-meaning family. They wanted the best they could imagine for me, but what they envisioned was a limited existence, trapped by walls and defined by my differences.

I'd be sitting in a mobility chair, most of the time. Later, I got powered legs, but people's habits were fixed by then. No one listened to what I had to say. The world would happen around me. All the decisions that affected my life were made whether I was listening or participating or not.

Until I escaped and took control of my own life.

The dream takes me through my memories. I remember being very young, sitting in a chair at the beach on a bright summer's day. I can see my brother and my father playing. They're digging with plastic spades, piling up sand and filling a collection of coloured buckets. They've just been in the sea; I can see the water glistening on my father's sun-browned skin.

A part of me always wanted to join them. I could have done it. I could have crawled or asked to be carried to where they sat. But in that moment, I looked up into the sky and I saw something else. A future beyond the limitations of other people's plans for my life.

None of them could have imagined I'd end up here.

There's an electronic beep. I open my eyes. *Someone's outside my door.* I don't know how long I've been dozing. A flick of a button disengages the straps.

"Come in," I say.

The panel slides back. "How're you doing, Ellie?"

I sit up and smile. "Coping, Sam. How about you?"

"The same, only I don't have all the facts."

"Neither do I."

"No, but rank has its privileges."

"It does indeed. Come in, that's an order."

He laughs and enters my room. Sam's a second-generation Martian. His parents were among the first people born on the planet in Jezero colony. We've known each other for nearly ten years, most of my life since I left Earth. When I got command of the *Khidr*, he was the first person I recruited. He's the quartermaster and runs the ship's stores, making sure everything's where it's supposed to be.

The door closes, and he moves to join me on the bunk, hooking a leg around the end and settling himself down. "So, what's going on?"

"I can't tell you everything, Sam, you know that."

"Sure, I'll get the details from the briefing, but I'm more worried about you and how you're managing."

His hand squeezes my shoulder. We were lovers in the past. That's not where we are now, but he cares, I know that. I care for him too. He's my friend. Probably my best friend out here.

"Things are difficult. The two incidents happening at the same time is a stretch for us all. Le Garre's leading the investigation into Drake's death. Duggins is prepping the teams for the *Hercules* rendezvous."

"Yeah, he's been down to see me with a requisition list."

"Good. That shows his mind is on the job." I rub my eyes; they feel sore. "I got a message from Dad."

"Hardly the best time. You watch it?"

"Yep. Jethry's cancer is back. They've taken him in for surgery."

"Jesus, Ellie, that's a lot for you to handle in one day."

"I know."

His arms are around me without my needing to ask. The warmth of his body is a comfort and a reassurance. I let go and the tears come, along with gut-shuddering sobs. Crying isn't much fun in zero gravity. The water forms into bags around my eyes, forcing me to wipe them away so I can see. Sam is my closest friend. He knows what I've been through to be here, what I still go through in terms of my baggage and stored-up guilt. He doesn't say anything more. I don't need him to.

As the straps re-engage around us, I let myself drift off to sleep. This time I don't dream.

* * *

The first manned spaceflight to the Moon took just over two days.

The first manned spaceflight to Mars took six months.

These days, we've shortened journey times a lot. Conventional rocket boosters have become more advanced and efficient. We also have a resonant cavity drive, which can be used when we reach sufficient speed. Six months becomes eight weeks, which is how a patrol like ours becomes viable.

I don't know how it all works; I don't have to. But like everything else, I have a rough idea, and I do know there's a lot of redundancy built in. There's also a feeling you get when they switch it on. A weird feeling in your stomach that I can't explain.

I'm awake with that feeling right now. Sam is gone. I'm alone. He must have left hours ago. The straps disengage as I sit up.

I glance over at the digital counter. I've another hour before I'm due on shift. There are no new messages, so I guess the ship has managed without me.

An hour is plenty of time for me to go through everything before I go back to the bridge.

Last night's correspondence is waiting for me. I drag each of them down from the mailbox and open them. Three are scientific queries – two from Earth and one from Mars. I find the data for the Earth queries on the system and prepare replies for each of them. The Mars query is a bit more complex. An ensign on the SETI station is asking about some minor communication and scanning anomalies he's discovered in plotting. I'm not sure why this has ended up with me. I forward the query to Ensign Jacobson and ask him to reply to the Mars Station officer with some comparative data.

The other two messages are military. The first, an inventory request, is easy to answer and update. The second...

Well now, that's strange.

Captain Shann,

This is a pre-authorised transmission. It was triggered when you made an inventory request on a classified cargo being transported from Phobos Station to Ceres.

Attached to this message is a data archive that outlines the purpose of these shipments. The clearance grade of this information is above your rank authorisation. However, it has been provided to you owing to your unique situation. You have authorisation to share this with senior crew on a need-to-know basis.

Good luck, Captain.

Fleet.

There's a file attachment. It's password encrypted. I have a set of flag passwords that are for rank-authorised files. I don't know whether they will work on this, but I assume they will or a way to access the information would have been provided. Much as everyone trusts that the communications officer on duty won't be reading private correspondence, additional security is required at times. In this case, I'm grateful for it, in light of what may or may not have been done to Drake.

I read the message again, carefully. The fact that it's been sent automatically after we requested the information about the *Hercules* piques my interest. The freighter wasn't named either, which suggests there's been more than one shipment between Phobos and Ceres.

Interesting…

CHAPTER FOUR

Shann

...protesters staged rallies across the country on Thursday, denouncing efforts by national governments to repeal the landmark Healthcare Entitlement law, which has extended medical suffrage to more than four hundred million of the world's poorest people.

Several thousand people gathered outside the intergovernmental building in New York City to deliver 'the Millions petition' to Earth's continental council. The veracity of the enormous list of written names has yet to be determined, but if it is genuine, this would be the largest signed document ever to exist.

"I feel sick today, but I came here because I'm terrified," said John Marlin, twenty-five – an unemployed San Franciscan who was diagnosed with cancer a year ago. "Politicians have the best healthcare in the world; everyone deserves the same."

Many demonstrators expressed outrage at the approval of additional funding subsidies for colony expansion on Mars and independent corporate ventures into the asteroid belt when basic subsistence incomes were under threat in Earth's poorest nations. "Wasn't the idea that going into space would make life better for us down here?" one man said. "Instead, they're living like kings while we rot!"

A spokesperson for...

★   ★   ★

"Captain on the bridge!"

There are two people up here – minimal crew for the transit. The metal shutters are down, and the lighting is low. Jacobson looks tired. I'm surprised to see him still in his chair. He should have been relieved by now. Or has he already had a break and come back? I make a mental note to check the duty roster.

"Situation update?"

"We're on course for the *Hercules* intercept. Resonance drive is engaged."

"Any problems?"

"One or two. A full briefing is on your screen."

I strap into my chair and start reading. Bogdanovic has finished his work in corridor six, and Le Garre's investigation has started. She's left me a series of interview requests, which I approve. They're mostly for people who were near where Drake was during the course correction.

"What's our ETA for *Hercules* rendezvous?"

"Four hours, Captain."

"How's she doing?"

"Listing a few hundred miles starboard of her approved course. Her position suggests a drive shutdown rather than a lockout. Duggins has updated his briefing."

"Have you slept, Ensign?"

"I did try, Captain, but—"

"You're relieved. Get three hours rest. We'll call you when things get serious."

"Okay, I'll give it another go."

Jacobson unclips himself and heads out. I look over to the engineer's post. Ensign April Johansson is sitting there, staring intently at her screen. I can hear noise coming from her headphones. I'm not sure she's even heard me come in, but that's typical of her. I've never met anyone so single-minded. Her Fleet profile has a write-up from her former XO about her not paying attention, but really her problem is the opposite: you give her a job and she forgets everything else.

I tap my screen and send her an alert. It pings right in front of her, and she immediately looks up and over to me. "Sorry, Captain Shann, I was listening to the transmission update."

"Best fill me in on that, Ensign."

"About thirty minutes ago, I initiated a broad range receive protocol so we could listen to any stray comms traffic from the *Hercules* or any other objects in the vicinity."

I frown involuntarily. "We're a long way out to pick up that kind of stuff."

"I thought it was worth a try, Captain."

"Okay, did you find anything?"

"Yes, Captain. Something strange." Johansson unclips the headphone from her right ear. "Want me to send you the recording?"

"Yes, please do."

The file appears on my screen. I open it up and listen to the first few seconds. There's a lot of static, and some strange interference almost like music, but here and there I catch what sounds like a male voice speaking fragmented words. "You think this is a transmission from the *Hercules*?" I ask.

"I can't tell," Johansson replies. "The resonance drive affects our ability to receive a clear signal, but I've applied a few filters to clean that up. What I can make out are two clearly distinct voices. They sound like they're talking to each other."

"A conversation?"

"Yes, Captain, that's what it sounds like."

I'm staring at the screen. It's pretty incredible that we're picking up anything that isn't directed at us at this distance, and we definitely wouldn't be picking up interior communication from the *Hercules*, so a conversation means one of two things. Either someone on the freighter went outside to fix something and was talking to the bridge...

...or there's another ship in near-field range to them.

"Have you checked the charts and course plot information?"

"Jacobson did just before you relieved him, Captain. There's no other ship due out this way for six days."

"Must be someone outside then – an EVA, or a background echo?"

Johansson nods. "That was my thought, Captain. I've been listening back and forth, trying to isolate a sentence or two to confirm what we're listening to."

Background echo is something that we've been dealing with ever since humanity started looking out into the universe. Broadcast signals have been bouncing back toward Earth since the 1930s, when radio transmission first became widespread. There's a swirling mass of three centuries of noise out here, which we have to filter out of any communication we're receiving. Usually, this wouldn't be an issue since targeted messages have a tight beam and set of handshake protocols, but here, we're listening in, trying to pick up anything we can, so all of those factors are part of the equation.

"These freighters usually have eight crew – two shifts of four, with three the minimal operational complement. If there was an emergency, they'd wake everyone. You think they'd try taking a walk outside to repair a drive shutdown?"

Johansson shrugs. She looks tired. Clearly, she's been at this a while. Her pale Norwegian face is almost ghostly in the low light. "Drive repair isn't my area, but I guess a two-person EVA would work if they have two specialists on board."

Interplanetary freighters are big, more than a kilometre in size. That's much bigger than the *Khidr*. While we have a larger staff and all sorts of different equipment to assist and repair other ships, the *Hercules* will operate mostly on automated systems with a tiny team. Any extravehicular activity, like an emergency repair, would stretch them thin. She's a huge cargo container, with engines at the back and a home for her crew in the front. Her typical journey would be back and forth on the same runs, which makes the classified message I read earlier all the more intriguing.

I'm half tempted to leave the bridge and start trying passwords on the data archive right now, but there are others who need a break more than me.

"When is your shift change due, Ensign?" I ask.

"In three hours," Johansson says. "I had the extra work with the doctor, clearing up what happened. We haven't rostered that in yet."

"Oh yes, you helped out with Drake." I've turned my seat, and I'm looking at her now. I remember the floating cloud of blood and worse. Even if she's had similar experiences before, a sight like that is traumatic. "Do you want to take some time?"

Johansson shakes her head. "No, I just want to find out what these signals are."

I stare at her for a few moments. She's clearly affected. The work is a distraction. I suspect she'll only dwell on what's happened if I send her away.

"Did you know Drake well?" I ask.

"I knew Jonathan, if that's what you meant?"

I let the matter drop. "I'll start analysing the last section of the file," I say. "If I find any words I can isolate, I'll shift them to your screen."

"Thank you, Captain," Johansson says. Her pinched expression relaxes, and she turns back to what she was doing, popping her earpiece back in.

"No problem," I say, knowing she can't hear me, and turn back to my own screen.

★　　★　　★

An hour later, Keiyho has joined us and I've isolated seventeen potential words. Three of them are in a sentence. I think I can hear *"...please don't...sir..."* I group everything up and send it to Johansson's screen.

"Thanks, Captain," she says.

A message alert flashes on my console. I open it. Le Garre is awake and wants a conversation in her room. I unstrap myself from my seat.

"You two carry on here," I say. "I'll be back in twenty minutes."

"Of course, Captain," Keiyho replies.

Le Garre's quarters are close to the bridge. I go past the entrance to corridor six. It's still sealed. She must have found something.

I press the announcer, and the door slides back a moment later. Music spills out into the corridor, some sort of atonal twenty-second-century ambient-synth that reminds me of the strange interference we picked up. Le Garre is in a chair at her desk. Her gaze is fixed on the screen in front of her. She has her hair scraped back into a bun. She looks tired as well, but there's a focus to her that suggests she's coping. She turns to me and raises her eyebrows.

"Captain?"

"Major. What have you found?"

"A few things." She picks up a portable screen from the table and hands it to me. "Drake is stored away in the cargo hold. We've photographed and recorded everything from the scene."

"Give me the headlines."

"Well, the straps weren't cut or burned through," Le Garre says. "It looks like someone triggered them to release."

"You mean an override?"

"I mean the emergency remote command. You remember the safety briefing?"

I try to cast my mind back six years to my basic astrospace training. "There's a remote trigger for any harness. It can be operated from the bridge or from a portable handheld device. Shuts down the whole system."

"Yes, apart from the magnets in our suits. They retain charge and connection."

"Duggins said they would have been enough to hold Drake in his seat on their own. Unless there was a lot of failure. Some kind of physical or electrical shock?"

"Or the electromagnetic system in the chair was switched off as well," Le Garre says. "I've asked Duggins to check."

I nod. "I've approved your interviews. Start when you're ready."

"Will do," Le Garre says. "Time for this may be an issue. My shifts might need to be covered."

"Yes, I understand. Johansson's had the same problem. We'll work it out. You going to be on hand for the rendezvous?"

"When is it?"

"Three hours from now."

Le Garre sighs. "I'll need to be."

"Did Duggins brief you?"

"Yes, he's spoken to most of the crew. With the updated information from Jacobson, he anticipates a shutdown, so his plan is a restart operation."

"How many people does that need?"

"Two on the outside, four on the inside."

"Something the freighter crew could do then?"

"Possibly." Le Garre glances at the screen again. "That wasn't why I messaged you, Captain."

"No, I guessed that. What's the issue?"

"Once I start the interviews, the crew are going to get nervous," Le Garre explains. "They'll already be talking, but this will spook them. It'll confirm we're thinking someone killed Drake. It'll let our killer or killers know we're thinking that too. We need to make a plan for their next move."

"Get ahead of them, you mean?"

"Yes."

I run a hand through my hair, feeling it as it floats in zero gravity. "There's still a chance the system failed, or the command was issued by accident. We need to get someone to quietly go through the execution routines on the bridge consoles."

"I can get Travers to do that," Le Garre says.

I shake my head. "No, it should be you, me, or Duggins. We were all there."

"You don't trust Travers?"

"Not with this. Not yet. I'm on shift. I can access the command history."

"Okay." Le Garre shrugs. "But we know who was on each station. My hunch is that we're looking for a remote device."

"Yes, but we need to rule things out."

"Agreed."

"The next step is the weapons lockers. We need to meet with Keiyho and authorise deployment of low-ballistic firearms to the officer group."

"Morale is going to suffer," Le Garre warns.

"Then we keep it quiet. And bring Keiyho into the group," I tell her. "He was on the bridge too."

"You trust him?"

"I will, as soon as we've cleared the console command history."

"So, we authorise firearms after that?"

"Yes." I chew my lip and hesitate a moment before making a decision. "We need to meet up again before we reach the *Hercules*. I need to brief you all on some classified information I received from Fleet."

Le Garre raises an eyebrow. "From Fleet? Interesting. Will it help?"

"I don't know; it's an encrypted set of data that I haven't looked at yet. Seemed to have been sent automatically too. I'm authorised to share it with the senior crew. I think we should all view it together and see if it's useful."

"We do that when we meet with the others?"

"Yes, I think that works best."

"Okay, Captain." Le Garre stifles a yawn and nods toward her bed. "Between now and then, I'm going to try to get some sleep."

"Good idea, you've earned it."

"Thank you."

*　　*　　*

I'm back on the bridge, lowering myself into my seat. Johansson hasn't moved. She's still at her station, listening to the audio recordings, but Keiyho nods to me as I settle in. "Nothing to report, Captain," he says.

"That's good to hear," I reply.

"Indeed."

My screen has gone into power-save mode. I swipe a finger across it, and the desktop restores, only it's not the same as before.

I frown. "Hey, has anyone been at my station?"

Keiyho raises his head and looks at me. "No, Captain, why?"

I'm staring at the isolated audio files. I'm sure there were six. Now there are five and they aren't where I left them on the bottom of the screen. "It doesn't matter," I mutter to Keiyho.

But I'm lying. It does matter. *A lot.*

I key up the command history. I find the missing audio file. It's the one with the three words. It was deleted twenty minutes ago.

When I wasn't here.

I scroll down the list, all the way back to the burn. There's a whole series of entries during the course correction. Commands issued from my console that deactivated four different acceleration seats across the ship. A cross-reference check with the crew report shows three of the chairs were unoccupied, one of them wasn't.

Drake's chair.

I didn't issue these commands. I couldn't have issued them during a course correction under five gravities. I wouldn't have been capable of doing so. No one could. They had to have been preprogrammed and set to go.

Routing them through my console was clever, but whoever did it had to have known someone would check. Why they'd move and listen to the audio files is anyone's guess.

Maybe I'm following a trail of breadcrumbs that have been laid out for me?

"Captain, I think I've got something," Johansson says. Her chair swivels around toward me. "I've isolated twenty-six possible words from the recordings. One of them sounds like 'Hercules'."

"Send it to me."

"Aye, aye."

The file appears on my screen. I listen to it. I can't be sure but think I can hear what Johansson has heard. It can't be coincidence, can it?

Can it?

CHAPTER FIVE

Johansson

"...please don't... sir..."

I'm listening to the message fragment the captain sent me. I've found thirty other words now, all parts of sentences. Nothing that I can link together.

Apart from this.

I've been a military communications and audio specialist for two years after I completed my basic astrospace training. At the end of this tour, I'll be sitting my second lieutenant exams. This is a long way from where I grew up in Bessaker, a stone's throw from the North Sea. I doubt anyone there thought I'd end up here.

I need a good endorsement from the captain so I can get a good posting. This is my opportunity to impress. That's why I volunteered to keep working on the problem. I find I can't sleep with something left unfinished. It's certainly an unusual situation, and the task in front of me suits my skill set. I've always loved working with sounds. I was a synth beat junkie when I was a child, making tracks late into the night and whenever I could skip school.

They don't need composers in the military. Audio engineers and communication specialists, though, they're a priority. There isn't much difference in running SETI tracking, reprocessing audio data dumps, communication line control and all the rest. Just different priorities with what you're trying to do. The task still requires you to be sat in front of a screen, listening to sounds.

I'm a detail person. That helps in this line of work.

The captain is moving toward the door, leaving me and Keiyho to look after the ship. It's a standing order that two members of the bridge crew remain on duty at all times. I'm exhausted, but I've agreed to stay. I can't let this go.

Keiyho is difficult to read. He's from Kyoto, the other side of the world to me. I've tried to get to know him – to impress him maybe? But I can't tell whether I've succeeded or not. If I ask for something, he reacts with the same shrug and humourless half smile that he gives everyone, apart from Captain Shann. There's a little inclination of the head Keiyho gives her. That's a Japanese tradition, left over from the bowing that used to be popular in their society – totally impractical in zero gravity.

Maybe one day, I'll command my own ship and men like Keiyho will bow to me.

I blink and focus on the sound files. They are neatly filed in a directory on my screen, little pieces of audio I've managed to isolate from the background noise. I've processed these files already, applying noise reduction filters, vocal enhancement tools, all sorts. I've named each one for what they are. There are two voices, both male. That was the first thing I noticed. If this is a communication between an EVA team and the bridge of the *Hercules*, then it's incredible that we've managed to receive any of it.

Have I missed something? I pull up the first file again and revert it to the original, setting it to play on a loop. I lean back and shut my eyes. It's easier to focus on what you're hearing when there's nothing else to distract you.

"...please don't... sir..."

There! In the background, really faint, but audible. *A whistling noise?* Sounds like music or old-school analogue interference. It's buried under the vocal layers of the recording. The computer will never manage to isolate it, but I know it's there. I pull up a second fragment, restore it to the original format, and listen again.

Nothing.

Dead end. *Oh well.*

Along with our other duties, SETI tracking requires a communication specialist to run all sorts of searches, angling a space station's receiver into deep space and processing whatever we find. Ever since humans started colonising space, equipment has been allocated to continue scouring the void for any trace of life beyond our solar system. According to the database, the project's been going since the last millennium. The job involves isolating small pockets of received audio and trying to find some meaning in them. We've always speculated that any aliens out there from distant planets would have to use powerful transmitters to get anything across the millions and billions of miles of emptiness between us. Either that or they'd have a method of sending messages that we just wouldn't know how to receive.

This isn't aliens. It's a human voice, but how did it get to us?

I play the sample again. There are definitely two sources, but I'm not sure this is conversation about an EVA mission. The frequency doesn't fit the ones we make use of, and the chances of a suit transmitter reaching us all the way out here is next to impossible.

"...*please don't...sir...*" – might be a request from someone in a spacesuit outside an airlock or whatever. There's a mention of the *Hercules* and a collection of *thes, ands, ofs,* nothing I can put together. I hear something else that sounds like *'glass'*.

Who is the other source?

I open another window on the screen and request an updated plot of all registered ships in the solar system. There's a lot of traffic. Mars, Ceres, Europa, the belt stations, all of them need continuous resupply. It's a lucrative business for nations and corporations alike. Green dots and their planned courses gradually begin to appear on a three-dimensional render of the region. According to the tracker, there are no ships missing. I key up and send a transponder request to verify all positions.

The door to the bridge opens. Jacobson is there. He glances around the room, smiles at me and nods. He knows what I've been up to. I take off my headphones and beckon him over. He glides across and settles himself into a chair, logs on to his screen and swivels the chair around to face me.

"How're things going?" he asks.

"Not bad. What do you make of this?" I nod toward my screen.

Jacobson leans forward. "You've found something else?"

"Possibly." I touch the tactical plot. "I'm checking where all the ships are in the region, asking for verifications of the data you sent me."

Jacobson frowns and gives me a sullen look. "Okay, that'll take a while."

"Yeah." I'm biting my lip and trying to avoid his eye. I just implied I don't trust the information Jacobson gave me. My people skills suck. I need to be better at managing egos if I'm going to earn a promotion.

I point at the files on my screen. "I think I've confirmed that these were from the *Hercules*. I'm trying to work out who they were talking to. That's why I needed the course information."

"You sure it was from the freighter? Not some stray reflections, echoing out of deep space?"

"I'm sure," I say. "One of the words is 'Hercules'. It has to be them."

Jacobson stares at me. He's still irritated. Those sparkly blue eyes of his are his best feature, along with his freckled cheeks. We've been sexual partners. In fact, we were together for a few weeks when I first joined the *Khidr*, we broke up. It was my choice. He was good and gentle. You have to be gentle in zero gravity.

"You need to get some rest," he says.

"I know, but I need to solve this."

"Looks like you already have. What else can you find out? You've analysed the fragments, deciphered them, and drawn a conclusion. That's the best we can hope for with limited information. Present that to the captain, let her factor it into her plans."

I can't fault his logic, and I know if I stay here, he'll just be annoying about it. "You're probably right," I say.

Jacobson reaches out and squeezes my shoulder. "Get some sleep, maybe?" he suggests.

"Sure, okay."

I turn back to my screen and send all the data to my portable device. Then I unstrap myself and nod to Keiyho, who gives me his half smile. "A wise choice, Ensign. You need the rest. You have permission to leave."

"I guess so. Thank you, Commander."

I'm out of the door and drifting down the hall. I make the turn toward my room and pass corridor six. I can't help but glance in that direction. The whole passage is spotless. It better be, with all the work we put into clearing up the mess.

Hard to think of all that blood and guts as a person.

Before I applied for astrospace, I was a medical volunteer in the Norwegian army reserve. I worked as a responder on road traffic accidents, sea rescue and veteran support. At the time, I did it to improve my profile and because I felt it was a way to put something back into a society that raised me and gave me a start. They say it's a common thing among my generation, to have a sense of gratitude and try to repay what we're given.

I've seen dead bodies, and I've attempted to help fatally injured people, but in nine months of medical work and two years of basic space, I never saw anything like the aftermath of corridor six.

Wounds in zero gravity can be problematic. Everything responds to the force exerted on it. Jonathan's body had been under acceleration strain, so he'd crashed into the far doors hard enough to shatter most of his bones. After that, when we stopped accelerating, his remains started to float around. That means a tough job trying to clean up, grabbing everything you can find by hand and bagging it up, until the whole sum of a person is collected into a set of bags.

I knew Jonathan. I guess that's why this was harder.

I've stopped moving. I'm staring through the glass, seeing it all over again. I'm not sure I can—

No, April! Focus. Move. Find something else to think about!

I reach my room door, place my thumb on the pad, and the panel slides away. I move inside and it closes behind me. Instantly my shoulders relax and a sob wells up in my throat.

I grab the desk as the grief takes me away. I need to let it out – to give in. That's how the therapist said you have to deal with it when it all gets too much. That's how we keep functioning. I don't have anyone to talk to out here, not properly. If I reach out like that, someone might see it as a weakness. I need this tour to go perfectly. *I need that promotion.*

But I know the bio-monitors will be registering distress. Doctor Bogdanovic will call me in response to an automated alert. I need to be ready to deal with that in a few minutes.

I can't control the sobbing. They turn into retching, the kind of crying that totally grips you. My hands are shaking. I can't get away from the image of the corridor and the bits and pieces of Jonathan. We joined the *Khidr* crew at the same time. He came from Scotland and grew up just outside Edinburgh, which I'd visited a few times. He had an older brother, who's also into plants. He's some important doctor on the Mars colony and—

"Bogdanovic to Johansson. Everything all right?"

The doctor's face is on my wall screen. I turn toward it and key up the response. "I'm fine, Doc, just pushed it a bit too hard, I think. Need a moment or two by myself to process."

Bogdanovic nods, but his concerned expression doesn't change. "Okay. Lieutenant Travers has amended the rota. It says you've got six hours downtime. If you can't sleep, drop by and I'll give you something to help."

"I will, thanks."

"I'll check in on you in an hour."

"Okay."

The intrusion is over, but it's done its job. The calm façade has returned. I've always been careful with whom I trust and let in. Bogdanovic is a nice guy, little older than me, but not someone I've opened up to in the past. Still, he asked me to help him and we shared that gruesome moment. Perhaps he'd understand?

No. He writes the psych evaluations for the Fleet promotional board. I can't risk it.

I'm staring at my hands. One is mine from birth, the other bought and paid for. I had the full integration operation with my prosthesis when I turned twenty. That was three and a half years ago now, after they'd assessed my physical development. I didn't want a 'corrective' like some people get when they grow a little more. The integration ring on this one should last forever. The prosthesis itself can be replaced or upgraded where necessary. I can barely tell the difference between my artificial fingers and my real ones these days, and that's the point. It took a while to unlearn some coping habits I'd developed as a child, but that didn't take long as I've been wearing removable units since I was ten. The main difference between those and the permanent system is the sense of touch. You don't get the same feeling of detail in a 'plug-on', without the hardwired connections.

My room has two bunks. By rights, I should be sharing, but there's a rotation in our extra capacity. The *Khidr* has to have space for twelve extra people as part of its mandate as a search and rescue patrol ship. There isn't a lot of point in leaving rooms unoccupied on a six-month patrol, so some of us don't have to pair up. That'll change in three weeks, when I'm due to move out and bunk in with Specialist Ashe. He's nice enough, but I'll miss not having my own space.

I'm out of sight of everyone else. That means I do what I was always going to do, carry on working. I pull out my portable screen and sync it with the wall device. The audio files and tactical plot appear in front of me. I check the frequencies and signal strengths again. This *has* to be a two-ship communication. There's no way it could be anything else.

I stare at the screen for a few moments, and then I have an idea. If this is ship to ship, how difficult would it be for us to plot positions from the fragments we've got?

I start running simulations, getting the computer to hypothesise the location of the transmissions based on our trajectory and relative position when we received the signals. Tight beam, energy-efficient broadcasting has been the protocol in space travel almost since we started climbing out of our atmosphere. The only exception to that is an emergency signal. When you're calling for help, you want everyone to know.

The computer starts working through the data. To start with, it can triangulate a possible range of positions for the second ship based on the audio information, the probability of receipt by us, and the position of the *Hercules*. The freighter is a huge ship and might affect the signal to block it or amplify it. These kinds of simulations are something I can understand, but working through the maths would take days or weeks for me, without factoring in any errors or checking I'd have to do on top of that.

Even with the ship's computer, the whole process will take hours.

I move to the lower bunk and lie down. The straps sense me and begin to snake around my body. I shut my eyes.

CHAPTER SIX

Shann

It's been nearly ten years since I left Canada.

My journey into space started with a call from the International Space Agency about my tactical and strategic simulation test scores. I'd always been into computers when I was a young child. Rather than see my interest in gaming as a waste of time, my parents encouraged me, pushing me toward the national and international military recruitment campaigns. I won a few regional events, but nothing serious.

I was invited to a meeting in Toronto. I sat three more tests and took two interviews before the agency officials explained exactly what they were profiling me for: the role of a space transit analyst.

I was offered a six-month trial secondment on Earth Station Five. I'd be monitoring and coordinating local orbit traffic around Earth and Luna. It took me about an hour to make a decision. I was packed up and flown to Vandenberg Air Force Base in California. I did six months of basic training and left Earth after that to start my new job.

Those first few days in microgravity gave me exactly what I needed. I'd found my place, my home.

I've never been back.

Six months vanished. A promotion and a second contract followed. Then I was invited to work in a senior coordination role on Luna. This would be a commissioned post, meaning I'd have to join Fleet officially. I did, passing the entrance exams and getting my ensign's bar. After nine months, I transferred to a mobile tracking facility, and worked there for nearly two years. From there, I got recruited as bridge crew on the *Baldr*. When the *Khidr*'s previous captain left, I interviewed for the captain's post and got it.

Sometimes, I wonder what life is like on Earth now. I get an impression from news articles and correspondence, but nothing visceral or current because of how far out we are. What goes on up here is pretty removed from the day-to-day politics and horse-trading I remember.

The resonance drive winds down. We spin up the rotational section. We're one hour away from the rendezvous, and I call another meeting.

When I get to the gravity deck, all the others are sitting around a table, waiting for me.

"I thought we were inviting Keiyho to this," Le Garre says.

"We were," I reply. "Something happened."

"You going to fill us in?" Travers asks.

"Yes," I say. "But first, I need to hear from each of you." I turn to Duggins. "Are we prepared?"

"Yes, I've briefed everyone," he says. "The team are ready to go as soon as we're in range."

"You think it's a shutdown?"

"Latest transponder information points to that."

"I've updated the rosters," Travers says. "We'll have all hands available at the rendezvous. We can plan for what's needed after that."

"Sleep deprivation may be an issue," I say. "We need to take care no one is pushed too hard, especially now people are talking."

Travers sighs. "Yeah, we're going to be vulnerable during the rescue – short-handed and with our eyes on other things. Perfect time for another *accident*."

"We think Drake's chair responded to an emergency override command from a bridge console, or a handheld device," Le Garre explains. "Captain Shann was checking the bridge command history for the last twenty-four hours. I take it you found something too?"

I nod. "I was about to bring Keiyho in and authorise personal sidearms, but when I got to the bridge, my screen had been tampered with. Only Keiyho and Johansson were there. Keiyho said no one had been in."

"Keiyho, you think it was him? Is that why he isn't here?"

"I hope it wasn't him," I reply. "However, I also found a set of commands executed from my console during the burn. They deactivated four different chairs across the ship. Only one was occupied. That was Drake's chair."

Le Garre frowns. "What about Johansson? She was there too."

I think about that for a moment. "She's so committed to Fleet and her career I can't see her as a traitor. When I got up there, she didn't even notice I'd come in. She's so focused on her work."

Duggins grins. "Yes, I put that in her file."

"Good, she deserves that. I can't be absolutely sure, but my instincts tell me she's not who we're looking for."

Le Garre's expression becomes thoughtful. "If you'd performed those commands, you wouldn't have told us. You'd have erased them and said the consoles were clean."

I smile at her. "It doesn't make sense that I'd try to murder my own crew."

Le Garre shrugs. "A random murder doesn't make sense either. The killer must have had a motive, personal or professional."

"Yes." I'm trying to think over the politics of this from the last intel briefing I read. There's nothing in Drake's file to suggest he would be a target for assassination, but taking out a Fleet tech while on board a ship, or even taking out a Fleet ship, would send a message. There are some Earth-based organisations that don't like us, but reaching us out here would be a stretch for them. "At this moment in time, let's not rule anything out."

"Probably for the best."

"If Keiyho is our main suspect, we have a problem," Duggins says. "He's one of two people on the ship with access to the firearms lockers. He might already be armed, and that means we're already at a disadvantage."

"Quartermaster Sam Chase is the only other person with access," Travers says.

I bite my lip and glance at Duggins. He knows how close Sam and I are. So do most of the crew, but not all. Duggins nods and gives me a reassuring look. "Captain Shann doesn't want to vouch for Sam as they were friends before he joined the ship's crew," he says.

"That's understandable," Le Garre says. "Do you trust him?" she asks me.

"Yes, implicitly," I reply.

"I'll interview him first then," she says. "We can call it vetting. Once we're confident he had nothing to do with Drake's death, we can bring him in."

"A good solution," Duggins says.

"It still puts us behind," Le Garre replies. "We have to anticipate that our traitor has already thought about this."

"I agree," I say. "When I looked at the files on my screen and the command history, everything was easy to find. There was no reason for files to have been moved and deleted. They were quickly recovered too."

"If someone had access to your screen with your log-in, they could have deleted all the clues, wiping out any trace of what they'd done," Duggins says. "None of us would know."

"So, what's their objective?" Travers asks. "I mean, if we're finding these clues, either they're sloppy or they want something else."

"Maybe distracting and dividing us is the objective?" Le Garre suggests.

Duggins grunts. "If it is, it's working."

"There's something else I need to share with you," I say. I reach across the table and activate the flip-up screen. I log in to the system, pull up my personal messages and select the one with the encrypted data archive. "This was sent to me from Fleet. It includes permission for me to share it with the senior officers. I've not accessed it yet. I wanted to make sure we all looked at it together."

"When we spoke before, you mentioned it was an automatic message?" Le Garre prompts.

"Yes, it seems to have been triggered when we sent the first request for the *Hercules*'s cargo manifest. There's no name, or sender."

The authorisation panel comes up. I input my Fleet ID and the highest authorisation code that I know. The whole screen goes black for a moment, and then a date flashes up – 22.02.2116 – just over two years ago. An Asian woman's face appears, and she's looking directly into the camera.

Then the image freezes and a second password box pops up. I input my codes again, but they are rejected.

"Why would you be given an archive that you can't access?" Travers asks.

"No clue," I reply.

"Perhaps the crew of the *Hercules* will have answers?" Le Garre says. "Maybe we were sent the information so they can provide us with limited access codes?"

"Possibly," I say. "A shame we don't have the answers now."

Duggins taps the screen. "We could try to crack it," he says. "Like you said, Johansson's focused and good with computers. Given some time, she might get through."

"We can't be sure of her yet, and I don't want to break regulations. We'll go by the book."

"Well, we don't know who sent us this. It might not be Fleet command."

"We'll assume it was for now," I decide. "Besides, Johansson's working on something else."

"Oh?"

I quickly explain the audio files and the isolated words. I can see Duggins absorbing the information and adding it to his plans. "Thanks," he says when I'm done. "That gives us more reason to think we're dealing with a drive shutdown."

"I wonder what 'please don't, sir' means," Le Garre muses.

"Could be anything," Travers says. He scratches his beard. "Have you had a complete report from Johansson yet, Captain?"

"No. She's being thorough."

"Will you share it when you do?"

"Of course."

I sign out of the system and look at each of my three officers. They're tired and confused, driving against an enemy none of us can name. We're two steps behind, trying to jump ahead. There's too much we don't know and too much at stake.

*   *   *

Humanity is a miracle and a solitary miracle at that, according to what we've found in the last three centuries of space exploration. Yes, we've found signs of extinct life on Mars, possible traces of life on Titan, but nothing to rival our own civilisation.

Our satellites and spacecraft continue to search the stars for habitable planets that we might travel to one day. They also look for signs of others who might exist like we do, imprisoned in their own solar system with an umbilical tether to the mother planet.

Earth isn't without problems in its past. Our home has seen five mass extinctions in its history, ranging from giant asteroid impacts to massive volcanic eruptions. Add in the World Wars and the twenty-first-century environmental crisis, and we've had three man-made disasters of nearly equal world-changing effect.

Many scientists and entrepreneurs have been on record in their endorsement of humanity finding ways to live on other planets. We have to expand into our solar system and devise technologies to take us farther into the stars.

The reasoning is straightforward: when the next giant asteroid heads our way, we must have the resources to deal with it. If we don't, we need to be someplace else; otherwise we'll be extinct. If the situation is worse, like a nearby star exploding, or our own sun destroying itself, we may not be able to save anything on Earth, Mars, or anywhere else around here. We can't afford to wait around and find out.

Settlements, outposts and colonies have to become self-sufficient to survive, and humanity can learn from all the mistakes we made on Earth. History helps us to improve ourselves, and it's working. You can tell because of our successes. The life you have today is far better than the lives people lived twenty, fifty, or a hundred years ago.

All we need is to keep looking forward and striving for the betterment of ourselves and our species.

Speech from Oludare Adisa, President of the United Astro-Physics Foundation.

CHAPTER SEVEN

Shann

I'm back in my chair on the bridge when Keiyho says, "*Hercules* within five thousand klicks, Captain."

Instinctively, I'm looking out into space. The shutters are up. The black expanse seems no different. It's impossible to determine our velocity without something to see moving past. I glance down at my screen. A red cross marks a spot in the top left corner; a set of decreasing numbers appears. "Time to rendezvous?" I ask.

"Thirteen minutes, twelve seconds."

"Increase braking," I order.

"Aye, aye."

My body is pressed against the seat straps. We're decelerating at just over one gravity, a gradual decrease in speed to match the velocity of the freighter. The *Khidr* has been prepped for the encounter. The rotation deck is stopped and locked, other deployed panels and antennae retracted. This won't be an easy maneuver. Our computers have been tracking the *Hercules* for hours, plotting its trajectory from a series of laser scans and transponder pings, but we can't be precise until we're very close.

I glance down at Johansson's completed report. Since we dropped out of resonance, there have been no further transmissions picked up. We can't be sure if the resonance drive affects the echoing, beyond the distortion we filtered out. There hasn't been enough research to determine whether travelling in that state enhances the sensitivity of our receiver systems.

Johansson isolated more than thirty individual words. Four of them might be 'Hercules'. That can't be a coincidence. The chance of the communication being an EVA transmission is tiny. There has to be something else in what she's found.

"There she is!"

Duggins is standing up in his seat, pointing. There are ten or more people on the bridge, with everyone called up for the rendezvous moment. I'm staring at where he's pointing. There's a bright silver box-like shape, growing larger and larger. Suddenly our speed is noticeable.

"Bring us in, Major," I say.

"Aye, aye," Le Garre replies.

The boxlike shape extends into an oblong. Details begin to appear. The freighter is huge and designed as a cradle, a vast scaffold structure with engines at one end and a habitat/control module at the other. Out here, there's no gain in creating sleek lines and pretty shapes. Cubes and cuboids offer the best storage solutions. When these ships are unloaded, they are empty shells; when packed with goods and supplies, they're a tame whale in space.

From here, the sense of scale is impossible to get straight in your mind. There's no frame of reference. I'm reminded of the old films where they tricked people into believing things were big or small by placing them near or far away from the camera. Forced perspective, they called it. Here, we have no perspective. I know the *Hercules* is still ten kilometres away, but I keep thinking I can reach out and pluck it out of the black background.

"We're detecting thrust wash," Keiyho says. "Their drives have been active recently."

"But they're not active now," Jacobson says. "There's no engines online."

The *Hercules* is listing and rotating slowly. This'll make docking with her pretty difficult. "We need more visual data," I say. "Get me a hull scan."

This is my eighth freighter rescue encounter in six years. Maybe that's a testimony to the robust design of these behemoths. Each encounter was different, presenting its own challenges and dangers.

The *Khidr* is approaching a little to the left of the *Hercules*. Le Garre adjusts our attitude for maximum view, and the freighter rolls around us so we're approaching from below. The major is overworked and tired, but still the best pilot we have on board. We close to single digits, and the engine section fills the upper half of the screen. Clusters and eruptions of hollow rocket cones, like the strange plants you see underwater on rocks.

"Any response to communications?" I ask.

"None so far, Captain," Jacobson says. "I'm increasing our transmission output as we get closer, adding frequencies, but there's nothing coming back."

"Not even the automated distress call?"

"No. Nothing."

That's strange. *Very strange.* Whoever sent out the call wanted someone to respond. *Why turn it off?* "Park us up near the habitat section," I say.

"Aye, aye," Le Garre replies.

The pressure on my straps eases a little. We're passing massive container after massive container, packed full of supplies for colonies and outposts beyond Phobos Station. This shipment maintains lives out at the dangerous fringe. Almost every commodity people on Earth take for granted has to be shipped out in continuous and consecutive runs every few months. The logistical planning for all this is done years in advance. The freighters themselves are a kilometre long and built to last for decades.

The *Khidr* is slowing noticeably now. We're drifting over the last of the storage. Next, there's the vertically mounted gravity carousel and in front of that a final cuboid – the control section.

"Wow. Imagine having to fix a problem on that thing," Jacobson says.

"You may just get your wish, Ensign," Duggins growls.

"The rotational deck isn't moving, Captain," Le Garre observes.

"Nice to see someone's paying attention," I say. "Any other signs of life?"

"Our ship's illumination profile makes it difficult to pick out anything, Captain," Duggins says. "I think I saw some exterior lights, but I can't be sure. We're not picking up any stray data from their internal network."

"Okay, send a wire."

"Wire, aye."

A 'wire' is a nonhostile projectile attached to a cable. It's fired from Keiyho's console and designed to attach itself to the hull of another ship to access its internal electronics. Once we're 'plugged in' we can begin a system diagnostic. The cable remains a loose and controlled connection, so if there's a movement discrepancy between the two ships that we can't fix, we can detach quickly.

"Wire deployed," Keiyho says.

We wait a few minutes. Then there's an audible ping on Duggins's console. "Connection established," he says. "Okay, this is unusual."

"What's unusual?"

"The *Hercules*, she's powered down, completely turned off."

The words float around the crowded bridge. I chew my lip. *Powered down?* Suddenly the mission parameters have changed. This is more than a rescue and repair. In all the previous freighter incidents I've dealt with, this has never happened. I can't remember an incident like it happening to anyone else, either.

I glance around. Everyone is looking at me, waiting for me to make a decision and get us moving.

"Keiyho, I want a security team assembled to board first, before the repair crew."

"Aye, aye."

"Duggins, assign one of yours to the detail. I'm going; Keiyho's in charge. Travers, you'll have the bridge until I'm back."

"Captain, are you sure that's—"

"It's decided. Let's get moving."

I'm out of my chair and moving before there are any more questions. I can feel the eyes on me, making their own judgements. Let them; the call is made.

★   ★   ★

Our airlock is correctly aligned with the *Hercules*'s habitat module. More 'wires' have been sent over to secure us. We could dock the two ships airlock to airlock, but that would leave us vulnerable. We'd be locked to their ship and its listless drift. *Khidr* engines would be no match for the *Hercules* if they suddenly reactivated and it would take time get us loose, so instead, we'll tether and EVA across.

I'm in a full astro-suit, wearing prosthetic legs and magged to the deck. The suits are standard issue, so the legs are required. I don't need them to move around, but without them, I'll be dragging half the getup with me.

The magnetic boots are another necessary burden. While it's safe enough to fly around inside our ship, outside I can't take risks. There's a voice in my head that says I'd be fine, but it's wrong. Another thing the human mind can't process properly.

Five others are prepped, Duggins and Keiyho among them. All I can see are people in suits and reflective visors, until Arkov, one of the techs, starts applying name patches to our shoulders. Someone is carrying a portable power unit. Someone else has a hull cutter.

We're all carrying low-velocity firearms.

"Team ready," Keiyho says over the comms.

"Wilco, team, depressurising the airlock now," Le Garre says from the bridge.

"Aye, aye."

Spacecraft have to make use of every resource available. Depressurisation of a room requires that room to be drained of air, which is sent back into the ship's reserves. Opening the compartment to the outside might be quicker and easier, but it's wasteful. So, we go through a gradual process of creating as near a vacuum as possible by bleeding the air back into the tanks.

Then we open the compartment door and the residual low-pressure atmosphere leaks out into space.

I'm clipped on to the cable with a motorised carabiner and connected to the other team members with a safety line. When we're all ready, the wheels on the carabiner will power their way along the cable to the *Hercules* habitat module airlock. Once we're there, Keiyho and Duggins will open the outer door with the emergency release.

Keiyho clips on in front of me and attaches his safety line to my waist. "Let's go," he says over the comms.

And with that, we're moving, out of the ship and into space.

My first proper EVA was during my six-month tour on Earth Five. There were only four of us on rotation at any one time, so anytime we needed a trip outside, all of us would be involved. One to do the work, one as backup, one monitoring from the bridge and one supervising from the airlock.

Back then, we were out cleaning solar panels and replacing a communications aerial.

This is something altogether different:

We're moving down the line. The *Hercules* is three hundred metres or so away, I guess. Lights from the *Khidr* are illuminating a large section of the fuselage, and as I get closer, I notice scars and pockmarks crisscrossing the freighter's shell.

"Captain," Le Garre says from the bridge, "we've identified a hull breach in the habitat section."

"How serious is it?"

"Pretty serious. According to the schematic, it's close to the pilot housing."

"Okay."

The information has been broadcast over the team channel. Keiyho and Duggins will know the same thing I do. The others all around me will know too.

We're close to the hull. Keiyho unclips himself from the cable and grabs the safety rail. He begins working his way along to the outer hatch.

I unclip myself and follow; everyone else follows me.

Keiyho grabs the emergency release handle for the hatch. He braces his feet against the hull and tries to move it.

No luck.

"Wait until we're all in position," I say. "Hopefully, we can apply a bit more brute force."

"Aye, aye, Captain."

I move hand over hand toward him. I go past him, securing a line to the safety rail on the other side. The other members of the team move up. I make room for them, and I switch channels to private. "Le Garre, what else can you tell me?" I ask.

"Not a lot, Captain," she says.

"If power on the ship is out, could there be any survivors?"

"We have some ideas," Le Garre replies. "If the *Hercules* was equipped with cryo-freezing tanks, the crew could have taken refuge in those."

"That's a stretch. Why would a freighter have that kind of tech on board?"

"Captain, with all the gaps in the registered manifest, anything could be on there."

I try to imagine a hull breach crisis and eight crew fleeing into a cubic kilometre of the cargo hold. "They wouldn't have had much time to organise something," I say. "But storage containers can be pressurised."

"Yes, sir, although not many are, as there's very few goods that require an atmosphere during transit."

"But the crew could pressurise a container?"

"It's possible." There's a scratching noise and some chatter on the bridge that I can't hear. Le Garre is talking to the others, I guess. A moment later, she's back. "Captain, Ensign Jacobson suggests an easier method of surviving would be to get into an EVA suit and plug into one of the atmosphere feeds."

I smile. "Tell the ensign those few hours' sleep appear to have woken him up. Good work. Can we check these feeds?"

"We can, as soon as Duggins restores local power."

"Okay, I'll talk to him about it," I say. "If we're going to search the cargo hold, we'll need to deploy drones. Otherwise we could be here forever."

"I'll let the technical team know, Captain."

"Thank you."

I turn back to the work at hand. The portable power unit has been cabled up to a mechanised arm magnetised to the hull. It's being operated by remote control, and as I watch, it grabs and slowly turns the emergency hatch release.

"Looks like we're in," Duggins says. There's a smugness to his words. I can almost hear him smiling.

"We'll make for the bridge first," Keiyho says. "We unclip now. Stay in sight of each other. I'll go first."

He clambers into the ship. The others begin disassembling the arm and the power unit. I follow Keiyho, stepping into the airlock.

It's dark in here. I can't remember ever having explored a spaceship without power. I activate my suit lights and switch my magboots to walk mode. They'll respond to the different ambulatory pressures of my prosthetic feet. This whole process isn't how I'd like to work, but for now it's required, so we're all moving at the same pace.

"Obstruction ahead," Keiyho says. I raise my head to see. The corridor looks like it's crumpled inward. There's a pile of crates wedged in here too, blocking our way. This is strange. Any crew gear wouldn't be stowed in an access corridor, and any cargo should be in the hold.

"It might be worth staying here, near the airlock, so we can link up the power unit to a terminal," Duggins suggests. "That way we can get a diagnostic before we move too far from our exit."

Keiyho turns toward us. "How long will that take?" he asks.

"About twenty minutes."

"We're tanked for three hours. I want to assess the bridge in that time."

The two visors turn toward me. "We should split the group," I say. "Duggins, you make a start here and call over the rest of your repair team when you need them. We'll move on toward the bridge."

"Aye, aye, Captain," Duggins says.

"Team to *Khidr*, we're splitting up," Keiyho announces. "Three heading forward, three staying at the entrance. Prepare the repair team to follow us in."

"Affirmative, team," Travers replies.

Tomlins moves past me. He's a lab tech by specialty, but also has seven years' experience as a marine, ideal for this kind of situation. I let him and Keiyho take the lead. The two of them move up to the crates and start moving them to one side. The job's more difficult in zero gravity; you have to have something to brace yourself against.

I wonder...

There's a knife on my belt. I draw it and clump over to one of the crates. I jam it into one of the catches, and it comes free. I do the same with a second and a third.

"What are you doing?" Keiyho asks.

"They shouldn't be here," I explain. "They've been put here to block off access from the airlock. I think the freighter crew were expecting visitors before someone blew a hole in their bridge."

There's a symbol on the lid. A sort of spiral inset into a circle in black and red. I make a mental note of it as I try to grip the handle with the thick fingers of my suit. Eventually, I get a finger into the gap and pull it open.

"Well, well," I exclaim. "That's a surprise."

CHAPTER EIGHT

Shann

Inside the crate are test tubes, hundreds of them. The contents are frozen. I pick one out. My suit lights illuminate something in the centre of it.

"They're carrying bees," I say.

Tomlins is beside me. He pulls out another. "I've seen these before. They're miniature cryogenic pods. There's an electrical current passing through the glass from a microcomputer in the lid. They have portable power units so they can carry on working for weeks, independently of a ship or laboratory. The military uses them to transport cultures."

I stare at the container. "Why are they transporting bees? What are they for?"

"The large hydroponics gardens on Mars use bees to replicate the plant fertilisation process," Tomlins explains. "It's more efficient than any kind of manual or mechanised system."

"Where could they be taking these? You think they're setting up a new garden on Ceres?"

"If they are, no one's talking about it."

I put the tube back in the crate. "We'll deal with this later. Let's get to the bridge."

Keiyho is still clearing the rest of the debris. Tomlins and I join him to help. Between the three of us, we manage to make a path and move into the access corridor.

Keiyho has a portable screen in his hands. "We turn right at the end and then climb up two floors," he says. "That should put us on the bridge."

"What are you expecting to find, Lieutenant Commander?" Tomlins asks. "If that's where the hull breach occurred, there may not be much to find."

"We still need to confirm that."

We move to the end of the corridor and make the turn. The access hatch to the upper decks is sealed. "We're stuck here," Keiyho says.

"Only for a little bit," I say. I activate a comms channel. "Shann to bridge."

"Bridge receiving, Captain."

"Deploy drones to the freighter. Send one up to us with a supplementary power unit and another cutter. Nothing too big, just enough for us to get through a door."

"Aye, aye."

"Might be quicker to bring the equipment up from the airlock," Keiyho says.

"It might, but then Duggins would have to stop what he's doing," I say. "Both objectives are necessary."

"Of course, Captain."

I turn to Tomlins. "If the *Hercules* was transporting classified hydroponics equipment, what else could we expect to find around here?"

"Seed catalogues, tissue samples, chemical fertilisers, soil, everything to supply a greenhouse, I'd guess," Tomlins says.

"But why would this be classified?" Keiyho asks. "Expansion to the lab gardens on any facility has to be a good thing that the public would be pleased to hear about."

"You'd think, wouldn't you?" I say.

We fall silent, waiting. My thoughts turn to Drake and the investigation. Le Garre can't make any progress while we need her on the bridge and I'm down here with one of our suspects. I'm watching both of my companions, holding back all the time. If Keiyho is our traitor, he's giving nothing away.

I look around. The chaos tells me this place has a story to tell. If we can get access to the computer systems, we might be able to obtain the security camera footage. Then we'll learn more about what happened.

A light appears at the end of the corridor. Instinctively, my hand moves to the low-velocity pistol on my belt, but then I recognise the drone and relax. "Le Garre, transfer control to Keiyho's screen."

"Aye, aye," she replies.

The drone floats past us all toward the hatch. Tomlins steps forward and detaches the portable power unit and the cutter. Both are smaller than the ones we brought up for the airlock.

"Keiyho, before we start applying brute force, can you do a scan of the chamber behind the hatch?" I ask.

"Sure," Keiyho says. "What am I looking for?"

"There must be a reason this door was blocked," I reason. "Perhaps this was a second line of defence."

Tomlins looks around, his suit lights illuminating the walls. "There's no sign of a fight in here," he says.

"Maybe they found another way through?"

"Or changed tactics," I say. "Just in case, run a scan."

"You think someone survived?"

"I think we need to run a scan."

Keiyho guides the drone forward. The controls are tricky to manage through the thick gloves of our suits, but he's done this before. A blue light bathes the wall as the machine moves through its repertoire of detection systems. Then it moves forward and lands on the hatch. The readouts scroll across Keiyho's screen, and as he reads them, he lets out a low whistle. "Quite a hunch you had there, Captain."

"What did you find?"

"There's micro-vibration and some kind of heat source behind there," Keiyho says. "The vibration is rhythmic. Could be someone banging on the door."

"Start recording," I say. "Get the drone to compare with our signal database. Could be Morse or a variation of it."

"Doing it now," Keiyho says.

"If there's someone in there and they've got atmo, it'll be hard to get them out," Tomlins says.

"We'll find a way," I reply.

"I have a translation," Keiyho announces. "You were right, Morse code. Message reads, 'HELP ME'. Looks like we have a survivor who needs rescuing."

"We'll try," I say. "We'll try."

*   *   *

An hour later, I'm back on the bridge of the *Khidr*, staring at the *Hercules*.

"So far, we've searched eight per cent of the cargo hold," Travers reports. "There's some signs of disturbance, either from the ship's listing or the crew breaking into some of the containers. We've found no other possible survivors so far."

"How's Duggins doing?"

"They've wired the power unit into the freighter's system. They're trying to isolate the data access from the emergency reboot sequence."

I nod. This was a problem we'd identified. Once they are activated, the life support systems of a spaceship are hardwired. Shutting them down properly requires a complex sequence of commands. If the *Hercules* lost power suddenly, then none of those commands will have been executed. That means the ship will try to activate all those systems the minute we hook it up. If that happens, our portable generator will be drained immediately.

To get around the problem, Duggins has been trying to isolate the computers from the rest of the ship's systems. He's working on a terminal near the airlock, which he needs to use to patch into the bridge computer that can tell us what was happening in the moments before the freighter lost power.

The whole process would be a lot easier if we could get to the bridge and access those computers directly, but the access corridor is blocked.

So, we have to do things the hard way.

"Captain, drone number six has entered the ship through the breach and reached the bridge," Travers says. "We've got a camera in there."

I activate the drone's feed on my screen. Roving torchlight reveals my worst fears. This is the aftermath of violence. The metal walls are rumpled and torn; there are bodies and equipment floating around the ruined space. Once people worked here, performing the kind of jobs we're doing now, and then in a flash, they were turned into this, so much charred flesh and dismembered limbs. I can only hope no one survived that moment, that for everyone, it was a quick end.

"Captain, we've got the photographic analysis of the habitat breach," Jacobson says. He sounds worried. "You're not going to like this."

"What's the computer conclusion?"

"Impact is consistent with a weapon impact."

"What?"

"Eighty-six per cent probability it's a weapon impact, Captain."

I feel cold. I look down at my screen. Jacobson's data has arrived, along with the analysis. I can see trajectory speculation, chemical compound residue testing, impact and damage evaluation. The words 'explosive compound', 'targeted pressure breach', and 'exterior close quarter battle launch' are listed underneath the animated diagrams.

What do I—

"Verify that calculation, Ensign," Travers orders from the pilot's chair.

"Lieutenant, the computer says—"

"I don't care, run the numbers again!"

I'm grateful to Travers. A double check gives me a moment to rally, to digest and comprehend what we're dealing with – the aftermath of a battle, an attack in space.

There's never been a moment like this in the history of human space exploration. The Cold War of the twentieth century was exactly that. The subsequent geopolitical proxy conflicts that became the death throes of the world's last two superpowers, America and China, in the late twenty-first century never had battle lines drawn beyond Earth's atmosphere.

Fleet's ships are equipped with weapons, but all the scenarios in which they've been deployed have involved encounters with asteroids, or stray debris. In those situations, we'd fire a guided rocket at range, or in close quarters we'd warm up the ship's laser. Any situation we've dealt with has involved an adversary that doesn't fire back.

There's never been an incident like this.

Who do I have up here? Which of them do I trust? Travers is in the pilot seat, Jacobson on navigation/communications; Ensign Chiu, Duggins's assistant, is in the engineering chair, and Ensign Thakur is on tactical.

These people are my crew. They are relying on me. I have to trust them until they prove untrustworthy.

"Communications?"

"Aye, Captain?"

"Once the verification is complete, I want a priority signal sent to Earth and Mars colony immediately relaying our findings. Package up all the supporting data we have. Engineering?"

"Yes, Captain?"

"How many of the crew are currently aboard the freighter?"

"Eleven, Captain."

"How many involved in the rescue operation?"

"Five."

"Inform Keiyho and Duggins of our findings. Tell them to prioritise the rescue. We can always come back for the data. I want an ETA on completion. Tactical?"

"Yes, Captain?"

"Start a field scan of our surroundings. I want our eyes outward. If there's anything out here, I want to know about it before it knows about us."

"Aye, aye."

"Ship-wide announcement, we're going to action stations. Get everyone in position. We're going to need them."

People start moving and disappear quickly from the bridge, leaving five of us in our seats. I think about Le Garre. When I got back, she left her seat to get some rest. This alert means she'll have to come straight back to take a position. Johansson was exhausted too, from completing that report. She'll have gotten some sleep before the alert will bring her back.

I look down at my screen. There's a whole selection of drone camera feeds, a view of Duggins's team at work in the airlock, and Keiyho's at work at the jammed hatch. The latter is a tough situation to resolve. The person on the other side doesn't have an EVA suit or any air reserve. That means they can't cut through the door without depressurising the space, but if they don't get inside soon, the survivor will be poisoned by the buildup of carbon dioxide. Keiyho's been trying to rig up a temporary ejection chamber, using one of the fabric corridors we have for ship-to-ship transfer. They've just got it pressurised and have started to cut their way through the hatch.

I'm still thinking about Johansson. I activate communications directly to her quarters. "April, this is Captain Shann, are you there?"

There's no response.

"Ensign, this is the bridge. Are you—"

Johansson appears on the screen. She fumbles with a headset and settles herself into the chair. "Yes, Captain?"

"April, I need you to go over your audio files again," I say. "We've new evidence that seems to validate your idea that the *Hercules* was talking to another ship. It looks like they were attacked. If that's the case, I need a fresh interpretation of the message fragments you picked up and a timeline, please. We may be able to use your work to get a picture of what happened."

"Okay, Captain, I'll get on that."

"Thank you. Stay in your room and alert the bridge if you find anything new."

"Aye, aye."

I touch the screen and close the window. I quickly flip through the drone feeds. We have twelve drones deployed; each one is going farther and farther into the cargo hold. The more of it they explore, the less we find. Everything looks undisturbed. That doesn't make sense. If attacking the *Hercules* was an act of piracy, surely whoever did it would try to steal things. Why has everything been left where it was?

Drone number five turns a corner, and its lights illuminate something in a corner. I key up the controls immediately and get it to stop. "Travers, bring up the camera on five," I say.

"Got it, Captain," Travers says. "I see it. What do you think—"

"That's an oxygen feed," I say. "Those pipes are looped into the container behind." I manipulate the controls, and the drone moves closer, picking out the equipment lying discarded on the floor. "Someone stowed away on the ship."

"That someone could still be there, watching our people," Travers adds.

"That's not an encouraging thought."

"Captain, Engineer Duggins has obtained access to the freighter's computer system," Jacobson announces. "He's initiated a data transfer. We're receiving an information dump now."

"Time to completion?"

"Three hours, forty-two minutes."

"Tell Duggins to clear his team out and set everything to remote," I order. "Brief his people on what we've found. They are authorised to use firearms if necessary. Get those people back over here as quickly as you can."

"Understood, Captain."

My hands are twitching. I'm struggling to stay here and sit in this chair. While I have access to all the information available on my screen, I feel powerless to help and act. Everything is too complicated and taking too long.

"Captain, drone number three is no longer transmitting."

I flick over to the relevant window. There's a blank screen. I wind it back thirty seconds. There's an open crate on the floor. It's huge, empty and filled with shaped foam. Some sort of large sphere has been in here, but now it's gone. A moment later, something obscures the camera and there's a whiteout. "Someone's doing this on purpose," I realise aloud.

I'm suddenly cold. I can see those bodies floating around the *Hercules*'s bridge. That could've been us, could still be us if I don't act fast and make the right calls.

"Captain?"

I blink twice; my left hand covers my right. The nail of my index finger digs into the back of my hand. Pain banishes the fog. *Get a grip!* Jacobson is still talking to me. He's waiting on an answer. "How far was drone number three from the rescue teams?"

"Five hundred metres or so, Captain."

I activate a communications line to Keiyho. "Lieutenant Commander, we have a hostile encounter. You need to complete what you're doing, very quickly."

"How long do we have?" Keiyho asks. His voice is calm. The Japanese inflection makes me feel calmer as well.

"About fifteen minutes," I reply.

"We'll make it," he says. "Prepare for five, plus one."

That's good news. I feel a sense of elation. If we can rescue the survivor, we may get some answers. "Relay that to Technician Arkov," I tell Jacobson, who nods. I remember what Travers said before – *we're going to be vulnerable during the rescue*. "Pull the drones back too. Get them in a perimeter, around Keiyho's people."

"On it, Captain. Shall I—"

At that moment, there's a loud and low bang. The klaxon alert sounds, and the ship lurches violently to the right. I'm jammed against my straps. Someone is screaming. Something has happened. We're...

...under attack!

CHAPTER NINE

Johansson

My head throbs and there's a ringing sound in my ears. A moment ago, I was working on my terminal analysing audio fragments, the next minute I was being slammed into the wall. The safety straps prevented the worst of the impact, but I still managed to whack my head against something hard and unforgiving.

I'm trying to untangle myself, but there's still shifting forces affecting me as the ship maneuvers. This is a complex burn. We must be under manual control. I can hear the alert klaxon in the hallway, and the auto-sensors don't want to let me go. We must be performing an emergency course change. *What's happened to cause this?* I'm struggling to reach the activation for my comms on my wrist or my neck, but I can't get to either.

There's an urge to panic. If I do, I know my heart rate will increase and my breathing will become rapid, alerting Bogdanovic again, who probably has more than enough to deal with.

I need to control the symptoms as much as possible. Part of this is psychological. I've done high gravity training, which simulates these kinds of circumstances. The changing directional pressure is confusing. The safety system is trying to protect me. I need to wait this out and focus on small objectives. Everyone on board will be going through a similar situation.

My right arm is trapped behind me. The strap has twisted around my prosthetic wrist. I can automatically disengage the arm to free myself, but then I'll be thrown around while the straps try to reengage. I need to ride this out.

I shut my eyes and remember the old fairground we used to visit every summer. It was in a field, right on the coast, just a short walk from my house. Every July, as part of the Fish Festival, I'd see the trucks arrive and watch the travelling families pitch their tents before they started assembling the rides. Circular metal tracks and painted cars would emerge from the back of transport containers. Men and women swarmed over them with hammers, drill drivers and wrenches, working long hours to make everything safe.

At night, the whole place would come alive with electric lights and music. Schoolkids from everywhere would queue up for hours just to get a few minutes whirling around on the rides, screaming with joy as they hurtled into the air and back down again.

I loved the fairground. Now I pretend I'm back there, being thrown about by the festival machines. I remember the view, looking out over the sea from the top of the 'magic carpet' or the Ferris wheel. I would try to get on as the sun set so I could see the water turn gold on the horizon.

Later, my school bought a whole set of synth experience pods, where you suit up and enter a visual emulation, with pulleys and platforms to make you think you're flying a plane or racing around a track in a fast car. It was never the same.

At the real fairground, you could ride in different ways. Scared kids would tense up, trying to fight the twists and turns; others would relax and go floppy, letting their bodies get thrown into every bump and shunt. Out here, I can't do either. There's a technique you have to adopt, letting your body move as the inertia dictates, but taking care to flex your muscles when necessary, to ensure the straps don't cut into your flesh, doing internal damage to bones and organs.

Back in those days of my childhood, I trusted I would be safe. The harness and belts were there to make sure we didn't get hurt while the machines flung us around. Later, it was the same with the experience pods, astrospace simulators and the 'vomit comet'. All of these were machines, designed to give you a thrill or test you within tolerable limits. That didn't stop people panicking or giving up their breakfast, but at least you knew someone had constructed the experience you were enduring or enjoying. There was a limit to the force you'd be subjected to.

Out here, the computer calculates a course correction and there's a similar safety threshold, but in an emergency, you've no idea what the pilot might chance. You're subject to the consequences of their choices. Those choices could be fatal.

At least I was strapped in when we started.

I'm thinking about the words again. I can see the file list in my mind. I start mouthing them, trying to work out what I've missed. I keep going back to the phrase Captain Shann found – *"...please don't...sir..."* I can picture someone saying it while in EVA, asking a technician to open the airlock, or something, but that doesn't make sense if we've got two ships talking to each other. 'Sir' implies a relationship, like they're in the same fleet or...

Maybe it's not 'sir'. Perhaps that's just part of a word.

How long was the pause? The dip between 'don't' and the next word. Long enough for there to be a word in between that we didn't pick up? I think so, but only a short one. Even with the fragmentation of the signal, the list of possible terms is small. A word with louder syllables would have a greater chance of being picked up. We've got nothing, just a gap. What could it be?

Please don't wait, sir?

Please don't...we?

Surrender?

I'm guessing, but it fits the facts. I need to tell the captain.

Just as soon as the ship stops spinning around.

CHAPTER TEN

Shann

"Report! What was that?"

"Some kind of depressurisation, Captain! A response team is on its way to hydroponics." Jacobson's voice is shrill and wavering. I'm reminded of just how young he is. His words register. An accident in hydroponics – where Drake worked. *Was he murdered because he found—*

"We're drifting away from the *Hercules*, Captain!"

"Travers, get us back in position!"

There's no answer. I look over. Travers is out cold, slumped forward in his chair. We're cabled to the freighter; if we don't correct, those lines will run out of play.

I key up the pilot controls. A mini-joystick flips out of the armrest. A graphic representation of the ship appears on the screen. The hydroponics compartment is flashing red. That means we're still venting atmosphere, still being pushed out of position.

I activate thrusters to compensate and set the computer to record and arrest our movement. There's a hum through the deck as the engines engage. We're slowing, then moving back. There's been no sign of the tethers snapping. The rescue teams will need those lines to get back. *Hopefully, we're in time…*

I can't be distracted. I'm mapping the *Khidr*'s original parking position, relative to the freighter. I instruct the computer to return us to that spot.

There's another lurch, this time the other way. "Hydroponics section sealed off, Captain," Jacobson says.

The thrusters reduce power and we're back. I unclip from my seat and launch myself toward Travers. There's blood on his face and the chair. When we moved, his head must have slammed into the side of the seat. I shake his shoulders. "Wake up, Lieutenant!"

"What happened? I…"

"You hit your head. We'll get Bogdanovic to take a look at it." Travers can't focus or look me in the eye. I can see he wants to help, to get it together, but he's a liability up here. "You're relieved, Lieutenant. Jacobson, tell Le Garre we need her, then escort Travers to medical."

"Yes, Captain."

I release Travers's straps and haul him out of his seat. Jacobson grabs him and guides him toward the door. Le Garre is coming in just as he leaves. Sam Chase is right behind her. His work suit is scorch-marked and torn.

"Thought you could use an extra hand, Captain," he says, "and an update."

"Both would be very welcome," I reply grimly. "What's going on out there?"

"An explosive charge detonated in hydroponics," Sam explains. He's moving toward Jacobson's vacant seat. Le Garre is settling into the pilot's chair. "We've sealed off the compartment."

"What's the damage?"

"No one hurt, but we've lost everything that was in there."

I'm doing the calculations even as he confirms the worst. Without hydroponics, we're on limited time. The necessary recycling processes facilitated by our garden allow a ship to stay out of port for weeks and months. We'll need to dock and repair. Thankfully, we're only three days or so out from Phobos Station. We can make it on our current reserves. "We need to assess all damage and work out where we are. Quartermaster, I need you to authorise and deploy firearms to all members of the ship's crew."

Sam stops and looks at me. "Is that a good idea, Captain?" he asks. "The last thing we need is more damage to the ship."

"The last thing we need is a terrorist running around destroying us from the inside," I say. "I need whoever it is found, Sam. With Keiyho off the ship, you're the senior firearms officer."

"Sure." Sam changes direction, making for the door. "I'll get to it."

"Thank you." I grab his shoulder as he goes past. "Remember, you're dealing with a murderer. Don't hesitate."

Sam nods. "I won't."

My screen flashes, another alert. Johansson's face appears. "Captain, something's come up."

"Is it urgent? We're dealing with a lot at the moment."

"Pretty urgent. Are you aware that we're transmitting?"

"Transmitting? What do you mean?"

"I'm picking up near-field communication from our ship to an unknown source," Johansson explains. "There's someone out there."

"Aboard the *Hercules*?"

"No, somewhere else." She frowns. "It's gone. I can't pinpoint the source."

"Get yourself up here," I order and close the screen. The ship graphic has calmed down now, but the hydroponics chamber is greyed out. I deactivate the pilot controls from my screen. "Transferring control back to you, Major," I say to Le Garre.

"Thank you," she replies in a pained voice. "Looks like you corrected our position just in time."

"We're still attached to the freighter?"

"Yes, I think so."

I open the camera feed from our airlock. I can see a mass of EVA suits crammed into the space – people arriving back, making their way through processing. The sight is a relief. I'm smiling in spite of everything. "As soon as everyone's aboard, get us ready to detach."

"Aye, aye."

My hands are shaking on the armrests. I know it's from the adrenaline and endorphins. My body's reaction to the crisis fired me up, and now, in a moment of aftermath, it's struggling to come down. I'm breathing carefully, managing myself. We're taught how to deal with these high stress situations, but there's a big difference between there and here. We've trained for crises, we have emergency procedures and protocols for an array of eventualities, but this situation is complex, more complex than anything I can think of.

"Duggins's team are aboard, Captain," Ensign Chiu says. "He's on his way up here."

"What about Keiyho's people?" I ask.

"They're at the freighter airlock," she replies. "They've had some problems."

I go over the drone feeds on my screen. Three of them have gone down. "What kind of problems?" I ask.

"Unclear," Chiu says. "There's a lot of chatter."

The bridge door slides back, and April Johansson is here and moving to take Jacobson's post as the navigation/communications operator. "Where's that field scan, tactical?" I ask.

"Just completing now, Captain," Thakur says. "I…errr… I'm not sure we've…"

"Send the data and the conclusions to me, Ensign."

"Yes, Captain."

The sweep appears in another window. It's a three-dimensional representation of our location and the region around it. I touch the screen and rotate the image. The *Khidr* is positioned in the centre, with a sphere of laser-scanned space all around us. The *Hercules* is a short distance away, and then there are a variety of other small objects picked up around it. I recognise them immediately.

"That's debris."

"Captain, I'm more concerned about quadrant six," Thakur says.

A section of the scan is highlighted in green. I zoom into that region. In the middle, there's a shape, roughly the same size as the *Khidr*.

"How far away is that object?" I ask.

"Ten thousand kilometres," Thakur replies. "There's some interference in our image out there. I can't be completely sure what we're seeing is accurate."

"What's the ratio?"

"Eight-two per cent accuracy, Captain."

"It has to be a ship," Le Garre says. "The ship that attacked the *Hercules*."

"And it's still here," I add.

"Looks like it."

I stare at the region around the object. There's a whole series of small dots identified by the scan. These are labelled as anomalies, driving up the computer's calculation of interference. "Run the sweep again," I order. "Make a positional comparison. Track those small dots and discount them from the accuracy analysis. Send the comparative image straight over as soon as you have it."

"Yes, Captain."

"Tactical, what countermeasures do we have aboard?"

Ensign Thakur shudders when I address him, like an electric charge has run through him and stiffened his spine. "Countermeasures, Captain? I'm not sure I—"

"Find out, quickly!"

Le Garre is staring at me. She looks confused. "What are you—"

"I think those are guided missiles," I say. "They are locked on to us, by some sort of tracking method – probably laser guidance, or our transponder."

The second image appears on my screen. I overlay the two. The small signals have moved. There are six of them and they're much closer to us. The larger signal is also heading in our direction.

"Chiu, isolate the objects from the two images and do a velocity calculation."

"Large object moving at fifty metres per second; smalls are...one thousand metres per second."

"Time until they reach us?"

"About eighteen minutes, Captain."

"Can we shoot them down with our own rockets?" Le Garre suggests.

I shake my head. "They're moving too fast. We need to give them something else to target."

"Captain, we could change our transponder signal?" Johansson urges. "They might be locked on to our ship identification code. If we change that, they might get confused."

"Do it," I order.

"If they're tracking us by laser sweep, like we're using, it won't make much difference," Le Garre warns.

"We try everything," I reply. "We don't know what tech they've got."

"Then we need to move position too," Le Garre says.

"We can't while we're tethered." I'm looking at the airlock again. More EVA suits are appearing in the room. I can see two people carrying a third figure. "Contact Arkov and keep an eye on our airlock, Major. Soon as you get an all clear, initiate a burn and get the freighter between us and the incoming hostiles."

"Will do," Le Garre replies.

"Tactical, what do you have for me on countermeasures?" I ask.

Thakur's face is pinched in concentration. "We have pressurised tanks and atmosphere bags for repairing hull ruptures. If we launch a tank inside a bag, we can inflate it and create another target for the missiles that's roughly the same size as we are. It may fool a laser scan."

"Will it work?"

"Depends how far away the missiles are when they detect the new objects and how accurate their tracking systems are."

"How many can we deploy?"

"Four, maybe five, depending on how much time we have."

"Get it done, Ensign. How many people do you need?"

"One for each, Captain."

"Get Duggins on comms and tell his people to make up what you need."

At that moment, a klaxon sounds, the ship surges, and the stars seem to fall like rain. I glance down and see the airlock door is shut. Le Garre is moving us up and over the *Hercules*, putting a kilometre of the freighter between us and the missiles. "We need to make sure we can deploy the tanks before we drop out of sight, Major," I say.

"Understood, Captain," Le Garre says.

We're banking and pitching; the magnets in my suit activate and the straps on my shoulders tense. A countdown clock appears on my screen – it's the estimated time it'll take the first of the missiles to reach us. "How long until we can jettison the tanks?"

"Duggins says three minutes."

I look at the clock. We have just under fourteen minutes. "Once we get to the other side, go dark. Switch off all non-essential power. We need them to think we're gone."

Le Garre grunts. "If this works," she says.

"It has to work," I reply.

CHAPTER ELEVEN

Sellis

The ship is moving, twisting, turning. I'm hanging on to a safety rail in corridor three, trying to stop myself from breaking an arm or a leg. The main lights are out, some sort of low power running required. Fuck Captain Shann and all those shitheads on the bridge! Why didn't they order us to chairs? Why the fuck are we being left to batter ourselves against bulkheads and walls?

All in the name of murdering some terrorist who wants to murder all of us? Fuck that! Worst fucking thing you can do, have the whole crew stumbling around, unarmed, waiting to get shot.

I was in the army before I joined Fleet. My mom loved me in the uniform. I remember her crying when 'Private Jake Sellis' shipped out.

I did basic infantry training in Utah before I got posted to Las Vegas. Some people laugh when I tell them that. "Why send soldiers to the casino city?" they say. Maybe they've never heard of the Nevada Army National Guard? I hadn't, before I read my transfer papers. All I could think of was the slots, the blackjack, and the poker table. Someone upstairs must have liked me back then.

Three weeks later, I was hooked.

There is no place on Earth like Las Vegas. The casinos are all part of how the city works. The hotels lay on huge buffet meals, where you can load up even if you're not a guest. Everyone wants you to save your money for gambling. The profit margin is much better for business when all you've taken up is twenty minutes of some card dealer's time. That's all you are to them – a twenty-minute trick, a thirty-minute trick. All depends on how deep your pockets are.

Maybe I struggled out there because of how I was brought up. Maybe that's why I struggle now. My hometown, Logan in Utah, was pretty conservative and insular. People looked out for each other back there.

There was a lot of 'sin talk' when I was a child. I'd regularly get fined or beat for cussing and such. These days, every profanity I hear or utter is a middle finger to my old man.

"Jake!"

I recognise the voice. Quartermaster Sam Chase is at the end of the passage, by the emergency doors. He's carrying a flashlight and shining it at me. Sam's okay. I owe him a couple of hundred dollars. Anyone who lends me money is okay.

"Yeah? What do you need?"

"You, with me, now!"

I sigh and start moving. The shifting around means it's like a weird mix of crawling and climbing. I have to trust our pilot won't get a twitch and get me battered. Sam's handling it all better than me. That's his way. The world never seems to make him break a sweat.

When I reach his side, I'm surprised. Sam's covered in blood.

"Fuck man, you okay?"

"Yeah, just been up and down these corridors for a while, chasing our little rat."

"You found him?"

"I think so." Sam has one of the low-calibre pistols from the arms locker in his hand. He's holding it upward, away from me.

"What are we doing?" I ask.

Sam points ahead to an open access hatch. "You're going to make your way down there, and I'm going to cover you."

"Okay." I move past Sam, toward the hatch. It's a standard tactical play – send the unarmed soldier forward while you cover him, then move up and check the open passageway. I played both roles during room clearance training back on Earth.

Doesn't mean I like being Sam's stooge, though.

I don't know how I ended up in space. I'm good with cables and repairs. My soldering is neat and clean, a tricky skill to keep up in zero gravity. Circuit boards and wiring are nice problems that sit right in front of you. I've always been good with that kind of stuff.

The same game doesn't work at the blackjack table, or on the slots, much as I wish it did.

I was three years into my posting in Vegas when I got told I was being transferred to Earth Station Two. I owed a lot of people a lot of money, so

I didn't argue. I just signed the papers and got on the next flight.

I worked on the orbitals for six years, until a woman tapped me on the shoulder and made me sign another form. This time she told me joining the crew of the *Khidr* would get some of my old debts forgiven. I might even get a chance to go back to Earth without being arrested at the space port.

In that moment, I started to get suspicious. Somebody was watching out for me, protecting me when the debts got too much and moving me on when it suited them. Strings were being pulled. I don't know how long they've been at it, or when they'll call time and ask to collect, but the cynic in me says they will one day. Sinners get punished, that's what the Good Book says.

In the meantime, best not to dwell.

I'm at the hatch. My hands are shaking. I can see a little way around the corner, but not much. This is where we need a camera drone, or someone needs to take a risk.

That won't be me. Not unless there's money on the table.

I can hear Sam moving up. He passes by me on the left, aiming his pistol into the open passage. "Clear," he says.

"Okay, what's next?"

"Same again. You lead, I follow."

I shuffle up as the ship turns, throwing us both forward and into the open room. We're near the gravity deck. The elevator access point is just ahead. The elevator isn't there; it's been taken up to the ring. There's no reason anyone would go up there during an emergency.

"You call the lift," Sam says. "Once it's down, we use the emergency override and keep it here. Then we call this in to the bridge."

There's a noise behind me. I turn around, my fists clenched, and Sam shines the flashlight back through the hatchway. "Who's there?" he calls out.

"Point that thing somewhere else, Chase." A figure emerges, also carrying a gas-powered pistol, which he's aiming at me. It's Tomlins. His left arm is bound up in a sling.

"Sorry, Sergeant," Sam answers. The two men are equal in rank, but Tomlins has seniority and tends to remind people when he does.

"You found someone?"

"Yeah, Arkov was away from his post. Sellis and I chased him in here."

Tomlins looks at me the same way he always does, as if he's examining shit on the bottom of his shoe. "We'll take it from here, Technician," he says.

"Sure, okay." I press the elevator call and move away into the passage, leaving the two of them with their prisoner – *Arkov*? Part of the technical club, like me. Vasili's harmless. We've shared a beer or two. He's from Turtas – some town out in the wilds of Russia. All his life he's wanted to work in space. I can't believe he'd be a terrorist and try to kill us all. There must be some other reason he ran away.

I've stopped in the corridor. The ship has ceased its maneuvers for now, so there's no shifting force to compensate for. I've half a mind to turn around and speak up for Vasili, to Chase and Tomlins, but I don't have any evidence he's innocent, and, well...I'm not going to get anywhere with the sergeant without some proof.

I need to let this go, for now.

I reach into my pocket and pull out a flashlight. I switch it on and hang it around my neck. I use this light for close work on circuit panels, so it doesn't illuminate much. I start making my way back the way I've come.

There's something not right about this.

I stop again, some way from the elevator access point to the gravity deck. I'm on my own here, but I don't feel like I'm on my own.

"Hello?"

There's no answer. Maybe I'm—

A rustling sound and a catch of breath. I'm turning toward the noise, but the illumination doesn't penetrate far enough to reveal anything other than wall panels and bulkheads.

"Hello?"

Still no reply.

I'm reaching for my comms to report in, but again, I hesitate. What have I actually seen? Nothing. So, if I initiate an alert, all I'm going to do is make a fuss over nothing. If they arrest Vasili, they won't listen to me if I'm jumping at shadows.

Go home, Jake.

I start moving again. I'm heading for my room now. I share with Ashe, but he'll be out somewhere doing the captain's shitty work. Fuck patrolling these corridors in the dark. Unless I get a call, I'm staying put and getting some sleep.

CHAPTER TWELVE

Shann

Six minutes to impact. Three atmospheric bags are deployed in our wake, and we're turning and descending on the far side of the *Hercules*.

"Chase to Captain Shann?"

"Go ahead."

"We've got a suspect cornered in the gravity deck."

I bunch the fingers of my right hand into a fist. A small moment of triumph. "Whatever you do, don't let them out."

"Going to be difficult with you shaking the ship around."

"It's important."

"Yeah, I understand that, Captain."

I switch channels and call Duggins. "Well done with the bags; leave it with three. We'll save the fourth one for later. Get yourself secured and ready to power down the ship."

"Aye, aye, Captain."

Le Garre is making the final adjustments, pivoting the ship, to change the shape of our profile should we be scanned. The side of the *Hercules*'s cargo section fills the view screen, and our exterior lights illuminate a mass of containers, all different colours, jammed together. If one of the missiles hits them, it'll send debris everywhere. We can't move away, because that'll make us a target again.

"We're in position," Le Garre says.

"Duggins, power down everything that's left."

"Aye, aye."

The exterior lights vanish. The freighter is suddenly a dark shadow. I glance at the screen clock – we have three and a half minutes until a potential impact. There isn't anything more we can do.

"Johansson, alert the crew to strap in before you take the comms offline."

"Doing that now, Captain."

The automated voice is a muffled echo beyond the bridge door. My screen flicks off. Only Le Garre's remains lit with the countdown in the corner.

"Time check?"

"Two minutes, thirty seconds."

We're powerless. There's nothing to do but wait.

I'm going over all the decisions I've made, looking for something I've done wrong, some kind of blame I can levy on myself.

We picked up the freighter's distress call; we responded, as we're required to do. When there was an accident and Technician Drake died, we investigated. When we found it wasn't an accident, we investigated further. We found the freighter; we explored and tried to work out what had happened. When we were in danger, I ordered an evacuation, and this improvised maneuver to keep us alive.

No, there's nothing I would do differently, given the information I had.

I wonder who'll discover we're missing. We sent a communication burst when we realised the *Hercules* had been attacked. We directed transmissions toward Mars and Earth. It'll take a while for either signal to be received. I remember a class on deep space communication interference during my initial training. If our enemy could get within the point-to-point line and broadcast their own signal, they could cancel out ours. They'd need to get an independent transmitter in the way.

What could Earth or Mars do? Send out another ship, probably. If they did, would they get stuck in the same situation we're—

"Thirty seconds, Captain."

I'm staring at the view out of the window. I'm searching the periphery, looking for any clue as to what's to come. The *Hercules* floats serenely in front of us. There's no sign of imminent destruction.

"Ten seconds," Le Garre warns.

I'm holding my breath without meaning to. There's a pain in my fingers. I glance at them. I'm trying to push them into the chair, through the padding on the armrest. "I just want to say thank you to you all. You've been magnificent," I hear myself say.

"Three...two...one...impact."

A glow splashes across the edge of the screen. It flares brighter, then brighter again. A moment of incandescent light and then we return to blackness and shadow.

We're alive.

We're *alive*.

I'm still not breathing. I can't force myself to. I remember moments when I was a child and I woke up from a bad dream. I'd think there was a monster in the room with me. If I moved or made a sound, it would know, and I'd be eaten.

In this moment, I'm a child again, scared to move or make a sound.

Another flash.

Another.

Silence.

"I only count five," Le Garre says. "There were six objects on the scan."

"Could it be wrong?" Johansson asks.

"Anything is possible."

I find my voice. It's dry and broken. "Start a countdown. No movement or power from here for ten minutes. Chiu, Thakur, thank you both for going above and beyond. You're relieved. Find Duggins and Keiyho and get them here. Move!"

All at once people respond, snapped into action by the words. We're alive; we have to make something of the time we've bought ourselves.

"Ensign Johansson, you came up here to report on the communications you intercepted."

At first, she doesn't hear me. She's still staring at the view screen, paralysed, I guess. I understand. I was almost the same. I reach forward and squeeze her shoulder. "April?"

She flinches, turns in her seat, looking at me over her shoulder as if I'm a stranger, but then the recognition comes back. "I—yes, I'm sorry, Captain."

"Johansson, your report, please."

She takes deep breaths, trying to steady herself. I notice her hands on the armrests. Her left hand is shaking. Her right is a cybernetic replacement for the one she lost as a child. We've talked about it before. The hand is hardwired into her nervous system and works just like an organic one.

It's shaking too.

"Take your time," I say.

"I went over the recordings again," Johansson explains slowly. "I looked for new patterns like you asked. I couldn't find anything else, but then I went over the phrase you sent me – '…please don't… sir…' I listened to that and broke down the gaps in the recording. We thought it was one phrase with a comma after the first two words, but it's not. There's a dip after 'please don't' and the third word is cut off. I think whoever spoke was saying, 'Please don't, we surrender.'"

I nod, thinking about what might have happened. "They didn't use long-range missiles on the freighter. They were right here. Right in front of it. They must have wanted to capture the cargo," I reason. "But what happened to change their minds?"

"Someone activated the distress call?" Le Garre suggests.

"Could be."

Keiyho and Duggins enter. "Looks like we're alive, Captain!" Duggins says with a smile. His slow drawl helps me relax. I can see he's exhausted and stressed, but there's a sense of victory and achievement along with it. "We live to fight another day."

"Something like that," I say. "What's the situation?"

"Not a lot we can see outside, but I did attach a camera to each of the atmospheric bags. We lost signal with all three. I think we can conclude they took the hits."

I nod and look at Keiyho. "What happened on the freighter?"

"We got the survivor out. He's in bad shape. Bogdanovic has him sedated for now. On the way back, someone attacked us. Tomlins took a bullet in the arm."

"There's more people alive over there?"

"Seems so."

I digest this. We're in a moment of pause, but there's so much to deal with. "We need to get ahead of this. Right now, we're reacting, not anticipating. We need a plan that puts us on the front foot; otherwise we're just surviving and sooner or later, they'll figure us out."

"At least they don't know we're alive," Duggins says.

"That lasts as long as we stay hidden or until they discover us. What will they do next?"

"If they think we're destroyed, they'll come back here for the freighter cargo and their people," Le Garre says.

"They'll also want to verify we're dead. Johansson, you mentioned you intercepted new transmissions?"

"Yes, near-field signals from a source inside our ship," Johansson replies. "I managed to set up some interference and then isolated the transmitter. Quartermaster Chase dismantled it."

"What about the people on the freighter? Could they signal the enemy ship in the same way?"

"Yes, they could," Johansson says.

"Can we stop them?"

"Only if we can get in the way, or destroy their equipment."

"That limits our time even further," Duggins says. "We've only got this breathing space so long as one of them doesn't see us."

"The ship will come here," I say, thinking out loud. "They're already on their way. At close range, our weapons may have a better chance against them."

"Captain, we don't know their capabilities," Keiyho says.

"But we know ours," I answer. "Our laser and our rockets are designed for targets we can image with our telescopes and the guidance systems on the ship. If we can get them into a range where we can fire back, we have a chance."

"Does make you wonder, though," Duggins muses. "Who builds a ship for the sole purpose of destroying other ships? Granted, there's plenty of that in fiction, but real space exploration and commerce has always been neutral and above all that."

"We should not rule out the possibility of extraterrestrial life," Keiyho says.

"We'll know soon enough," I say and look up at the counter on Le Garre's screen. "In six minutes, begin a gradual power up of the ship's systems. If the people on the *Hercules* have a transmitter, I want some solutions for finding and taking it out that don't involve further risk to our crew."

"Will do, Captain," Johansson replies. "I have some ideas."

"In the meantime, I'm going to the gravity deck to see the rat in the cage," I announce and unclip my straps. "I'll be back in thirty minutes, or before if something comes up."

"I'll come with you," Le Garre says.

I shake my head. "We need someone here who can pilot the ship if we have to make a move."

"Keiyho can handle that, or call me back," Le Garre counters. "Need I remind you, Captain, you made me responsible for the investigation into Drake's death?"

I stare at her. There's a dullness to her eyes that comes, I guess, from lack of sleep. She's pulled more shifts than all of us in the last twenty-four hours, but the steel is still there. She's not going to take no for an answer.

"Okay, we both go," I decide.

"Good."

★   ★   ★

In the dark, the passageways of my ship are familiar and unfamiliar. Objects loom from the shadows, leaping out at us as we make our way through the different corridors and hatchways. The occasional item floats free, the result of being left behind and our emergency maneuvers.

I know these places. I've pushed and pulled myself through them for the last three years. The *Khidr* is my home – our home. The fact that everything I am and everything I might have been could be wiped out in an instant... That's still something I'm adjusting to.

When you sign for Fleet, you recognise a lonely death is a real possibility. Humanity is not meant to live in a vacuum; only our technology allows us to survive. We can't conquer space; it's too vast and too empty for us. The best we can hope for is to endure it, while we journey to where we want to go.

The job is an anomaly. Our continual existence between places is to enable the journey of others. We're a lifeboat, dispatched into a storm of absence, where one wrong move will unmake you, unmake everything around you too.

Dying out here is something I accepted. Dying out here and leaving no trace of who I am is not what I accept.

I'm thinking of my parents and my eyes fill with tears. I wipe them away with my sleeve. Mom is gone; Dad is old. My brother, Jethry, is not well. Soon we'll all be gone too. No trace of us beyond our fleeting presence in other people's lives.

"Captain?"

Le Garre's in front of me. She looks concerned. I nod, grimace and wave her on. She opens another hatch and we're here. Sam Chase and Tomlins are standing by the entrance to the gravity deck elevator. They both have torches. Sam turns his on me, making me flinch and blink.

"Oh, it's you, Captain."

"You expecting someone else?"

"No, but we're being cautious, given the circumstances, and this place in the dark…well…it makes you paranoid."

Sam is bloody and bruised, but seems intact. Tomlins has a cut on his forehead and his left arm in a sling. They're both carrying small, gas-powered pistols.

"Who do we have in there?" I ask.

"Arkov," Sam replies.

"Arkov?"

"Yeah."

Corporal Vasili Arkov is our airlock technician. He's a diminutive and enthusiastic dark-haired Russian, with an easy smile and energetic diligence about his work. Thinking of him as a traitor who would try to murder us all is difficult, but then I've shared months with all of these people and I thought I knew them all.

Right now, I want through that door to tear at him with my hands and nails for what he's put us through.

"Is he talking?" Le Garre asks.

"Not to us," Tomlins says.

"What's your evidence then?"

"He was away from his post when the engineering team arrived back," Sam explains. "When I challenged him about it, he ran."

"That's everything you have?"

"Pretty much."

I'm glad Le Garre wanted to come. She's being methodical, evaluating the information. I should be doing the same, but I can't.

This bastard tried to destroy my home.

"Have you seen him since you chased him in here?"

"He was at the door when we locked it," Sam says. "He screamed at us through the glass until the ship started moving. He disappeared after that."

"Do you know he's still there?"

"Yeah, I didn't leave the room. Tomlins was with me when the ship went dark."

"That was pretty dangerous," I say to Sam. "If we'd had to pull some g's..."

"You'd have been scraping me off the walls like Drake, I know." He smiles. "You gave me an order, Captain. That's important to me."

Lights are beginning to come on. Duggins must have started the power-up sequence. "We need to get Arkov in a secure space where I can question him," Le Garre says. "Someone will have to go in and bring him out."

I look at each of them. They're waiting for me to give another order and send someone through the hatch. I'm not doing that. "Tomlins, give me your sidearm," I say.

"Captain, you can't—"

"I can, and I am, Major; the order is given."

Le Garre bites her lip. Sam glowers at me but says nothing. Tomlins hands me his pistol. "Quartermaster, you follow me through. I'll move on; you wait there. If I shout, you come running."

"Understood, Captain." Sam moves to the hatch and touches the lock release. The door slides away and I enter the elevator. The emergency exit at the top of the compartment has been opened. Arkov must have gone up there. I grab the edge of the panel and pull myself up.

"Vasili?" I call.

There's no answer. As the gravity deck has been retracted, the lift shaft is about ten metres long with an exit into the rotational ring at the top. If Arkov has a firearm, I'll be an easy target floating up there.

"Vasili? It's Captain Shann. I'm alone!"

I can hear Sam in the elevator below me. I look down; he looks tense and worried. "I'm going up," I say.

"Are you sure that's wise?"

"We'll soon find out," I reply. "Besides, we don't have any choice."

"Okay, Captain."

I start up the lift shaft, pistol in hand. I move through zero gravity better than most. The trick is to just use a hand to steer and let my first push-off do the work.

I'm moving slowly, freely, gun aimed at the disembarkation point. "I'm coming up to you, Vasili! I just want to talk."

There's no answer.

I reach the end of the shaft. The door is wedged open. The recreation room is beyond it, and beyond that is the strategy room, where I last met with the senior crew before we encountered the *Hercules*.

It seems like a lifetime ago.

If Arkov wanted to shoot me, he could hide behind a table or one of the exercise machines. As soon as I go through the doorway, I'm vulnerable.

"Vasili, I'm here. Where are you?"

The door to the strategy room is open. It's also wedged. I push my way toward it.

Technical operative Vasili Arkov is sitting at the table inside. His hands are on the table where I can see them. He's staring at me as I approach.

"Vasili, I just want to—"

"To talk, yes, I heard you." There's a flatness about his voice and despair in his eyes. He has a red mark on his cheek. His hands and his forehead are bloody. "Did you come alone?"

I nod, keeping the pistol trained on him. "The others are waiting for my signal."

"I'll surrender to you," Arkov says. "You can take me back, but I didn't do this."

"Why weren't you at your post when Duggins's team came back?" I ask.

"Because somebody called me away."

"And who did that?"

"Quartermaster Chase."

I'm staring at him, trying to read a lie from his face, but there's no tell or twitch. He's exhausted like all of us, but if he was a traitor, he could have locked the airlock rather than abandon his post. Then he'd have stranded half the crew in space. "You best tell me your version of events," I say.

He relaxes a little. "I can do that," he says.

"One moment." I activate the comms bead on my lapel, making sure I'm on an open channel. "Shann to Chase?"

"Receiving, Captain. You okay?"

"We're both fine. Arkov has surrendered."

"You want me to help you bring him down?"

"No, we'll both be along in a minute." I switch the bead to personal record mode and gaze at Arkov. "Okay, I'm listening."

"I didn't sabotage the hydroponics compartment, Captain. I didn't kill Drake either."

"Just start with what happened when we ordered the EVA teams back. Where were you?"

"Just outside the airlock, at my station." Arkov is breathing hard. His hands are gripping the table. He's trying to stay calm, but I can tell it's a struggle. "I got an automated request on the terminal to go to stores. It said there was an important set of equipment I needed to bring up for Duggins and his people."

"So, you went to the stores?"

"Yes."

"And?"

"There was no one there. I was on my way back when there was an explosion, and, well…you know the rest."

I fix him with a stare. "Is it usual for you to get an automated message like that?"

"Sure, happens all the time. Is it usual in the middle of an emergency? No, but Sergeant Chase outranks me, so I followed the order."

"And you didn't see the quartermaster at all when you got there?"

"No, he was missing. That's why when he started accusing me, I ran. Maybe I should have stood my ground, but…well…I panicked."

"We've all had our moments in the last few hours," I say. I touch the comms bead again, turning off the recording. "We'll head down now. You'll be placed under arrest and confined. Major Le Garre will want to interview you. Tell her what you told me and anything else you remember. Don't hold anything back."

Arkov nods. "Okay, I will. Thank you."

"You have my word we're not going to prejudge you, Vasili," I say. "We'll get to the truth."

Arkov sighs. "I sure hope so," he says.

CHAPTER THIRTEEN

Sellis

The electronic chime of my door sounds, and I'm swearing to myself again. It feels like I've barely shut my eyes since I was—

"Technician, let me in, please."

The voice is muffled, but authoritative. Whoever's out there outranks me. I get off my bunk, move to the security panel and enter the keycode to unlock it.

Major Le Garre is outside.

I've always had a thing for the major. She's a bit thin and younger than me, but we share a few hobbies. She likes a game of cards and a fine whisky, but she knows when to stop on both counts, particularly when the captain's around.

"How can I help you, Major?"

Le Garre gives me a thin-lipped smile and with a few words stamps on my hope that this is a personal visit. "The quartermaster said you helped him corner Technician Arkov."

I sigh. "Yeah, I was with him when we got to the gravity deck access point."

"You see Arkov do anything suspicious?"

I shake my head. "I didn't even know it was Arkov we were following. Chase mentioned it when Sergeant Tomlins arrived."

Le Garre nods. "You think Arkov is our traitor?"

"No, Major. You know him as well as I do. He wouldn't harm the ship. He loves it here."

"Yeah, that's what I thought." Le Garre looks up and down the corridor. "What did you do after?" she asks.

"After?"

"After Tomlins sent you away."

"Oh, yeah." I rub my face. "Came back here, tried to sleep, failed."

"See anything?"

I hesitate. "No," I say at last.

"Okay, good."

She's still here. Maybe I'm going to get lucky after all. I pull out my top-drawer smile. "Listen, if you're sticking around, Major, I could put some coffee on? Or something stronger if you like? You can question me all you like over a cup or two."

Le Garre stares at me, her expression stony. "It's not going to happen, Jake."

"Sorry? What I'm—"

"I know you are."

I look away and the silence gets awkward. "Is there anything else, Major?" I ask.

"No, not for now."

"Okay then."

The door slides shut between us. I wait a few moments, listening to her move away. Then I turn toward my empty bunk.

The screen on the wall flickers. "Incoming message," the computer says in its usual calm, measured tone.

I glance in that direction and maneuver myself around so I can read the screen. I'm drifting in midair in front of it. "Display," I order.

The screen brightens. A list of information starts scrolling upward. I blink, focus and start to read. These are transaction numbers. I can see my bank account ID and my name against each of them. *Fuck, this is my entire credit history, all the money I owe people in Logan, Vegas, on Station Three, everywhere!*

The transaction list continues for a long time. After that, names and addresses appear. My sister's address, my parents, my uncle Sal from Maine, even some of my friends from school, technical college and army basic.

Even my ex-wife and my daughter.

What is this?

The list stops. There's a short message at the bottom.

We have everything on you. We will act against all of these debts and individuals if you do not cooperate.

Shit!

The screen goes blank.

CHAPTER FOURTEEN

Shann

"How is he, Doctor?"

Bogdanovic looks up at me as I enter his room. Behind him, there's a sealed chamber on one of the beds. Our new guest, rescued from the *Hercules*, is inside. "Unconscious and staying that way for the time being," Bogdanovic says. "I know you have questions for him, but he was hypoxic and suffering from carbon dioxide poisoning. While he's out, I can regulate his breathing and gradually bring down the inflammation of his lungs."

"How long?"

"An hour or two, minimum." Bogdanovic holds up a hand. "I know the risk to us. I'm aware of what's going on here. If I push the timetable up any further than that, you'll get no information from him at all."

I sigh. "It is what it is," I say. "What other casualties have you had?"

"Two gunshot wounds and an assortment of cuts, bumps and bruises; plus Travers has a bad concussion. Tell that crazy Frenchwoman she needs to drive more carefully, next time."

I smile. "I might have been piloting for some of all that."

"Good of you to admit it. Same advice to you then," Bogdanovic grunts.

There's a silence between us. The doctor is busying himself, but I sense he's waiting for me to leave. "I wanted to ask how things were for you, during it all."

"No, you wanted to ask me if I saw anything suspicious." Bogdanovic is looking me in the eye. It's an intense stare. I return it evenly, determined not to flinch. "I think you need to be careful, Captain. You've asked the major to handle the investigation. Best you don't go around doing her job."

"That's not what I'm trying to do."

"Might be worth you seeing it from the other side then?" Bogdanovic suggests. "Let her do her job."

More silence, more stares. "Okay," I say at last.

★　★　★

When I get back, the bridge is quiet. Jacobson has returned. Duggins has left.

"Situation update, please, Lieutenant Commander Keiyho," I say.

Keiyho swivels his chair toward me as I move to my seat. "Power-down time expired, so we began the start-up sequence as you ordered. Systems are coming back online. No sign of detection or further hostility."

"Do you have a solution to the transmitter problem?"

"We do." Keiyho nods toward Johansson. She looks like she's recovered from her moment of crisis. Having a manageable task to solve may have helped.

"We're adapting a drone," she tells me. "It'll be piloted, fitted with a signal detection unit, a cutter and some explosives. Duggins has gone to finalise it for launch."

I glance toward the view screen. The cargo containers of the freight blot out almost everything. "Will the drone give us eyes on the other side of the *Hercules*?"

"Yes, they should. We've added a portable sweeper. It won't have as much range as the *Khidr*'s laser scanner, but it'll mean we have some warning if another ship gets close."

"We'll need that," I say.

"Captain, they may just stay out there," Jacobson says. "They think we're dead, and we don't know who or what they are. Why risk coming back?"

"Because I think they want something from the freighter," I explain. "I think that's why they left people on board. The distress signal disturbed them before they could find what they were looking for, so they abandoned a team and set up an ambush for us."

"If they stay at range and keep an eye on things, eventually they'll figure out we survived," Keiyho says.

"They won't do that," I reply. "They're on the clock, just like we are. They were coming in behind the missiles when we last got a reading. They won't have changed course."

"If they do come in, should we try to talk to them?" Jacobson asks. "Perhaps they'll be reasonable?"

I shake my head. "They've committed a hostile act in what they did to the *Hercules*. They launched missiles at us. We have a tactical advantage, and I'm not giving it away in the hope they'll want to talk."

The comms bead in my ear crackles. "Duggins to Captain Shann."

"Go ahead."

"You get briefed by Johansson on the drone plan?"

"Yes, we're chatting about it now."

"Okay, we're ready to deploy down here. Am I cleared to go ahead?"

"Yes, you are."

"Great."

I glance at Jacobson. "Now we've got power, have you run an analysis on the freighter's position?"

Jacobson looks confused. "No, should I—"

"Yes, you absolutely should, Ensign. We need to know if there's been any change. Could be a sign of a missile impact. We're so close to the cargo section we won't get much warning if things start drifting toward us."

"Right, I'll do that." He turns away.

"See that you do."

Johansson is focused on her screen, no doubt waiting for information from the drone. Keiyho is still looking at me.

"Captain, we need to plan some warfare scenarios," he says.

"Agreed. What are your initial thoughts?"

"I think we assume we're going to be fighting a human controlled and constructed ship," Keiyho says. "Otherwise, we'll have nothing to base our tactics on."

"Yes, that makes sense," I say. "But we adapt, if we find out we're wrong."

"If we assume the ship is Earth made, it makes sense that most of its capabilities will be similar to ours," Keiyho says. "We know they have better long-range weaponry, but we think the technology used on those missiles is the sort of thing we could readily manufacture. That means it's unlikely they have other advantages in acceleration, power distribution, or maneuverability."

"So, at short range, the odds will be even."

"More or less."

Keiyho pushes a tactical representation of our position over to my screen. "If we obtain tracking data from the drone that enables us to determine the position of our enemy, we can maneuver out from behind the freighter and fire every weapon we have that's in range. The drone and the ship will be able to maintain a target lock, in a similar way to how we deal with rogue asteroids. We need to hit as hard as we can and as fast as we can."

I look at the calculations and numbers. The plan is simple. The best ones are. "What happens after that?" I ask.

"We close in," Keiyho says, "and pound them with everything we have."

"That'll mean they'll be able to do the same," I say.

Keiyho smiles and there's a glint in his eye. "Yes, just like some sort of seventeenth-century naval battle. It's dangerous, but if we don't hit hard and fast while we have the element of surprise, they'll grind us to dust."

"If their oxygen tanks rupture, or something else ignites, we could get caught in the debris."

"It's a risk, but in any engagement at range, we'll lose."

"Yes, I see your point." I tap the screen with my finger. "What other scenarios have you prepared for?"

Keiyho shrugs. "Mostly reactive situations. If they find out we're alive before they get close, we'll need to hug the freighter and try to get behind them to target their engines."

"They won't destroy the freighter to destroy us," I say.

"Yes, I agree with you on that."

I'm thinking out loud, sharing my ideas as they come. "One thing we need to prepare is some communication updates. If we go down, we need to ensure Fleet and Earth know exactly what's happened out here."

"We could use one of the buoy satellites we have on board for that," Keiyho suggests. "They're preprogrammed with homing coordinates for Earth and Phobos Station. If we launch them as we go in, they're less likely to be detected."

"That would work," I say. "Can we prepare them in time?"

Keiyho shrugs. "Currently, we don't know how much time we have."

"That's something we can work on." I turn my chair. "Jacobson, when you're done with the freighter position, run a projection on the large object we identified in the laser sweep. I want to know its ETA."

"Already done, Captain. It'll arrive in just under thirty minutes."

I nod to Keiyho. "That's how much time we have. They'll have to factor in some deceleration, but it won't make a lot of difference. We need to be weapons ready by then."

"I'll need to talk to the crew," Keiyho says. "I may need to pull a few people off other duties."

"Do what you have to do," I reply. "But don't compromise our security."

"You mean the traitor?"

"I mean the investigation. No one's proven guilty, yet."

Keiyho starts to make his way out. I see a new window flash up on Johansson's screen a moment before she announces, "Drone online, Captain."

I key up the same window on my own monitor. There's a wide expanse of black; the freighter is positioned on the left. The drone rotates, then descends. The *Hercules* disappears from view.

"Moving us to the far side," Johansson says. "No transmission signals detected so far."

Dark shapes appear. The drone's headlights illuminate them. They're fragments of twisted metal, spinning in random directions. "That's debris," I say.

"Yes, and it's small and light, which suggests the missiles took out our decoys," Johansson replies.

"Can confirm freighter trajectory has altered zero point five metres," Jacobson says. "That's consistent with proximity to the explosions, but no impact."

"Best-case scenario for us then."

"At the moment, Captain, yes."

A thought occurs to me. I open a comms channel to Duggins from my screen. "Commander, is the data connection to the airlock terminal on the *Hercules* still open?" I ask him.

"It was last time I checked," Duggins says. He's replying from his desk, and I see him glance briefly at a portable unit. "Yes, it's still going. The transfer will be complete in just over two hours."

"What's the range on our connection?" I ask.

"Not massive. It's a standard point-to-point stream. I optimised it to about one hundred and forty per cent of its specified range. I guess just over one and a half kilometres."

"We may need to maneuver past that," I warn.

"Well, both units are set up to auto-pause and resume if we do," Duggins says. "The partial transfer will also be useful, if we don't get everything."

"Okay, thank you." I end the connection. Throughout the conversation, I've had half an eye on the progress of the drone. Johansson's picked up a larger object on its scanner and rotates the little craft so we can see it.

I recognise it immediately.

"That's a missile…the one that didn't explode."

Since their development in the 1940s, missiles have always been sleek, oblong projectiles. The warhead and guidance is packed into the nose, the engine and fuel crammed into the end. There's a tradition of making these projectiles sleek and aerodynamic. None of that matters in space, but old habits die hard. What we're looking at could have graced the pages of a history book.

I think back to my conversation with Keiyho. "We can confirm they're human," I say.

Keiyho flashes me a tense grin. "Looks like it," he says.

"Captain, I'm still reading telemetry from the warhead," Johansson says. "It could still be live and reacquire us with its near-field detector when we emerge from behind the freighter."

"Can we disable it?" I ask.

"If we do, we'll lose the drone," Johansson says. "We can't move far enough away and destroy the missile."

"You mentioned it's still sending out a signal," Keiyho says. "Can we hack that signal? Turn it into a weapon we can use?"

Johansson bites her lip. "I think I could do it, but not in thirty minutes."

"Why would it stop?" I ask. "All six missiles were travelling at high speed; this one decelerated." I tap on the screen. "There's no sign of a braking thruster, so whatever stopped it must have been a freak impact."

"Like it's got a concussion," says a voice from behind me. I turn around. Travers is in the doorway. He's blinking a lot, trying to focus. "Lieutenant Bill Travers returning to duty, Captain."

"Did Bogdanovic clear you, Lieutenant?"

"We had an argument. I came here. You need me."

He's right, we do need him. Without Le Garre, we're short on pilots, and she's busy interviewing Arkov. "Take the chair, Lieutenant," I say.

"Thank you, Captain."

I catch Keiyho's eye and we both nod. We need to watch Travers. He's clearly not at his best, none of us is, but he has more reason. "We need to decide what we're doing about the missile," I say. "Options?"

"Disabling the thruster with the cutter might be something we can do," Keiyho says. "However, we can't grab it or stop its rotation. It may be a waste of our time."

"We could target it with the ship's laser the moment we have a point-to-point solution?" Jacobson suggests.

"Or we leave it," Johansson says. "If it was dangerous, it would correct that spin."

"Option two and option three," I decide. "Flag the location and update our tactical display."

"Aye, aye." Johansson flicks the controls, and the drone spins away from the missile. The *Hercules* reappears in our view.

"Estimated time to second ship arrival?" I ask.

"Twenty-four minutes, Captain."

The battered metal side of the freighter's containers is illuminated by the drone's searchlights. Here and there I can see dents and scarring. "Must be peripheral blast damage," I muse out loud.

"Looks like it," Johansson agrees. "I'm moving us closer so we've less danger of being picked up in a scan. Once we're positioned, I'll turn around and then we can wait for the other ship."

As if on cue, the proximity indicator flashes and Johansson flips the drone around. We're staring out into the black now. A new window opens with a display of the little machine's near-field scanner. The laser that the drone can emit is small and lower powered. We'll get poor resolution from it compared to the *Khidr*'s sweeper, but any advantage we can get...

A thought occurs to me. I open another private comms channel to Duggins. He picks up quickly, still sitting at his desk. "Yes, Captain?"

"Your terminal access on the *Hercules*. Is it locked down, or can you still issue commands?"

"I can issue commands, but it'll be slow going as the computer's copying its whole database to us. What's the need?"

"Could we power up the freighter's scanner for a single sweep?"

Duggins chews his lip. "Possibly, if it's still functional. The system is isolated; however it will drain the portable power unit we installed. Also, any ship approaching will notice."

"They might think it's a signal from their own people."

"True."

"How quickly could you get it done?"

"I can start it now."

"Do that. We need the eyes."

"Okay."

I close the channel.

"Any sign of transmission from the *Hercules*?" Keiyho asks Johansson.

"None so far," she says. "If they've spotted us and got comms, they're leaving it late."

"I've authorised Duggins to try to patch into the freighter's scanner," I tell them. "Discount that from your readings, Ensign."

Johansson raises her eyebrows in surprise, but nods. "Will do, Captain."

An orange dot appears on the drone's camera view. It's tracked from a similar dot on the scan. "Possible object identified," Johansson says. "It's close by and moving at the requisite velocity."

"Send the data to Duggins," I order. "If we can narrow the field, he can target the *Hercules*'s system to match and preserve some power in the portable generator."

"As ordered," Johansson answers. "I'm also targeting our second sweep."

The orange signal moves forward as the screen updates the top right corner. The computer gives me an analysis of the object's velocity. "They're at one hundred and forty kilometres per hour. I guess they're decelerating on approach."

"At least that means they'll hold still while we shoot at them," Jacobson mutters.

"No excuses if we miss," I say.

A third update of the screen, this time narrowing into a thin wedge around the orange dot. Again, it jumps forward. "One hundred and thirty-five klicks," Johansson announces.

"Time to arrival?"

"Twenty minutes, Captain."

"That has to be them," Keiyho says. "I'm comparing with our earlier scans. It matches all of our previous data."

"Agreed," I reply. "Adjust our position and sound action stations to the crew. Let's be ready. This time we start the fight, and we finish it."

CHAPTER FIFTEEN

Shann

The walls feel like they are closing in.

One of my first memories as a child was a sense of helplessness in my own room. I was always an early riser. I'd wake up in the morning and have to wait for other people to come before I could get up. Granted, there was an alarm and a support worker available, but I didn't want to call them. I wanted to do things for myself.

I remember trying to manage without help. The falls out of bed, the bruises and bumps that I'd get and how they were discussed by visiting doctors and nurses. There would be changes each time. A new handhold or bar would be installed to help me get up and out. The carpet got replaced three or four times with softer and softer material.

Later, I recall a conversation where my parents told me how I'd been an angry child, pushing away their hands. "We struggled to adjust," my mom said. "But we soon learned you didn't need our pity."

At night, I'd go to bed, seeing the room around me as a challenge. I'd plan my route and the things I'd want to do when I woke up. Clothes would be laid out nearby; books and portable screens would be kept near the bed. My auto-chair would be positioned so I could get in on my own.

When I was a little older, the chair went away, and a set of prosthetic legs appeared. They were a novelty for a time and I wore them everywhere. I discussed having the permanent nerve implants and internal wiring adaptations with my parents. They were all for it and so was I, but the doctors urged caution. My body needed to settle and stop growing; otherwise the whole system would have to be replaced. "There are a few subtle things that develop in our bodies when we're in our twenties," I remember someone telling me. "Once that's done, we can proceed."

However, before that happened, I discovered space and changed my mind. There were a lot of reasons really. These days, I feel like I'm a different person – liberated and empowered in this world of pressurised containers and zero gravity.

Now, I'm strapped into a seat in a dimly lit room with a window into the darkness. Every bump and curve of this place could be dangerous. This metal and plastic box keeps me alive, but in less than an hour, it could also become my tomb.

I'm not alone, though, there's that.

"High-resolution laser image coming in from the *Hercules*," Johansson announces. "We have confirmation. Our object is a spaceship and it's closing fast."

The image loads onto my screen, and I get my first look at our enemy. The data is colour shifted and some of the details smeared away. The computer is enhancing the image as I manipulate it, turning and twisting it around to see what we can learn.

"Very similar to us," Jacobson says.

"Indeed," I say. "Looks like you were right, Keiyho; that's an Earth-manufactured ship."

I zoom in, tracking across the hull of the mysterious ship. There is a word etched into the fuselage – 'Gallowglass' – that must be its name.

"Jacobson, run a commissioned vessel database check on 'Gallowglass', please."

"Aye, aye." It only takes a few moments. "There's no record, Captain," Jacobson confirms.

"The ship has four additional thrusters compared to us," Keiyho says. "I can see two laser housings, and three rocket clusters."

"Two and three, to our one and four?"

"Yes, I think so, Captain."

"What's the range?"

"Four kilometres. She's slowed to thirty klicks per hour and is still decelerating."

"Is she in range of our weapons?"

"She will be in laser range in approximately ninety seconds."

"Lieutenant Travers, warm up the engines. Prepare for a Z positive burn. Six hundred metres elevation. Ready the crew. Jacobson, give me a countdown on approach."

I'm thinking about our saboteur. Both attacks came in moments where we were vulnerable, and we're about to be very vulnerable. I'm not sure we have the right person in custody. I remember Arkov mentioning the message he received on his terminal from Sam. He'll mention Sam was away from his post too. I need to stay away, focus on this and set aside my personal feelings. Someone accessed my computer as well. Hopefully, Le Garre can follow up on all of it and find our traitor.

"Thirty-five seconds, Captain."

"Travers, initiate burn. Keiyho, get ready to target rockets and laser. Hit with everything, just like we discussed."

"Aye, aye."

We're moving upward. I'm pressed into my seat. The main view screen is like being in an elevator with cargo container after cargo container going by. Then we reach the top and a dark expanse. Beyond it, the sun's light reflects off an object in the distance. It's the size of an apple, but getting closer.

The *Gallowglass*.

"We're in range and I have a firing solution," Keiyho announces.

"Do it," I say.

"Firing now," Keiyho replies.

In space, you can't see a laser apart from when the light reflects back at you. That only happens when the laser encounters something, a solid object, gas, or liquid. At this distance, I think I can see the ship called the *Gallowglass* flash with green for a moment, but I could be fooling myself.

What I don't imagine are the loud thumps and alert klaxons that herald the launch of our guided rockets. Four shapes jet away from us, their thruster engines aglow as they head straight for the oncoming ship.

I'm leaning forward in my chair, staring at our innocuous metallic neighbour. "Jacobson, activate the shutters. Travers, aim us right at them and boost to fifty klicks. Keiyho, recalibrate, reload and aim a second volley. Johansson, monitor impacts and any attempt at communication."

There's a chorus of affirmations. I'm pressed up and back into my chair as we maneuver and accelerate. A straight charge, like a joust. The distance between ships will disappear quickly. The element of surprise got us a first shot at them. If we can be quick and they are slow, we might get a second shot in before they can fire back.

"Captain, I'm detecting a change in telemetry on the rogue missile," Johansson warns. "We also have a course change from the *Gallowglass*. She's slowing and rotating to track us."

"Adjust targeting to compensate," I tell Keiyho.

"Aye, aye."

There's a flash from the approaching ship. Could it be an explosion from the laser? Or something else?

"I'm detecting retaliatory rocket launches, Captain!" Johansson says. "We're being targeted and there's some sort of—"

She doesn't finish the sentence. There's a tearing sound against the hull, and the decompression alarm goes off. The screen in front of me flashes red, and the schematic of the ship appears over the top of all the other windows.

"Laser impacts! We're being hit on the gravity torus and the starboard thruster!" Jacobson yells over the noise.

"Travers, calculate a spiral maneuver that maintains our course!" I order. I open a comms channel. "Bridge to Engineering?"

Duggins's voice in my ear is loud and urgent. "We have a lot going on down here, Captain!"

"We're about to have more," I say grimly. "Can you launch the last inflatable decoy we kept back?"

"We'll find a way, Captain Shann," Duggins says. Then he cuts the link.

For a moment, the tearing sound stops. I start thinking about the damage that's been caused. We might already be dead, our ship venting its crucial atmosphere and reserves into the darkness. The *Khidr* is built to endure, with multiple redundancies and reinforced hull plating, but I doubt the designers considered a circumstance like this.

"Rocket impacts confirmed!" Johansson shouts.

"Second volley loaded and away!" Keiyho adds.

Another round of low thumps and rumbling as the rocket engines ignite. I switch my screen to an external camera view. The *Gallowglass* is right in front of us and clearly visible. Our ordnance will be launching at almost point-blank range.

Suddenly, the ship shakes. I'm thrown against the straps and everything tilts ninety degrees. "We're hit!" Jacobson yells. "Multiple hull breaches! There's a fire in corridor three!"

"Seal compartments," I order. "Lock us in. Travers, rotate our profile as we pass the enemy. Keiyho, if you get a chance for a third shot, you take it!"

"Aye, aye!" Keiyho is staring at his screen grimly.

"Captain, I'm analysing the Gallowglass for damage," Johansson says. "We've hurt them, but...I'm...I think they've got some kind of shielding..."

"Shielding?"

"Yes," Johansson explains. "All four projectiles from our first salvo were direct hits, our laser tore a hole in their hull, but I'm not seeing enough damage. I think our warheads may have detonated before impact."

"We can't take much more of this, Captain," Jacobson warns.

"Bring up a navigation chart. Is there anything else out here?"

"Demios is thirty-six hours away," Johansson says, confirming what I already knew. "There's nothing until we get to the asteroid belt."

"Deploy prepared comms and plot a course toward Phobos Station," I order. "Get a damage confirmation. If they're still intact, we—"

The ship shakes again, and I'm slammed into the side of the chair. The rending sound of the laser returns. It's much closer, probably cutting into the corridor outside or a compartment nearby.

"Rotate and come about!" I scream.

We turn, and the Gallowglass is right in front of our rocket launchers as we drift past them, less than a kilometre apart. The proximity alarm goes off. Keiyho is firing anything he has, including the rail guns. On my screen, I can see scarring along their hull. A container rips away from the ship and disappears in a flash-fire explosion.

Sharp strikes rattle the view port shutters. I'm wincing and ducking in my seat instinctively. "Soon as we're clear, Travers, make for Phobos at the best speed you can manage. Alert the crew that we're going for a burn."

Travers nods, but doesn't reply. "Automated alert active, Captain," Jacobson says.

Another flash-fire explosion erupts from the Gallowglass, somewhere near the engines. Might have been fuel or an engine. "Johansson, get me everything you can on how much damage we've inflicted!"

"Aye, aye!"

I watch the collision counter numbers increase at the bottom of the screen. We're at two and a half klicks distance, and the *Gallowglass* is struggling to turn. She must have lost positional thrust. The tearing sound of her lasers raking across our hull rings out as we move away. I can see rockets heading toward us. One dissolves into flames, which quickly disappear in the vacuum. The other keeps coming, right at the screen.

"Brace for impact!" I yell.

I'm rammed into the seat. The breath in my lungs is gone in one big cough, and I feel something snap in my chest. I can't inhale. There's a roaring noise. I can't hear anything over it. For a moment, I think we're done. There's been a hull breach here, on the bridge, and all the air has been sucked out into space, but then I realise the other signs of explosive decompression aren't happening. *It's just me; I'm winded.*

I smell burning; the screen in front of me is on fire. My hands fumble with the armrest, and I pull out the micro-extinguisher. Foam snuffs out the danger and coats the ruined electronics.

The roaring noise is fading. I can hear voices again, but they're hard to make out. *"Captain, we're at four klicks; what's your order? Do we disengage?"* Travers is in my face, his dark skin and beard inches from me. I can smell his blood and sweat.

I nod. I try to speak. "Phobos." I don't know if he hears me, but he moves away.

A moment of nothing. Then pressure. I'm thrown around in my seat, before a constant force builds on me, pushing me back into the chair. My chest hurts; my lungs scream.

I…

*   *   *

Patrick Schuffer, the first man to walk on Mars, told lawmakers Thursday that the end of the 'nations era' has left the international human spaceflight programme to face a difficult future.

"Corporate partnership is a good thing, but we have to look at the balance. As of next week, we will have no access to, and return from, low Earth orbit unless a corporate partner authorises that trip. I can foresee a time when a

conflict of interest may arise that puts lives in danger," Schuffer told the Annual International Conference on Science, Space and Technology.

When asked to elaborate, Schuffer did: "After several false starts, humanity is beginning to expand its reach, at last. We're looking at permanent Moon settlement, permanent Mars settlement and beyond. There's an absolute need for corporate partners in all that, but somewhere down the line, the question of sovereignty is going to come up. When a commercial company is paying all the bills and providing all the materials, why shouldn't they own the buildings and the land? In that moment, you don't have an international conflict; you have the potential for an interplanetary conflict. It's a question of looking ahead."

Schuffer was part of a four-member panel of space experts who told delegates that the international coalition needs a stronger vision for the future and should focus on an 'end-game strategy' that 'fostered the most collegiate working environment in space that could possibly be achieved'.

"We're in danger of selling out completely," said Afriki Affuno, who commanded the Artemis 6 flight to Ceres in 2186. "Most people think that's about marketing and exhausting the brand, but in space travel and space colonisation, it's a different issue. We're talking about shaping people's lives for generations. We have to redefine ownership and property for people who've never been to Earth. Why would they see some allegiance or loyalty to us if they were born on Mars or the Moon? If we want to have a say in the future of these new nations, we have to share the risk and the cost. That's why there needs to be a partnership."

CHAPTER SIXTEEN

Johansson

Alarms wail around the bridge. I'm triggering the emergency release in my seat. As the straps retract, I grab one with my left hand and use it to swing myself around, getting a look at the damage in here.

There's a fire near the door, close to the atmospheric equaliser. The emergency system hasn't kicked in to deal with it. If the flames get to the oxygen tanks, the whole bridge will explode.

It's hard to move. The ship is accelerating. I could die doing this. One little slip and I'll get thrown into the walls, over and over, until my bones break like sticks.

There's a darkness at the edge of my vision and a throbbing in my head. I'm reaching for the emergency extinguisher packed into the side of my chair. Keiyho is also out of his chair, moving toward the captain. We exchange glances and he nods. I continue toward the fire, raise the extinguisher in my right hand and press the button, dousing the flames with foam.

"I've set course for Phobos Station!" Travers shouts over the alarms. "Captain's last order!" He's struggling out of his chair as well, turning toward Shann. Only Jacobson remains in his seat, leaning forward intent on his screen.

A small, cynical voice in my head says I should be helping the captain too. I glance in that direction. She's injured and unconscious, her chair is tilted at an angle, and her screen is covered in extinguisher foam. If I'm seen to help and by her side while she's disorientated, that could help with my letter of recommendation when this tour ends. I'd be doing myself a favour if—

No. That's shitty behaviour. Cut it out, Ensign.

I remember Captain Shann's last order to me. I need to focus on that and do my duty. The senior bridge officers will see to her.

I'm back in my seat. I bring up the bridge operations screen and mute the alarms. There's a whole list of flashing systems and ship functions that are going to need attending to, but that'll wait for a moment. The *Khidr*'s computer states our hull integrity is okay and the engines are functional. Everything else is secondary.

The tactical display shows the relative positions of our ship and the *Gallowglass*. The computer is running a damage assessment as I instructed before the hit. Snapshot photographs open and close in different windows, green boxes highlighting the possible damage we have inflicted. There is a finite window for this assessment. We're moving farther and farther away from the enemy ship, so image capture will become difficult and detail will be harder to determine.

There's a list of prioritised photographs appearing in another window. I open the one on top. It's a picture of the side of the *Gallowglass* that was closest to us as we passed by. There are six different boxes, highlighting impact and damage assessment. Some of the smaller engine cones are ruptured. That means they may struggle to maneuver, but there isn't nearly as much damage as I'd expect to see from the amount of ordnance we fired at their ship.

I track back through the footage recorded on our exterior cameras. There are a couple of freeze-frames of rocket explosions. I manipulate the image, zooming in. There's clear distance between where the warheads detonated and the side of the enemy ship.

Why did our rockets explode before they hit the *Gallowglass*?

The pressure of acceleration is easing. The burn Travers initiated to aim us toward Phobos must be nearly complete. I glance over and notice Jacobson is still working away at his console, his hands flashing across the screen. We're the only two people left on the bridge.

"Something wrong?" I ask.

"Travers didn't factor deceleration into his executed course plot," Jacobson says. "I'm correcting his work. If I don't, we'll be out of fuel and unable to stop."

"Understandable, given the pressure of the situation," I say.

Jacobson shakes his head. "There's no excuse for incompetence, particularly when it could get us all killed."

"Gunnar, you should cut him some slack."

Jacobson spins around in his chair and glares at me. He looks angry and points a finger at me. Those baby blue eyes are icy, and his pasty white skin is red. He opens his mouth to speak, but stops himself and sighs. The tension seems to run out of him. "You're right. We're all tired. I should let it go."

"Yeah, you should." We're friends. I've seen this before with him. Jacobson's a perfectionist. That's a trait we share. I used to think all his passion and enthusiasm was guileless, but it isn't. That's why we aren't lovers anymore.

Jacobson runs a hand through his hair. "How did the captain look?" he asks.

"I didn't see much. I think she was unconscious."

"She'll be all right, though, yeah?"

"I hope so."

I'm thinking about Captain Shann. If she weren't my superior officer and fifteen years older than me, we'd probably be close friends, or rivals. In her career, she's achieved so many of the things I want to achieve, and she's standing in front of a lot of doors I'd like to kick open.

That cynical voice in my head says I could do without her dying. I can't help but agree.

"We're outmatched by that ship," Jacobson says. He nods toward his screen. "They'll be wounded, but they'll come after us. With those tracking missiles they have, we'll need ideas if we're going to survive."

"Where did they come from?" I wonder out loud. "I've never heard of a *Gallowglass*. You said they're not on the Fleet registry. Are there any private owners who it could belong to?"

"If there are, they're breaking interstellar regulations," Jacobson says. "No ship that large could be built without making use of the shipyard in Earth orbit or around Mars, unless we don't just have this to deal with."

He's suggesting there might be another, secret shipyard, somewhere else. "That's a worrying thought," I say.

"Yes, it is." Jacobson leans toward me and lowers his voice. "Something like this is bigger than us. The captain's made choices that put us in the middle of a whirlwind."

"She was following procedure."

"That won't do much good if we all get killed."

I'm concerned at where this is going. "We're military. We don't question orders. We follow them."

"Sure," Jacobson replies. "But we need to stay alive and work out how we're getting out of this."

"I have faith in your abilities," I say and turn back to my console.

★   ★   ★

Fifteen minutes later, Travers returns.

"Captain's okay," he says. "Bogdanovic is with her."

Something in me loosens. I find myself smiling even though there's very little to smile about. "I'll start putting together an initial damage inventory," I say.

"Please do, and send it through to Duggins when you're ready," Travers orders. "He can start sorting out the work details."

I nod and initiate the internal damage sweep. While I'm doing so, the assessment calculation for the *Gallowglass* finishes up. I save the files. The captain will want them later.

I look around the bridge again. The damage is extensive. The captain's chair is wrecked, all but torn from its mooring. There's an inward bulge in the wall next to the main view screen too. Something hit us there from outside. We were very lucky the hull wasn't breached here, leaving us all to be sucked out into space.

Others on the ship weren't so lucky.

The quiet after all that frenetic activity is disturbing. It's a strange lull; we're safe for the moment, but in imminent danger if we make a bad call. People are talking in whispers, as if making a noise will somehow bring back the threat. There's a seductive quality to the silence, to hesitation as well. We're on a precipice. For now, we've no captain. Any decision taken in her absence might not be the decision she would make and might not fit into her plan. The captain always has a plan; that's part of the myth you make yourself believe so you can trust the chain of command.

Maybe Jacobson's right. Maybe we've gone wrong. If we have, when will the moment come when I make a different choice and defy what I'm told to—

My screen flashes; the initial damage assessment is complete. I key up a transmission window and send it to Duggins.

CHAPTER SEVENTEEN

Sellis

Jake,

I'm sorry it had to end like this, but you left me no choice.

I've packed all my things from the closet and left you with enough food for a day or two. My brother will be around tomorrow to collect the rest of my things.

There's many things I could say, but none of them will do any good; that's been proven. You've not changed after the last time we spoke about your problems, so I have to make a decision that's right for me and our unborn daughter.

You're not ready to be a father yet. Maybe one day you will be, but right now, no.

Please don't try to contact me. We're done. If you do, I'll have to take legal steps, and neither of us wants that.

Helen.

"...corridor nine needs a full system diagnostic. Currently, there is a power spike in panels four and six. You'll need to remove them to see what needs to be repaired."

"Yes, chief."

"That's it for now. Keep your portable comms active and I'll update you."

Lead Engineer Duggins's face disappears from my wall screen. I open the overhead locker above it and pull out my toolbox. After the war, comes the work. The ship won't fix itself.

The screen flashes, turns blue, and a small text appears in the top left. This time it's a short message and doesn't scroll. I lean in to read it.

Disable camera monitoring in corridors four, two and eight.

I stare at the words. The meaning is clear. Is this how it starts? How I'm blackmailed, and I compromise myself?

To be fair, I've done worse. When I owed money at the Nevada barracks, I sold all sorts of things out of the quartermaster's inventory.

When I was a kid, I sold my bike to pay off David Sansen, the class tough guy, and told my mom it was stolen. I'm not proud of those things, but I accept them. I'm pragmatic about the situations I end up in.

I leave my room and head toward corridor nine. I'm thinking about what I'm going to do. Turning off cameras while the crew are making repairs is clever thinking. Duggins and anyone monitoring on the bridge is likely to think it's a system malfunction. I can access the security network from any terminal and get it done. Given time, someone might check who logged in and 'did the deed', but right now, we all have other priorities.

I've no idea what my mysterious messenger wants to do. Could be that it's harmless. Then again, why now?

No. I don't think this is harmless.

How involved am I if I do this? What do I lose if I don't?

I think about Drake and the mess they had to clean up in corridor six. *Yeah… Fuck that.* There's no choice really, particularly as they've mentioned my ex-wife and daughter. That list gave me my daughter's name – Jane. I never met her while I was still on Earth. Helen left before she gave birth.

I reach the terminal at the end of the passage. I log in and bring up the camera feeds. I switch monitoring to manual and deactivate them, one by one. Then I go into the command history and delete all my entries.

I need to be quick with this. Duggins will have sent out the entire repair team. They'll be all across the ship. The minute someone finds me here and not where I'm assigned, questions will be asked.

Before I log out, a blue window appears with another message.

Thank you. Memorise this code – 0bXhuj7693a

Well, shit. Fuck you very much too.

I stare at the digits. When I was at school, I'd get a part in the stage stuff they'd put on. I wasn't the best actor, but I was good at memorising lines. I could visualise each page of the script by staring at it for a while and repeating the words. Instinctively, I'm doing that now. Doesn't matter whose side I'm on; this is self-preservation.

I make my way down to corridor nine. The lights are flickering – a sign of the power fluctuation Duggins mentioned. There are scorch marks all along the deck and the bulkhead. There's foam in here too, floating around. Must have been a fire, put out by the automatic extinguisher. I expect that one of the cables shorted, either from the flames or the foam.

I remove panels four and six, and suddenly the world becomes a much smaller place – always does when I get into fixing things. Circuits and cables speak to me in ways that people can't. I remote into the *Khidr*'s system and deactivate the power. The lighting flickers once more, then dies. I unscrew the safety cover, switch on my flashlight, and lean in to examine the damage. This is the kind of job they can't ask a computer to do. AIs might be able to diagnose a fault, but unless they go all android, they'll never replace the repairman. Human beings are cheaper and more expendable, will be forever, no matter how much the tech improves.

A portable vacuum cleans out the compartment. Then it's a case of crimping and switching the wires. In zero gravity, we use a chemical solder compound. Cut out the bad cable, expose the ends of the replacement and the old section, wipe on a little of the magic paste and hold it all in place while everything joins together. Still fiddly, but a lot easier than trying to scrape a bubble of liquid metal onto bare wires, like we did back when I—

"You okay, Sellis?"

I look up. There's a flashlight in my face, making me blink and cover my eyes. "I was fine until you came along," I grunt.

My bunkmate, Technical Specialist Jahad Ashe, kneels down beside me. He's three years younger than me and has been trying to get out of sharing our room ever since we were put together three weeks ago. It's *nothing personal*, apparently. *Yeah, fuck you, shithead.*

Ashe is second-generation Sri Lankan American and an optimistic pain in the butt. He's got these watery blue eyes and super metabolism. He eats every chance he gets, but you wouldn't know it to look at him.

"Duggins gave me corridor five," Ashe tells me – like I'm supposed to care.

"You all done then?"

"Yeah. Just a malfunction in the atmospheric processor."

"Why are you bugging me then? Duggins will have more for you to do."

Ashe flinches from my glare and looks uncomfortable. There's something off, but he's not talking about it. "I just wanted to check on you…" he mumbles.

"Bullshit," I reply.

"I mean it, I…" Ashe looks around, then moves in closer. "You can tell me if anything's wrong, you know that, right?"

"Sounds like there's something you want to tell me."

"No, I…" Ashe swallows, biting off what he was going to say. "They say Captain Shann was injured in the attack."

I shrug. "I bet plenty of people were hurt and killed."

"Who'll take charge?"

"You know who. Travers is XO. The senior crew will rally around him."

"You think they can get us home?"

"You think they can't?" I chuckle. "You know as well as I do they believe they can. They have to. That's what being an officer is all about, making choices and standing by them, even if you're wrong. We march in line. That's what soldiers have always done."

Ashe looks at me again. His eyes are watery, and there's a redness about his face that I didn't notice before. He's been crying. "Hey, you sure you're okay?" I ask. "Come on, if you need to talk it out, I guess I can—"

"No, it's nothing." Ashe wipes his face. The moisture clings to the back of his suit sleeve. The comms badge on his wrist flashes. "I need to get to my next assignment. I'll see you later." He turns and drifts away.

I'm left wondering what he wanted.

Maybe someone's approached him, like they did with me.

I replace panel four and move on to panel six. There's some residual extinguisher foam in here. I take out the micro-vacuum and scrape away all traces of it. These compounds are designed to insulate circuits and cut off the power in the event of a fire. A quick circuit test indicates no further repairs are needed.

Good.

The rest of the damage to the corridor is superficial. We're in the middle of the ship, so it was probably protected from the worst of the attack. Cleanup will come after we've fixed the worst of the damage.

I'm done here. I'll have to check in with Duggins and get my next assignment.

CHAPTER EIGHTEEN

Shann

I'm alive.

I'm not alone.

We're alive.

The pressure on my chest is easing. I feel fingers working at the straps around me. There are voices too. I recognise the words and I should understand them, but I'm too tired to link everything together.

Hands are under my arms; I'm being lifted from where I was, floating in the air. An arm wraps itself around me, guiding me away from where I was.... I remember the captain's chair...on the bridge of my ship... the *Khidr*.

It's all coming back gradually. I hear the word 'relax' said by a familiar voice over and over again. I try to do what I'm told and not force my head to make sense of everything – just let it come naturally.

"Captain Shann, can you hear me?"

The words make sense, so I nod. I'm lying down. I can feel more safety restraints, but they're not constrictive. *How did I get here? How long have I been here?* There's a time gap. *Was I asleep? What did I miss?*

I open my eyes. I'm in my own room and I recognise Doctor Bogdanovic. He's leaning over me. There's dried blood on his cheek. I can't see a wound. I guess it's not his.

"Hello, Captain Shann. How are you feeling?"

"I—" Opening my mouth to answer brings the pain. A crushing headache that feels like a vise is gripping my skull. My mouth is dry, my voice hoarse and broken.

Bogdanovic smiles. "Good, better than I thought you were and better than some of the others. The painkillers will kick in shortly and you'll be able to function." He's holding a small torch and staring into my eyes, watching how my pupils react. "You know, I watch a lot of retro-Earth sports entertainment? You ever heard of boxing? Awful game where two athletes would enter a roped-off space and inflict as much head trauma on each other as possible. All for money and a gaudy belt. The medical professional in me hates the idea, but there's something about it that's strangely compelling. Right now, you're exhibiting the same kind of symptoms as one of those poor saps. Thankfully, you're not making a career out of it."

I notice there's an IV line in my left arm at the elbow. My right hand is wrapped in a tight blue glove. "What happened to—"

"You've broken two ribs, banged your head really hard and fractured your left wrist. I've set the bones, but you'll be managing a fair amount of pain for the next few weeks. Provided we survive that long, of course." Bogdanovic moves away from me toward the door. "Give yourself twenty minutes or so to let the medication get into your system, then unplug the IV and you can return to duty. Given the power failures and damage, I'd suggest you make use of your own terminal for the time being."

"How bad is—"

"Bad enough, but manageable. You can start dealing with it when the drugs kick in."

"How long have I been out?"

"About an hour. You should eat something."

I lie back and hear the door open and close. I'm alone now, listening to my heart, my breathing and other noises. The life beat of the ship, louder now she's hurt, I guess. There's a throbbing, fitful hum that I don't remember from before. It doesn't sound healthy.

I go through what I remember. There was a missile aimed at us. I know it hit the *Khidr*. We were already moving away, and there was that horrible press of high g's. Travers must have gotten us clear. The engines must still be working, at least enough to give us a chance.

The headache starts to recede, and now I can feel the muted dull ache of my wrist and my ribs. The painkillers make me feel distant too, as if I'm not really here. That won't help.

I don't know whether twenty minutes have passed, but I can't wait any longer. With my left hand, I pull out the IV and sit up.

I'm immediately dizzy and disorientated. It's like the first day of zero g training all over again, but this time I'm not going to vomit. I undo the straps and push off with my left hand, catching myself on the back of my chair with my right. My injured wrist protests at the use, but I ignore it and drag myself into the seat.

There's a ship schematic on the screen. Several compartments are labelled dark red. That means they're either gone or irreparable. Hydroponics is among those, so are at least half of the crew compartments. We're in bad shape.

My hands are shaking as I manipulate the screen. *Do I want to know how bad?* No, not really, but I have to know. It's my job, my responsibility.

A damage summary appears and scrolls in front of me. We're down to twenty-four per cent of our oxygen reserve, twenty per cent of our nitrogen. Thruster fuel is at thirty-three per cent. The laser scanner is offline but being repaired. Our laser turret has been destroyed. Two rocket launchers are also inoperable. Half the ship's thrusters are no longer functional. We have six unidentified pressure leaks, and fourteen members of the crew are injured and five dead.

Five are dead.

Tomlins, Thakur, Lendowski, Andelman and Orritt all *killed in action*. After the freighter crew and Drake, the first casualties of a war in space.

I stare at the photo IDs of the dead crew, and it hits me. I honestly thought we were past moments like this. Sure, there have been tensions between different factions, but Fleet exists to represent humanity as a whole. We're supposed to be united; that's the difference between us and the national militaries. Conflict between nations has always been an 'Earth thing' – I've heard many people say that. People who've been trying to lead, shape and define what being a human being in space means. What our non-Earth societies are, and are going to become.

What possible motive could these...*murderers* have?

I can see my own face reflected in the glass. I look awful. There are little nicks and bruises along my forehead and down to the right side of my jaw. My eyes are watery, and I'm struggling to focus. Battered, but not broken. Not yet.

I remember what Bogdanovic said before he left – *you should eat something.* My stomach growls. He's right. Despite feeling like crap, I'm hungry.

Food in space is never going to be an occasion. On some ships they've tried to have sit-down meals and everything, but it doesn't work too well. Astronauts are used to liquefied meals they can squirt and swallow without too much ritual. Zero gravity means any fluid or object that isn't strapped down will move around. A lot of mixed liquids get sticky without gravity to keep them in line and don't like leaving their containers. So, a lot of clever designing has been needed to get around all these problems.

But, even then, food is functional.

I suppose we could eat a scheduled meal on the gravity deck. But for it to approximate the same ritual on Earth, we'd have to prepare everything up there and keep the torus spinning for a long time. Cooking is wasteful. In space, you can't afford to be wasteful, so we're left with preprocessed and preprepared liquefied paste. Better than ship's biscuits, gruel and rum, I guess, but not by much.

I eat, if you can call it that, quickly. The hunger subsides, but I keep eating until the plastic pack is empty and I can drop it in the recycler. No waste is a good habit, even if our ability to reuse and reconstitute our supplies has been compromised.

The signal chime sounds at my door. I look down. I'm barely dressed. Someone has had to get me out of my work suit and into a surgical robe. "Hold on!" I say and open one of the compartments above my head. There's fresh clothes in sealed and magnetised bags. I pull out what I need and quickly change. "Come!"

The door slides back. The person waiting there is someone I don't recognise.

"Captain, I'm Technician Kiran Shah, from the *Hercules*. Doctor Bogdanovic and Major Le Garre gave me permission to come and speak with you?"

"Of course, come in."

Shah enters. He's as beat up as I am, but his dark hair and dark skin conceals it better. He's much older than me, in his late forties, I guess. There's a thick bandage around his head, and he winces when he moves. I offer him the chair and he takes it with a nod of thanks.

"I guess you've told Le Garre what happened to you?" I ask.

"Yes, I've gone through all the details with her. She wanted to talk to you first, but the doctor said no. He gave her something to help her sleep. Apparently, she can't do that."

"I don't think any of us will be getting much sleep."

"No, probably not."

I'm staring at Shah as he gathers himself, working out where he wants to start and what he wants to say. I don't rush him. My own brain is struggling to cope with the basics at the moment.

"Firstly, I wanted to thank you for coming for us. I mean, I know this hasn't turned out how anyone wanted, but we called for help and you came; that means a great deal."

"We did what we're supposed to do, Technician," I say.

Shah shrugs. "Okay, well, it still means a lot to me. I was a long time out there thinking I was going to die, suffocating in a metal tube. I very nearly gave up. Seeing your people... Well...I'll never be able to say thank you enough."

"Were you on your own?" I ask gently.

"At the end, yes," Shah says. "They couldn't find me after we set the distress call."

"That was you?"

"Me and Peters. We were down in the manifest when they attacked the bridge. We ran away and hid, then came back and activated the beacon. They found us and shot him."

"They came aboard?"

"They were always aboard. They attacked us from inside and out. When the captain wouldn't surrender, they launched missiles."

"You think their plan was to capture your ship?"

"At the start." Shah chews his lip for a moment. "When we first picked them up on the scope, the captain called us into a whole crew briefing. He gave us a set of codes and made us memorise them. Said they'd be needed if we were rescued. Major Le Garre said I should talk to you about that?"

Realisation dawns in my fog-filled mind. "Yes, you should," I say.

*   *   *

"Welcome to the executive summary of Project Outreach. I am Doctor Aki Kuranawa from the University of Kyoto. If this is your first viewing of our proposed strategy, I recommend accessing the relevant data and reports provided alongside our presentation, so you can follow our methodology and see the evidence behind our conclusions.

"A summary of our findings is as follows:

Within ten years, Earth governments will no longer financially support manned spaceflights.

Colonial settlements will require regular shipments of life-support resources for the next century. Mars might become self-sufficient before this, but it will still need essential resources.

Solely commercial space operations will not be financially viable for at least twenty years.

A solution for the above issues will need to be found; otherwise our settlements on Luna, Mars and Ceres are in danger of being abandoned.

"Project Outreach looks to provide that solution by establishing an independent infrastructure base away from Earth. The project has already identified possible replacement sources of the essential components we currently ship from Earth. A selection of new technologies will be required to obtain these resources quickly, as the environments they exist in are not ones we can quickly make suitable for human habitation. Therefore, extensive autonomous technology must be constructed and shipped out to these sites to begin the necessary work.

"Our detailed plan explains how this will be done. We hope you will agree with our findings."

The image disappears from the screen, and we're all left staring in silence.

We're back in the strategy room on the gravity deck. The torus is damaged and no longer able to rotate, but we can access the compartments. This is as good a place as any to discuss our next move.

The lack of gravity changes this place for me. I'm not shackled or restricted by having to wear prosthetics. We're clustered around the table, but there's no need to sit and obey some sort of meeting ritual anymore. I know the others would prefer things the way they were, but I like it like this. Although, I wish the circumstances that brought us here were different.

The group has expanded. With me are Travers, Le Garre, Duggins, Keiyho and Technician Shah, who supplied the correct code to unlock the files.

"The corporations are building a claim for independence from Earth," Le Garre whispers.

"Looks more like an insurance policy to me," Travers says. "If the conclusions from the data are right, we'll all need a backup plan when this goes down."

"Did you know what your ship was carrying?" Duggins asks Shah.

Shah shakes his head. "I've been a freighter tech for eight years. We check cargo under security supervision according to the agreed protocols. We don't open containers without permission."

Duggins sighs. "It occurs to me, Technician, we've only got your word for all this. You might very well be a saboteur from your own ship."

Shah stares at him, expressionlessly. After a moment, he says softly, "You think I'd intentionally seal myself in that corridor? Let myself be poisoned by the air, just on the off chance someone would rescue me?"

"I don't know what to think," Duggins says. "But I guess you're right."

"Thank you."

"I think we need to assess our current place in this," I say. I take a breath and start going through it all, aloud. "We've responded to a distress call from the *Hercules*. The ship that attacked it is not on any manufacturing or construction manifest. We now know the freighter was transporting secret supplies for the building of an illegal colony. The *Gallowglass* acted to stop it."

"By killing innocent people," Duggins says.

"The point is that we're caught in the middle," I say. "There's no right path. This is the start of some kind of secret war between two factions that we don't understand or belong to. We're trying to follow orders that don't take any of this into account."

"Whatever we believe is right, we have an enemy ship following us that's trying to ensure none of us survive," Keiyho says.

"You best update me on our situation," I say.

Keiyho shrugs. "We're moving at fifteen thousand metres per second, the fastest we can manage and also decelerate in time when we get close to Phobos. The resonance drive is gone, so this is our best speed. With rationing of air, food and water, we can just about make it."

"How long until we get there?"

"Approximately four weeks."

"The *Gallowglass*?"

"She's in pursuit. We damaged her drives, but I don't know how much. We've got a lead. We may keep it; we may not. If they catch up to us, then we may have some tricks, but judging from the readout Johansson got of their ship, we won't last long."

"What did we learn about them?"

"The ship is based on the same design as ours," Duggins says, "in that it's a set of joined modular containers, all filled with specialist equipment and linked together with access corridors. She's got at least one hundred and fifty per cent of our power. I estimate they're using larger fission reactors, or they've got three to our two. There's an additional rocket cluster and some experimental weaponry, as we've experienced. The reason they're able to do all that and be about the same size as us is because they aren't carrying all the rescue equipment and extra reserves we have aboard. That said, the only reason we're still alive is because of those reserves."

"Tell me about the weapons."

"Guided missiles and some kind of signal interference net. That's why some of our rockets detonated before they hit the ship's hull," Duggins explains. "Any sort of electronic detonation appears to be affected by it – a neat trick. When we have time, we'll adapt our warheads so they don't use systems like that."

"Okay." I turn to Le Garre. "What about your investigation?"

Le Garre sighs. "I questioned Arkov. His reason for leaving his post and panicking when Quartermaster Chase confronted him seems plausible, particularly after what you told me about your workstation on the bridge."

"Did you speak to Chase?"

"I started to, but then everything around here went to shit. He's my next interview, as soon as I leave here."

"Do you think Arkov is innocent?"

"I don't know," Le Garre says. "What I do know is that while he was locked up, we had no further incident during the altercation with the *Gallowglass*."

"We're short-handed," Duggins says. "We can't spare people to watch him."

"Then we don't watch him," I say. "We make sure he has everything he needs, but we keep him in his quarters under security override."

"Fine," Le Garre says.

I glance at Duggins. "What do we need to repair?"

"Everything," he replies with a humourless smile. "To begin with, we need to stop losing atmosphere. The leaks we have are microscopic cracks, the sort that a construction crew finds with a sweep before or during shakedown, but that's not our situation. I need as many people as possible going over this ship to find them."

"After that?"

"After that we look at trying to repair things that'll keep us alive," Duggins says. "We've no external communication and we're currently flying blind. The only reason we know we're pointed in the right direction is that your ensigns on the bridge are using all sorts of old-school tricks."

Travers chuckles. "Heaven forbid you praise Jacobson. He'll be impossible to manage afterward."

"What can you repair in the way of weapons?" I ask.

Duggins looks at Keiyho. "Two rocket launchers are functional," he says. "We've discussed rotating and adapting a third to drop explosives behind us."

"You mean, like mines?"

"Yes, it makes sense," Keiyho says. "The *Gallowglass* is starting from the same position we were in, so their course will be almost identical to chase us down. According to Johansson's damage assessment, they've lost some manoeuvering too, so that'll help. We don't need an increase of speed; we need deceleration. That may take as much fuel, but it doesn't require as much aiming to get right. The more our explosives decelerate, the quicker they'll encounter the enemy ship. If they detect them, they'll have to slow down or adjust course. Either way, we'll increase our lead."

"Four weeks is still a long time," Travers says. "Too long, if you ask me."

Those words hang in the air. No one disagrees.

CHAPTER NINETEEN

Johansson

"You're relieved."

I look up. Ensign Chiu is next to my station. She looks tired, but her voice is firm and insistent. "Travers says you've been here since the attack and you pulled extra time before. You need a break."

"You're not qualified for the comms post," I say.

"Combat protocol means bridge crew rotates," Chiu replies. "That's the priority. I can handle the basics."

I lean back in my seat, getting a better look at my screen. It's filled with windows, half-finished tasks I've started and got distracted from as new problems arose.

What am I achieving? Looks like nothing.

"Okay." I start unstrapping myself from the chair. I've never really got on with Chiu, but then when you're on a tour of duty with the same twenty-five people, you learn to be polite and professional about these things. I know she's Korean, from the reclaimed territories. I can't imagine what life could be like there. Perhaps one day we'll swap stories.

For now, though, no.

I leave the bridge. The damage in the corridor outside is extensive. There are scorch marks on the walls and sealant foam in places. The *Khidr* has an automated control system, which activates in the event of a hull breach. There are sensors embedded throughout the ship that can trigger emergency measures. Redundant systems and backups upon backups are all part of the design of a spaceship. They always have been, all the way back to Vostok and Apollo.

My head knows all that, but I've some kind of gut feeling of being vulnerable and powerless. There's a big difference between a fabricated section of the ship designed and tested to hold pressure and a repaired section of the same. All the compartments will need to be checked and assessed again. In the meantime, we're hoping it holds. These walls might crack and blow out at any moment.

I guess that's what happened to Tomlins or Thakur, or any one of the others. One minute they were in a lit atmospheric compartment, and the next they were out in the dark, drifting away with no air. They say one of the things you feel is the saliva on your tongue bubbling and that you black out pretty fast, but even so, that moment of knowing there's nothing to breathe…

No one deserves to die like that.

Still, at least we got confirmation about the captain's condition. Apparently, she's already back to work.

I'm making my way back to my room, but then I have a thought. While I'm exhausted, I know I won't sleep. I feel guilty for taking a rest while everyone else gets on with the job. I know it's irrational, but that's part of how I am. Doctor Bogdanovic can prescribe sedatives during a combat protocol without a comment on my file. They might give me a chance of at least resting, or switching off.

I turn around and start heading toward medical. As I get close, I hear Bogdanovic talking, but when I round the corner, he's on his own, examining a set of vials he's just pulled out from a shelf. He looks up.

"Help you, Ensign?"

"I, uh, yes. I've just been sent to rest. I'm not sure I can."

"So, you came here for a sedative?"

"If possible, yes."

Bogdanovic nods. He looks at me, but when I meet his eye, his gaze flicks away to somewhere else. "Well, you're not the first person I've seen about this since our little altercation. I can give you a shot, or a couple of pills. Depends how you're feeling and how long until people will need you."

"Just the pills, thanks. Hopefully, I can get a couple of hours."

"Okay." Bogdanovic turns to a screen on the wall and brings up my medical record. "Says here you have a ketamine allergy?"

"I do."

"Best we keep you away from that then."

I glance around the room. Something's not right. There's no one here, so who was he talking to? Bogdanovic is exhausted just like the rest of us, but he's being very careful in what he says to me. We're not close, but he asked for me to help with the Drake analysis and cleanup, which means he rates me. We would be closer, I guess, but I try to avoid anyone who might find cause to mark my card. Still, it'd be strange not to say something now.

"Something troubling you, Doctor?"

He turns toward me, his expression stony, but then he forces a smile. "Just tired," he says. "We're all up against it."

"I'd offer to help, but…"

"Yeah, you're too busy already. I'll manage. When people die, it all gets…real? We have to detach a little bit to handle it all."

"I get that."

"I know; that's why I'm telling you. Other people…" The doctor hesitates then continues. "Other people expect you to show you care, like everyone's a favourite puppy. They don't realise you can't do that in this job. It breaks you if you do, makes you feel personally responsible. I'm sorry that sounds harsh—"

I hold up a hand. "No, I understand, I've been there." Bogdanovic knows my background. He doesn't need me to elaborate.

"Sure." Bogdanovic hands me a container. There are four pills in it. "Take one and see how you do. You can take them all without a problem, but you might not wake up for a while."

"I'll be careful, thanks."

"No problem."

I make my way out and back toward my room. I think I hear sounds of talking again. I've half a mind to stop and listen, but that's not me. If Bogdanovic is coping by talking to himself, then fine. I totally get his point. All medical professionals try to establish that professional distance. It's an ongoing struggle to maintain it, particularly when you see some of the things your patients are going through. It has to be harder when you're locked away with the same people for months, like we are on tour. Each face is someone you get used to seeing – a part of your routine and your daily life. When they go, that's a change, a little destabilisation. We get used to it and move on, but in these moments, where everything is threatened, it's hard to accept these things properly and process them. The missing people are like the damage to the walls. We're structurally weaker without them. All we can do is plaster over the cracks and hope.

I reach my room, open the door and move inside. This feels like a safe space, but really, there aren't any safe spaces, not anymore.

CHAPTER TWENTY

Shann

Three hours later, I'm back on the bridge and the medication is wearing off.

Gradually I'm learning more about what happened at the end of the battle. The missile I'd seen coming toward us struck the deck just below the bridge, destroying a water purification compartment. The impact tore my chair from its moorings and sent me crashing into the wall. Travers and Keiyho had to free me and get me to Bogdanovic.

The bridge is a wreck compared to what I'm used to. Screens and consoles have been replaced with temporary equipment from store. There are cables trailing everywhere, like snakes floating in water. They'll need to be bolted down, but for now they're a necessary hazard while we get on with more urgent repairs.

A replacement chair has been bolted into where mine was. I'm in it, shifting around uncomfortably. Duggins is in the engineering chair and Jacobson is acting as navigator. Le Garre is about the ship with her investigations, and the others are asleep.

It's quiet. I can hear the fitful throbbing of the ship from before. She's labouring along, weakened and limping away from a bloodied enemy who has licked its wounds and is coming back for more.

Since the meeting, we've got the laser scanner back online. Communication is close to being repaired, but only if someone takes a walk outside. Currently we have no functioning airlock, so that'll have to wait a while longer.

My screen flashes. An incoming private communication request from Le Garre. I slip on my headphones and pick it up. "You finished with Sam?"

"Yes, finally." Le Garre frowns into the camera on my screen. "He's admitted to being away from his post. Says he heard something in the cargo hold and went to see what it was. The door closed and locked on him, and he was too embarrassed to mention it. When he got back, nothing had changed, so he didn't think it was important."

"You believe him?"

"I think if it was a lie, it'd be more elaborate."

My instincts aren't reliable around Quartermaster Sam Chase. He's my closest friend in space and the person I've known longest aboard the ship. I'm not sure I could think of him as a traitor, responsible for the deaths of my crew. I'm trying hard not to let those feelings affect my judgement. Le Garre has responsibility for this investigation. I need to give her space to work through it all.

"Okay, let me know if I can help."

"Will do."

I end the call and pull off my headphones. "Jacobson, give me an update on the position of the *Gallowglass*."

"She's in pursuit and increasing speed," Jacobson says. "She's gained sixteen kilometres on us in the last hour."

"How long until she catches up?"

"At the moment, eleven days. If she has a working resonance drive, that'll come down significantly."

"Yes, of course." I turn to Duggins. "Can we get any more speed out of our engines?"

"Not if we want to be able to decelerate into Phobos orbit," Duggins says. "The *Gallowglass* doesn't have to factor that braking into its course as they have no intention of going there. They only need to decelerate to a speed in which they can launch missiles at us."

I nod. "If we accelerate to our maximum possible speed, we won't be able to stop?"

"Not without killing everyone aboard," Duggins says. "We could aim for another destination, but we'd only be prolonging the time until the *Gallowglass* hunts us down. There's also the issue of fuel. We have to make sure we have enough to brake."

"Okay." Something else is on my mind. "How much of the freighter's records did you get?"

"About forty-five per cent." Duggins looks at me. "You think there's something in there we need to know?"

"I'm not sure," I say, thinking aloud. "Our enemies wouldn't have boarded the ship if they didn't want something from it. Perhaps they wanted the lot, perhaps there was something specific, but we're more likely to find that out from the files in the secure transmission. Right now, I'm more interested in the flight records."

"You want to know where they've been?"

"No, I want the active records, right before the *Hercules* was attacked. There must be camera feeds, scans, all the saved data from the ship's and crew's last few hours."

"Okay, now I see what you're thinking." Duggins manipulates his screen. "I've got a partial download of the recorded system data from the last two hours before the freighter lost power. Sending it to you now."

"I'll take a look at it in my quarters." I unbuckle myself from the replacement chair. "Let Bogdanovic know I'll drop in to see him on my way."

"Aye, aye, Captain."

I'm through the door and into the corridor. I'm in pain. My left hand is awkward, and I fumble my grip on the safety rails. It's a long and frustrating trip into the lower decks, more difficult than the journey up as painkillers have worn off.

There's no one around in the passageways. The strip lighting buzzes and flickers, intermittently. One of the security team should be on duty, patrolling between here and the cargo hold. Probably Sam, Keiyho, or someone else they've pulled in to help. Tomlins would have been the one taking the third shift, but he died, doing his job, burned alive and sucked out into space during the altercation with the *Gallowglass*.

I'm passing an intersection when I feel pain in my right shoulder, like a bee sting, sharp as a needle. My arm goes numb, and I crash into the hatch at the far end. I struggle to turn around, groping with my left hand.

My back is against the hatch. My heart is pounding, lurching. I see a figure emerging from the side passage. I can't see their face. I can't keep my eyes open. I can't move.

"It had to be you, didn't it?" A man's voice. "I'm sorry, Captain Shann."

There's a shout and the sound of a gunshot. A hand grabs my arm, shakes me. "Are you—"

"I'll be okay, leave me! Get after him."

When I was a child they had to operate on me as I grew. There were complications with my bones and the necessary plugs for the use of my prosthetics. They gave me all sorts of sedatives and anaesthetics for the surgeries. I know the signs.

My headache fades into a buzz, and the pain in my wrist disappears. I'm floating physically and spiritually, soaring outside myself up and above.

I want to go to sleep, but I know I need to stay awake. Dimly I can hear alarms. There's shouting and another gunshot. I force my eyes open. Two figures are grappling with each other in the passageway in front of me. Someone is wounded; there's blood spiraling around them both in a trailing stream.

I gather myself and push off from the wall with my broken wrist. I hear the bones grind and crunch. I'm flying toward the two people, screaming a wordless challenge. I slam into them both, trying to grab hold of someone, anyone, but I have no strength and drift past, bouncing off the deck and on down the corridor.

Another figure appears in front of me. It's Duggins. He's by the intersection. I gesture wildly. "He was in there!" I shout.

Duggins enters the storage compartment. He shouts something and the hatch closes, locking him in. There's more shouting behind me and I hear people moving. They're getting farther away. I try to push myself up, but my right arm isn't useful, and my left isn't enough. I can't go after them. I'm—

"Captain, you've been shot."

Le Garre's in my face. She's calm. She's holding me in her arms. "Some kind of tranquiliser," I say. "You can't let him get away."

"Don't worry; half the crew's chasing him. Did you see who it was?"

"I didn't get a good look."

"Well, he's got nowhere to go. We'll get him."

"You need to check on Duggins," I tell her. "He went into the storage compartment the traitor was coming out of. The door sealed after him."

"Okay," says Le Garre. "I'll take a look."

She lets me go. I'm still struggling to focus and move around, but I make it to the hatch and down a deck before Bogdanovic finds me. "Le Garre said you'd been attacked," he says.

"Yeah. Injected with something." My breathing is fast and shallow. I try to hold on to him, but my fingers won't grip.

Bogdanovic guides me into the medical bay. There are three patients already here. Ensign Chiu is sitting up on one of the beds. "You all right, Captain?" she asks.

I nod and concentrate on breathing. Chiu helps Bogdanovic get me onto the vacant bed. My eyes are starting to lose focus again. "You need to stay awake," the doctor says, "at least until I figure out what to do with you." He waves a needle full of blood in front of me. I didn't even feel him take it. "I'll do a quick scan to see what you've been injected with."

Ensign Chiu is in front of me. I can feel her fingers on my face. She's talking to me, trying to keep me awake. "I never thanked you properly for selecting me for the ship's crew, Captain. I wanted you to know, no matter what happens, how proud I am of getting the chance and how proud my family were when I gave them the news..." Chiu continues talking, but I don't understand the words anymore. I try to keep nodding and keep my eyes open. They're rolling all over the place, wanting to close, wanting me to sleep. I—

"Okay, I think I know what it is. I'll give her a shot, and then you can let her sleep it off."

This time I feel the needle in my left arm. It's the last thing I feel.

I pass out.

★   ★   ★

I'm staring at a man I don't know through reinforced glass.

The *Khidr* doesn't have a prison cell. When we detained Arkov, he was restricted to his quarters, after those quarters had been searched. Now I'm gazing through the door slot of the late ensign Thakur's room. The man who is in the room is the man Lieutenant Commander Keiyho captured in the corridor, after he assaulted me.

This is a man who knew my name and spoke to me as if we were acquaintances.

I do not remember this man.

There's a hand on my right shoulder. I can feel it now that the tranquiliser has worn off. I'd been injected with enough to trigger a heart attack. Thankfully, Doctor Bogdanovic got to me in time.

"You were very lucky," Le Garre says, echoing my thoughts.

"He said something to me after he stuck me with the needle. I think I disturbed him; he didn't want me dead."

"Duggins says he was wiring up the compartment to explode," Le Garre says. "That room was storing all the replacement communications equipment. If it had gone up, we'd have never been able to contact Phobos and we'd have decelerated significantly, meaning the *Gallowglass* would have caught up to us much more quickly."

"He knew where to hit us then?"

"Seems like it. He's well trained too. Keiyho shot him, but he says if you hadn't barreled in when you did, we'd be short another crewman and he'd have gotten away."

"I didn't know what I was doing," I say.

"Well, you did the right thing," Le Garre says.

"Thanks." I point at the man in the room. The drugs have mostly worn off, but my left arm still feels awkward when I move it. The shoulder twinges and there's a dull ache in my hand. "What else do we know about him?"

"Not much," Le Garre says. "He was carrying some unusual items, including a sidearm and portable near-field communications. I think that was the source of the transmission Johansson detected. Otherwise, his face doesn't appear in any crew or passenger registration document from the interplanetary files or the colonial citizen registration system."

"He's from Earth then?"

"I'd guess so, but he's been trained to operate up here by someone. We need to question him and find out who that is. Are you up to it?" Le Garre asks.

"You want me involved?"

"We're dealing with ship security and an ongoing tactical situation," Le Garre explains. "This isn't just about investigating a crime. You need to be a part of talking to him."

"You lead then, Major."

"Understood."

Le Garre opens the door. I switch the comms bead in my ear to record mode, and I follow her in. The man at the table looks up and smiles. He's a well-built Caucasian, in his midthirties with dark hair and eyes. The only sign he's been shot is the slight bulge of a bandage on his shoulder, beneath his tight black shirt. He's strapped into a chair with restraints that are designed to hold him and protect him should we make any course changes.

"Captain Shann, I'm glad to see you survived. That'll make what comes next a little easier."

I don't reply; instead I settle myself into a chair. Le Garre is carrying a portable screen. She pulls up some information and gazes at our guest. "What's your name and rank, soldier?" she asks.

The man sighs. "Do we have to stick to formalities, Major?"

Le Garre scowls. "You know who we are; I'd like to talk on equal terms."

"I suppose that's fair," the man replies. "My name is Kieran Rocher. I was a special operations officer in the *Kommando Spezialkräfte*, but that isn't relevant to this conversation."

"You're an assassin," Le Garre says.

"I'm a messenger. Everything else is part of the way in which the message is delivered."

"Very well, what's the message?"

Rocher smiles again. "It's not for you." He points at me. "It's for her."

CHAPTER TWENTY-ONE

Shann

Le Garre laughs. "If you think you're going to get any alone time with my captain or anyone else on this ship, you're deluding yourself. Whatever you have to say, you can say to us both."

Rocher shrugs. "Very well. I'm here to persuade you to join us."

I stare at him. His smile hasn't disappeared, but there's a fierceness in his eyes, something that makes me believe he's serious. There's a game being played, but it's for stakes I don't entirely comprehend.

I need to see where this goes.

I hold up a hand. "You'll get your chance to make your case," I say. "We have questions; we'll start with those."

"I'm sure I have answers that will help you," Rocher says. "But you'll forgive me if I'm not entirely obliging."

I ignore the barb. "When did you board this ship?" I ask.

"While you were boarding the *Hercules*," Rocher replies.

"Were you alone?" Le Garre asks.

"Perhaps. Perhaps not."

Le Garre snorts. I hold up a hand. "Why did you really come here?" I ask.

"I have said, to deliver a message that will make you see we are on the same side."

I look at Le Garre and she looks at me. "You came from the *Gallowglass* then," I say.

Rocher shakes his head. "I stowed away aboard the *Hercules* when she stopped at Phobos. We survived in a pressurised cargo container for three days and then made our move on the crew. Unfortunately, some of them decided to resist."

"How many of you were on board?"

"With me? There were three of us, but I don't know if there were more."

"How does the *Gallowglass* fit into this?" Le Garre asks.

"They were to escort us to the rendezvous point."

"Which is where?"

"I was never told."

I nod instinctively, digesting the information. "Was it you with the portable transmitter?"

Rocher smiles. "An automated signal to indicate I had infiltrated your ship."

I sigh and wave a hand. "Okay, speak your piece."

"As I said, I'm here to invite you to join us." Rocher taps his hands on the table. "The circumstances in which we find ourselves meeting are not quite the ones I would have chosen, but they'll have to do. You're out here running out of options."

"And you're here to present a new alternative?"

"I am." Rocher gazes at Le Garre and then stares at me. "By now, you must have an idea of what you've gotten involved in. The *Hercules* was carrying supplies for a new colonial mission. Those supplies were being hidden and illegally transported under the authorised agreement between Earth's nations and the off-world settlements. We had every right to stop and seize that freighter."

"Fleet has authority to intercept supply missions," I say. "Last time I checked, the *Gallowglass* was not on the Fleet roster."

"Our mandate comes from a higher authority," Rocher says.

"Name them."

"You already understand," Rocher says. "If we had not stopped the *Hercules*, you know what would happen. This is the first step in a war between those who seek a united humanity and the fools who want to divide us. The people who I work for want to keep us together, moving forward for everyone's betterment. A secret colony, beyond the reach and authority of Earth, would change everything. It cannot be permitted."

"Your answer is to murder people in space."

"Far better than letting thousands die who have never left the ground. When you're up here, among the stars, it's easy to lose sight of the true objective."

"And what is that?"

"To improve the lot of all of us, every human being who is born, lives and dies. This cannot be a future for a privileged few."

"You're not an idealist," Le Garre scoffs. "You're a contract killer."

"We're all military people here, Major," Rocher replies. "We follow orders. I have mine. You, however, have two masters pulling you in different directions. You have a standing order to patrol and maintain the trade route between colonies, outposts and Earth. You have evidence that someone is breaking the international agreement to supply these colonies. You know this is systemic – it's not just one cargo shipment. This is just the first we have caught. You received a detailed manifest before you encountered the *Hercules*. That wasn't from me; that was from people in Fleet who know what's going on."

"You murdered the freighter crew," I say.

"They refused to surrender and to be placed under arrest."

I'm trying to process this. Rocher's position is implacable and it raises questions about ours. "What is the option you're giving us?" I ask.

"It's simple," Rocher says. "Decelerate and let me signal the *Gallowglass*. The two ships will rendezvous, and we can discuss what's happened. We'll then communicate with our contacts in Fleet and agree on an incident report. Your crew will be briefed on the real situation. After that, things will have to change out here. It'll be rough, but we'll make it through. In the meantime, no one else on the *Khidr* needs to die."

"If that was your message all along, why didn't you just tell us, rather than try and wreck our ship?" Le Garre asks.

Rocher laughs mirthlessly. "I'm not a fool, Major. You'll go away and discuss what I've said and probably reject the proposal; we'd anticipated that. Soldiers often respond best when they are given the least-worst option. My orders were to ruin your ship and give you no choice but to surrender. Right now, you still think you've got a reason and rationale for what you've chosen to do. You think you're right, morally, and you still have hope – you think you can beat us. The deaths of your people and the freighter crew are clouding your judgement. That was always going to be the case. Sabotage offered a better percentage."

I've heard enough. I move toward the door. "Le Garre?"

She's glaring at Rocher, but he doesn't flinch or turn away. She backs up, opens the door, and we both leave.

"I want you, Travers, Duggins and Keiyho on the gravity deck, now," I say when we're clear.

"Understood, Captain," Le Garre replies.

*　　*　　*

Silence in the strategy room.

I'm looking at my senior officers. No one meets my eye. The expressions around me are variations of shock and horror. They echo my own feelings. It's one thing being alone in space, knowing you're thousands or millions of kilometres from society and civilisation; it's quite another to find the vocation that brought you here questioned and undermined.

On the table between us is my communications bead. It has just finished replaying our interrogation of Kieran Rocher.

"Given what we know now, I'll understand if any of you think I've made a wrong decision in the last few hours," I say.

Keiyho looks at me. "Captain, you must be careful not to take this man at his word," he cautions, his soft voice instantly soothing my soul. "He has much to gain by you accepting everything he has said exactly as he has said it."

"We can't dismiss it, though," Duggins counters.

"No indeed," Keiyho says. He holds up a finger. "Our intruder has knowledge of us. He has obtained this from Fleet records. That means he is Fleet, or has been briefed by someone who works for Fleet." Keiyho extends a second finger. "Our intruder is aware we received a classified data dossier about the *Hercules*. He knows we have accessed it and that the dossier confirms the freighter was carrying materials and resources to set up a secret colony."

"We didn't mention any prior incidents of sabotage or what happened to Drake," Le Garre adds. "There was nothing in Rocher's responses to suggest he knew anything about that."

Keiyho nods at Le Garre and extends a third finger. Then a fourth. "Our intruder claims to have boarded our ship while we were boarding the *Hercules*. We must find out how and where this was done."

"Without cutting into the hull, which we'd have been alerted to, I'd say the airlock or the drone garage," Duggins says. "The rocket pods are also possible, but again, cutting into the ship from there would have triggered a depressurisation alarm." He accesses a tactical map of the ship. "I can get someone to check the garage, but it'll be hard to distinguish between Rocher's work and the pounding we took from the *Gallowglass*."

Keiyho nods to him and extends his thumb. "Our intruder claims the authority of Fleet and that we must trust him over our standing orders. We must verify this, as soon as possible."

"The EVA then?" I say.

"Yes, the EVA."

"We're missing something," Le Garre says. "Rocher knew where to find the replacement comms rig. We only caught him because Captain Shann happened to pass by and disturb him. Someone must have told him where the equipment was being stored."

"That means our traitor might still be on the loose," Travers says.

"And that Arkov is innocent," Duggins adds.

I sigh and run a hand through my hair. "Or, that we have more than one person trying to destroy this ship from the inside." I gaze at my senior team again. "Before all this started, had any of you heard rumours about an independence movement, some sort of secret colony or covert war?"

"We've all seen news reports where people are complaining about public money being put into space programmes," Travers says. "Given what information we have, it's not surprising people out here want to preserve and protect what they have."

Le Garre rounds on him. "You agree with this?" She gestures at the hydroponics compartment, greyed out on our ship's schematic. "This is the result of division, of partisan politicking with people's lives."

"And you're defending the armed and murderous response then?" Travers says. "Takes two sides to make a war."

"And we're in the middle," I say, glaring at them both. "All of us, together, no matter what we decide."

"Apart from those who've already tried to sabotage our ship," Duggins mutters.

"And because of that, we need to be able to talk this out," I say. "The five of us are all that's holding this crew together."

Keiyho taps a finger on the table, drawing my attention. "You have all met here before, without me, when this started," he says. "I am interested to know why I was excluded."

"We were going to include you, but then someone interfered with my computer," I explain. "You were on the bridge at the time."

"You thought it was me?"

"I had no way of knowing," I reply.

Keiyho smiles. "Your doubts were reasonable. And now we find ourselves swirling amid doubts." He looks at Travers. "We four were on the bridge with Jacobson when Drake died. You were not."

"Are you accusing me of—"

Keiyho holds up his hand. "No, please, I am making a point about suspicion." He turns to me. "You and I were together on the *Hercules* when the hydroponics compartment was blown up. Duggins was only a few metres away."

"Both Travers and Le Garre were on bridge comms," I add. "In sight of each other."

"Indeed," Keiyho says. "But it is easy to lose track. A reminder that we all have good reasons to trust one another is important."

"I see where you're going," Travers grunts. He looks more relaxed; they all do. "What about the time just before we caught Rocher?"

"Duggins was on the bridge with me," I say. "I spoke to Le Garre on comms, and Keiyho arrived to capture our guest."

"Where were you?" Keiyho asks Travers.

"Asleep until I heard the alert," he replies.

Keiyho nods. "I, too, cannot provide a definitive answer for my actions at the time the captain's screen was tampered with. However, my actions during this situation are cumulative, as are yours. I am not a traitor to this crew."

"Neither am I," Travers says.

Keiyho smiles. "None of us are traitors," he says. "That is the basis on which we must proceed. If any of us were, we could have already destroyed the ship."

"It's also important we consider the information bubble we're in," I add. "We've had a limited digest of news from Earth and the colonies. It'd be pretty easy for someone with an agenda to play on our hopes and fears."

There are murmurs of agreement around the table, and I'm feeling relieved. We're all exhausted, but at least our suspicions of one aother are alleviated.

For now.

"Rocher was right about one thing," Le Garre says. "We do have to make a choice."

I shake my head. "The minute you start considering things that way, he's won. We have our orders; we fulfil them."

Duggins nods. "If Fleet wanted us not to intercept the *Hercules*, or to back away from a confrontation with the *Gallowglass*, they had ample time to send orders. Yes, the situation is complicated, but our role in it is clear."

Le Garre shrugs. "We all know being an officer in battle means being prepared to make the wrong decision and lives to be lost because of it. Captain Shann will have to answer for whatever we decide."

Travers grunts. "If we survive."

"We must survive." I glare at him. "What happened here must be reported. Only then can the right decisions be made on the matters we've uncovered."

Le Garre leans over the table and brings up a crew roster alongside the ship schematic. "If we discount all of us and those who we've lost, we're down to the rest of the crew."

"What about Technician Shah?"

"I've checked the crew manifest," Le Garre says. "I've also interviewed him. I think he's legitimate."

"He wasn't here for both of the main incidents," Travers adds.

"I was on my way to review the data dump Duggins gave me of the last two hours aboard the *Hercules* to check his story," I say. "I'll go through that when I leave here. I think we can consider him loyal, for now."

"What about Arkov?" Duggins asks.

"That's a more difficult decision," Le Garre says. "His story about leaving his post matches the information I got from Chase."

"So, it's either the truth or a very plausible lie?" I ask.

"Yes."

"If you're in agreement, I'd like to release him," I say to Le Garre. "We place him on supervised duty for now and keep him away from Rocher."

She gazes at me for a moment, but then nods. "Yes, let's do that."

"Good."

"I'd say we try to ensure everyone is supervised," Travers says. "All crew stay in twos at least, whenever possible. That may give us a chance of finding our traitor."

"Most of our people are exhausted," Duggins says. "Mistakes will be made."

"I'll speak to the doctor and authorise the use of stimulants," I say. "We're going to need to work all the hours we can to prepare for the next round." I lean over the table and cancel the ship schematic and roster, replacing them both with a trajectory map. "This is what we should concern ourselves with at the moment. The *Gallowglass* is still accelerating. She'll catch us before we reach Phobos orbit. She'll have to decelerate to engage, but she can still pass us at speed, launching guided missiles."

"I think we can assume she won't look to repeat what happened before," Keiyho says. "Their speed is dangerous to us, but also an advantage. They will have less time to make course corrections. The advantage range they had is also nullified, to a point."

"To a point?"

"They can still launch their guided missiles at us when they get in range," Keiyho explains. "However, those missiles will be travelling at a higher velocity, which means course corrections may be more difficult for them. Our rocket mines will be slowing down, not speeding up, and they don't have the same kind of guidance systems. We're relying on the fact that the *Gallowglass* can't change course because they'll lose us."

"We need other plans and scenarios," I say. "They must be considering their options."

Keiyho and Duggins exchange looks. "We'll see what we can come up with," Duggins says.

"Talk to Johansson," I tell them. "She seems to be having a lot of good ideas."

"I will," Duggins promises.

*　　*　　*

An hour later, I'm back in my room, eating and drinking through a tube and looking at the data dump from the *Hercules* that Duggins sent me.

Much of the information is continual maintenance content that won't help us. I scan through, looking for security camera footage. There are hundreds of files. Sorting them by date narrows the selection, but there's still a long list categorised by camera code number.

I stifle a yawn. The pain medication and everything that's happened has taken its toll. I'll sleep soon, while I can.

I open video file after video file, checking the time stamps and speeding through the footage. I pause one when I recognise the crumpled corridor from my EVA visit to the ship. There are three people manoeuvering containers into the passage.

Wait a minute. Three people? Shah only mentioned two…

Suddenly I'm awake. I watch carefully, spooling backward and forward through the clip. Another three have the same time stamp and I open those as well. In one, several shadowy figures move toward the camera. A face appears, inches from the camera, and the footage ends. I wind back and pause the feed on the frame before.

It's Technician Shah. He's taken out the camera.

Why?

CHAPTER TWENTY-TWO

Sellis

Well, *fuck*.

I'm staring at the blackened interior of the communications housing. The whole system is ruined. There's no way I can fix this.

Duggins's damage assessment of the *Khidr*'s broadcast antenna on the outside of the ship is that it's ruined. We'll need to construct a new one, go outside and attach it to the ship to replace the old one. The problem is that there's nothing to connect it to.

Without an antenna and relay, we can't contact anyone. We're out here on our own.

Black flakes float out of the open electronics housing, and I can smell the charred particulates in the air. The whole ship stinks of burned cables and circuit boards and will for a while as the atmosphere recyclers ingest and redistribute gases into every compartment. I know the scrubbers will filter out the fragments, and really, I'm probably not breathing as much of this scorched-up plastic as I might think, but that cold rational voice doesn't make a lot of difference, right now.

I reach out and scrape the back of the housing with my nail. More black dust comes away to float in the air around me. There's not much between this and the outside of the ship.

"Sellis to Duggins?"

"Go ahead."

"The communications processor is a bust, completely destroyed. We're not going to be able to repair this. We'll need to seal up the box too. It could give way at any moment."

"I'm seeing your feed," Duggins says. That means he's looking at the same thing as me through the camera strapped to my forehead. "You're authorised to make the repair. Nothing we can do with this."

"Sorry, chief."

"Yeah, me too."

I pull out the foam gun and activate it, filling the housing with grey paste. Within twenty minutes, it'll set and harden, turning the old box into a reinforced slab, which will strengthen the wall against any residual damage. The only problem is, if we have to get to any of the cabling behind it, we'll have to smash our way through. The foam has some flexibility to it, but it's a temporary solution.

I'll need to open up everything else, but that's not an urgent priority. The atmospheric sensors are broken, but the portable kit tells me we're not losing air in here. There are repair crews all over the ship, trying to repressurise essential areas. Duggins is leading the effort to rebuild the airlock personally. I really don't want to end up working on all that.

The last briefing organised the majority of the crew into three different repair details. Thankfully, one or two of us are needed to sort some specific small jobs. I volunteered for those because I suck at telling anyone else what to do.

My own space. I've always liked to be on my own, working alone, my way, talking to the broken machines, bringing them back to life. Other people get in the way.

Being here, with no one around, gives me time to think.

There are a few people exempt from repair duty. A rotation of the bridge staff are needed to keep us operational and on course. I can contact them if I need a system checked or tested. Doctor Bogdanovic and the security team are exempt from shifts too. They have to be now we've caught the intruder.

I shudder just thinking about him. What was his name? *Rocher*, that's what they said. Le Garre has him locked up for questioning. I think about the message I got on my screen. Could that have been him? When I turned off the security cameras, was I helping him? I have to believe I was. If I was and he mentions my name, they'll lock me up too.

Should I confess? March up to the captain and tell her all about the computer messages and everything? If they find out some other way, I'll be in the shit. Fleet laws are severe, particularly in deep space. There's even a regulation that allows the ranking officer on a ship to execute someone as a 'waste of oxygen'. Looking around at the state of the *Khidr*, that might be a factor.

They'll probably keep the intruder alive. He's probably more valuable as a source of information. I don't know anything other than that I'm being played. I'm useful to whoever sent that message so long as I don't start squealing and no one else squeals either.

If that guy Rocher gives me up, I'll be arrested, but as long as no one's come for me, he hasn't given me up. This is a gamble, something I'm familiar with. My life's on the line, but then it was every time I owed money to bad people and when I stole from army stores. This is nothing new.

Shit. Why is it things always get complicated when I'm not on my own, repairing machines?

I key up my comms. "Sellis to Duggins?"

"Go ahead."

"I'm done here for now. Moving on to hydroponics."

"Affirmative."

I drift out of the chamber, toolkit and emergency metres dragging behind me on tethers. It's not far to the garden chambers, but I know what's waiting for me won't be a pretty sight.

I reach the sealed hatch at the end of corridor seven and look through into a ruin.

The hydroponics compartment was where the bomb was. The *Khidr*'s systems reacted immediately to the explosion, sealing off a large section of the ship. In the aftermath, we left things as they were. The portion of the ship I'm in now has no essential combat facilities, so there was no need to assess what we have left.

Now though, with the amount of structural damage we have from taking on the *Gallowglass*, it all needs checking out. It'll be a lonely task and it'll take a long time.

Just the kind of job I like.

The walls, ceiling and floor are blackened and marked. There are tears in the inner metal membrane; I've no doubt there are tears in the outside layers too. Both ships were equipped and firing automatic weapons at each other. Bullets can act like pins in a balloon when they pierce a pressurised section of a spaceship. Thankfully, modern hulls are designed with multiple layers that can flex and react to damage. There's a process a bit like blood clotting, where some of the fabrics in the middle of the ship's skin will turn sticky and gum up an abrasion or tear to prevent it spreading.

Of course, none of that works when you're dealing with a laser, designed to cut straight through everything.

My atmospheric pressure detector starts to go off. There's a leak in here and I'll need to find it quickly; otherwise we'll lose our oxygen reserve and suffocate. According to the repair diagnostic, there are at least six leaks the computer has detected all across the ship that we've yet to fix.

I turn around and seal the hatch, containing the compartment. Then I reach for the emergency 'ox' mask in the corner of the room and turn off the pressure regulator, which has been maintaining the room's atmospheric balance. The pressure loss rate has been analysed by my portable metre. It's pretty small, so I should be safe enough to work in here for a bit, and the gradual reduction will help me find the leak.

I grab the metre and switch programmes, activating the air disturbance pictograph. The device runs, and a scan and three-dimensional representation of the room appears. There's a coloured swirl around me and the door, showing where I've come from. That'll settle down and fade away. What I need to find are other areas of moving air, which might indicate where the atmosphere is escaping from the room...

There it is! Right in the corner, at the back of a storage unit. I open the panel, empty out the contents, bring up my foam gun and fill the space. Once I'm done, I shut the container and wait. After a few minutes, the pressure metre beeps. The leak is sealed.

Damn, I wish they were all this easy.

I reactivate the pressure regulator and replace the 'ox' mask in the safety box. I take a drink from the water feed attached to my work suit. Corridor seven is as far as we can go. Beyond it, all that remains is jagged debris. The whole biological facility that contributed to the *Khidr*'s recycling and reclamation system is gone. In terms of food and water, we're running on whatever stores we've got, unless Duggins can work out another way to wash piss and process shit as fertiliser, but that's a way down the priority list right now.

I look out through the hatch's DuraGlas screen again, out into the remains of the other compartments. If I wanted to destroy the ship, I'd have put explosives in the oxygen feed. Every section of the *Khidr* is connected by the atmospheric piping. Pure oxygen is highly flammable and has to be constantly mixed with other gases to compensate for our respiration. There would be no coming back from that. Whoever blew up the laboratory knew exactly what they were doing to damage the ship, but not blow it to pieces.

I'm thinking about the intruder again. Was he on board when this happened? Had he stowed away when we were last in dock on Phobos? If that was the case, even if he could have avoided being picked up on the cameras, eventually the computer would have picked up his presence and registered a change in atmosphere comparable to an extra passenger. No, he had to have come over here recently. Maybe got on board while we were tethered to the freighter.

That means he can't have killed Drake. Was that an accident? If it wasn't, we've got two traitors on board.

Fuck.

CHAPTER TWENTY-THREE

Shann

I wake up some time later, still partially sitting in the chair. My alarm is going off. That means I'm due on shift in thirty minutes. I feel awful. Doctor Bogdanovic said I might. The amount of different drugs I've had in my system has thrown my body out of whack.

The screen in front of me brightens as I move. The last thing I was looking at appears. It's Technician Shah's personnel file, listing all his qualifications and experience. Everything looks fine and checks out.

Why didn't he tell me about the third person and the camera?

I'm nauseated and hungry at the same time. I need to eat; I know that. There are vacuum-packed plastic meals in a compartment across the room. I pull out two and open the nozzles. I make time to consume all of it.

I'm chewing through the last of my meal when the screen flashes up a comms request. It's Le Garre. I open it. "Yes, Major?"

"Captain, can you stop by? I may have something to share."

"That makes two of us. Are you in your room?"

"Yes, and there's coffee."

"Great, I'm on my way."

I extricate myself from the chair and make my way out. The trip to Le Garre's quarters is without incident. She opens the door, greeting me with a tense smile.

"Come in."

"Thanks."

Le Garre hands me a portable screen and one of the zero gravity cups. The coffee is warm through the membrane. I sip it carefully while looking at the screen. There's a diagram with crew names dotted across it. They're connected with lines and notations. "Keiyho's little speech last night let me know he was thinking along the same lines as me.

I've been correlating people's locations and alibis for each incident. The conclusion is interesting."

I frown at the screen, trying to make sense of it. "Who's your chief suspect?" I ask.

"No one," Le Garre replies.

"What?"

"No one," Le Garre repeats. "Every surviving member of the crew has verified evidence of being somewhere for one or another of the incidents through camera footage or unprompted witness testimony from someone else."

"Where does that leave us?" I ask.

"Facing the prospect that we're not dealing with an individual. We're dealing with a mutiny."

The word makes me shiver. No captain ever wants to hear it. Out here, in the cold void, we're far from any institutions or support at the best of times, and these aren't the best of times.

"I found something too," I say. I switch the screen to display the security camera feed and pause the footage on the last frame. "That's Shah," I say. "Did he mention disabling the security cameras to you?"

"No, he did not," Le Garre says. She's staring intently at the image. "Why would he want to conceal this?"

"We'll need to ask him," I say. "Otherwise, do we need to be watching our backs?"

"I think so," Le Garre says. "Now we're sure of Keiyho, I'd recommend we revisit the deployment of firearms to the senior officers. Particularly in light of what happened to you."

"Makes sense," I agree. "Can you handle that while I speak to Shah?"

"Yes," Le Garre says. "I'll be discreet. We'll also need a contingency plan. I'll run some ideas past him and Duggins."

"Good." I hand the empty coffee cup back to Le Garre.

★   ★   ★

Technician Shah has been given Tomlins's compartment. Shah's off shift, so he should be in. I press the door buzzer and hear a muffled grunt.

"Shah, its Captain Shann, can we talk?"

There are sounds of movement from inside. I'm worried for a

moment; I've been attacked, and Le Garre is talking about us needing personal weapons. Now here I am waiting to question a complete stranger about why he's lied to me.

I touch my comms bead, switching it to record mode. The door opens, and I swallow my concerns. "Can I come in?" I ask.

Shah smiles. "Of course, Captain," he says.

I enter and wait until the door is closed and Shah is back in the middle of the small room. "How can I help?" he asks.

"I need to clear something up." I pull out Le Garre's portable screen with the frozen image of him. "What can you tell me about what's happening here?" I ask.

Shah's face crumples into a beaten expression. He sighs. "That was a shameful moment," he says. He looks at me. "Please, Captain, I would rather not talk about what happened."

"I understand you've had a traumatic experience," I say. "But if we're to trust one another, I need the truth."

Shah nods; his head drops. "I thought I'd been careful," he says. His hand goes to a chest pocket on his work suit. "You'll want to view this as well." He holds out a data chip.

I take it and plug it into the screen. There's one more video file, a better angle on the three figures moving the crates. I watch as the scene dissolves into a struggle. One man pins another to the floor. The third goes to the wall and disables a camera. "That was me," Shah says. "I'm not proud of that, or what comes next."

I watch as Shah in the video moves back to the other two. Light gleams off a knife. A hand raises and falls, raises and falls, again and again. The man on the floor writhes as he is stabbed multiple times.

"That was you," I say.

"Yes," Shah admits softly. "I did that, but I had a reason."

"Explain."

"I told you, they were already on board our ship," Shah says. "Specialist Hutton was their inside man. He opened their container and tried to lock the rest of us out of the computer system. I... I had to do something."

"You killed him."

"Yes. Peters and I went with him to the airlock, and then we did what the captain asked us to do. I didn't mention it because...I didn't want anything to sully their names. Hutton deserves… He deserves to be forgotten."

"You've taken a life," I say. "That's a hard thing to deal with."

"I'll cope," Shah says. He smiles at me sadly. "This should be the least of your problems. I want to help."

I nod. "Technician, you know the situation we're in. I need to be able to trust you. Is there anything else you haven't told me or Major Le Garre?"

Shah shakes his head. "I can't think of anything, but if something becomes important, I'll tell you straightaway; you have my word, Captain."

"Okay," I say. "Let's hope it doesn't come to that." I pull the data chip from the portable screen and hand it back to him. "I've taken a copy. I can't promise we'll cover up all the stuff about Hutton, but I'll only use it if I have to."

"I appreciate that, Captain, thank you."

"Of course."

A moment later I'm outside and deactivating the recording from my comms bead. I make my way to the bridge. Jacobson is there with Travers and Chiu. Travers nods to me as I enter and unstraps himself from the command chair. "Update is the airlock has been repaired and we're about ready to attempt the EVA for communication repair, Captain," he says.

"Thank you, Lieutenant," I reply. "Who are our volunteers?"

"Johansson and Chase are in suits and ready to go. Technician Arkov is at his station to assist."

The mention of Arkov's name makes me tense. I think back over our conversation. I believe what he said to me, but did he tell me the whole truth? Le Garre was right; no incidents occurred while he was confined, until the situation with Rocher, but she's also right to point out everyone has alibis. I want to trust Arkov.

I'm strapping myself into my seat and logging in to the system. I glance at Ensign Chiu. "Anything else I need to be aware of?" I ask.

"Not from me, Captain," she says.

"*Gallowglass* has increased speed," Jacobson says. "She'll be on us in one hundred and eight hours, Captain."

"Okay, bring up communications with the EVA team," I order.

"Open a channel between them and us. Also, activate working external cameras."

"Aye, aye," Jacobson says. A collection of options appear on my screen as he initialises all the feeds. I select the ones I want, prioritising external views of the new transmitter site and the mission briefing Duggins has prepared. He's picked a fresh position, abandoning any attempt to repair the old system. As I read through his instructions, this makes sense. The *Khidr* is a huge electronic network, beneath the outer hull. The new position is a redundant access point to that network, requiring minimal cutting to connect up to. It's also sheltered by the torus section. Once the exterior equipment is planted and patched through, Duggins and his people can do all the wire fixing inside the ship. They can test as they go, which should eliminate any need for further EVAs to check faults.

At least, that's the theory.

"Bridge to EVA, all set?"

"Receiving, bridge, this is Chase. We're ready."

"Proceed."

"Thank you."

Ensign Johansson is the best person for this job. Her expertise with our communication system is past proven to me. She has a rare talent. I worked a similar post to hers when I was on Earth Five, so I can appreciate and admire her gift and dedication, but she's not experienced in EVA repair. Duggins or Keiyho would have chosen to send Sam with her. I trust him implicitly. I wonder how things were between him and Arkov before he went out. I'm sure Sam would have settled it up front, like he does with most things.

"We're outside," Sam says over comms. "Moving toward the site."

"Copy, we have you on feed," Jacobson replies.

For the most part, a space walk is the same whether the object you're walking on is travelling at speed or not. I've always found that difficult to get my head around. When it's you outside, you don't have any sense of movement; there's no frame of reference. The sensations you might get on a skydive, of the air rushing past or the ground coming to meet you, don't exist in space because there is no air or ground. Or, you think about driving a car, on a road – there's no visual frame guide. You can't look out the window and see things moving in relation to your position. Yes, there are things in space, but most are so far away all the time the small change in where we are isn't something our eyes and brains can usually detect.

Velocities are relative, so you're travelling with your ship. Pushing off and floating forward is you travelling a bit faster, and so on.

The whole concept goes against your instincts. A space walk on a moving ship sounds like it's more dangerous and there are greater risks if someone falls or slips, but actually the risk is almost the same as when the ship's stationary.

"They've reached the new plant site, Captain," Chiu says.

"Okay, proceed as ordered," I reply. In this case, there's a whole set of extra reasons we don't want too many EVAs. Our airlock is patched together with a temporary foam sealant designed to seal pressure leaks, but an airlock is different. It's subjected to changes in pressure during each time of use. One trip is a risk; two is worse.

Something else is on my mind. I shift the monitoring cameras to the left of my screen and bring up the other working exterior feeds. There are twenty working units out there. I'm sure Duggins has scrolled through them all, assessing the damage to the ship. I can see dark scars and ruptures where laser fire from the *Gallowglass* cut through our hull and twisted metal where her missiles caught us. The smooth manufactured surfaces I once glimpsed are a thing of the past. This is an unfamiliar landscape, one of injury and endurance. The *Khidr* is the most important member of our crew, and here I see just how much she is suffering for us as she grits her teeth and powers on.

I'm thinking about Rocher and our speculation of how he got aboard the ship. I access the exterior camera to the drone garage. The compartment is wrecked, but the monitoring camera is operational. I issue commands to it, getting a three-sixty pan across the section. There's a cable trailing out of the entrance. Evidence to back up our suspicions.

"EVA team to *Khidr*, we're almost done out here," Sam says.

"Copy that, EVA," I say in response. "How's your oxygen level?"

"Got about an hour left each, Captain."

"Good. I wondered if you could check something else for me."

"I guess so." Sam sounds hesitant but willing. "Makes sense to do it while we're out here."

"Can you take a walk over to section thirty-three? The drone garage exterior launch."

"Sure, we'll finish up and do that."

"Thank you."

I switch windows to Johansson's head camera. She's threading connections through freshly drilled holes in the hull plate. Sam's hands appear. He's got the seal dispenser. When she's done, he draws a line of paste around each cable, sealing the new breaches.

"EVA to Duggins?" Sam calls. "Ready to test."

"Testing now," says Duggins over the comms. He must be in his room or somewhere else accessing a console. A moment later he confirms. "We have a working connection."

"That's excellent news," I say. "Great job, everybody!"

"Thank you," Duggins answers. "It'll take some time to configure the system, but we have confirmed power to the new antenna."

"We're moving over to section thirty-three, bridge," Sam says.

"Copy that," Chiu replies.

I'm viewing both head cameras and the monitoring feed from the external device. Sam and Ensign Johansson come into view. He is leading and kneels down in front of the broken access hatch. "There's a snapped cable here, not one of ours," he says. "It's secured inside. I'll see if I can find where."

"Be careful," Johansson warns. She pulls out another tether and anchors them both to a clip on the hull.

"Will do," Sam says. He's looking into the torn remains of the launch bay. The entrance doors are twisted. His hands reach out and grab at one, levering it away. He moves forward, into the space. His helmet torch illuminates the darkened recess. "What am I looking for?" he asks.

"I think our guest Rocher entered the ship through there, before it was wrecked in the fighting," I explain.

"I'd say you're right," Sam replies. "I've found something that shouldn't be here." His torch focuses on a small box secured to the wall. There's a data screen in the middle. I can't read any of the writing on it, but it shouldn't be there. Sam's hands reach out—

"Don't touch it!" Duggins warns over the comms. "I know what that is! It's identical to the device I found in the storage compartment."

"It's a bomb then?" I ask.

"Yes," Duggins says. "It's a bomb."

CHAPTER TWENTY-FOUR

Shann

I'm back in the room with Rocher. "Tell me how to defuse and remove the device!" I demand.

Rocher smiles. He's barely moved since I last saw him. "Ah, you found something that you believe belongs to me?"

"Cut the crap," I say. "If that thing goes up, you die with all of us!"

"As Major Le Garre pointed out, I am not an idealist; I am a contractor."

"Then you'll never get to spend any of the money you're being paid."

"Your interpretation of my profession is interestingly narrow." Rocher raises his hands. "I told you my objective before. I need you to realise that you have no alternative to surrender. Your crew, your ship, you and I are a small calculation in a much larger context. If you return to Phobos with a story of piracy, destruction, secret colonies and the rest, you'll bring much of what's going on out into the open. Perhaps that would be a good thing, but my employers calculate that we aren't ready for such exposure. You and the drifting *Hercules* with all her cargo are assets with assessed value. If you threaten another asset, such as the existence of a covert military ship, we'll have to dispose of you."

I stare at Rocher. What can I offer? What will work to change the situation? I should have known he would have a contingency. Where is the compromise? "What will it take to get you to disarm your explosives?" I ask.

Rocher shrugs. "You know the answer. You have a working transmitter now, right? Signal the *Gallowglass*, reduce speed and surrender to them at a location of their choosing."

I don't reply to that. There's nothing to be gained from this conversation. I exit the room. Keiyho is waiting for me outside.

"Chase and Johansson have about forty minutes of air left," he says. "That includes their emergency tanks. What do you want them to do?"

"What do we know about the other device Duggins found?" I ask.

"Only that it wasn't primed," Keiyho says. "We didn't do much work on it, as we've had other priorities."

"Where is it?"

"In storage."

"We need a clear space to work. Get it and meet me in the strategy room. I'll ask Duggins and Chiu to join us."

Keiyho nods and disappears. I send an urgent comms requests to Chiu. She'll have to leave the bridge. I guess Duggins is still in his quarters. Two minutes later, I'm outside and he's opening the door.

"Come with me now and bring your toolbox."

"Where are we going?"

"To diffuse a bomb."

I'm moving quickly through the corridors and hatches to the torus. I'm into the elevator and out through the hatch into the shaft, then up and through the gym into our meeting space. I activate the screen on the table and pull up every camera feed I can find, along with an open communications microphone.

"Chase, Johansson, this is Captain Shann."

"Receiving," Sam answers. "What's the plan?"

"We're bringing up the device we found in storage. Hopefully we can use it to talk you through disarming the one in front of you."

"Okay, wouldn't someone better qualified be—"

"You two are what we have," I say. "Can you make the space big enough so you can both work in there?"

"Yes, Captain, I think so."

"Good."

"If this is going to require fine motor skills, I'm not rating our chances, Captain," Johansson says. "To get any kind of grip on components, we'll need to get our gloves off."

I glance at Duggins, who nods. I agree with them. Our EVA suits have inner gloves that are similar to those used by scientists examining specimens in sealed boxes. There's no explicit danger in removing the outer glove, provided the astronaut is in a controlled environment.

The ruin of the drone launch bay is not exactly that, but it is better than being on the side of the hull. "Okay, do that," I say, "but be careful."

"Aye, aye."

Keiyho enters, clutching the deactivated explosive device. Chiu is right behind him. I beckon her over. "I need you and Duggins to take this thing apart and explain to Johansson how to do the same to the armed device that's attached to our ship," I say. "You have about thirty-five minutes to sort this."

"Chase to Captain Shann?"

"Go ahead."

"If we need more time, we can re-tank?"

I mute the channel and look at Duggins. He guesses my question. "Another airlock operation would be risky. Our EVA suits run live estimates on how much air remains in the primary and emergency tanks. The estimate recalibrates based on a continual measure of the astronaut's breathing rate. We can't be absolutely precise about how much time people have. We calculated the mission at four hours and provided oxygen supplies accordingly. There is also a spare tank in the airlock that they can access and share if they need it. Metabolism, stress and exertion can be contributing factors. They can both stretch a bit if they stay calm."

"Okay," I say. I unmute the channel. "Sam, proceed as instructed for now. Your job is to be Johansson's extra hands."

"Got it."

"Good."

Duggins is unscrewing the cover of the half-prepared explosive. "Looks like a custom-made shield," he says. "Modular internal design, which makes decommissioning it a little easier for us. They didn't plan for these to be tampered with."

Chiu leans over the open case and points at a box in the top left corner. "That's the detonator." She traces the wires to a second section below it. "Control unit and power is here."

Duggins nods. "The issue will be whether there's some kind of dead man's switch that triggers an explosion anyway." He leans toward the mic on the table. "Johansson? Best to start by examining the box lid catches and how the unit's secured to the wall."

"Aye, aye," Johansson replies. In the head camera screen, her plastic gloved fingers reach toward the box. She's holding a small metallic object. It looks like a mirror. Torchlight from her helmet reflects back at us, whiting out the screen for a moment. "Two catches at the bottom," she says. "Looks like some sort of chemical reactive resin on the wall."

"That's useful," Duggins says. He flips over the box on the table. There are no holes on the back. He places it right side up again. "I think there's no anchor trap. That'll mean we should be able to cut it away from the ship."

"Should?" Johansson asks.

"I don't know yet if there's a tremble sensor," Duggins admits. "The vibration from us removing the resin could set the bomb off."

Chiu has taken a powered driver to the side of the detonator casing. She's looking for screws. None are obvious. I pick up a mini-torch from Duggins's toolbox and hold it over the table. "Thanks, Captain," Chiu mutters, but the light doesn't reveal anything that I can see. "The cabinet is molded and sealed. We'll need to drill in." She picks up a metre. "There's polarity in here. That means there's a charge."

"Which means it's live," Duggins says. "Damn. We can't cut into that."

"If there was a motion sensor, it would be affected by the ship," Keiyho reasons.

"Risky to assume anything," Duggins warns. "That said, I'd think you're right. It's a shell defence to prevent us cutting into the unit."

"Then we don't cut into it," I say. "Sam, can you hear me?"

"Aye, Captain."

"Cut away the wall plate. Make the section as large as you can manage to feed out of the launch bay," I order.

"Are you sure, Captain?" Sam asks. I glance at Duggins and Chiu. Duggins shrugs, but Chiu refuses to commit herself.

"Yes, do it," I say.

Sam moves away from the box. I see him produce a handheld cutter. "I've got thirty-five per cent charge left. Might not be enough."

"Do your best."

"Aye, aye."

Sam applies the cutter to the wall. I see the metal plates part as the invisible laser burns through them. They curl away from each other, leaving a ragged gap. Lasers are always strange to watch as there appears to be no cause for the damage. But this is inch-thick steel. Sam is working methodically, drawing a line of torn metal around the black plastic shape.

"Halfway," Sam says.

At three-quarters, the work gets harder. Sam has to retrace his marks several times. "We're pretty much out of juice," he says. "We've fifteen minutes of air left."

"If you use the drill and make consecutive holes along the final section, it might be enough," Keiyho suggests.

Duggins shakes his head. "It'll take too long. Better to stick with what we have. Johansson, can you run a cable to the new antenna? We can power the cutter from there."

"Yes, I think we brought enough."

"You'll need to do it quickly," Chiu says.

"Okay."

There's movement and Johansson is back outside, flying across the hull. She's moving hand over hand – risky, but needs must. She reaches the antenna quickly, grabbing the safety rail to lose her momentum, and opens the power unit they've just wired up, ripping out the cables. She attaches a new lead from a long drum and makes her way back to the drone garage.

"Chase, here!"

Johansson is outside the drone garage, reaching in with the end of the cable. The wire is passed between the two astronauts. It's strange to watch it happen on two head cams and an external view. Sam plugs the cutter in and repositions himself.

"Okay, let's finish this."

He begins working. I glance at the time counter. "You've eight minutes," I warn.

"Almost there," Sam replies.

I watch the numbers recede. There's a brief moment of achievement when the wall section comes away. Johansson manages to grab hold of one end. She's replaced her gloves. Together, she and Sam begin manoeuvering the jagged sheet of metal out of the launch bay.

"Slowly and gently," Duggins warns.

My hands are gripping the table as I stare at three different windows. I'm viewing the external camera feed and both head cams. The astronauts are at either end of the cut plate. I can see strain and exhaustion on their faces. We've all been pushed beyond the point of reason. If our lives weren't at stake, we'd be ordered to rest.

"Three minutes," Chiu says softly, almost in reverence.

Slowly, the plate inches out of the ship. Both Johansson and Sam appear on the outside camera feed. I sigh with relief. The dangerous bit is done and there's been no explosion.

"You'll need to give it a push," Duggins says. "We can't just let it go; otherwise it'll float alongside the ship."

"Aye, aye," Johansson replies.

"Then make your way back to the airlock quickly. You've got about ninety seconds of air left," Chiu says.

Four hands let go of the metal simultaneously. The black box drifts away, serenely, a process that belies its purpose. "Well done. Get yourselves back indoors," I order.

"On our way," says Sam.

"Wait!" Johansson says. "We need to re-plug the antenna!"

"We don't have air, Ensign, wait—"

Too late. Johansson is already moving, propelling herself across the hull at speed. I'm gripping the desk, wanting to order her back, but she knows the risk. Women tend to use less air than men. There's a chance she has a bit more left in her suit tank. That might give her enough time.

I see her return to the transmitter site, yank out the trailing cable and fumble with the comms power plug. I can hear the emergency oxygen level alert going off in her helmet. She restores the connections and heads for the airlock.

She's at minus forty-five seconds of capacity.

It'll take another three or four minutes for her to get back to the airlock. I activate another communications channel. I pray she's got enough left in the tank. "Arkov, have you been monitoring?" I ask.

"Yes, Captain."

"Make sure Bogdanovic is notified. They'll both need a check over."

"Will do."

The four of us are left in the strategy room, staring at the camera feeds and the bomb components on the table. Success is somehow an anticlimax; Johansson is still out there. There's no sense of achievement in finding a way to live for a while, until the next crisis.

"Well done, everyone," I say, but the words feel empty. "Let's get all this tidied up."

"We still need to test the antenna," Duggins says.

"We'll worry about that in a bit," I reply.

CHAPTER TWENTY-FIVE

Johansson

I must be mad.

The alarms in my helmet are a constant hammering torture. I can't switch them off; I haven't time. I'm throwing myself across the outside of the *Khidr*'s hull, racing for the airlock.

Carbon dioxide poisoning is a strange way to die. It's not like drowning or being in a vacuum where there's nothing for you to breathe. You keep breathing, but every moment that you do, you're killing yourself. Your body doesn't really understand this. You can breathe the contents of your helmet, so you do. Only a conscious effort of will keeps you trying to restrict your intake, and that's fighting your body's natural instinct to gulp down more air as it realises you aren't getting enough oxygen.

Everyone's hypoxia symptoms are different. We're trained to recognise the signs in our own body and take action to deal with them as they occur.

There's a handhold, just outside of the exterior hatch. I'm reaching for it. I grab it with my prosthetic hand and brace myself as my momentum takes the rest of my body onward. My upper arm is a little numb, but the sudden pain as I'm pulled around sends a jolt through me, keeping me awake for a few more seconds.

I have a thumping headache. The throbs of pain come in rhythmic waves that match the suit alarm. Ahead, I can see the hatch. Quartermaster Sam Chase is inside. He's not moving. I realise Arkov couldn't repressurise the damaged compartment twice. They've had to wait for me.

Then he turns and gives me a thumbs-up. I can see he's plugged his suit into the extra tank we left behind. *Fresh, tasty, new, breathable air!*

"Come on, April, you can do it!" he urges over the comms.

I grit my teeth and pull myself forward.

I remember a lecture from two mountain climbers in my first week of basic astro training. They'd been part of a commercial touring group who worked on Mount Everest, before the quake in 2084. They came to talk about oxygen deprivation and how you can train yourself to keep functioning when you recognise the signs. Hypoxia is all about gradual brain death. Above 25,000 feet on Earth, your body is dying. You have to try and function, knowing every move you make will be exhausting. That's my moment, right now.

Thankfully, space helps. I'm not fighting gravity; I just have to aim myself at the right place and…

"Got you!"

Sam's got hold of my shoulders. He flips me around and unscrews the emergency valve on the neck of my suit; then he plugs in a new feed to the emergency tank. I can hear a hissing noise and the alarms subside.

"Arkov, get us inside!"

The outer door begins to close. A sense of euphoria washes over me, but right now is when I need to be most careful. My EVA suit's atmospheric processor needs to rebalance the nitrogen, oxygen, carbon dioxide mixture that I'm breathing. It'll take a few moments. If I don't wait, I might do more damage and pass out. I must breathe only when necessary and keep my heart rate down.

"April, what the fuck were you thinking?"

Sam has me in his arms. He's not letting me go. I'm quite touched by how much he seems to care. Maybe he's attracted to me? We've lost so many people in the last few days it's difficult not to feel a bond between those of us who remain. Perhaps that's what motivated me to go back and finish repairing the transmitter.

It's difficult to process my emotions. I'm kind of detached and dislocated. Could be it's an effect of the carbon dioxide. What I just did was madness, but at least I'll get the letter of recommendation I want when we get back to Phobos.

Is that what motivated me?

No, I don't think so. Not anymore.

There's a clunk against my helmet. I blink and focus on Sam. "Hey there," I say.

"Hey yourself. You're nuts."

"It needed to be done."

"Not at the expense of your own life."

I think about that for a moment. "The stakes are pretty high right now, and they're only going to get higher. If we don't start taking some bold risks, we'll all die out here."

"Is that why you did it?"

"I don't know. I just… I made a choice."

The atmospheric pressure indicator beeps, and a green light comes on. I fumble at the seals around my helmet, but my fingers don't want to obey. The prosthetic ones won't even move. "Sam, I—"

"It's okay; give me a moment and I'll sort it."

I try to stay calm. This awkwardness will be temporary. Bogdanovic can check me over and sort me out. Just because neurons in my brain have died due to a lack of oxygen doesn't mean I've lost any motor skills. Neurons in our brains die all the time. The ordeal is over. Panic will not help. Panic will not—

There's a clump and squeak as Sam unlocks my helmet and pulls it off. I let myself take a deep breath and smile. "We did it," I say.

"Yeah, we did. Live to fight another day, eh?"

"Damn right."

Sam is working around me, disconnecting the spare tank from both of us and unfastening my backpack. I let myself drift, doing nothing. I've earned it.

"You're right, you know."

"About what?"

"About how we have to take risks, fight for what we believe in – all of us." Sam sighs. "We're bound by procedures and protocols. They're getting in the way. If we're going to survive this, we have to set fire to the rule book."

I turn my head and look at him. "You want to be careful," I say. "You're talking about disobeying orders and breaking the chain of command."

"I'm talking about using some fucking initiative."

"Don't use my screwup as your justification for going AWOL, Sergeant Chase."

The use of his rank and surname makes him flinch. It reminds him of his rank and mine. He looks hurt for a moment, then covers it, but the closeness we had a moment ago evaporates. "I'm sorry, Ensign, I didn't mean—"

"No, you didn't."

The door opens and Arkov comes in; he's smiling at me. "You two were amazing!" he says.

"Had to be done," I reply. "I'll need to apologise to the captain."

"Why? You saved the ship!"

"I went back to fix the transmitter, disobeying a direct order. Captain Shann gets to decide what that means."

Arkov's smile cracks. He glances at Sam, then looks away. There's still a tension between them, from when Sam accused him of being the traitor. "Yes, of course, procedures and all that."

I nod. "Yeah, procedures. Sometimes that's all that keeps us from going insane."

Arkov shrugs. He approaches me and starts to work on getting me out of the EVA suit. "The captain's on her way," he says. "She wants a quick debrief here, if you're up to it?"

"I should be," I reply. "I'll need a medical assessment after."

"Something wrong?"

"Yeah, the neural transmitters in my artificial hand have stopped working." I try to lift my right arm. The bit I was born with responds awkwardly, but the prosthetic attachment doesn't move. "Something must have got disconnected."

"I'm sure Bogdanovic or Duggins will sort it."

"Let's hope so." My breathing is easier now, but my throat is sore and there's a wheezing catch each time I inhale. "You'll have to help me get out of this suit."

Arkov's smile returns. "Now that I am qualified to assist with," he says.

CHAPTER TWENTY-SIX

Sellis

I'm halfway through foam sealing another bulkhead in corridor two, when my requisition alert goes off.

I finish foaming the join, holster the gun and turn to the terminal. I log in and check the message. *Technician Sellis requested on the bridge.* There's no signature, and while it's a priority call, which got routed through to my wrist comms, I can't tell who's asking for me.

Okay. That's pretty strange…

Looking at the schematic, I see my work plan has been altered. Some unspecified bridge repairs are now top priority. I'll need to head straight up there.

It's a fair distance, and this time I can't let everything trail behind me. I begin packing up my kit, storing everything into boxes and satchels that are strapped to me. If I'd been in gravity, I'd never be able to carry everything, but up here, there are different problems; manoeuvering around corners can be tricky.

Still, orders are orders.

I make my way to the bridge. Progress is slow but steady. I don't see anyone on my way. With the crew grouped into repair teams, it's likely they're all busy in specific parts of the ship.

I get to the door and activate my comms. "Sellis to bridge, I'm nearly with you."

The comms clicks in response, indicating it hasn't acquired a receiver. That doesn't usually happen. Maybe one of the relays has broken down. Might be why they called me.

I push the door release and the panel slides back. The bridge lights are off. I move inside.

I've walked right into the middle of something here.

"Close the door, Technician, and move toward the viewer."

There's a young blond officer holding a gun and pointing it at the XO – Lieutenant Travers. I can't remember the name of the young guy. "What the fuck are you doing, Ensign?" I ask.

"Technician, best you keep your mouth shut right now," the ensign replies. I remember his name now, Jacobson, a Swedish guy, I think. "Just move over to the view screen."

"Technician, do what he says," Travers says. He's got his hands raised, like he's in a zero gravity stickup. It would be funny, if this wasn't serious.

"Ensign, you're holding a low-velocity gas-powered pistol," I say very slowly. "If you discharge that weapon in here, you'll risk all of our lives, given that the ship's hull is pretty fucked up right now."

The blond shit doesn't even look at me. "Technician, you've been given an order."

I shrug and move my way across the room. I see there's someone else in here. The young Asian engineer, Chiu. She's still in her seat, her gaze on the floor.

"Jacobson, don't do this," Travers says. "You're throwing away your career. You both are."

"And you're throwing away our lives," Jacobson replies. He waves the pistol toward the door. "In a few minutes, some more people will join us. You're going to stay right there, and if you give me no cause, we might even let you leave."

"This is mutiny, Ensign."

"History is written by the winners, Lieutenant."

I'm out of my depth here. I don't know why I've been called up. There's at least half a conversation I'm missing. "Listen," I say. "If you can just tell me what you called me up to repair, I'll do my fucking job, while you folks argue it out."

"You weren't called to make repairs," Chiu explains. "You were called because you're going to help us."

"I am? Why should I—"

"You already know why."

I glare at Chiu and get an unflinching bruised stare in return. Instinctively I know we share something. "I don't like being used," I say.

"We all get used," Chiu says.

The door peels away again and Ashe enters. When he sees me, he freezes and looks confused. "What are you doing here?" he asks.

"Same question to you."

"I got a priority repair call."

"So did I." I look at Jacobson. "You want to give us an idea of what's going on?"

"You two and Chiu are going to help me take over the ship," Jacobson replies.

"Begging your pardon, Ensign, but why the fuck would we do that?" I'm chewing my lip and looking at the people on the bridge. Chiu, Jacobson, Ashe, Travers and me. There's a broad skill set here. Each person has intimate knowledge of an area of the ship. This group looks carefully planned. "What happens if we don't help you?" I ask.

Jacobson keeps his gaze and his pistol trained on Travers. "You know what happens, Technician Sellis. They've got a file on you stretching back fifteen years."

My hands clench into fists. I've half a mind to throw myself at him, but I can't be sure of my situation. Who else here is being blackmailed? Who is taking this guy's side because they want to? I've roomed with Ashe for months; the only moment he's gone weird on me was the chat earlier. Was that a cry for help?

I look at Travers. He's okay. A bit distant, and a cold fish at cards, but I've never had any trouble with him as XO. Those dark eyes catch mine and I can't hold them. Does that make me a traitor? I don't know.

"This can't work out well for anyone," I say.

"It'll go fine, so long as we all do what we're told," Jacobson says.

Suddenly, Travers explodes into motion, closing the distance between him and Jacobson. The two men crash into the back of the pilot's chair. The lieutenant's hands grab for the gun, but Jacobson's twist it away and punches him, hard, in the ribs. There's a crunch and Travers goes limp. Jacobson grabs his head and smashes it against the seat.

"Don't kill him!" Chiu shouts.

Jacobson turns to her. "I'm not going to," he says. "But we need to play for time." He activates the exit release and manhandles Travers into the passageway. The lieutenant is groaning and barely conscious.

I can see blood in the air, swirling, spiderlike trails drifting around the lieutenant's forehead.

Jacobson seals the door. "More people will be arriving soon. Then we can get to work."

"You sent me those messages," I say. "You threatened my family."

"I forwarded a set of communications to you as I was instructed," Jacobson replies. "I don't know what you received."

"We all have our secrets," Ashe adds.

"If you're not in charge of this, who is?" I ask. I glance at Chiu, but she shakes her head.

"You'll find out soon enough," Jacobson answers. He moves over to his console and accesses the screen. A minute or two later, he raises his head. "Okay, I've disabled all the recording in this room and deleted the previous entries. Chiu, I need you to lock Duggins out of the priority engineering access system. If you don't, as soon as they know something's up, they can trap us in here with no means of accessing the rest of the ship."

"Hold on, fucking *wait* a minute, we can still stop this," I say. "When the captain arrives, we can just walk out of here and give up."

"People I care about will die if I don't do this," Chiu says. "If that's not the same for you, then it might be better if you step outside."

I remember the message, the list of transactions, debts, names and addresses of everyone I care about. "They can't go through with their threats. If they do, they lose their leverage."

"Are you prepared to take that risk?" Ashe asks. "Do you want to watch the people you care about get murdered, one by one?"

I scowl at him, then at the others. All my life I've been a gambler, risk-taker, chancer – whatever you want to call it. Those bets were never about winning; they were always about the uncertainty. It's in this moment, right now, that I see it all clearly. I don't like winning, I don't like being lucky or unlucky. I like the risk, the step out into the unknown.

The consequences never mattered to me until after. I've lost my money, other people's money, stolen shit, sold shit, anything to get my fix. Something had to be on the line to make the bet real; otherwise it didn't matter. Am I prepared to call someone's bluff here? Someone I don't even know? It's just like the slots, trying to game a system when all the variables aren't on the table. I can feel that sweet tension right now as I hesitate, the same as the wheels rotating, the roulette ball bouncing around, the cards about to turn.

This is higher stakes; it's other people's lives. There's no straight choice or risk. It's all dangerous.

Something cold and metallic is pressed against my forehead. Jacobson has closed the distance between us. "At this range, I won't miss, and I won't damage the ship," he says in a low voice. "Don't make the mistake of thinking this is all about you."

CHAPTER TWENTY-SEVEN

Shann

There is a moment's lull. A time given by fate for success, perhaps?

Field operations in the military require hard evaluative clarity. You can't bask in a victory, any victory. There's a need to set aside the congratulations and praise while an enemy remains to oppose you.

Wars might be won by winning all your battles, but if you lose one, you can lose everything.

I'm outside the airlock in the EVA storage area. With me are Arkov, Johansson, Duggins and Sam.

"Incredible job," Duggins says. "I'll start running calibration tests. Thanks to you two, we'll have working communications in an hour or so."

"We also haven't exploded," I add. "Which is also down to your work."

"Thanks," Johansson replies. She looks pale. Her eyes are bright and wide. She's trying to help Arkov remove her suit, but there's no strength in her fitful efforts. I glance at Sam; he seems more able, shedding the hard gorget without difficulty.

"Where's Doctor Bogdanovic?" I ask. "Did you contact him?"

"Yes, Captain," Arkov replies. "I signalled his office and his personal comms."

"You didn't talk to him in person?"

"No, I was busy getting ready for these two."

I tap my comms bead. "Captain Shann to Doctor Bogdanovic, are you receiving?"

There's a click, like an acknowledgment, but no reply. I try again. "Doctor, we're down in airlock exit. I'd like you to look over Chase and Johansson after their EVA. Can you come and join us, please?"

This time there's no answer at all. I glance at Sam. He reads my concern. "I'm sure it's nothing to worry about. Probably dealing with a medical complication."

"Could be." I turn to the wall console and bring up a ship schematic. I activate the comms bead tracers. Gradually, the two-dimensional map populates with the locations of all the crew, each a blue dot with their name appearing underneath them. A cluster of dots represent where we are, another cluster on the bridge, two more in medical. None of them is Bogdanovic.

Then his location appears. Outside Ensign Thakur's quarters. Where we're holding Rocher.

"We have a problem," I say.

Sam moves over to join me next to the screen. "Shit," he says, "you think—"

"He has no reason for being there," I reply.

Duggins touches his comms. "Duggins to bridge, we have a situation. Can you lock down corridors three and eight, please?"

Again, there's a click in response but no actual answer. I look at the screen. Jacobson, Chiu, Sellis and Ashe are on the bridge with no senior officer. The latter two have no business being there. Travers, who should be in charge, appears to be in the corridor outside. His dot isn't moving.

I activate my comms bead again. "Shann to Travers?"

There's no answer at all.

I tap the names on the screen. "This doesn't look good."

"What do we do?" Sam asks.

"You don't do anything." I point at him and Johansson. "Sit here and lock yourselves in if you need to. The three of us will handle this." I turn to Arkov and Duggins. "He'll make for the bridge with Rocher. We need to intercept them."

"Corridor six," Duggins says. "But we'll need to hurry."

I'm already moving. "Do you have your sidearm?" I ask.

"Yes," Duggins replies.

"Good. Arkov, hang back. If we catch either of them, be ready to jump in and assist."

"Yes, Captain."

I'm moving fast, faster than the other two, leaving them behind. My left wrist is still a hindrance, but I'm coping, compensating. This is my world, racing through metal tubes in zero gravity. More speed, less safety.

There could be a reasonable explanation for what's going on. Bogdanovic might need to see Rocher for something, might then have business on the bridge. Sellis and Ashe may be helping with repairs and some essential maintenance. Travers might be outside for some important reason. *All these things are possible.*

I reach corridor six, the place where Drake died a lifetime ago. I peer around the corner at the end. My low-calibre pistol is in my hand and the safety is off. I can't see anyone. Did I get here first? If Rocher and Bogdanovic were making for the bridge, they'd be in a hurry to get there while we were all out of the way. They won't necessarily know we're on to them.

I'm listening for sounds of movement.

I can't hear anything.

Slowly, I inch my way out.

There's a loud bang and I duck back. The hiss of escaping gas behind me makes me glance around. There's a bullet-sized hole in the nitrogen vent. An alarm goes off and the emergency doors start to seal. I push off from the wall and glide through, just as the passage seals itself.

I see movement ahead. Two figures, making their way through the next hatch.

I lean into my comms bead. "Shann to Duggins?"

"Go ahead."

"I've found them and Rocher's armed. Your route is blocked because of a bust nitrogen seal. Get in there and patch it, then catch up."

"Understood, Captain."

I push on, reaching the end of the passage. There's no sign of anyone at the intersection. I've missed them.

I pull myself around the corner and do the last few twists and turns to the bridge. Again, I peer around the corner, gun in hand.

The bridge door is shut. Floating in front of it is Travers. He's unconscious. There's blood swirling around his head.

I'm tempted to go to him, but I know the people on the bridge will have me on camera by now. If I step out into the passageway and concentrate on rescuing Travers, I'm vulnerable. I need to wait for backup.

I hear sounds of people. I turn to see Duggins and Arkov making their way through an access hatch and coming toward me.

"What's the situation?" Duggins asks when he's close enough.

"Looks like we weren't quick enough," I say. "They've dumped Travers outside. We need to grab him and take him back to medical."

"Who's going to look him over if Bogdanovic has gone rogue?"

"We'll figure that out in a bit, but we can't leave him where he is."

"Sure."

Arkov joins us. Duggins nudges him. "Vasili, can you get Travers? We'll cover you."

Arkov looks at me. He appears nervous, but nods and maneuvers his way past. I'm reminded of how we treated him, locking him up in his room while Le Garre continued her investigations. Can I trust him now? I think so. He edges out into the passage, Duggins moves to the other side of the corridor and I train my gun on the door to the bridge.

Arkov gets his hands around Travers's left foot. Travers groans. That's an encouraging sign. Slowly, Arkov pulls him back toward us. The blood trails behind Travers, like tendrils. I'm watching them out of the corner of my eye, everything else focused on the bridge door, ready to shoot if someone comes out.

"Okay, I've got him," Arkov says. He's behind us, holding Travers, who's still unconscious, his face grey. "What now?"

"I'm not sure," I say. "Check Travers. Is he carrying a sidearm?"

Arkov points to an open holster on Travers's waist. "Looks like he was," he says.

"That means one of the people inside is armed," Duggins reasons.

"And that they're likely waiting behind the door for us to try to get in," I add. "They'll be watching and listening on the security feed, no doubt."

Duggins nods. He points at the camera by the door and beckons Arkov and me in close so we can whisper. "This is a mutiny. We need backup, but we can't leave this intersection unattended. Who can we trust?"

"At the moment, Sam and April," I reply. "But, hopefully the rest of the crew as well; otherwise this lot wouldn't have clustered up here." I touch my comms bead, but it clicks uselessly. "They may be rerouting the central communication system to stop us warning the rest of the crew. We need to find them and inform them."

"Agreed," Duggins says. "But that's not the highest priority, Captain. You need to think about why they're in there." He nods in the direction of the bridge door.

Inwardly I'm cursing. "Of course, you're right," I say. "What do we need to be worrying about?"

"Well, shutting down the internal comms is a problem, but hardly the worst we can expect," Duggins says. "Control of the bridge systems gives them full control of the ship. A course correction without warning would probably kill us all."

"That'll have to be a plan they're considering," I say.

"Absolutely," Duggins replies. "I'm surprised they haven't done it already. We're on borrowed time."

"Rocher has been trying to get me to agree to surrender," I reason. "I think they'd still like that to happen. Maybe they think this will change my mind?"

"Or there's a disagreement and they're not all prepared to be murderers," Arkov says.

"Whatever their motives are, right now, speculation won't help us," I decide. "We need to warn the rest of the crew and take back control." I hand my gun to Arkov. "You stay here. Guard the door. Arrest anyone who comes out."

"Okay, Captain."

"Duggins, you find yourself a good space with a console and acceleration chair. I need control of my ship back."

"Aye, aye," Duggins says.

"What are you going to do, Captain?" Arkov asks.

"Alert and arm the crew," I say. "I'll find Keiyho and Le Garre first and get the weapons lockers open. Once that's done, I'll send someone up here to relieve you."

Arkov nods. I leave him there, pushing myself back down the corridor and away.

*   *   *

I'm alone in corridor six, moving toward the hatch at the end.

"Hello, Ellisa."

I stop. The tinny-sounding voice is coming from the wall speaker. I recognise it. I grab a handle on the wall to arrest my forward momentum. "Rocher," I say.

"I wanted to thank you for our last conversation," Rocher says. "It was most…enlightening."

"You need to open that door and surrender to my crew," I state coldly.

"Thanks for the offer," Rocher replies. "But, as you may have noticed, circumstances have changed."

"You think I've changed my mind?"

"I'm hoping you have. Otherwise, this conversation may be very short."

I grimace. I'm staring at the speaker, hating the person speaking through it, but it's just a speaker, a conduit for his voice. They'll be watching my reaction, reading my expressions to gauge my emotions and how they affect my responses. This has become a chess game – move and counter move.

"What's the plan then? Murder us all with a surprise deceleration?"

"It's an option," Rocher says. "However, the calculations are complicated. If we use up all remaining fuel to do that, the *Gallowglass* will be unable to rescue us, so instead, we'll be making a course correction shortly. If this conversation goes as I hope, we'll notify you when we begin the burn. If you don't give me the right answers, well… you don't get any warning."

"You appear to have this all worked out," I say.

"There are a few things we're still trying to iron out," Rocher says. "We don't want any more deaths, Ellisa. You can help us save lives."

I don't reply for a while, thinking over what's being offered. I don't believe Rocher's compassionate motive. That means he wants something from me that he doesn't currently have.

That means we have a bargaining chip.

"How long do I have until you need me to make a decision?" I ask.

"I'll give you about an hour," Rocher says. "That should give you long enough to talk to the rest of the crew. I'd suggest you gather in your strategy room, where I hear you have all your secret meetings."

He's laughing at me. I can hear it in his voice. I'm supposed to react, reply with some angry impulse comment, but I'm cold inside, detached and withdrawn. I need to be better than this, to outwit Rocher and his traitors. Otherwise we'll only survive while we're worth something.

I don't answer. Instead I'm moving again, heading for Le Garre's compartment. I'm going to need her help.

CHAPTER TWENTY-EIGHT
Shann

"So that's the situation."

I'm gazing at a group of desperate faces. Everyone who's left alive and loyal is sitting around the table, apart from Duggins and Arkov. Eleven people here, including me, and counting our missing two – thirteen of us, against six on the bridge. We have weapons, numbers, experience, every advantage.

But they have control of the ship.

Johansson came in here before everyone else. She disabled the cameras and the audio recorders. She took all our comms beads and left them in the lift shaft. Unless Chiu or someone else left a bug in here that we didn't find, we should be safe to talk and plan.

"Hard to accept all this," says Keiyho. "We were sitting here with Ensign Chiu less than an hour ago."

"She was busy watching everything we were doing," I say. "They made their move right when we were vulnerable, in the aftermath of diffusing the bomb."

"We don't have any options," Johansson says. She looks beaten and exhausted. "The minute we organise to take the bridge, they'll vent the air, initiate a course correction or something else that we can't stop them doing."

"That doesn't mean we give up," Sam says. "We just need to think our way around the problem."

"I don't see how," Johansson says. "I've served with Jacobson for two years on this ship. If he's a sleeper, he's had all that time to shortcut his way around the computer system. The minute we start trying to hack them out, he'll know what we're up to."

Johansson's saying what we're all thinking. Rocher's an unknown quantity, but the rest of the people up there have betrayed us. They've been colleagues and friends for a long time. I'm thinking back over moments I've shared with them. Chiu talking to me in the medical room, confessing her pride in being selected for the crew, Jacobson's easy smile and hard work to help us navigate. Are these the people who will kill us?

"We're going to agree to their demands and surrender," I say.

There's resistance. I expected it. No one speaks, but I can see it in the glares I get as the words hang in the air. "Ensign Johansson, can you alter the personal communication beads so they don't use the ship's system?" I ask softly.

Johansson frowns. "Yes. The beads are designed to switch to peer-to-peer mode when the ship isn't in range."

"Can you encrypt or isolate what's being sent?"

"I should be able to. Yes, but that won't help us if—"

"Technician Shah, can you teach my crew some simple Morse signals? Just a few words we can use, not the whole language. Some of them know it already."

"Of course, Captain."

"They can still track our location through the beads," Keiyho says.

I smile. "Of course, we want them to know where we are, until we don't want them to know where we are."

"So, when you say surrender, you mean for now?" Travers says. He's sporting a bloodstained bandage, but otherwise, he doesn't look much worse than the rest of us.

I nod. "Ensign Johansson is correct. We can't retake the bridge in less than an hour. We have to use their tactics and work toward a moment when they're vulnerable and we can make our numbers count."

"That means we'll have to accept their course change," Le Garre points out. "We'll be going into another fight with the *Gallowglass*."

"Yeah, but I don't think we have another option, unless Duggins can lock the bridge controls in time."

"He won't be able to," Travers says. "That's too big a job."

"We worry about the *Gallowglass* later. This is our fight right now," I say. "We need options."

"The weakest moment is when we're all vulnerable, during the course correction," Keiyho says. "They have a disadvantage at the moment. There are six of them locked up tight on the bridge, but only five chairs. If they initiate a burn, someone in that room will die."

"Rocher won't care," I say.

"But if there are any doubts among his companions, that will affect them," Le Garre says. "Think about it. Working together with people, being their friends, all of it, cuts both ways. One or more of that group murdered Drake and blew up the hydroponics laboratory. They were committed against us the moment they did either of those things. Why was it Rocher who spoke to you, not one of them? They know you better. It would have twisted the knife."

"You think he's trying to keep them in line?"

"I think he has to. He's the outsider with the plan."

"If that's the case, there might be something we can exploit," I say. "Can we get access to the bridge consoles? Communicate with them directly?"

"You mean like some kind of back channel?" Keiyho asks.

"Yes, something like that. You're close to Chiu. Maybe if you talked to her through that, we might find out more about their situation."

Keiyho looks doubtful. "It's worth a try, but I'm not sure I trust her after this."

"You don't need to trust her; you just need to help us get an advantage."

"Yes, I understand." Keiyho looks at Johansson. "What about you and Gunnar?"

Johansson can't meet his eye. "I guess I could try talking to him," she mumbles.

Keiyho glances at me and winks. He knows the two of them were close. I start to smile but think better of it and disguise the expression with a cough to clear my throat. "Anything that gets us a possible advantage is useful."

I lean over the table and bring up the ship schematic. As expected, access to live data updates has been cut off. "I want you all dispersed. No grouping or congregating. The bridge must be watched at all times. They might have control of our ship, but we aren't letting them out of there without knowing what they're up to." I look at Sam. "Empty the weapons lockers and disperse everything around the ship. All members of the crew are to be issued sidearms. When I give the word, hide them somewhere."

"What about me?" Shah asks.

"You're my crew now," I reply.

★ ★ ★

"Your hour is almost up, Captain Shann. What is your decision?"

I'm back in my quarters, strapped into the chair and staring at the screen in the corner of the room. I'm watching *Celerity*, the thirteenth-century Japanese period drama series I subscribe to – a war between the north and south royal dynasties over who should be emperor of the kingdom. Shoguns gallop across the land on horseback, waging war even as they scheme in the great courts, every one of them self-interested and morally compromised in one way or another.

I pause the video file. "Yes, we've made our decision," I say. "You win. We surrender."

"I'm glad to hear that," Rocher says. "I hoped you'd see sense."

"Call it whatever you want," I reply.

"Two of my people will be leaving the bridge and going to the airlock access. They'll visit the medical room on their way. I want your crew to let them pass and stay away from them," Rocher says. "I'd advise your people to strap in. We'll be initiating a course correction in just under twenty minutes."

"You've disabled our access to ship-wide communications," I say. "I'm not going to be able to tell them all in time."

"Don't worry, this little conversation is being broadcast; they'll know."

"Good. Thank you."

"You're welcome. We're all one crew now."

I bite back an instinctive angry reply. "What's the gravity rating and duration of the burn?" I ask instead.

"Up to seven g," Rocher says. "We'll be correcting for fifteen minutes. Doctor Bogdanovic informs me we won't be needing sedative injections to cope with that, but I'll want everyone strapped into their chairs on time."

Seven gravities. Highly dangerous for anyone to try to function under those conditions. The force change will be gradual and unpredictable to anyone without access to the trajectory plot. I bet

Rocher will try to surprise people with some anaesthetic medication anyway, so even if anyone is conscious, they'll be fighting off the drugs as well. "Okay," I say. "If we're talking to everybody, for the record I'm ordering all crew to their acceleration stations."

"Thank you, Captain. That's very helpful."

"What guarantees do we have that you won't repeat what you did to Drake?" I ask.

There's a pause. I can hear someone talking to Rocher in low tones. I can't make out what's being said, but I think he's being told what happened. That could mean a lot of different things. Eventually, Rocher replies, "You have no guarantees, Captain, but you should note I've been entirely honest with you since we met. If the crew are compliant, they will be unharmed during the course correction."

"I guess that's the best I can expect," I say.

"Yes, it is."

The comms channel goes dead, and I'm left to think about what I've heard. I gaze at the frozen Japanese nobles on the screen. Alliances, betrayals, violence. Is humanity hardwired to divide and squabble over anything that has value?

I try to put myself in Rocher's position. He will come for us, using the comms beads to track the location of each member of the crew. Bogdanovic will have prepared sedative injections for everyone. They'll wait until people are strapped in, and then he'll dose everyone up. Depending on what he uses, the next time I wake up might be when the *Gallowglass* arrives.

We can't rely on tolerances. Bogdanovic knows the medical records of everyone on board. If we're going to make something of the circumstances, we need to accept that we're going to be injected. There has to be something else we can do to change the situation.

I pull up the ship schematic again. Outside of the bridge there are six more acceleration seats, which are pretty close. Close enough? I don't know. I don't think anyone's tried to move around a spaceship for an extended period under that kind of gravity load. Minor work operation tests were part of my training on Earth Five, but what we're considering here is on a whole different level.

I'm thinking about old field medic techniques, things you have to do in an emergency when there's no other option. Take the injection but cut off the blood supply to the limb. A tourniquet made out of rope or cloth, something that could be concealed under a suit?

That might work.

Next thing is to get around the need for mobility. How can we get onto the bridge and take over the ship without having to fight our way around? I think back over the things we've done since we found out about the *Hercules*. I'm picturing Keiyho and Tomlins outside the sealed hatch when we rescued Shah. There's something about what we did, something I'm missing.

Then the idea comes to me.

Yeah, that might just work.

CHAPTER TWENTY-NINE

Sellis

"This is shit."

We're crowded on the bridge with our new warlord, Kieran Rocher, sitting in the command chair. Ashe and I are keeping busy, fixing what we can of the damage. I had thought I'd try and sleep, but being part of a mutiny doesn't help.

I'm wired and pissed off.

Rocher spins around in his chair and favours me with a challenging smile. "Something you want to talk about, Technician?" he says.

"I said this is shit. There's no way the captain has agreed to what you want."

Rocher's smile widens. "I think you'll find Captain Shann has no choice. This is the best solution for all of us."

"What guarantees do we have that—"

"She's an honourable woman. You know her."

I glare at Rocher, but he's not backing down or looking away. I don't like my chances taking him. He has the pistol from Jacobson, and the way he moves tells me he's had advanced zero g combat training. He's not told us anything beyond his first name – *Kieran*. Bogdanovic broke him out of the room they were keeping him in. I can see blood on the doctor's knuckles. Looks like that wasn't easy. Right now, I don't trust any of these people. I can't be sure how far they're prepared to go.

"What are your people trying to do?" I ask.

"Right now, save lives." Rocher runs a hand through his hair. "This way, you people survive and the people giving me orders get what they want."

"You make it sound easy. Like there's no consequences for killing those people on board that freighter, or anyone on this fucking ship."

"What are we in space but assets?" Rocher points to the door. "If you think Captain Shann won't execute people who prove a burden to the running of her ship, you are wrong. Out here, mercy and generosity only go so far before an enemy becomes a waste of precious resources. I will not be kind to my enemy if they are breathing the air that I need to live."

"That's cold."

Rocher shakes his head. "Sellis, I've read your file. You don't give a damn about anyone apart from yourself. I'm surprised threats to your family even worked on you. The reason you're angry now is because you're worried about your own situation, not anyone else's."

"All the same, it might be useful if we all had an idea of your plans," Bogdanovic interjects.

There's silence. We've got everyone's attention now. Even Chiu has given up pretending she's invisible and is watching Rocher, waiting for him to talk.

Rocher looks at each of us in turn. "I'm under no illusions here," he says. "This is a difficult situation for you all. Leverage and incentives have been applied to make you help me, but you'll find this is the right course of action."

"You're asking for trust," Ashe says. "We don't know you."

"True." Rocher unstraps himself from his seat. "You've heard what I want. We'll be altering course shortly, lining us up for a rendezvous with the *Gallowglass*. Once we have confirmation of Captain Shann's surrender, we will notify the *Gallowglass* that we are in charge. There will be a peaceful meeting between the two ships, and everything will be straightened out without further bloodshed."

"What possible incentive do those bastards have to keep us alive?" I ask.

"If they wanted you dead, you'd already be dead," Rocher replies. "The benefit of keeping the *Khidr* and its crew intact outweighs any other option."

"So you say."

"Yes. Again, we come back to the matter of accepting my word." Rocher taps the holstered pistol at his side. "Your decisions are made. You are wasting energy and effort questioning the situation. Make the best of it and help me. You will not regret it."

"What about the *Hercules*?" Bogdanovic asks. "What will happen to her?"

"The freighter will be impounded," Rocher says. "They were guilty of smuggling illegal goods, something members of this crew might have been involved in. That's one of the reasons I'm here."

I scowl. "One of the reasons…"

"Yes, one of them."

"You're aware that one of the *Hercules* crew survived?" Bogdanovic says. "He's been debriefed by the senior officers."

I glance at Bogdanovic. He's not supporting me; he's playing his own game. It's like blackjack when two of you are up against the house. Everyone likes to see the house beaten, but that doesn't put any money in your pocket.

"I'll want Shah confined to quarters," Rocher replies. "We'll have to deal with him."

Bogdanovic frowns. "What do you mean deal—"

"Mister Rocher," Jacobson says, interrupting the conversation, "we may have an issue."

"Issue?"

I glance at Jacobson. He's hunched over his screen, intent on whatever he's discovered. "There's an anomaly," he says. "Some sort of minor calculation error when I'm trying to plot our new course."

"Is it Shann, trying to interfere?"

"I don't think so." Jacobson's fingers are flying over the keys on the screen as a list of data scrolls by. "It's a tiny error, some kind of scan and position discrepancy. I can't believe I didn't notice it before…. Maybe I did, but didn't realise…" He seems oblivious to us and the irritated Rocher, who is now looking over his shoulder.

"Will it stop us making the burn?" Rocher asks.

"No…we should be fine."

While they're talking, my hands are in my box of tools. The chemical cutter is a precision instrument, designed to heat up at a moment's notice and burn through steel plate. Might not be needed, but I'd rather have something in my pocket.

Rocher is speaking to Jacobson. "Okay, we've given them long enough. I want a list of all the occupied acceleration chairs. I want to know where every member of the crew is when they prep for the burn."

"Okay," Jacobson says. "I can do that."

"Good." Rocher looks at me. "You can escort the doctor to the medical room. I want sedative injections given to every crew member. You'll then proceed to the airlock and let us know you're strapped in. As soon as you are, we'll initiate the course correction."

The mission is a pretty good excuse to get out of this room. I'm keen on that, even if the rest of his plan is shit. "What if we run into trouble?" I ask.

"Good point." Rocher reaches for his holstered pistol. He takes it out, flips it and hands it to me, butt-first. "That should take care of things."

I accept the gun and stare into his eyes. I'm tempted to end him, right there and then, but I don't. Instead, I mumble, "Thanks," and turn toward the door.

"My pleasure," Rocher replies. "See you on the other side."

CHAPTER THIRTY
Shann

Twenty minutes are up, and I'm strapped into my chair in my quarters. The magnetic locks are all engaged. I'm ready. The necessary instructions have been sent out in Shah's simplified Morse. Hopefully, everyone else is ready too.

The chime of the emergency override goes off. My door opens and Bogdanovic appears, accompanied by Specialist Sellis, who levels a pistol in my direction.

"Thought as much," I say.

"I'm sorry, Captain Shann, but this is for the best," Bogdanovic says. He looks uncomfortable, like he's aged five years in the last couple of hours. "Just lie back and let me do my work."

"You're a doctor. You spend your life trying to help and heal people. How can you countenance this?" I ask.

"I'm a soldier first and foremost, Captain," Bogdanovic says stiffly. "We're all trained to kill. Besides, you won't die from this injection."

I sigh and do my best impression of looking defeated. Acting was never a specialty of mine, but a silent glowering expression is something I can manage. Bogdanovic doesn't want to be here anyway. He unzips the medical access in my right sleeve, finds a vein and jabs me with the needle, unloading the syringe into my arm. "We'll talk again after," he says.

"Count on it," I reply.

I shut my eyes and look away. The room door closes. I'm still being observed on the ship's cameras, so I have to be quick and discreet. I unstrap my left arm and reach for the rope tourniquet concealed around the upper part of my right arm and yank it tight, cutting off the circulation. Next, I tap my comms bead, signalling to the rest of the crew that I'm set and that the plan is in motion.

There's an acknowledgment reply from Keiyho and Sam, who are positioned near the bridge. One by one, other people check in too.

I strap my arm back in loosely, so I can free it again when needed, and settle down to wait.

* * *

Thirty minutes later and I'm still waiting.

Something must have gone wrong. Rocher and his people have found something, or they're preparing a contingency we haven't thought of.

I've no way to check or do anything without jeopardising the plan. I need to sit here, stay calm and ride it out. Whatever is going on, I can't help or hinder.

I close my eyes and I'm back in my room at home. It's dark and I'm five years old waiting for someone to help me after I've woken up from a nightmare. I've pressed the alarm, but I can't hear anyone coming. I'm stuck here on my own.

A rational part of my mind knows there's a light sensor, portable screen and other devices within arm's reach, but another, louder part just wants my parents to be here. If I turn on the light, I'll see what's hidden in the darkness and it'll see me. It'll know me.

There is a power in blind ignorance. A power of possibility that we feed with our imaginations, our speculation and our fear. Planning, strategising, preparing, anticipating. All of it magnifies what could happen, what might happen, leeching away our ability to shape and control events.

While I guess and wonder, I expend time and energy countering things that may never happen. I empower Rocher and his traitors by overthinking all this. For all I know, everything may have gone wrong for them. Le Garre or Keiyho might have retaken the ship. *Could that be—*

No. There would have been a signal or something...

My right arm is numb and sluggish, just like before, only this time it's because of what I've done. Any attempt to restore the circulation will speed up the effect of the sedative. I need to stay awake; people are relying on me.

Two clicks in my ear from the comms bead. There's a hum and surge in pressure. It's begun. I'm pushed into the straps as the ceiling becomes the floor. For a moment, I can't breathe, but then the training kicks in. Little sips against the building constriction. I must move. I must execute the plan.

Keiyho's portable screen from the EVA to the *Hercules* is tucked under my right shoulder. I lift it out with my left hand. Even if Rocher's people are watching, they won't be able to leave their chairs and make it all the way down here to stop me.

All drones are activated and operated from the bridge consoles. Senior officer authorisation is required to switch control to a portable device. Le Garre did that when we found Shah. The drone slaved to this screen comes equipped with a cutter and a portable power unit.

However, this drone wasn't designed to work in a gravity environment, so Duggins had to make some changes. Hopefully, he's done everything needed for our plan to work.

The screen is cabled to the back of the chair, so I don't drop it. I have one hand to operate it with. I slide it carefully into a mounting arm on the seat. It's an effort to turn my head to see the display, but failure is not an option, so it has to happen.

The drone is a green dot. I touch it and draw a line through the ship to where I want it to go. There's a beep and the green dot begins to move. Very, very, slowly.

I bring up a live camera feed. The drone is pitching and rolling through a corridor. Trying to climb, roll and maneuver along the walls, floor or ceiling as the ship shifts and twists. Duggins has fitted wheels, claws and a grapple to the frame. He's also welded the portable power unit onto the back, meaning it's all one device. The onboard guidance has been hacked to accommodate the new upgrades, but it's cobbled together. The gyroscope at its heart still operates in the same way, working to correct its orientation. I hope the new code is good enough to do the job.

Better to let a machine do the climbing than risk the crew, but in this case, we'll need both.

I tap the comms bead in my ear twice and receive the same acknowledgment back. Someone else is still conscious and working on our plan. Both Sam and Keiyho are near the bridge; it could be one of them. I hope it's one of them.

There's a red haze at the edges of my sight, a little like the visual distortion people get with migraines. I know what it means. I need to fight it off and stay conscious, or otherwise we lose. *Otherwise*—

The screen beeps confirmation that the drone has reached its destination.

Right outside the entrance to the bridge.

I activate the magnetic clamps, anchoring the vehicle in position. Then I target the door and switch on the laser cutter. There should be enough charge to cut through the door, and once the instruction is given, the drone goes into a preprogrammed sequence to complete its task. I can just about see the metal peeling away in the shaking camera window.

There are two more clicks in my ear. The gravity shifts again, and I'm pressed back into the seat. A sequence of clicks follows. I'm trying to make sense of them, recalling Shah's set of codes.

In corridor. Chiu is helping…. Stop cut…

That must have been from Keiyho. He must have gotten through to Chiu on the back channel. Maybe she was being coerced or threatened. Who knows?

I instruct the drone to cease its work and wait. A moment later the door slides back. I guess Chiu has unlocked and opened it?

The bridge is dark, apart from the flickering screens. I tell the drone to enter and mark up its next position. I could turn on the mounted torch, but that'll alert the rest of the bridge crew to what's going on. We need to hurry; the force of the course correction is easing, meaning they've nearly completed the maneuver. They'll soon know we've gotten onto the bridge anyway, and they'll be out of those seats the moment they feel threatened.

There are more clicks in my ear – *Right behind you.* A shape moves in front of the drone. I can't see who it is, but the microphones are picking up shouting and there's the sound of gunshots. The force pinning me to my seat is lessening with every second. The camera shows chaos, bright and dark blurs, the pattern of a seat and then someone's surprised face.

Jacobson. He's strapped into his chair. The drone is right in front of him. For a moment, I think there's been a miscalculation. I was supposed to get to Rocher, to confront him before he could get out of his seat. Then I realise Jacobson is in the captain's chair, not the pilot seat. He's struggling, but the drone has him pinned down, its grapples following preprogrammed instructions. Eventually, he'll get loose, but we have a moment, a chance to retake the bridge.

I can't hesitate; people's lives depend on me. I press the button and activate the laser cutter. The tool positions itself, aiming for his chest.

"No, wait, I didn't—"

The cutter is designed to slice through metal plate. It makes short work of a pressure suit, skin, flesh, bone and the back of the chair, slicing right through all of them. Jacobson is screaming in agony, his eyes bulging as he pours out his pain directly into the camera.

I want to look away, but I can't. I have to watch. I owe Jacobson that. He might have betrayed us, but this is an awful way to die. I made the call. I pushed the button. It's my responsibility. I'll never forget what I'm seeing, a man dying, screaming in my face. I know it'll haunt me forever.

He goes limp. His eyes dull. It's over.

★   ★   ★

"...joining me to discuss the way ahead for the space industry is Doctor Jan Halpern of the Intercontinental Research Institute, and Richard Isaac, consultant for Sovereign Reform – an advisory organisation who supports individual governments in attempting to retain their independence from globalisation initiatives. Mr. Isaac, if I can put the question to you. What is the future of the space industry as you see it?"

"Well, fundamentally, it needs to be smaller. We've overreached ourselves again and we're neglecting the basics. People on Earth are struggling in their day-to-day lives. Why should money be poured into these hugely expensive subsidised colonies?"

"You're referring to the intergovernmental financial levy?"

"Yes, that and other things. I mean, what are we getting out of this? What do hardworking families gain from paying for unsustainable colonies on Mars, Luna and Ceres?"

"I'd like to put that question to you, Doctor Halpern. What do we gain?"

"If you mean in tangible terms, there's a hundred examples I could give, but I think it's worth considering what this argument is really about. If you think withdrawal of funding from the levy and the other programmes that individual governments signed up to more than a generation ago, then you're mistaken.

What Mr. Isaac isn't saying is that the lives of these families will get any better when or if these initiatives are closed down."

"You're suggesting there is another motive?"

"Of course. This is about power and control. The commercial interests of a particular set of wealthy individuals rely on division and self-interest. No one will gain from us turning our back on the solar system."

"It's pretty disingenuous of Doctor Halpern to predict the future. No one is saying anyone will turn their back, just that people here on Earth need to be the priority. We can't reach for the stars when people at home are suffering."

"All very emotive, but the only change those people can expect if we stop funding the colonies is for their lives to worsen. Humanity came together to explore the stars. Division is a breeding ground for greed and war."

"And you're accusing me of being emotive! The thing is..."

CHAPTER THIRTY-ONE
Sellis

Oh *shit*.

I'm in the airlock, strapped to one of the chairs. Bogdanovic is on the other side of the room. The acceleration has eased off. That means the course correction is over, but something's wrong. Rocher said he'd contact us at the end of the burn, but neither of us has received a signal.

I stare at the doctor; he stares at me. Eventually, he shrugs.

"What do we do?" I ask.

"Whatever we need to," Bogdanovic replies. "If things haven't gone to Rocher's plan, then we'll have to adapt to what comes next." He touches the comms bead at his neck, and it clicks. "Still working and set on the right channel. We definitely should have heard from them by now."

I start unstrapping myself from the chair. When I'm free I make my way to the door and press the release. The lock beeps and a red light comes on, then disappears. "It's been locked from Arkov's control room," I say.

"You mean we're trapped in here?"

"Yeah, looks that way." I'm thinking about the door mechanism. I can probably get through it, but what will that achieve? If Captain Shann has retaken the bridge, then we'll be traitors. There are only so many places you can run and hide when you're stuck on a spaceship. "We'll need to surrender," I think aloud. "We can't—"

"We're not surrendering until we know the situation," Bogdanovic says. "Whatever's happened, the *Gallowglass* is still coming for us. There's nothing Shann can do to stop that. If she's taken the ship, it's only a matter of time until we're all dead."

My eyes stray to the pistol at his belt. He took it from me when we got in here and I had to check the condition of our seats. "What did you do?" I ask.

"Excuse me?"

"What did you do for Rocher to get a hold on you? I mean, it doesn't take much for people to work out my issues. You've seen me at the card table, and you've probably talked to people who I owe money to. Fuck, I owe money to most of the ship. But you, you've always been a cold and careful fish, Doctor. So, what's his lever?"

Bogdanovic glares at me. "Whatever deal you had going with them or have going with them, I don't want to know about. I'd like you to show me the same courtesy."

I nod. "Okay, but if Rocher's gone, they'll be wanting to question us about why we agreed to help him."

"Telling you anything doesn't change that."

"No, but if we stick together, we can—"

"Oh, we'll stick together all right." Bogdanovic is laughing. It's all effort and spittle with no humour. "You'll keep your mouth shut about everything; otherwise I'll make sure whoever did the arm-twisting will find out you betrayed us."

I hold up my hands. "Hey! I'm just trying to work out our best way through this."

Bogdanovic shakes his head. "There's one person you care about. Just remember, if you tell a story, I tell a story. Besides, we don't even know if—"

There's a *crunch* against the door. I look through the glass. I can see someone. It's...

Vasili Arkov, the airlock technician. Our eyes meet, and then he turns away.

Fuck. We. Are. Screwed.

Bogdanovic is over my shoulder. "What is it? You see someone?"

"Yeah, we're in the shit. Vasili's out there."

"Vasili? You mean they've—"

"Must have done, yeah."

Bogdanovic scowls. "Might not be the case. Rocher could have had other agents. Arkov was arrested and interrogated before. Maybe he was kept back to help?"

I shake my head. "I don't think so."

Bogdanovic moves away. I see another figure in the corridor. I can't make out who it is. I press my face to the glass, and my breath steams up the transparent surface. If they come in, I plan to surrender and back up into a corner. If the doctor wants to fight it out, that's up to him.

"Can you get control of the outer hatch?" Bogdanovic asks.

I turn and face him. "Suicide is not something we're doing."

"Rocher anticipated Shann might try something. We were sent here so that the airlock would be guarded for when the *Gallowglass* arrives. All we have to do is stay here and make sure the door gets opened when they dock."

"That's not going to work," I say. "Sure, there are emergency access protocols on the terminal we have in here, but even if I could override Arkov's exterior control console, they can just vent the room. We'll be dead or unconscious in minutes." I look out of the window again. "I expect they're already locking us out of the system."

"They need the airlock! We can say we'll blow it up! Rupture the oxygen pipes or—"

"Anything we threaten to do will just convince them to act and exchange this prison cell for something else. Face it, we're on the wrong side. Like you said, we need to adapt."

Bogdanovic flinches and looks around the room. I realise I'm watching somebody fall apart. It's a weird situation. Usually, I'm the one having a meltdown owing to the shit decisions I tend to make, but this time, it's not me.

"You have to let go," I mumble. "It's over."

I don't think he's heard me. Bogdanovic has always come across as being in control. Now he's powerless. Sometimes in life you need the lemons, or otherwise you never learn how to make lemonade. I know what it's like in those moments where everything piles on top of you. Those are dangerous moments. I don't want to be here with a man who's going through that.

And who has a loaded pistol in his hand to boot.

I don't remember seeing him draw the gun, but he's holding it loosely as he settles back into the acceleration chair. He's staring at it, turning it over in his hands. "Throughout history, prisoners of war have been made to work for their captors in the most dangerous and unskilled situations. They built railroads, broke rocks, dug mineshafts. I'm not built for that kind of work. I can kill with the slightest surgical slip or with a change in medication. The slightest injury is an opportunity for me to execute my enemies. Captain Shann can't risk that."

"You think she'll space you?" I ask. "You really think she's got that in her?"

He raises his head and fixes me with a dead-eyed stare. "I've worked in conflict zones. You have to make hard choices based on percentages. Who gets the morphine? Who gets surgery? The soldier who'll bleed out in twenty minutes, or the one who'll bleed out in fifteen? In times like that, you realise you only have one set of hands and you can only save one person. Shann may not even realise she's capable of making those kinds of decisions. It all depends on how far she's pushed. We're nothing but a threat, and the *Gallowglass* is coming. In the end, we'll be a waste of oxygen."

CHAPTER THIRTY-TWO

Shann

The aftermath is difficult. The tourniquets have to come off, but when they do, people will lapse into unconsciousness. We have to rely on Ensign Chiu to help. She wants to do everything she can, but it's hard to trust her, given the circumstances. Unfortunately, we don't have much choice, particularly with Sellis and Bogdanovic locked in the airlock.

I couldn't stay in my room. It's a violated place now. Every time I close my eyes, I see Jacobson's face and what I did to him. In my mind, I'm still doing it; there's no death release and end to the pain.

I'm in the medical room, watching the recorded camera feed from the bridge. I see Sam and Keiyho enter after the drone. They divide up. Keiyho, moving like a spider, goes past Chiu and moves towards Ashe, who is trying to release his safety straps. The Lieutenant Commander does not hesitate. There's a flash and suddenly Ashe is limp with a bloody hole in his chest.

A second feed shows me what happened to Rocher. Before Sam gets to him, he manages to get his arms free. He grabs for Sam's gun, but misses. Sam tries to right himself to get a shot off, but suddenly, Rocher is loose and pushing off towards him.

There's another flash and our insurgent is dead; a hole blown right through his skull.

We had no choice. I had no choice. Those words have become a mantra that I mutter to myself under my breath when the memory is too much, which is any moment I'm alone. Of the four traitors on the bridge, only Chiu survived and that was because of her message to Keiyho. Four targets. Three dead, one surrendered. I ordered the executions and I killed Jacobson myself.

We were the right three people for this bloody business. Both Keiyho and Sam had the combat ops training, and I am in charge. In this, I needed to take responsibility. I couldn't ask anyone else to operate the drone anyway. There was a chance we'd have to kill the mutineers, and we did. That has to be on me.

Now Bogdanovic and Sellis are holed up in the airlock, locked in and refusing to come out. I don't know why Rocher sent them there, but they've managed to override the door control, making it a standoff. We could cut our way in, but only when people have recovered. For now, Duggins has disabled their terminal. They can wait.

Chiu's here with me now in the medical room. My tourniquet's been removed, and I'm lying down, recovering from the sedative Bogdanovic loaded me with. I've been asleep, but I don't know how long. I want to vomit, but apparently that wouldn't be helpful. The drugs need to mix and balance.

Chiu looks terrified. She clearly has something she wants to say. I wait her out.

"That day we were here last time. I tried to tell you," she confesses. "I held your hand while the doctor injected you. I wasn't sure what he was doing. I thought you might die. That's why I stayed with you, so someone would be here, as a witness."

My mouth and tongue feel uncooperative. It takes me a couple of tries to form the question I want to ask. "Why did you help them?" I manage eventually.

"My family is on Earth, in Hangzhou. I was told they'd get Mars passes if I did what I was told. Later, they said they'd hurt them if I didn't obey."

"Le G-Garre will need to...question..."

"I know. I've written down everything." Chiu bites her lip. "They'll court-martial me when we get back."

"If...we get...back."

"What I said to you, Captain, I meant it," Chiu says. "If anyone can get us out of this, you can."

I look away from her. She's risked everything changing sides; she knows that. Her career in Fleet is over if what happened here gets out. This blind loyalty is all she has left, but there's something else, something I see in all of them, the reliance on a captain, a leader whom they can trust to have a plan, to know what to do.

"We'll think of...something," I say. The words are coming more easily now. I try to smile, but I'm not sure how successful I am at it. "What's the situation out there?"

"Quartermaster Chase is guarding the airlock with Technician Arkov," Chiu explains. "Ensign Johansson and Lieutenant Commander Keiyho are on the bridge."

There's something nagging at me, a question. "Chiu, why did Rocher want us alive?"

"He wanted the ship. That was his mission."

"While you were locked in the bridge, he could have cut off life support to the rest of the ship. Why didn't he do that?"

Chiu shrugs. "I don't know, Captain. He never suggested it."

But why not? There's a reason. There has to be a reason why he wanted us alive. I'm getting up, pulling out the IV in my arm and undoing the straps that hold me to the table. "Where's Duggins?" I ask.

"Engineer Duggins is asleep in his quarters, Captain."

"Wake him up and get him to meet me in Strategy."

"Aye, aye."

★　　★　　★

When Duggins arrives, I'm staring at the screen over the table. The data archive we received and Shah unlocked for us fills the screen. "Rocher talked a lot about the value of assets," I say. "He didn't care if we lived or died. He was trying to get information. There has to be something in here that he wanted. That's the reason we're still alive."

Duggins grunts. "I took a look at what was sent. The compression's interesting. You've got a mass of raw data there. Without knowing what we're looking for, it could take a lifetime to figure out what they want."

"But they must have known the keys to the archive were on the *Hercules*," I say. "They must have been trying to capture the crew to get them."

"And they must have figured out we had the archive," Duggins says. "Or had a copy of it themselves."

"Rocher implied that they sent it to us, but I don't know if I believe that. Maybe they already have the information and just need the key code?"

Duggins nods. "Very possible. Do you think Shah knows this was what they were after?"

I think about the last time I spoke to Shah. I shake my head. "Someone on the *Hercules* knew and prepped everyone before they were boarded." The pieces start to fall together in my mind. "That's why they had to kill Hutton! He'd been given access codes! They had to kill him before he could tell anyone."

Duggins sighs. "It's all going past me, I'm afraid, Captain."

"Doesn't matter," I say, waving my hand. "The point is, Rocher needed us alive for this information. That means the *Gallowglass* people must want us alive as well."

"Stands to reason," Duggins says. "But that's not something I'd like to take a chance on, begging your pardon, Captain."

"Me either." I access the navigation database and pull up a course plot. "This is where we're heading?"

"Yes, Captain. Gunnar Jacobson set a programmed deceleration into the system." Duggins reaches over my shoulder and taps on the screen. "We're scheduled to come to a dead stop, here."

"How much fuel will we have left?"

"About one or two per cent of total tank. Enough to push away, but…well…it'd take weeks for us to get anywhere where people could see us. We'll be out of oxygen and long dead by then." Duggins runs a hand through his hair. "The communications are calibrated, though. We can broadcast our situation to Phobos. They may be able to send someone after us."

That plan doesn't work for me. "We don't want to put another ship in the same situation we were in with the *Hercules*."

"True, but I don't see any other option."

I'm looking at the data archive again. "They want access to this. That means they're still willing to negotiate. Until they arrive, they'll still think Rocher's in control."

"The minute we don't reply to a message from them, they'll know."

"Then we make sure we reply," I say. Then something occurs to me. I bring up a search box on the archive and type in 'Gallowglass'.

Immediately a list of files appears and I'm smiling.

"Perhaps they don't want the specifications and origin of their ship revealed to the whole of humanity," I say. I tap a finger on the files. "Do you think you can do something with that?"

Duggins nods. "We can at least make a plan," he says. "They might outgun us, but by knowing what we're up against, we have something to work with."

I select the files with my finger and flick them to Duggins's user profile. There's a ping from his portable screen confirming the copy. "Start pulling it all to pieces," I say. "Get Johansson and Chiu to help you."

"Aye, aye, Captain." Duggins is up and moving. I see a light in his eyes. At last, we're not reacting and fixing; we've gotten some advantages – a few cards we can play.

I touch Duggins on the shoulder before he leaves, getting his attention. "When you're done, copy those files into our message for Phobos. We'll hold off sending them until the last moment, but this time we'll make sure people know what kind of ship we're facing."

"Could be something to threaten them with?" Duggins suggests.

"Yes, I'll be sure to mention it."

Duggins leaves and I'm alone in the room.

Except I'm not really alone, am I?

Jacobson's face is etched into my eyelids. I can almost see him screaming as I look around the room. What I've done won't leave me. Talking to others and thinking about the problems at hand are all I have as a distraction.

The next conversation may not be so productive.

I leave the room and start making my way to the airlock.

★　　★　　★

Keiyho and Le Garre are waiting for me in Arkov's control room outside the airlock chamber. They both look old and ragged, driven to this point by the events of the last few days. As I enter, I can see two figures in the chamber itself.

Bogdanovic and Sellis.

"Any developments?" I ask.

Le Garre shakes her head. "They've been locked out of the system. Bogdanovic says he wants to talk to you. He won't talk to anyone else."

Keiyho grunts. "I wonder what he thinks he has left to negotiate with. We can open the airlock at any moment."

"He'll be aware of that," I say. I move forward and activate the two-way speaker under the window into the chamber. "Shann to Bogdanovic, I'm here, Doctor, and ready to listen."

Bogdanovic looks up at me and smiles. There's something cold in his expression that I've not noticed before. I'm reminded of the amount of times I've been strapped into a chair under his supervision. He could have killed all of us, anytime he wanted. I wonder why he didn't.

"Captain Shann, glad we finally have your attention. When are you going to let us out of here?"

"What makes you think I'm going to do that?" I ask. "Right now, I'm waiting for you to give me a reason not to space you both."

"An empty threat, Captain, which we both know." Bogdanovic moves across the room to the window and steadies himself when he reaches it. "You will not kill us because we share the same sensibilities. I didn't kill you or anyone else when they were under my care."

I glare at him. "Who killed Technician Drake, Doctor? Rocher wasn't on board when it happened. It had to be one of you two, or one of the others from the bridge."

Bogdanovic's smile slips. "Ah. That. A sorry mess where no one did the right thing. Drake discovered our preparations. We couldn't let him live."

"You killed him yourself then?"

"Jacobson initiated the programme. We had no choice."

"A man's life for your ideals," I say. "The death of the others is on your conscience too."

"And I expect you killed people on the bridge. This is war, Captain. Surely, you see that by now?"

I glance at Le Garre and Keiyho. They look like they've been through a war, and I guess so do I, probably. "Whatever way you try to frame your actions, Doctor, they are still crimes against the commitments you made to your fellow crew members," I say.

"Only history can judge us, Captain," Bogdanovic says. "But right now, you have more immediate problems. The only thing that can stop the *Gallowglass* from blowing this ship to pieces is us."

I nod slowly, swallowing the anger. "Okay, what are you offering?" I ask.

"When they arrive, surrender immediately. Let me speak to them and they'll know your order is legitimate," Bogdanovic says. "After that, let them dock. I will vouch for the crew. Everyone will be given the opportunity to join us."

"And if we refuse?"

"You become prisoners of war."

I stare at Bogdanovic. He's reaching. He has no idea what will happen if we refuse to switch sides. There's never been a war in space. The necessary management of resources makes taking prisoners a costly business. We're coming down to the wire. Both ships are damaged, running on finite supplies of oxygen, water, food and everything else. Every living individual on our ship and their ship consumes more supplies. The *Gallowglass* has been ruthless so far in murdering anyone in their path. I've no reason to trust they'll keep us alive.

But I've also no reason to play my hand here.

"Let me discuss this with the crew," I say to Bogdanovic. "We'll make a decision after that."

"Don't take too long," Bogdanovic warns. "There are pieces in play that you are unaware of. I cannot control what may happen next."

I smile at the doctor. "Thanks, I'll bear that in mind."

CHAPTER THIRTY-THREE

Johansson

"You all right?"

I look up. I'm sitting in the medical room on my own. All my patients are gone. Quartermaster Sam Chase is at the open door, staring at me. I force a smile. "Fine, I guess."

"You guess?" Sam points at the medical terminal. "You run the checks?"

I nod. "Oh yes, sorry. My lung capacity appears to be unaffected. Some residual soreness, but that's to be expected. No issues otherwise." I sigh. "I guess I'm just a bit frustrated being stuck down here."

Sam nods. "I'm sure it'll just be temporary. We don't have anyone else with medical experience now Bogdanovic is locked up."

I glance down at my right hand and the surgical plug where my prosthesis had been plugged in until an hour or so ago. The neural connections need resetting after my trip outside, and we've no one trustworthy who can do it. "I feel useless stuck here."

"You're the opposite of useless. That's the point."

"Sure."

Sam scowls at me and moves into the room. "I mean it. I actually stopped by to thank you."

"For all that with the transmitter?" I shake my head. "We've been through this. It was a bit of stupid bravery that's best not encouraged. This is my penance."

"No, for what you said after, about respecting protocols and the chain of command," Sam replies. "You were right. I was out of line. Thanks for calling me on it."

"No problem, it's forgotten."

"Thanks, but I won't forget," Sam says. "I owe you."

"Don't mention it. We all have our moments."

Sam looks around the room. "What are you supposed to be doing?"

I shrug. "I'm on hand in case there are any issues with the sedatives and the tourniquets. I've taken blood samples and screened them. It doesn't look like Bogdanovic left us any surprises, but if anything happens in the next hour or so, someone needs to be on hand. Captain Shann says I should get used to everything and work out how the doctor has it all organised."

"Haven't you worked with him before?"

"A bit, but the captain's right. Someone needs to know where everything is." I remember something and smile. "Last time I was here, I almost offered to help him, but I'd been ordered to rest."

Sam nods. "Well, you're right; you're wasted in here right now. I know most of the inventory as I signed all the requisition transfers. I can put together a stock plan to make this easy. Let me deal with it."

"You sure?"

"Of course. What would you do with yourself if you had the free time?"

"Probably take a look at some of the data we have on the *Gallowglass* so we can find a tactical weakness?"

Sam smiles at me and flips me a salute. "Sounds like a much more productive use of your abilities."

A few minutes later, I'm back in my room and logging in to my screen. The half-finished work from before appears, the audio fragments that we found what seems like a lifetime ago. There's a complete repair assessment, which I sent to Duggins before the mutiny, and there's a capability assessment of the *Gallowglass* as well, which I had the computer run based on the images of the damage we did to her. There's a selection of conclusions saved in a file. I open that up and take a look.

Interesting...

I've already reported on the anti-collision system they've got that intercepted our torpedoes but the computer has concluded there's a reaction time pattern to all the maneuvers and actions they're making. We'd see a certain amount of this on any ship, since the level of automation between an instruction being enacted by a crew member and the system making that action takes a bit of time. However, there should be a certain amount of difference as people hesitate and change their minds.

In this analysis, there are differences, but so many patterns. *It's almost as if the same person is making all the decisions...*

I need a second opinion. I call up Duggins. After a few seconds, his dishevelled face appears on the screen.

"How can I help, Ensign?"

"Before Rocher initiated the mutiny, I had the computer run an analysis on the *Gallowglass* based on all available information from our last encounter. Some of the conclusions took a while to complete, but I've got them now. I wondered if you'd take a look?"

"Of course, happy to."

"Great. I'll send them over."

Using the computer with one hand is weird. It takes me back to when I was really young, when I didn't want to wear the powered gauntlet I'd been given. Still, I've always been able to manage, and I get the relevant files packaged and sent over.

"Received, thank you," Duggins says. "I'll take a read and let you know my thoughts." His window disappears.

All the remaining clutter on my screen makes it look like a warzone of tasks and incomplete work. I'm usually organised, but the last few days have been impossible. I'm thinking about the last time I looked at all this, Chiu's reassuring touch on my shoulder.

Oh yeah, *Chiu...*

She betrayed us, but she then betrayed the mutineers. I don't know her motives either way, but she'll be facing charges. By rights, the captain can space her if she wants. *I wouldn't object.*

That realisation is chilling. This situation has changed me, made me hard and uncompromising. It's the binary of war – allies and enemies. Out here, in space, there's even less room for a grey area in between.

I start into the rest of the processed reports and gradually get more and more depressed with the evaluations. The data is quite clear. We were outgunned and out-armoured when we went into the last altercation with the *Gallowglass*. In that fight, we took more damage, so we're even more outgunned now.

All of this makes me think about what I said to Sam and what I did outside. *If we're going to survive this, we have to set fire to the rule book.* He was angry when he said that, but he wasn't wrong. Maybe

I was wrong to shut him down. The only way we're going to win is if we do something risky and unexpected.

I turn away from the screen and close my eyes. They want to shut for just a second. Maybe I'll...

"Johansson, you there?"

I blink and look at the screen. An hour has disappeared. How did that happen? Duggins is back in front of me; he still looks tired, but there's an energy about him I didn't see before. I key up the receiver. "Sorry, Chief, must have dozed off."

"No problem. I've taken a look at your data. Can you meet me on the bridge?"

"Sure, on my way."

CHAPTER THIRTY-FOUR

Shann

"It's all automated! The whole ship!"

I'm on the bridge, sitting in the replacement chair. We've turned all the seats around into a huddle. Myself, Keiyho, Johansson and Chiu are listening while Duggins talks, his eyes shining as if he's just discovered the world is round.

"Take a breath, Commander," I say.

Duggins's face colours, and in a moment he's become a schoolboy who's just been told off. "Sorry," he says. "Captain, I believe I've found a weakness in the *Gallowglass*. The ship is running a large number of systems on remote. The plans indicate it's been designed for a crew of six."

"Six crew?"

"Yes, Captain, I believe so."

"That means we outnumber them more than two to one, despite our casualties."

"Yep."

"Captain, there's something else," Chiu adds. "That level of automation means there must be a more advanced internal system making decisions for the ship."

"We have some of that," I say. "Every ship has to rely on its computers, even the Apollo missions."

"Yes, they do, but not every ship will have active computer control of so many systems," Chiu explains. She looks at Keiyho, who nods his encouragement. "We can look for patterns, predictable behaviours."

"I wouldn't rule out hacking their system either," Johansson says.

"That's a long shot," Duggins replies. "But we should go over all the data we have from the last engagement. We may be able to find an automated system that we can exploit to our advantage."

"They will have manual control of weapons and manoeuvering," Keiyho says. "We must look for something less obvious."

"Okay," I say. A plan is forming out of these component parts. I don't understand it all yet, but I can see some of the moves. "Duggins, is the message to Phobos ready?"

"Yes, Captain."

"Will the *Gallowglass* detect a transmission if we send it?"

"Depends on their position," Duggins says. "The replacement communications rig is just that, a replacement. I can't narrow beam our signal in the same way I could have done with the original."

"What if I want them to see it?" I ask.

Duggins stares at me. Then he smiles, and the light from before returns to his eyes. "I think I can manage that," he says.

I nod and push myself out of my chair. "Okay, work on it here and then help the others. I want all of you working on a tactical weakness in that ship. Keep it quiet for now. I'm going to gather up the rest of the crew and prepare them. I'll link you up to the meeting when I'm ready."

"Captain, given that we're running out of time, you may want to think about our priorities," Keiyho says. "All four of us here are needed to prepare the *Khidr* for battle. If we're tied up working on this, you may not have any weapons to use against the *Gallowglass*. Similarly, if the crew are called to another meeting, we lose time. You can speak to them over the intercom."

I stop and stare at Keiyho. I'm about to reply sharply, but then I see his point. He's right. I'm tired and not considering all the options. "Thank you, Keiyho. Apologies, I'm not thinking this through." I remember Bogdanovic's words – *There are pieces in play that you are unaware of.* Are there more traitors among the crew? Whether there are or aren't, I'm doing exactly what I said I'd do when I spoke to the doctor. I need to change the game and hold something back.

I force a smile. "I guess I need to start trusting people to do their jobs."

Keiyho nods. He glances at Chiu and squeezes her shoulder. "It can be difficult," he says, favouring her with a reassuring smile. She flinches and looks away.

"I should be doing something too," I say. "I'll head up to the torus and go over the data myself."

"I'll come with you, Captain," Johansson says.

*　　*　　*

Fifteen minutes later, Johansson and I are floating around the strategy room with a copy of the archive spread across the table and additional screens. "Permission to speak freely, Captain," Johansson asks.

"Go ahead," I reply.

"I don't trust her. I think she's lying to us."

I'm turned away from Johansson so she can't see me frown. "You mean Ensign Chiu?" I ask.

"Yes, Captain," Johansson replies.

"Why would she turn again?" I say. "Her only hope is that we accept her back."

"If it was preplanned, she could regain our confidence and betray us," Johansson explains.

"That would require a lot of foresight," I say. "The *Gallowglass* isn't in contact with us, and I don't think Rocher was planning for his own death."

"There could be other traitors, though," Johansson says. "We still don't know who set up that transmitter we found right before we encountered the enemy."

"Yes, you're right."

We're staring at each other now. I can't read her expression. "Is this why you wanted to accompany me here, Ensign?" I ask softly.

"No, I—" Her voice quivers. She clears her throat. "No, Captain, I have a few ideas on our situation."

"Then let's have them."

"Right, sure." Johansson reaches out to the display of the *Gallowglass* schematic and brings it into the centre. "According to the data, as Duggins said, the ship has six stations, but a normal shift would need three people, if our crew rotation is anything to go by." She touches the image of the *Gallowglass*'s bridge with her hand, and the room expands. "I've tried to identify what the crew roles might be. I'm guessing a pilot, a maintenance officer and a captain. One of those would need to double as a medic and communications specialist while on duty."

"With other roles being taken up in an emergency?"

"Yes, exactly that. For example, a weapons specialist is not going to be needed unless there's an emergency that requires it, so in that situation, a member of the second shift crew would take on that responsibility. Could very easily be the other pilot, or someone like that."

"Okay, so by knowing what people are up to, we get an idea of what other systems on the ship are automated?"

"Yes, but also what systems they may not pay attention to as much as we do and how vulnerable they are if members of the crew are taken out." Johansson touches the screen, zooming in on the bridge. She gestures awkwardly, and the model moves into the air between us as a three-dimensional projection. "One that I think we can target is the respiration system." Her fingers highlight the environmental pipes in the walls of the bridge. "If we can change the oxygen mixture in this one location, we can take out half the crew."

"How hard would that be?" I ask.

Johansson shrugs. "On this ship, it would be impossible. There's too many of us all over the ship. The *Khidr* is designed to breathe in reverse. The system detects the level of carbon dioxide in a room and removes it, replacing it with the correct ratios of oxygen, nitrogen and the rest. Three crew members have responsibility for monitoring the system, with regular portable sampling done every twenty hours. However, according to the data archive, the *Gallowglass* doesn't have the crew to manage the same rota. They're relying on the computer sniffers without a secondary check."

"All of this relies on us finding a way to access their computer system?" I say.

Johansson nods. "Yes. Again, almost impossible. Our network can be accessed through a hardwired connection, just like we did with the *Hercules*, and, as you know, there's a set of auto-docking protocols as well. The signal gets sent, and a space station tech takes over our final approach. That doesn't help us much with the *Gallowglass*, but I might be able to modify it."

"Either way, we'd have to be in contact or within a kilometre of their ship to have a five per cent chance," I say. "If you're suggesting this, you must have an idea of improving on those odds."

"We could launch a propelled vehicle and deploy a team onto their hull," Johansson suggests. "There are enough parts in the hold to adapt a drone and rocket to make what we need."

I shake my head. "That's still a lot of resources to commit to a slim chance. If they have an autonomous intelligence, there will be several layers of additional security to bypass. Besides, if we managed to hack their computers, we would be in control of their ship."

"A slim chance is better than no chance, Captain." Johansson manipulates the image again, returning it to the flat screen to show our position and course. She keys in a sequence, and a second line appears that intersects ours. "This is the projection of our intercept. We've been told the *Gallowglass* wants us alive. If we can get them in close without starting a fight, the percentages change."

"Agreed, but we need more control over this encounter." I examine the intersection. "What's out there?" I ask.

"Sorry?"

I tap the cross on the screen. "That location. Is it the optimal interception point or has it been chosen for some other reason?"

Johansson's forehead pinches in concentration. "I'm not sure, Captain. I'd guess a judgement was made to exhaust our fuel reserve as much as possible, making it more difficult for us to fight back."

"What about if we don't slow down?" I ask.

"Then we drift out into deep space." Johansson widens the view on the screen. "We've been turned away from Phobos to make the interception easier. We won't pass a trade lane or anything. The farther we go, the less chance we'll have after we fight the *Gallowglass*. Besides, if we don't stop, they'll know something is up. They'll get in range and fire more guided rockets at us."

"Sort of like the situation we were in before, but without a place to run to."

"Yes. The *Gallowglass* could just stalk us for weeks in the darkness, waiting until we run out of air and water. Then close in and wipe us out."

"Okay, but can we alter this a bit?" I ask. "Decelerate faster so they have to maneuver to find us or slower for the same?"

"Slower might be possible. However, if they scan our position, they'll adjust accordingly." She traces a new line across the screen.

I nod. "If they do that, we lose the advantage. We need them approaching in a straight line, along a path that's almost the same as ours."

"We can counter that if we drop some explosives along that

trajectory," Johansson says. "Just a case of plotting the course of their approach."

"You mean like the mines plan Duggins suggested?"

"Yes, we could use it to discourage their course change. My recordings indicate we damaged their manoeuvering anyway. Drop a rocket with a guidance system on board to get to the run position and then go dark. They'll either detect it and adjust their heading, or run over it and take the damage."

"Either way we gain something." I'm thinking out loud now, using Johansson as a muse. "What about our destination? Are there any known objects or markers nearby? Anything bigger than a spec of dust that we can use?"

Johansson touches the console. "Strategy, to bridge?"

"Bridge receiving," Keiyho replies.

"Commander, the captain is asking if we have any scan data on our rendezvous point."

"We can initiate a sweep. Is that authorised?"

Johansson looks at me and I nod. "Yes, it's authorised," she confirms. "Can you stream the results to us here as you get them?"

"Will do."

"Of course, we can make our own debris if we want to," Johansson says.

I tap on the cross. "Yes, and that's made easier if we adjust our course to overshoot in a straight line so they'll follow our path."

"Giving us more control," Johansson says.

"Exactly." I'm staring at the graphical representation of the *Gallowglass* on the map. "Duggins said they'll get into communications range and expect a reply. Bogdanovic has offered to talk to them, provided we surrender to him and Sellis first. We can make the course adjustment before we agree to anything."

"You're going to surrender?" Johansson asks. "Like we did with Rocher?"

"No, I'm trying to work out the constants and variables," I reply. I'm thinking over what happened when we responded to the *Hercules*. I had to make choices based on the information available. I need to put the *Gallowglass* in the same position. "Could you synthesise a voice based on the ship's recordings of Bogdanovic?"

"Possibly," Johansson says. "But wouldn't they think of that?"

"They'll have to play the percentages like we are and take some educated guesses," I reason. "A quick scan of the *Khidr* will tell them we've had to replace our transmitter. No visuals and intermittent communication might be a result of that."

"What if they have a secondary protocol, or a code?" Johansson asks. "No synthesiser is going to get around that."

I nod. "If they are insurgent cells, they may not even know who they're expecting to meet, other than Rocher. Bogdanovic seems confident, though. I think you're right; there'll be a code." I pull up the archive again, putting the file list in the centre of the screen. "We still don't know why they want us alive. If we did, we'd know how much of a risk we can take. There has to be something here or on our ship that they want."

"Another problem is, we don't know how badly they want it," Johansson says.

CHAPTER THIRTY-FIVE
Shann

An hour later, the deceleration begins.

It took a combination of Le Garre, Chiu and Johansson to hack Jacobson's programming. The kid was supremely talented, and he's a big loss to us any way you look at it. The only way they could convince the braking thrusters to ease off was to persuade the ship we weren't travelling as fast as we are. That's meant ship-wide calibration inaccuracies.

But it'll be worth it.

The Art of War is a famous military textbook that had survived and stayed relevant to us for more than two millennia. It was supposedly written by Sun Tzu – a Chinese general who lived in the fifth and sixth centuries BC, so more than 2,600 years ago.

In the late twentieth century, the principles of Sun Tzu became motivational words for business talks and the mantra of commerce go-getters. The cheap comparison of war to trade implies the stakes in both arenas are the same and that we're fighting to survive every day of our lives. A revered military text becomes the ultimate capitalist dogma, creating a competitive culture that trivialises the taking of a life by comparing it to making a living.

Out here, Sun Tzu's writing is useful in its original context. *Warfare is based on deception*, he says. That means holding things back. I don't know if I can trust the remains of my crew. It's surprising how much you have to adjust your thinking, particularly when you live with the people you're holding back from for months and years at a time.

That's why I'm in here alone, separated from the rest. I need to establish distance and detach myself if we're going to get through this. Later, I'll go back, but for the moment, here is where I feel comfortable.

The Art of War also has a section about 'shaping the enemy'. This is all about choosing your battlefield and trying to control the condition of your opponent as they come to the fight.

The final part of the laser-scanning data comes into the strategy room as I'm strapping myself in. I'm disappointed. Keiyho's found nothing we can use, just a whole lot of big empty.

But that doesn't mean it needs to be empty when the *Gallowglass* arrives.

"We're ready to launch the powered mine, Captain," Le Garre tells me.

"Launch when ready, Major," I reply.

"Aye, aye."

The push of braking is light but constant, around half a g or so, I guess. I close my eyes and try to relax. The crew have their instructions. By the time the preparations are finished, we'll be at a dead stop at the end of a debris field.

"Captain to bridge."

"Bridge here, go ahead."

"Keiyho, what's the last recorded position of the *Gallowglass*?"

"She's about two hours from our scheduled stop, Captain."

"Okay, thank you." I'm working out the distances. The slow deceleration means we can still work. We need the time for running repairs and improvised upgrades. In a few minutes, the *Gallowglass* will scan us and know we've overshot the rendezvous point. They'll start looking to change course, turning inside our vector, but their scan will pick up the mine we've deployed. That'll leave their captain with a choice – stay on course and assess the gap when they're on the same course plot, or turn and engage the mine with their own weapons.

If it were me, I'd do the latter, unless…

"Shann to bridge."

"Bridge here."

"Begin transmission and increase deceleration."

"Aye, aye."

Warfare is based on deception. A patchy broadcast of voices, stitched together by Johansson from whatever she could find in the ship's data archive. I gave her permission to check every recording for samples of Rocher, Bogdanovic and the rest. There are recordings of the fighting too, screams of people wounded and dying, all put together to create the narrative we want them to believe: the *Khidr* is decelerating, someone on board the ship is transmitting, trying to get the attention of the *Gallowglass*, while the crew and rebels fight for control of the ship.

Dead traitors like Jacobson, Ashe and the others will perform one last loyal service to help us.

"Bridge, wait ninety seconds, then execute phase three."

"Confirmed."

The last part of the plan. Every piece of cargo, debris and rubbish we can find has to be flung out of the airlock and jettison tubes. Sections of the ship that were damaged in the last altercation have already been sealed off and cut away, with small explosive charges detonated to remove them and push them away in our wake. When we're done, the *Khidr* will come to a stop at the end of a trail of destruction.

This is the hard part. We've thrown away everything we could find. That includes the dead. Technician Drake, joins his comrades, Ensign Thakur, Sergeant Tomlins, Lendowski, Andelman and Orritt, who were all blown into space during the last altercation. The crew don't like it; they understand but don't approve. There's an emotional debt we'll all pay in the end when we have to second-guess some of the choices we're making, if we survive.

When we survive.

I remember conversations with veterans during my basic training. They said war never leaves you. Once you've been there, forced to choose your life over someone else's, your life changes. There's a clarity that comes with making that kind of choice, a framing in your mind that makes everything binary – good and evil, right or wrong.

One of the old men I spoke to told me how embracing that frame made everything bearable when he had to make the shitty decisions, but he warned me too. *Afterward, you have to be able to come back*, he said. *You have to be able to let go.*

I guess it's like being colour blind in a way, only about perception and judgement, not sight. I can feel the trauma waiting for me, lurking in the back of my consciousness. I know it's there, but staying at war, defining the world as *them and us* keeps it away and justifies my actions. Jacobson's face in those last moments is there. He's staring at me, accusing me. I have to ignore him, but sooner or later I'll have to stare back.

Right now, I need this clarity. But it can't define the rest of my life. My portable screen is synced with the displays around the table. I pull up the tactical plotting. A line-drawn, three-dimensional image of the *Khidr* appears in front of me. The velocity numbers are descending; they aren't accurate, but the rate of change is.

"Bridge, can you detect any alteration in the *Gallowglass*'s course?"

"Nothing yet, Captain."

If I die out here, it'll be right. Space is where I've lived – where I came to life. I'd have been happy being left in the void, like Drake or one of the others. If my dead flesh could give my crew one more second, one more minute to survive, I'd call that a worthy end.

There. That's said. That's how much they mean to me. My people, forged in vacuum and betrayal. There's no point in doubting them now, waiting for another traitorous act. We have to play the hand we're dealt and see how it all turns out.

Don't get me wrong. I don't want to die. But I have to accept it's an outcome.

My body is pushing against the chair straps. The deceleration has increased. I can see the fuel reserve readout flashing. We should be left with about three and a half per cent. More than we'd first thought. Whatever fuel we have if we survive will be used to push the ship toward Phobos. If we're not found, we'll reach there in about eight months.

Of course, we'll all be long dead by then. Killed by traitors, asphyxiation or starvation, or a mixture of all three.

"Shann to Duggins."

"Duggins here."

"What's our weapon status?"

"Three launchers are now configured to fire."

"You managed to fix one?"

"Yes, Captain. We cannibalised some parts before we began ejecting debris. The launch tube is now powered, so we can use it just like the other two."

"Good work."

"Thank you. We're working on the improvised weapons as agreed. I'll give you an update on those when we have them."

"Great."

Three working rocket launchers. That's the same number that the *Gallowglass* had when we fought them. The difference was they also had two laser turrets. We had one, and lost it in the fight.

Both types of weapons are dangerous. If a rocket breaches the hull of either ship, the flash-fire explosion could end things pretty fast. On top of that, the *Khidr* isn't built to withstand laser cutting. There's a nanotube ceramic coating over most of the hull, which helps, and some sections are plated with aluminium oxide, but ship-mounted lasers are powerful enough to break through these enhanced materials. If those weapons hit us for an extended period of time, they'll cut right through corridors, rooms and the rest, just like they did before. Once they are within two hundred kilometres or so, the only real defence against a laser is to get out of its way or shut it down.

Again, the straps bite a little harder into my shoulders, and I notice the fuel reserve tick down, past four per cent. We're nearly there.

"Bridge to Captain Shann."

"Go ahead."

"Captain." It's Travers over the comms. "We've received a priority message from the relay point. It's addressed to you."

I blink. "Lieutenant, we have been radio silent other than the broadcast to the *Gallowglass*, correct?"

"Yes, Captain."

Then what could this possibly— "Okay, patch it through to the screen here."

"Aye, aye."

The main display fades into black, and an encryption box pops up. I tap in my authorisation code, and the United Fleet flag appears. The words 'authorised admiralty transmission' are in white underneath the logo.

I'm paying attention.

A man appears on the screen, staring straight into the camera. I recognise him by reputation. It's Admiral Langsley, a member of the Defence Committee, back on Earth. He's balding, with liver spots across his pale forehead. His eyes are red and watery. He looks every day of his seventy-plus years. He's wearing a military uniform, but the collar is undone, making him look even more dishevelled. This isn't the way he usually appears in the media broadcasts.

"Captain Ellisa Shann. I hope this message finds you in time. My office has received word that you and your crew are intending to investigate a distress call from the freighter *Hercules*? I'm recording and sending this message to you immediately telling you to stand aside and ignore the transmission. We have reason to believe this signal is false. The *Khidr* is to continue with its regular patrol, while Fleet determines an appropriate response to the signal. I…"

There is a pause. Langsley's eyes flick nervously to someone behind the camera. I lean forward in my chair, staring at his face, trying to read what's going on.

Langsley's head dips, in a barely perceptible nod, as if he's receiving instructions. He licks his dry lips, blinks rapidly and then resumes. "You are ordered to maintain your current heading and provide an update transmission in twenty-four hours confirming your position."

Abruptly the screen goes black. A moment later, the data displays I had available return.

I'm left to contemplate what I've just been told and assess what remains of my resolve.

"Shann to Travers."

"Receiving."

"What was the date stamp on that transmission, please?"

There's a moment's pause. "According to the log, just under twelve hours from when we sent our request for the *Hercules* inventory." There's another pause. "Actually, Captain, it's exactly the same date stamp as the data archive you received."

"So, we were definitely in range of the communications buoys to receive it back then?"

"Yes, Captain. I don't understand why we wouldn't have—"

"Don't waste time on it, Lieutenant. You have plenty to be getting on with."

"Aye, aye, Captain."

At face value this is an impossible situation. If I'd have received these orders when they were sent, the *Khidr* would have been en route to the freighter and I would have had a decision to make over continuing on, or obeying the order, correcting course and returning to our patrol. As it is, we know Admiral Langsley's information was incorrect; the *Hercules* was indeed under attack from a hostile ship – the *Gallowglass*.

I think the only person on board who has seen this message is me. My security clearance opened the file. The only other way to get into it would be to break the encryption or use some sort of authorised back door. If there's another traitor on board, they could be in either category.

What I do with the information now is crucial. It could mean life or death for all of us.

I'm thinking about the way Langsley looked. How he was behaving. The video file had the right encryption and titles, but the truncated ending isn't what I've seen in any other flag briefings. Also, he isn't my immediate superior at Fleet. Why would he be sending this message? Who would be giving him orders?

Who was behind that camera?

There are pieces to this puzzle that I'm missing. Events have moved on. If I order the *Khidr* to stand down and surrender to the *Gallowglass*, there's no guarantee we'll be allowed to live, despite what Bogdanovic says, but at the same time, if I continue on without paying Langsley's orders any regard, I could be court-martialed.

Military officers aren't supposed to be put in a position where they have to interpret orders.

The communications system buzzes. "Captain, I errr... We've detected something." It's Travers again. I'm almost glad for the distraction.

"What have you found?" I ask.

"I think you better come to the bridge and see, Captain," Keiyho chimes in.

I consider the difficult trip from the strategy room, down the lift shaft and through the rest of the ship while we're still decelerating. "How long until we're in position?" I ask.

"About forty minutes, but this won't wait."

"Okay, I'm on my way."

I sigh and disconnect the control linkage between my portable screen and the displays in the room.

CHAPTER THIRTY-SIX

Sellis

"Okay, I think we're ready."

I'm in the acceleration chair again, the straps and buckles all connected, as instructed. Bogdanovic appears to have done the same. I can't see the pistol anymore. Maybe he's hidden it somewhere.

The airlock door opens, and Quartermaster Sam Chase comes in. He's carrying a pistol, aimed at me. Behind him, Commander Keiyho aims a weapon at the doctor.

I think something's coming. Bogdanovic hides it well, but he's desperate. I glance at him, but he's not meeting my eye. Instead, he's looking down, his chest rising and falling rapidly.

Do I say something? No. That would be betrayal.

And courageous. *Fuck, I'm such a coward.*

Arkov slips past both men to the side of my chair and presses the release. "Get up, slowly," he says. I do so, raising my hands as I float out of the chair.

"You are with me," Keiyho says. He gestures toward the open hatch. "You go first."

Carefully, I back toward the exit, making sure I'm facing everyone, my hands raised and palms outward. I still have the chemical cutter in the pocket of my suit, but there's no point in mentioning or drawing attention to it now.

Keiyho's gun is trained on me all the time I'm moving, and Chase is still covering the doctor. If Bogdanovic kicks off, I have to hope everyone will think for a second before shooting me.

"Nice and slow," Keiyho says.

I nod and try to smile reassuringly, but I'm not sure it comes out how I wanted. I meet his hard gaze, but then I see movement over his shoulder and his attention flicks away from me. He turns around as Bogdanovic screams and raises his gun, aiming at Chase.

Then everything goes to shit.

For some reason Chase doesn't fire, but grabs for Bogdanovic's arm. The gun goes off; the recoil noise is deceptively quiet. Arkov cries out in anger and pain, just as Keiyho reaches them. He seizes Bogdanovic's other arm and reactivates the emergency strap restraint mechanism. Suddenly, the doctor is held fast by the chair's automated acceleration safety protocol. He's struggling against it, but that nylon fabric is like steel, manufactured to withstand twenty g's or more. The gun, taken from Travers and given to me by Rocher, floats free. Chase plucks it out of the air with his left hand and points his own weapon at me.

"You stay right there," he snarls.

I haven't moved since it started, other than to gently drift backward with a forced grin on my lips.

"Vasili, you okay?"

"I'll manage." Arkov is clearly in pain. He's breathing in gasps, and there's a thin spiral of blood leaking out of his work suit into the air. Keiyho holsters his own gun and takes Bogdanovic's weapon from Chase. He gets hold of the airlock tech's collar and pulls him backward, past me and toward the exit.

"I didn't do anything," I mumble.

"No, you didn't," Chase replies, scowling at me. "And right now, you're going to keep on doing exactly that."

A minute later Keiyho returns. "We've sealed the wound and called for Ensign Johansson," he says. He points at me. "Best I take this one and come back to help you with the doctor."

Chase nods. "Sounds like a plan, Commander."

Keiyho touches my shoulder, and we start moving for the airlock once more. He's still got a gun aimed at me, but really there's no need. Any last thought of resistance drained away when I saw what Bogdanovic tried. Sure, there'll be consequences for my family and my career, but I can't live waiting for some nameless fucker to act on all that. I've made up my mind on what I'm going to do right now – that's play along and behave. There's really no point in doing anything else.

We're out of the airlock and into the passage. "Take a left turn at the end," Keiyho says.

I do exactly as I'm told, facing him, keeping my hands open and my movements slow and deliberate. "Look, I'm really sorry about—"

"No talking, just keep moving."

"Oh, right, sorry."

We take several lefts and rights. Eventually, we get to corridor four, near where I was working on sealing off the wrecked hydroponics section. There are a couple of storage rooms just before the worst of it. Keiyho gestures for me to enter. I do so. It's a small space. All the boxes have been cleared out, apart from one to sit on. Major Le Garre is standing inside. She's also carrying a pistol.

"Everything okay, Commander?" she asks.

"We had a little trouble with the doctor," Keiyho replies. "I need to go back and help deal with it."

"No problem. I can handle Sellis."

"Great."

Keiyho departs and I'm left alone with the major.

The silence is pretty awkward. I'm fucking ashamed of myself. Of all the senior officers on the *Khidr*, she's the one I respect most. Sure, I'm attracted to her too, but that's a separate issue. She's always dealt me straight and honest.

"What's going to happen?" I ask softly.

Le Garre looks at me and shrugs. "In the short term, that depends on you. In terms of the investigation into Drake's murder and everything else that's happened, I'll produce a report and hand it over to Fleet Intelligence when we get back."

"You mean, *if* we get back? There's a lot that could see us dead in space long before that."

"Of course. Your friends on the *Gallowglass* could wipe us out, but I'll still be writing my report."

"They're not my friends."

"Okay, then what are they to you then?"

It's a straight question. I take a deep breath and start explaining. Once I get going, it all comes out in a confessional rush. I go over all the information that appeared on my screen, the deactivation order I gave to the cameras and how I was summoned to the bridge. While I do, Le Garre nods and listens silently, giving nothing away. When I'm done, she gives me a thin, humourless smile.

"Sounds like you did your best to dodge your way through all this. Of course, we only have your word for it."

I sigh. "I can understand you thinking like that. If Bogdanovic and I were the only survivors, then—"

"You weren't the only survivors."

I stare at her and realise my mouth is hanging open. *You weren't the only survivors.* Bogdanovic has lost it. I don't trust him to back up my recollection of events unless it suits his interests, which it won't. However, if someone else is still alive who was there, then they'll be able to validate my story.

For whatever reason, Le Garre has thrown me a bone by mentioning it.

I regain control of my jaw and bite off the instinctive questions that I want to blurt out. This isn't some kind of pity fuck. It's an incentive to do the right thing. I can't be totally desperate; that'll make the situation worse, and she's not going to wave a magic wand for me.

"I fucked up," I say at last. "I had no idea all this was coming."

"Perhaps," Le Garre says.

"It's on me. No one else is going to fix it."

"You can't go back, Jake. Some bridges are burned."

"Yeah."

I run a hand through my hair. It's slick with sweat. My face is oily too. There's been no letup since all this went down. "What's the water situation like?" I ask.

Le Garre shrugs. "We'll ration it. The scrubbers can cope for a while."

I tap the empty bottle attached to my shoulder. "Enough left for me to have some then?"

Her lips quirk. "Yes. One moment."

She steps outside and turns her back on me. While she's away, I pull the chemical cutter out of my pocket, activate the little magnet on its side and put it against the wall. Then I quickly return to my seat.

Le Garre comes back in with a replacement water bottle. I point to the cutter attached to the metal panel between us. "I kept that back from my toolkit, in case Rocher or Bogdanovic decided to get dangerous."

"Would you have helped them?" Le Garre asks.

"I'd have defended myself," I reply truthfully. "I didn't help the doctor when he decided to get violent just now."

The major plucks the cutter from the wall, deactivates the magnet and puts it in her pocket. "I'm glad you gave this up," she says.

"Just give me a fair hearing. That's all I ask."

"The more you cooperate, the easier things will be."

"I have to think about what they're threatening to do to my family and friends. I hope you understand that."

CHAPTER THIRTY-SEVEN

Shann

There was a day when I was seven or eight years old when I was left alone in the house.

I don't remember why, but I do remember waking up and pressing the call button beside my bed and no one answering. I waited for half an hour or more and started shouting to get someone's attention.

But still no one came.

I crawled to the end of the bed and tried to get into the auto-chair, but somehow it slipped out of the cradle and I couldn't reach it from where I was.

I recall looking over the edge of the bed, judging the distance. The carpet was thick and soft, but I knew I'd have to fall onto it. The trick would be to fall the right way. I'd done it before, but not when I was alone in the house. If I got hurt, there would be no one around to help.

The impact was a shock. I managed to land and roll, but I hit my head on the side of the auto-chair cradle. There was a bit of blood and some disorientation, not too bad as it turned out, but enough to give me a fright.

By now, I needed the toilet. I struggled into the chair, but because it hadn't been securely placed in the cradle the night before, the power unit had run down. I had to struggle out again and make my way down the hall to the bathroom.

It wasn't very far, but the urgency and loneliness made everything twice as hard. All the while, I kept wondering where my parents had gone and why they'd left me behind.

About an hour later, I found out why when they returned. My brother had run off, forcing them both to go and search for him. By then I'd managed to reseat the auto-chair to get it charging and made my way downstairs. They were surprised to find me in the lounge.

I never told them how frightened I was.

Now, in this moment, I have to make my way back to the bridge. I didn't expect to be moving while the ship would be decelerating, so I didn't bring my prosthetic legs with me to the strategy room.

No easy task.

The braking means I'm drawn to the far wall of the room, pushing against the straps like I'm hanging above the ground. The door is to my right. I'll have to work my way around toward it. My hands close over the safety release and I hesitate. I'm remembering what happened to Drake. The fall for him had been under six g. For me it will be less than one, but it's still dangerous.

I press the button and raise my arms. There's a shrill alarm from the chair, and the wall rushes toward me. I manage to avoid hitting the table and bump into the wall. The impact is sudden, but not too painful. I manage to roll, using some of the momentum to get closer to the door. I crawl the rest of the way and manage to climb up the wall to press the door access. The panel slides away, and I grab hold of the frame with my fingertips, lifting myself up.

The passageway is fairly easy to manage. I can feel the shifting of our ship's braking. It makes the sensation strange and not like Earth gravity at all. You get little shifts in a generated gravity environment too, but they aren't this pronounced.

The large lounge gym will be much more difficult to get through. We don't usually come up here when the torus isn't spinning. There are fixed tables and chairs that are sideways to me, acting like a crazy climbing frame. Small indentations in the floor help too. I think I can see a path to the lift shaft.

Navigating the *Khidr* like this would test anyone. We've had some practice in orientation training, but Fleet designs its ships to ensure you don't have to move far in the event of an emergency. That's why there are safety seats in every space, just in case of sudden acceleration or deceleration. You might need to move around if you had to get to an escape craft, but even then, the ship is designed to prevent that. Rooms and corridors are sealable containers with emergency air and water, ensuring you're already in a lifeboat all the time.

"Shann to Keiyho."

"Yes, Captain?"

"I'm in the rec room. This better be worth it."

"It is, Captain, trust me."

I'm getting a better sense of my ability to fling myself around. I get to the end of the corridor and reach out, ensuring I have a good two-handed grip on a chair base and then pull myself off the edge of the door. Once I'm balanced I reach out again, this time to grab a chair.

Progress is slow, steady and exhausting. Someone with legs would take more risks, leaping or jumping the gaps, but there's danger in doing that. For me, it's no option, so my journey is gradual and repetitive across seats, tables and couches.

A fresh challenge comes when I get to the end of the recreation area. There's an open space in front of the lift shaft. I'm looking for handholds on the floor that has become a smooth, manufactured cliff face. There are fingertip holds between metal floor tiles and DuraGlas plates, but it's too far to rely on those. Instead, I rip open the emergency tab on my suit sleeve and activate the interior magnetics. There's enough charge to polarise all the contact points in my clothing to hold me suspended on the floor. The difficulty will be ripping away from each connection to continue to make progress.

This was the method Chase and Keiyho used to get to the bridge, only they had boots and gloves designed for exterior traverse. All I have is my suit's emergency charge that isn't designed to be flipped on and off. Still, needs must.

I make it to the lift shaft. I'm able to slide down it on my backside and tumble out into the deck at the bottom. Shah is there with a plasma torch, working on reinforcing a bulkhead. He's strapped into a bracing harness. He turns toward me, pushing up his safety goggles.

"You need a hand, Captain?" he asks.

"Have to get to the bridge," I pant in reply.

Shah nods. He slips off his mag-gloves and hands them to me. "Looks like you've done the hard bit," he says. "I can manage without these. Might make the next section easier."

"Thank you," I say and make my way out.

"You're welcome, Captain," Shah calls after me.

★　　★　　★

Ten minutes later, I'm through the bridge door and climbing into the spare seat. I take out my portable screen and plug it in. "All right, Travers, this better be good."

Travers spins around in his chair as I'm strapping myself in. It's just him and Keiyho on the bridge. "We've picked up an object on the closer range scan. It didn't show up on our laser sweep."

"Didn't show up? Why?"

"It appears to be made of an ultra-absorbent material, Captain." Travers's fingers sweep across his console, and a short-range scanning plot appears on the screen in my hands. "You can see, the original laser sweep was hitting it, but just disappearing, leaving a small blind spot in our plotting field. Occasionally there are glitches like that, so I think our computer system was filtering it out as a data error. However, we're a lot closer now and…well…it's there."

Laser field sweeps are designed so any reflection, diffusion or refraction of the beam is detected by the instrumentation. This is what gives us an accurate picture of our surroundings. However, some materials are known to absorb light to such a degree they look like holes. "Does that mean our scan was inaccurate?" I ask. "We can't know if anything was behind this object, can we?"

"Well, we do now," Keiyho says. "Our change of course meant the local communications relay's position changed in relation to ours. It passed behind the object and disappeared for a moment. That's what caused us to find it."

"How far away is it?"

Travers checks his screen. "We'll pass within six metres in about… five minutes."

"How big is it?"

"We estimate it's a complete sphere, the size of a large beach ball."

"And our relative velocity?"

Keiyho smiles. "If you mean are we travelling slowly enough to grab the object, Lieutenant Travers and I have already come up with a plan to do just that. We were going to raise you on the comms to make a decision about it if you didn't make it here in time."

"Good thinking," I say. I find myself smiling too, despite my exhaustion. Keiyho's expression is infectious. "What's your assessment?"

Keiyho shrugs. "Truly, Captain, I have no idea. It could be an explosive charge, but I've never seen one like it. I did a cross-reference check with the data archive you unlocked, and there's no mention of a weapon designed like this."

"Maybe there should be. Super dark chemical coatings aren't difficult to produce."

"No, they're not, but there is nothing to indicate we're looking at a weapon."

I glance around the mostly empty bridge. "Who else knows about this?"

"Just us, Captain," Keiyho replies. "Although anyone you met en route might be curious as to why you were called here."

Another marginal decision to make. "Okay, let's do this," I order.

"Of course." Keiyho swivels away from me and hunches over his console. After a moment he announces, "Bafflers deployed."

The ship's bafflers are large steel nets designed to harvest objects from our immediate vicinity. Ships use them to capture and clear away debris or to pick up samples for analysis. In this case, they'll do the job, entangling the object and drawing it into the collector so we can bring it inside. The only danger will be our speed. An encounter at high velocity would tear right through the metal mesh.

"Time to dead stop?" I ask.

"Twenty-eight minutes," Travers says.

I turn to the screen in front of me and key up some of the readouts from the strategy room. I'm thinking about the message from Admiral Langsley and his harassed face on the video file. Keiyho and Travers won't ask about the video, but I know they're curious. The choice is made. I can't tell them what I saw and heard. Instead, I try to get my mind on the issue at hand.

The laser scan is on my screen, and now that Keiyho has removed the computer compensation, I can see the gap in the readout. It's like a dark wound in the spherical sweep, getting wider as it moves farther away from the ship, as if there's something out there blocking our view of anything behind it. Some complex triangulation has verified the object's position, but we still can't be completely sure of its exact coordinates owing to its ultra-dark surface.

"Distance to baffler intercept?" I ask.

"Twenty-five kilometres," Travers says.

I'm staring at the data. "Has it moved? It seems very convenient that it would pass this close to us, unless there are lots of them out there."

"There's no suggestion that it has altered position since we detected it, Captain," Keiyho says. "As a precaution, I'll be keeping it outside of the ship and we'll do a thermal conductivity test."

"Good plan," I say.

"You're not wrong about this being a lucky find, though," Travers mutters.

"Our albatross," I muse. "Only it's supposed to arrive before we're becalmed, so we can bring the curse upon ourselves. Maybe we did that anyway."

"If you say so, Captain," Travers replies, clearly not getting the reference.

"Never mind."

The numbers descend and the bafflers rotate into position. Keiyho is having to run an isolated calibration to operate them, as we're currently fooling the *Khidr*'s computer into managing our slow deceleration. I pull up an exterior view. Many of the cameras were knocked out in the last altercation with the *Gallowglass*, so the angle isn't great, but I can see the nets.

"Time?"

"Forty-five seconds."

I don't know whether the object will hit the section I'm looking at, but I can't take my eyes off the window on my screen. There's something strangely enticing about trying to spot something you know is almost impossible to see.

"Fifteen seconds."

I glance at Travers and Keiyho. They are both fixated on their screens. The last moments evaporate in silence until there's a catch in Keiyho's breathing. That's the only sign of his achievement.

"The object is collected, Captain," he says.

CHAPTER THIRTY-EIGHT

Johansson

Arkov's bullet wound is minor. The slug grazed his biceps. Thankfully, as it came from a low-velocity firearm, there wasn't much danger of explosive decompression. That's why they have these gas-powered guns. Body armour in space is pretty impractical, so the military thinking is that any combat would involve unarmoured opponents and that the integrity of a pressurised environment needs to be preserved. In a zero g atmosphere, there's less degradation of velocity, so there needs to be less velocity to start with, provided there's still enough to punch through flesh.

Pretty awful business when you think someone had to work all that out.

I seal the wound with a solvent strip. Battlefield injuries have been treated with a variation of this stuff since the 1970s. These days, the bonding agent is designed to degrade in a specified time, so in seventy-two hours, I'll be checking Arkov's injury again.

If we survive that long.

"You'll do for now, Vasili. Take it steady and you'll hardly feel it. I'll come find you when the seal needs to be changed."

"Thank you."

Once he's left, I open up the tactical and strategy information on my portable screen. The conversation with Captain Shann was frustrating. I put together the audio she asked for, but even if we herd the *Gallowglass* in, just as she wants, we're still at a disadvantage.

We need something else.

I played chess as a child. I loved the board and all the game components, particularly the tall queen. When I was very young, I would make up stories about her as the real power in an imaginary kingdom, ruling alongside an ineffectual king. However, when I played, my tactical game would fall apart when there was a need to exchange and sacrifice my pieces for my opponents. I'd made up characters for the knights, the rooks, the bishops and the pawns. I didn't want to lose any of them.

I really didn't want to lose the queen.

Maybe there's something of that in Captain Shann. After losing so many of the crew to a mutiny, betrayal and warfare, maybe she's clutching hold of us too tight. Sometimes leaders have to order their soldiers to take risks, or follow an order that'll probably get them killed.

I go through the data again, looking at the captain's proposals. Our chances are better, but they're still not good enough. Of all the ideas I've had, the propelled vehicle with someone going EVA still offers the best increase in our odds. That said, I was definitely wrong about sending a team. We can't afford to lose more crew.

However, we could send one person.

Me.

I use the screen to locate and alert Sam Chase. He's returned to the ship's stores. I don't try to message him, just send a request for him to meet me in medical.

He arrives a couple of minutes later, looking a little irritated at being summoned.

"Something you want?"

"You said you owed me a favour?"

"Yes, although I thought I'd paid it back by sorting the medical inventory."

"Ah, okay then, I need a favour from you."

"What do you want?"

I'm hesitating to make my request. Once I say what I want, I can't take it back. This is a crazy idea, the kind of risk heroes and fools take. I'm neither.

"You remember you said we needed to throw out the rule book if we were going to survive?"

"Yeah, and you set me straight." Sam gives me an inquiring look. "You want to open up that discussion again?"

"Not really." I pull out my portable screen and hand it to him. "I need you to help me make these modifications, in less than an hour, without telling anyone."

Sam stares at the screen. I know how much he's read by the changing expression on his face. "You want to do... This is fucking nuts."

"I've done the calculations. It's the best chance we have to improve our odds against their ship. Can it be done?"

"What's the chance you'll survive?"

"Not...great."

Sam glares at me. "Either way, I get court-martialed for letting you try and kill yourself." He hands the screen back to me. "In answer to your question, yes it can be done. The oxygen tank and manoeuvering thrusters you want can be rigged up pretty quickly because we've already stripped out a couple of torpedoes. I doubt Duggins will notice one of them going missing."

"You'll help me then?"

"I didn't say that."

I glare at him. "I'm not doing this to die. I've done the math."

"I don't doubt it." Sam sighs and rubs his face. "If we do pack you into an empty torpedo with an oxygen cylinder and a couple of thrusters, wired up to a portable screen, we make a very neat little manned carrier. If we weren't going into combat, I'd consider doing this and adding some of our robotic tools from the drone garage to make a really awesome little repair and rescue vehicle. But there's a big difference between doing this then and doing it now. What the fuck do you think you're going to do out there?"

"Did you scroll down?" I ask.

Sam smiles. "No, I stopped when I realised you were trying to murder yourself."

"If I can get close enough to the *Gallowglass*, I can make use of the information we have on their ship to interfere with the control system. We can win."

"And if they notice you?"

"That's the risk I have to take. Our chance of defeating the *Gallowglass* without taking a chance like this is next to zero."

"Has it occurred to you that someone else might already have a shit crazy plan and that by going all lone gun, you're getting in the way?"

"That's a good point," I say. It is a good point, a really good point. Maybe I am being arrogant, thinking Captain Shann or Engineer Duggins haven't already come up with some special sauce to go on their strategy that they're not telling us about. "I don't want to get in the way, but if we don't know what they're doing…"

"My turn to remind you about the chain of command."

"That's fair." I look at the screen again, trying to figure out what Shann or Duggins could be planning. I can't see anything that would make a massive difference. "How about we put this together and make a go or no-go decision when we have a better idea of what's happening?"

"So, we prepare our insubordination and choose whether to disobey orders if we don't like what's going on?"

"No one specifically told us we shouldn't be doing this."

Sam laughs. "That's a game of words and you know it, Ensign. Captain Shann will see right through it." His expression grows serious. "I'm not going to let you kill yourself, April."

He's looking at me. The appeal is honest and frank. He's right; there's no point in me taking a mad risk that'll make no difference to whether we all live or die. But then, if we have to die out here, at least I can choose my ending.

And besides, I genuinely believe this will work.

"It's a tough task. I'm under no illusions about it, but I'm not planning to die. If I was, I wouldn't be asking you to help me."

Sam scowls, but he's nodding now. "All right, we put this together, but if there's another way—"

"If it ups the odds, of course, we go for it."

"Good." Sam pulls out his own portable screen. "There's a whole set of issues you haven't thought about, though."

"Like what?"

"Like how are you going to launch your little ship?"

I nod and smile. He's partially right, but it costs me nothing to concede the point. "I'd thought we'd mix me up with the other torpedoes being launched as mines."

"That would work, but unfortunately, Duggins has fixed the launcher, so the ignition velocity would likely tear your little ship apart. Even if it didn't, you wouldn't have enough thrust to maneuver toward the *Gallowglass* from an undirected position. No, you need a low-powered launch, aimed in the right direction."

"Okay, can we do that?"

"Thankfully, yes, as I'm operating one of the launchers. Before that, the captain wants to jettison another load of debris, which I need to total up and sign off. That'll give me some time to work on these changes."

"Great."

Sam gestures down the corridor. "In the meantime, Shann's called some of the crew to the airlock. We should show our faces before we do this."

"What does she want?"

"We should go and find out."

238 • ALLEN STROUD

CHAPTER THIRTY-NINE

Shann

"The *Gallowglass* is thirty minutes from range."

The *Khidr* is at dead stop at the end of a self-generated debris field with just over three per cent of fuel reserves left. The moment we arrived, I gave orders for Bogdanovic and Sellis to be moved so we could bring in what we snagged in the bafflers. Now, I'm outside the airlock, with Quartermaster Sam Chase, Technician Arkov, Major Le Garre and Ensign Johansson. We're staring at what I know is a round sphere, but my mind refuses to accept this. Instead, it looks like a hole in the middle of the room.

"It's so strange," Arkov says. "No matter what angle you look at it, you can't get a sense of its size or shape."

"We determine shape by the way light reflects off things," Johansson explains. "There's no discernible reflection, so there's no way our eyes can work out the dimensions of what we're looking at. The sensors say it's a sphere, and I guess if we could touch it, we'd feel that."

"The question is, what's it doing out here?" Le Garre asks.

"No idea," Arkov says, "but we are registering a temperature drop and a small atmospheric drain in the room. The object appears to be absorbing both the heat and the gas around it."

"Like it's feeding or breathing." I'm thinking out loud.

"Was it wise bringing it on board, Captain?" Le Garre asks. "Our course change to this location can't have been a coincidence."

"It probably wasn't a coincidence," I say. "The *Gallowglass* must have known about this being here. However, the conductivity tests don't register any kind of residual output."

"None at all?"

"No. Not even a heat trace, which is very unusual."

Johansson looks at me; she seems annoyed. "Do you think there were more of them? I mean, we only noticed this one because Keiyho and Travers spotted the anomaly in our scan readout. The computer would have passed detecting this off as a glitch."

"You think there's a chance we missed a few others?" I ask.

"Well, yeah." Johansson runs her hand through her hair. "Our scan records go back weeks. We might have missed hundreds of them."

"Something to analyse when we have more time," I say.

Le Garre turns away from the window. "What are you going to do with Bogdanovic and Sellis?" she asks me.

"I want Bogdanovic on the comms telling the *Gallowglass* we've surrendered."

"How're you going to convince him to do that?"

"I'm not sure yet."

Johansson taps on the DuraGlas. "What's the plan with that, Captain?" she asks, pointing at the black sphere.

I shrug. "Again, I don't know. I saw something on a drone feed when we were exploring the *Hercules* just before it went out. There was some kind of packing crate that held objects like that."

"You think they had these on the *Hercules*?"

"If they did, people allied to our enemies stole them. Like you said, Major, it can't have been a coincidence we picked this up here. The *Gallowglass* must know it's in this location. They must have planned to retrieve it or for us to retrieve it."

"We can't spare the time to analyse it beyond the basics," Le Garre says. "If it's some kind of weapon they left for us, we've done their job for them."

"The decision is made. We'll see what they say about it," I say.

Johansson frowns. "It's completely laser absorbent, right?"

"Yes, the surface is more light absorbent than any material talked about on Earth."

"Could we fire it at one of their turrets? Jam it right in front of their weapons?"

"I'm not sure how we'd do that," Le Garre says.

"When we solve that, we start considering it as a tactic," I reply. "Arkov, can you get it to the rocket ordnance chamber?"

"Yes, of course, Captain."

I turn to Johansson. "How much longer do we have left on your little composition?"

Johansson grins. "About ten minutes; then we go radio silent. You'll want to get Bogdanovic talking to them before they reach weapon's range."

I nod. "Time I went down there then."

"Probably," she says.

★   ★   ★

The storeroom has been emptied, but it's still cramped with three people inside. Bogdanovic is blindfolded and strapped into the acceleration chairs. Chase is standing by the door with Taser in hand.

I've prepared myself as best I can. The personnel files on both of our prisoners are extensive. Bogdanovic has worked as a doctor in a variety of off-Earth assignments for the last fifteen years. Sellis is career military, a specialist on system maintenance drafted in from the army, and was one of the reasons the *Khidr* has stayed intact after we faced the *Gallowglass* the first time.

Or at least, that's what I thought back then.

"Is that you, Captain?" Bogdanovic asks as the door closes behind me.

"It is," I reply. He looks pathetic, confined as he is, but we've no choice but to manage things like this. "I need your help."

"You've considered my offer?"

"I need you to tell the captain of the *Gallowglass* that we have surrendered to you. I need you to use the code words you were given to ensure him that our surrender is authentic and that you have full command of this ship."

"Why would I do that, Captain Shann?"

I hesitate and glance at Sam. He nods, encouraging me to go on. "You'll do it, because if you don't, you'll die here, blindfolded and strapped to a chair."

Bogdanovic forces out a laugh. "Not much of an incentive. I don't believe you'll murder me."

I sigh. "Doctor, you need to realise this is the only option on the table. I'm going to lead the *Khidr* into battle with or without your cooperation. If you help, the odds of your survival go up a bit. If you don't…" I pause, leaving the sentence hanging for a moment or two. "I'll go next door and tell Sellis you're helping us."

Bogdanovic's sweaty face pinches. "Sellis won't believe you," he says. "You left it too long to play that card, Captain."

"Perhaps," I say. "But we'll only know if I have to try. I spent a fair amount of time digging into his background and yours, looking for something to work with. Did you know he owes some pretty dangerous people a lot of money?"

"It doesn't matter whether I did or didn't."

"Okay, well you have nothing to worry about then."

I move away and out of the room. Tomlins's old place is a few metres along the corridor. I go inside. Sellis is in there, similarly strapped into a chair with Le Garre standing over him. I remove the blindfold. Sellis stares at me and I stare back.

I'm trying to remember what I know about him. He's always been in the crowd, behind others when it came to volunteering for anything. A classic second, probably a good place to be when you're trying to hide something.

"Seems you got yourself in a lot of trouble, Specialist," I say.

Sellis flinches but doesn't reply.

"I'm here to offer you a way out, if you'll take it."

Two blinks. I can't read anything from that.

I decide to lay out my cards. "Sellis, I need you to tell the *Gallowglass* we've surrendered to you and give them whatever code word they've told you to say. If you don't, I'll fight them anyway and our chance of winning will be less. If you want a better chance of surviving, you need to lie to these people."

Sellis blinks again, and for a moment, there's a spark of something. Could it be hope? "I don't care about surviving," he says. "This isn't about me."

I nod, remembering the records. "You had a wife and a daughter, right?"

"Yeah."

"And you're divorced."

"Uh-huh."

"You're worried about them?"

Sellis grunts. "More than worried. The minute I do anything, they'll be executed. You can't protect them. No one can."

"What's your way out?" I ask.

"Huh?"

"What are you trying to do to get safe and away from these people? You must have some kind of plan."

"I thought they'd stop. I never dreamed I'd end up in a situation like this."

"Bullshit." I lean in until our faces are inches apart. "You've played this well, but you have to have a way out. What did they offer you?"

Sellis flinches again, looking away from me toward Le Garre. I turn to her and she shakes her head, slowly and deliberately. "They said I could disappear," he mumbles. "After this tour, I would be totally out. No debts, new identity, the works."

"And what guarantee did they give you that they'll leave you alone?"

Sellis doesn't reply.

I look at Le Garre. She shrugs. I turn back to Sellis. "Do you know the people on the *Gallowglass*?" I ask.

Sellis shakes his head. "No, only Rocher did. Bogdanovic introduced him to us and said he'd verified himself."

"Do you have a code to verify yourself to the *Gallowglass* if you took over the ship?"

"Yeah. I think we all do, or did."

"Sellis, you know these people will keep using you. They'll make you betray everyone you care about until there's no one left. Your daughter will only be safe if you find a way out, a proper way out."

"What are you suggesting?"

"After this fight. We'll register you as dead. After we get to Phobos, you can disappear. Your family will be safe if everyone thinks you're dead."

Sellis stares at me. There's that spark again. It stays for a while this time. "I can't trust them. Why should I trust you?"

"Because you've been on this ship with me; you know me. Have I ever lied to you?"

"No...you haven't..."

"You agree then?"

"Yeah, okay."

I turn to Le Garre. "Get him out of here and in a room with access to comms. I want Ensign Chiu there as well. When the moment comes, they can both send the message with their verifications."

Le Garre nods. "I'll get to it, Captain," she says.

I'm at the door. I look at Sellis. "You're doing the right thing, Specialist," I say.

He tries to smile, but the expression is twisted and painful. "I hope so," he says.

★   ★   ★

Humanity has always been fascinated with the concept of extraterrestrial life. Our religions constantly looked to the stars to explain our origins. Later, artists and writers flouted the constraints of dogma to imagine heaven and hell beyond this world, tying all things into a series of mythologies that could not be disproved with the evidence at hand.

Later, religion was forced to retreat as our knowledge disproved much of the speculation of great thinkers. Our world expanded but became less and less defined. We were forced to adopt an evidence-based approach to our understanding, and this enabled our advancement.

However, our imaginations remain a part of who we are. We still look into space and try to explain the unexplainable. In our colonisation of the solar system, we have reached out farther and farther than ever before and discovered xenobiological life, but not intelligent neighbours. So, the mythology remains and we continue to imagine answers to the question, are they out there, or are we alone?

When this question is considered, another argument becomes prominent: do we know all there is to know? Conspiracy theories about alien encounters have swirled around since Roswell in the 1940s and before. Interpretive opinion that links ancient societies together claims either that we came from the stars or that we were fostered by aliens, alternately, depending on which paranoid fantasy is popular at the time. There are stories of military cover-ups, abductions, mysterious recordings and more. Some fragmented half-truths make us see shadows in the darkness. Evidence-based research is supplanted by fiction, and we return to the same speculative storytelling as our ancestors, huddling together and dreaming of the possible.

A mysterious intelligence, existing beyond our world. Lurking and observing us. Leaving clues for us to find, assessing our responses. Recording their observations and assessing our technology before deciding to reach out...

CHAPTER FORTY
Johansson

I remember being five. I was on my own at home. It probably wasn't for long, maybe an hour or so, but for me, it felt like forever.

I was playing with my toy cars in my room. Something happened and one of them ended up under the bed, out of my reach. I lay on the floor and stretched out my left arm, getting my fingers to it, but I couldn't pull it out.

I remember looking at the gap between the frame and the floor. There was enough room for me to be able to squeeze under there, so I did, wriggling my way right up to the car and grabbing it.

It was only then that I realised I couldn't get back out. For some reason, I just couldn't push myself back the way I'd crawled in.

By the time my mother came home, I was screaming. She heard me and lifted the bed so I could escape. Afterward, she hugged and scolded me, saying I should never do anything like that again.

Now, I'm disobeying her.

The metal plate under my feet is hot. I have to keep shifting my toes so they don't get burned through the soles of my heavy-duty EVA boots. I know what's causing it. Sam Chase is busy with a welding iron and chemical sealant, wedging me into the hollowed-out body of a torpedo, along with a drone's manoeuvering thruster, a portable data screen and an oxygen supply.

My field of vision is intentionally limited. The helmet of my EVA suit faces the touchscreen display. My left hand is bent up in front of my face so I can operate it by moving my wrist and my fingers. For now, I have my visor up, which makes things a bit less claustrophobic. I'll need to pull it down before I get outside.

I must be crazy thinking this would work, but there's no turning back now. We have ten minutes and there are still three plates to fix.

"What are you doing in here?"

The words are muffled but spoken with an inflection of surprise. I shift my head as much as I can to look out of the gap that Sam has yet to weld shut, but I can't see the speaker. I hear shuffling as Sam gets up.

"Vasili, please, this has nothing to do with you."

It's Airlock Technician Arkov. He's turned up at the worst possible time. There's silence. I know the two men are staring at each other. I recall what happened between them before; Sam accused Arkov of being a traitor and chased him into the gravity deck.

I'm trapped in here. I can't get involved. Whatever they decide will be my fate.

"Okay, I'm not going to rush to any conclusions," Arkov says coolly. "But, in light of everything that's happened, you'll understand why I'm going to need an explanation for what you're doing."

"You don't want to be involved," Sam says.

"I'll be the judge of that. Tell me the plan or I buzz the captain."

After another pause, Sam begins to talk, grudgingly. "Johansson's in here. It's her plan. She wants to use the torpedo as a vehicle to get over to the other ship. She thinks she can disable it, if she can get close enough."

"And you're going along with this?"

"I owe her a favour."

"And you're repaying that by letting her kill herself?"

I'm not waiting for this to resolve itself. I tap the screen, activating the comms panel, and buzz Arkov directly, enabling the secure channel protocol. Under normal circumstances, all comms traffic would be monitored and recorded, but no one has time right now. The ship's computer will flag the secure encryption for the attention of the bridge officers, but it'll be a while before someone picks it up.

"Vasili? It's me."

"April. This is crazy, you know that?"

"It's a little crazy," I concede. "But I've done all the calculations. There are good margins for doing this. That's why Sam's helping."

"He says he owes you."

"Yes, he does, and so do you."

Arkov laughs. "If you mean your patching up of my arm, I'm grateful, but come on! Assisting a suicide is not a comparable transaction."

I sigh. "We don't have time for this. Make your choice."

"Sorry?"

"I said make your choice. Report me or help me. The *Gallowglass* will be here in minutes. I'll not waste more time fencing with you." I shut down the comms.

After a minute, I hear muffled voices. Sam and Vasili have moved away to talk about me. That's fine, but they need to hurry up and decide. I shift my position a little, easing the pressure on my shoulders, but causing a section of the casing to dig into my ribs.

A metal plate comes down over the gap near my face, and there's a chemical smell. *Decision made.* I flip down my visor and try to move my head away from where Sam is working. I can feel the heat on my neck through the EVA suit, but it's bearable. Whatever Arkov has opted for, we're carrying on.

That means I just have to wait.

It's dark in here, like it was under the bed. I remember closing my eyes and trying to think of another way out. A part of me couldn't stop thinking about the frame and mattress pressing down on my skull and my chest. If someone sat down above me, I'd be crushed. Which of my bones would break first?

Looking back, I stoked myself up into a panic. It was a ridiculous, delusional fear. No one would have gotten on the bed without seeing me and hearing my cries for help. My feet were probably sticking out and would have been the first thing my mother saw when she came home.

This time, it's different. I'm safe enough for now, but once I get out in space I'll be at the mercy of the speed at which I'm ejected from the *Khidr* launch tube. Most of the drone jet fuel will be needed to slow me down. Otherwise, if I somehow manage to be pointed in the right direction, I'll crash into the *Gallowglass* and the metal shell of the torpedo will crumple in around me, breaking my bones a lot more easily than any mattress might have done all those years ago.

We might have been able to avoid that risk if we'd launched earlier. Captain Shann has deployed several torpedoes as maneuverable assets in the debris field. If I'd been one of those, I would have had more control over my velocity, but we weren't ready, and I'd have been out in space too long. My oxygen supply would never have lasted, and the *Gallowglass* would have had a lot longer to identify me, acquire a target solution and turn me into dust.

I reset the screen to its previous window, the tactical position plot of the *Khidr* and the *Gallowglass*. Sam has mounted a tiny camera to the exterior of the torpedo's warhead casing, along with a drone arm, which I can control from here. The problem is both additions are pretty obvious to spot. He'll need to smuggle me into one of the launch chambers and load me up before anyone notices. That'll require some quick work and quick thinking.

I run some basic calculations again, making sure all the files I'm working with are locally hosted. If all goes well, in a few minutes, I'll be far away from the *Khidr*, so making use of the central storage drive won't be an option. It's surprising how you can become used to having all these resources at hand and forget about what you're using after months and months of working with the same equipment.

I touch a finger to the new metal plate, pushing against it. There's no movement. The weld is solid. A moment later the casing around me shifts and I hear a muffled thud. Sam has detached the torpedo from the clasps he was using to hold it while he worked on sealing me in. He must be moving me to the launcher.

That means Arkov must have at least agreed to look the other way.

I flick up the visor and breathe carefully, trying to stay calm. All of the crew have biomonitoring, and although Bogdanovic is not going to be monitoring the screens while he's locked up, the computer system will alert the captain if my heart rate goes too high. Being chucked out of a torpedo tube might be cause enough to trigger that, but by then it'll be too late. What I can do without is any kind of alert beforehand that ruins my chances of getting clear.

There's a beep in my ear, and my screen registers an incoming comms request from Sam. It's unencrypted. I key it up. "How's things going?" I ask.

"All on schedule now," Sam replies. "We've gained an extra pair of hands."

"That's helpful," I say.

"Yeah, it'll help with a few of the difficult jobs coming up."

"Great." The channel clicks off.

I bring up the exterior camera. There's something partially covering the lens, but I do get a slanted image of the corridor we're moving down. I run the adaptive visual recognition system, and text and lines start appearing around each blurry object, identifying and cataloguing everything it can see. I'll need this when I'm outside in the dark. The computer optics are far superior to anything I can eyeball.

The screen goes dark. I hear muffled voices again and there's another *clump*. I'm being packed into the firing tube, I hope, or I'm being put back on a rack and this isn't going to plan. There's a comms channel click on the screen, then another one. That'll be from Sam, two clicks for success, three clicks if something's gone wrong.

I wait for a third click.

It doesn't come.

CHAPTER FORTY-ONE

Shann

"She's here, Captain."

"Broadcast the message."

"Aye, aye."

I'm on the bridge with Keiyho, Le Garre, Chiu and Travers. Duggins is lurking somewhere in the ship's bowels. The rest of the crew are at battle stations. Chase is with Sellis. The message he prerecorded with Chiu has been sent. All we can hope is that the *Gallowglass* crew believe what they hear and that our two traitors haven't sold us out.

This time, we're prepared. Everyone is wearing emergency suits, with a portable oxygen supply. If any compartment of the ship is compromised, the crew will have a chance to survive.

The bridge shutters are drawn back. I can see into the darkness. We're drifting in a field of our own debris. There's something serene and peaceful about it all. The silence of a lethal void that waits for us, *waits for me…*

"Two minutes since broadcast, Captain. No change of heading."

I can't see the enemy ship. I won't be able to see her until she's almost on top of us. "What's her trajectory?" I ask.

"About fifteen metres leeward of where we'd hoped," Keiyho says.

"That's acceptable. Adjust targeting to compensate but do it slowly. I don't want them working us out."

"Aye, aye."

The *Gallowglass* is in range. We can attack. But, if we do, they'll return fire. We must be absolutely sure we can hit them hard enough so there will be no retaliation.

"What's their velocity of approach?"

"They're decelerating. Four hundred metres per second and slowing."

"Shann to Arkov, are you ready down there?"

"All prepped, Captain."

"Good."

On the high seas, warships were at their most effective if they could bring all their cannon to bear. These were situated belowdecks on the port and starboard sides. A man-of-war would have to turn to attack, raking her enemy as she came alongside. Of course, this made her vulnerable to the same broadside. The only way to win was to create an advantage. For a time, that lay in the training of gun crews, with one ship faster at reloading than another. After that, came ingenuity and innovation. Ironclads, rifling, breech loading, manufactured ammunition and others. The range of combat increased. Invention outstripped construction, resulting in mismatched battles between obsolete ships and modern killers.

And now, here we are, the obsolete ship, waiting for the enemy. The only way we can win is to ensure the fight is on our terms.

Up close and personal.

Le Garre is hunched forward over her controls. The minute we need to move, we'll be relying on her. Like me, she'll be matched against her opposite number. Reaction time, manual dexterity, perception, anticipation, all of these will be factors in their intimate duel.

I'm the same, competing for survival against an unknown enemy. Both of these duels are related to a whole host of other factors, meaning any victory might not be decisive. The technology available to us compared to that exhibited by our enemy weighs the engagement in their favour.

I can see Le Garre's hands trembling. She's been operating on minimal sleep, like the rest of us. We're all trained to deal with fatigue and exhaustion, but it'll still affect her responses. She'll make mistakes; we all will. So will the people out there, trying to murder us.

I think about Johansson. Her fine mind for detail would make her an asset up here, but she's the only person we have with decent medical experience. We need her downstairs. Besides, right now, we need to be a machine. Her EVA actions tell me she's a little too ready to use her initiative. I need people who won't exceed their responsibilities. Travers can manage her post and he won't go off plan. Keiyho won't do that either. Chiu definitely won't do that. I can tell by the shame she can't keep from her face.

"*Gallowglass* is two hundred klicks out," Keiyho says. "Still slowing on approach. I'm getting signs of weapon discharge. They're clearing a path to us."

"Good." I shift around in my chair. Our plan requires a careful series of actions performed in sequence to give us the best possible chance. There are two objectives. The first, to survive this encounter; the second, to survive a return trip to Phobos. We can't do either without some on-the-fly innovation of our own. We'll need to adapt to whatever happens as well. No plan ever works perfectly.

"Shann to Duggins, are we ready?"

The exhausted Texan's face appears on my screen. "As ready as we'll ever be, Captain," he says.

In the totality of assessment, there is only loss and pain to come. War is always about cost. Resources will be destroyed; people will be wounded, maimed and killed. However, if we do not fight, we will die. I can't accept there is any other possible outcome. The compromises of surrender, perception and responsibility are behind us.

This is where we are; this is our path.

The *Khidr* shudders. I look at Keiyho, who shrugs. Could have been a small collision with some of our debris. "Start a visual scan of the hull," I order.

"The *Gallowglass* is still out of range. It's likely to be nothing, Captain," Keiyho replies.

"I know, but we can't afford to take that chance."

Keiyho initiates the sweep. I begin checking the exterior cameras as well. The process keeps me occupied and calms me. We don't have full coverage anymore, but we have to check as much as possible.

Our plan is not without precedent. Superior enemies have been lured into traps throughout history. Moments like this, before the fighting begins, are difficult to bear.

"Range, one hundred and twenty kilometres," Chiu says. "*Gallowglass* is still braking. Speed now one hundred metres per second."

"At that speed, it'll be twenty minutes to point-blank range," Le Garre says.

"They'll slow down further. Otherwise they'll overshoot," Travers replies.

"If we're unfortunate, that might be their plan," Keiyho says.

I'm watching the windows on my screen. The *Khidr* has rotated away from the *Gallowglass*'s path, but I have the tactical plot in front of me. The velocity and distance numbers are reducing fast. Our system is also tracking the drifting objects between us. One after another disappears as the *Gallowglass*'s point defence systems destroy each potential collision hazard.

With each moment that they don't open fire on us, our chances improve.

"Update on our assets in the field."

Three tags appear on my screen. "All dormant and intact, Captain," Keiyho says. "They've not passed any of them yet."

"Any reaction or targeting?"

"Not that I can see."

I'm staring at the tactical ID of the *Gallowglass*, trying to imagine what their captain might be thinking and deciding. What would I do in their place, faced with an enemy ship that appears to be dormant? "Are they trying to make contact?" I ask.

"They are," Travers replies. "There's a constant loop auto-broadcast. I expect they'll go to actual if they get a reply."

"Let's hear it," I order.

Travers nods and after a moment, a synthesised male voice echoes through the bridge comms. "Fleet patrol, this is *Gallowglass*. We acknowledge your transmission. Stand by for further instructions.... Fleet patrol—" Abruptly, the sentence cuts out.

"That's on repeat," Travers says. "I didn't think you needed to hear a second round of the same."

"Doesn't give anything away," Le Garre remarks.

"*Gallowglass* is about to pass the first asset," Keiyho says. "Your orders, Captain?"

"Maintain position," I tell him. "We need their full attention on us before we make a move."

"It'll delay the response time."

"We'll manage that," I reply.

"Range is ninety kilometres," Le Garre says.

"Speculation on their planned defence?" I ask.

Keiyho spins around in his chair, so do Le Garre and Travers. "They'll have their electronic interference net deployed," Keiyho says.

"If they see anything that might be hostile, they'll activate lasers first and try to cut us apart."

"Primary target?"

"Here, the bridge. If they can destroy or isolate our controls, the rest of the ship is defenceless."

"Other usual targets will be power and propulsion," Travers says.

"They think we're out of fuel," Le Garre points out, "and they won't want to damage the cargo by blowing up a nuclear power unit."

"Last resort then," Travers says.

"If they're sending a boarding party, how many can we expect?" I ask.

"Two, maybe three. We can handle them."

"And without that number of crew, they might be weaker." I turn to my console, activating the comms. "Shann, to Arkov. Time to depressurise the airlock."

"Aye, aye, Captain," Arkov replies.

I turn off the comms channel. "We need to wait until they're aboard; then we attack."

"Analysing their tactics so far, there's no reason to believe they'll hesitate to murder their own people," Keiyho says. "Whatever they want from this ship is what's keeping us alive."

I nod. "It's a matter of percentages, but there's the added incentive that reducing their crew will reduce their effectiveness."

Le Garre shakes her head. "They must be anticipating a hostile situation and planning for it. They know they have minimal crew. Would you divide your people?"

I frown. "You might be right."

"On the *Hercules,* they didn't need a boarding party," Le Garre says. "The infiltrators were already in the storage container. They're anticipating that they'll have the same advantage here."

"When things went bad on the freighter, they blew up the bridge," Travers adds.

"That was the reason I mentioned it," Keiyho says. "If they'd had a contingency, we'd have seen evidence of them using it when we were there."

"Seventy kilometres to contact," Chiu announces. "I'm detecting a launch of some kind. Could be another guided missile."

Immediately, the rest of the bridge crew turn back to their screens. "The projectile is not accelerating," Travers says. "It's moved away from the *Gallowglass*. Seems to be smaller than the projectiles we encountered before."

"Impact of an explosive charge at one hundred metres per second will still tear the *Khidr* to pieces," Le Garre says. "If we don't deploy countermeasures, that object could be enough to end us."

"They wouldn't make all this effort and just destroy us," I reply. "Tag the projectile and monitor it for signs of deceleration."

"Aye, aye, Captain."

"Get a profile scan as soon as possible. Might be we can work out what it is by the shape."

"Will do."

I'm watching the tactical display on my station screen. The new object appears beside the *Gallowglass*. The rates of deceleration are comparable, but the new tag is gradually inching ahead.

"Range is fifty-five klicks," Travers says. "Passing the second asset, now."

The ship has rotated a full turn, and the main exterior view is pointed in the right direction again. I lean forward in my chair. There's a bright circular object, a bit bigger and brighter than the visible stars. "There she is," I mutter.

The *Gallowglass* gets closer and drifts across the screen as we turn away again. Everything is so quiet. The peaceful serenity of space belies what is about to happen. The ripping and tearing of metal, flesh and plastic, the rupture and venting of gases. All of these things deserve noise. We'll hear them, and as long as we can hear, we'll be surviving. The minute it all goes silent is the minute we die.

"Time to intercept?"

"Eleven minutes. Projectile will reach us in nine."

I shift in my chair and touch my screen, moving one of the external cameras so it picks up the *Gallowglass*. The smaller object isn't visible yet. I know Travers wants me to give the order to launch a missile, but I can't. The minute we do, the game is up. I have to bluff this out. "Chiu, drop our power output down as far as you can without compromising us. Suspend life support if you have to. Let's not make it easy for them to identify targets."

Chiu grimaces but nods. A moment later, the atmospheric and thermal cycling alarm appears. She's drawing the air out of the pressurised compartments, back into the central reservoir.

I activate the ship-wide comms. "Go to suit oxygen, everybody," I order and clip my emergency supply to the port on the side of my chair. I flip the visor of my helmet down, and the internal audio speakers activate automatically. There's a faint hissing sound as the suit system starts working to balance the atmosphere around my mouth and nose. The compartments of the *Khidr* will remain pressurised, but plugging in means people survive if the room they are in is suddenly breached. I think back to what Johansson said about manipulating environmental controls. If anyone wanted to wipe out my crew right now, this would be the way to do it. Inject a little nitrous oxide into the supply tank. With us all on pipes, everyone would be unconscious before the alarms—

"*Gallowglass* is decelerating further," Travers says. "Three minutes to point-blank range."

"What about the projectile?"

"It's also decelerating and manoeuvering. Course plot suggests its aiming for our airlock. Looks like you were right, Captain."

I wince. There's no time for points scoring. "Prepare for arrivals."

"Aye, aye."

"We're also being hailed."

Showtime. "Inform Specialist Sellis it's time for him to go to work."

CHAPTER FORTY-TWO

Sellis

I'm strapped into an acceleration chair in corridor four with a portable screen in my hands, waiting.

And waiting.

It's dark. All I can hear is the sound of my own breathing into the emergency mask. If I look up and to the left, I'll see the guy, Shah, from the *Hercules*. They've assigned him to watch over me and given him a weapon, just in case.

Oh, how the fucking mighty fall... They trust me even less than some hypoxic stranger found in a tin can. Still, I'm doing better than Doctor 'Sociopath', who they've sedated and prepped for cold sleep.

The fate of the ship and everyone on board is in my hands. When the *Gallowglass* opens a comms link to talk to us, I'm supposed to convince them I'm in charge of the ship.

I have no idea what I'm going to say.

I can guess what Bogdanovic would do if he were in this position. This would be his chance to alert Rocher's friends on what to expect. He'd start all sugar pie and then try to blurt out some information to give the *Gallowglass* a strategic advantage. Not that they need one; we're screwed anyway.

I have to think about that and consider it carefully. This moment is about making the right choice for *me*, not anyone else. That means evaluating my survival chances and working out who I care about. In the past, it was all about me too – another fix, rolling the dice again, for the next roll and the next. But this... It's the same but different. I can't explain why.

I'm thinking about what Captain Shann said to me – *you need to lie to these people*. She might be right. Lying is the only way I have any power and can keep something back. I'm used to lying, but it doesn't make it easy. Good liars commit to their argument and don't try to fill in too many details. It's strange that this time I'll be lying to help people, not just wriggle out of my own issues. If I go with Rocher's people, it'll only be a strategy to stay alive longer.

Either way, there will be a battle and I reckon this time, only one ship will survive.

I remember when I was first told I was being posted off planet. It was a Friday, right at the end of my duty shift. I'd already booked leave, so I went home that night and started bingeing on science fiction. I watched films, played the immersion sims, everything. That whole weekend was a blast of starships, multicoloured laser beams, strange aliens and galactic adventures. It was like old fireworks in the night sky, a huge epic spectacle. All the colours and flashes distracting you from the mass of death and destruction being advertised as entertainment. Of course, no one really died; it wasn't real space. Most of what I watched and interacted with had been made on computers or recorded in film studios.

It was fun.

Astrospace training on Orbital Station Two was nothing like any of it. I decided there and then, reality out here sucks. My first combat situation in space, when we escaped from the *Gallowglass*, might have been colourful and epic on the outside, but when you're powerless in a pressurised metal can, restrained to keep your body from being smashed against the walls, you don't feel much of the spectacle.

Now we're going to war for a second time and I guess it'll be just like the first time, only I'll be strapped into a chair out here instead of my bed in my—

"Specialist Sellis?" It's Travers on the screen. "We have the *Gallowglass* hailing us. Are you ready?"

"I…uh…yeah, sure."

"It's audio only, but we'll be transmitting video. They'll be able to see you."

"Understood."

Travers's face disappears and the window goes black. The words 'exterior comms established' begin flashing in the bottom right corner of my screen.

"This is *Gallowglass* command," says a distorted voice. "Who am I speaking to?"

"This is Specialist Jake Sellis," I reply.

"Do you have an authorisation code, Specialist?"

"Yeah, it's zero, B, X, H, U, J, seven, six, nine, three, A."

There's a moment's pause before the voice answers. "That code is confirmed, Specialist. Can you report the status of your ship?"

"Ensign Chiu and I are in charge. There's still some resistance, and we've had to lock up a lot of the crew. We'll need help to secure the ship and deal with the prisoners."

"Support will arrive shortly," the voice says. "You will need to allow our transport to dock. When our assets disembark, you must both identify yourselves with your recognition codes."

"Understood."

"Thank you for your loyalty, Specialist."

"I…err…yeah…okay." Even as I say the last words, the conversation ends, and after a moment or two, Travers's face reappears. "You get all that, Lieutenant?" I ask.

"We did, yes. Well done."

"I kept it simple."

"Probably for the best." Travers rubs his bandaged forehead, and I suddenly feel guilty for not helping him on the bridge when I had the chance. "If they contact again, we'll alert you."

"Sure. I'll be here." *Where else am I going to go?*

Where indeed?

The comms window disappears and I'm left to consider my options. They are coming, and they'll expect me to be in or around the airlock. I'm doing nothing strapped here, other than waiting for another call. The advantage of staying put is that I'm safe if Captain Shann decides to start moving the ship, but I guess she won't do that until whatever Rocher's friends are sending over has nearly docked at least. Shann wants the *Gallowglass* vulnerable, or at least as vulnerable as she can make it.

That means I have a little bit of time.

I've changed my mind. I start unstrapping the buckles on my chair, but something distracts me. There's a red light flashing a little way away, over by Shah. He looks at me and removes his own restraints. He moves in my direction, drawing a weapon, aiming it at me.

"What are you doing, Specialist?" he asks.

"I might ask you the same."

Shah's hands are trembling. He's holding a Taser – a good choice given the circumstances. No chance of explosive decompression if he misses. I'm surprised they left him looking after me. He's a civilian contractor, probably has some firearms and security experience from back on Earth, but I doubt he's discharged a weapon or fought somebody up here. That said, Shann probably doesn't trust him either. I bet she couldn't think of anything else to do with him.

"I want to go to the airlock," I say. "You heard the comms transmission. They'll be expecting me to be down there."

"You told the lieutenant you'd stay here."

"Yeah…well, then I thought about it. I need to be in the airlock."

"That's not what you agreed."

I sigh. "You want to buzz them and get permission? Haven't they got enough on their plate right now?"

"I was given orders to make sure you—"

"Look, the only reason you're alive after what happened on the freighter is because you made some independent choices. We're in the same position, stuck out here with them coming in. You know what's next."

Shah chews his lip in thought, but he doesn't lower the Taser. "You're talking about two different things," he says at last. "What I did on the *Hercules* was for my own survival. Captain Shann is trying to make sure we all survive."

"So am I," I counter. "I want to go to the airlock because they'll expect me to be at the airlock. If I'm not there when they arrive, it'll get messy."

"There's a team at the airlock. They'll deal with what's to come. If you and I go down, we'll just complicate things."

"And based on your experience, you think they can handle what's coming?"

Shah doesn't answer. The Taser in his hand wavers. He looks even more unsure. I'm out of my chair now. If I wanted to choose a side right now and make a move on him, I think I'd succeed. First thing would be to take away that Taser and put him out with it. If the master-at-arms gave him a second cartridge, I'd take that and make my way down to the airlock to get rid of the others as well.

However, if I want to stay neutral or go the other way, I need to keep him on my side, for now.

I hold a hand up. "Okay, you buzz Travers. Get him to make the call. I'll wait."

He touches his comms bead with his left hand, while keeping his weapon trained on me. He taps the bead twice, like a code, not what I expected. "Hey, what are you—"

He fires the Taser and the points hit me in the chest. A moment later, the charge is delivered and I'm thrashing around, twisting myself up in the cables. My sight starts to blur, but I can see the weapon has been torn out of Shah's hands. He leaps for it, grabs it and presses the trigger a second time.

"I'm sorry, Mister Sellis, you were right. Better not to bother the bridge, but settle this ourselves. Turns out you were a traitor after all and…"

He's still talking. I can see his lips moving, but I can't make out the words. Then everything goes dark and I…

CHAPTER FORTY-THREE

Shann

The *Gallowglass* is right in front of us. The computer says there's two and a half kilometres between the ships. I can see the smaller object now, still approaching, rotating toward our airlock. We know from what was said it contains some kind of boarding party, but there has to be a twist to this. The enemy ship has a smaller crew than ours. They can't want to increase that disadvantage by dividing their personnel.

"Chiu, can we get a reading on what's in that pod?" I ask.

Chiu shrugs. "If I activate a scan, Captain, they'll notice."

"Okay, hold fast on that. Are Chase and Arkov ready?"

"Yes, Captain," Keiyho says. "They report everything is prepared."

Now is the moment when I need to make a choice. We can't find out anything more about the object unless we allow it to dock. The enemy ship is in range, but still outguns us. *Do I wait, or do we make a start?*

"Keiyho, do we have firing solutions for all of our torpedo launchers?"

"We do, Captain."

"Then let's begin. Order the crew to battle stations."

"Aye, aye."

In the old films, there would be a red light or some kind of alarm. We have a klaxon and automated announcement in the same dry ship's voice that we're all used to hearing. There's a reason for that. The lighting on a spaceship is kept at an optimum level for working. Changing that level or colouring it for any reason would be a distraction.

We don't need distractions.

"Bring tubes to bear and fire a broadside when everyone's ready," I instruct.

"Aye, aye," Keiyho replies. There will be a moment when the enemy registers what we're up to and reacts. We have to hope we can be quick enough to—

"They've started moving, Captain," Le Garre warns. "Looks like they might be on to us."

"Power up and get ready to evade!" I shout. "Close quarters, Major!"

"Close quarters, aye."

There's a noise, like a thumping, and I start to feel the acceleration pressing me into my seat. The torpedoes are away, and we're heading toward the *Gallowglass*, trying to negate their firepower advantage by moving in as close as we can. It's an aggressive move, maybe an obvious move, but we'll see what they do.

"Three successful launches, Captain," Keiyho says. "The fourth is behaving...erratically."

I turn my chair. "Erratically? Something we need to worry about?"

"There appears to have been some sort of problem with the launch," Travers says. I can see him opening windows on his screen. "Projectile is clear, but decelerating."

I'm relieved. An armed warhead stuck in a launch tube might have finished us, but it's still confusing. "How can it be decelerating?"

"Some sort of guidance misfire," Travers says. "I'm monitoring it."

Ahead, a flash of fire on the main viewer snatches my attention. There's debris around the *Gallowglass*. Then there's a second flash and a third. "Three clean hits!" Keiyho shouts.

"Detecting return launches," Travers says. "They're trying to adjust to our position."

"Angle and rotate!" I order. "Use whatever we have left in the manoeuvering thrusters!"

The *Gallowglass* is getting larger as we move toward it. The rotational jets kick in and I'm pulled to my left in the chair. I touch my screen and the shutters begin to close. I activate a feed to the external camera and a window pops up on my console. The distance between the ships is counting down, closing rapidly. "Do we have anything left for deceleration?" I ask.

"Not much," Le Garre replies.

"Do what you can," I urge and activate the ship-wide alert. The klaxon blares out again, and then the computer speaks.

"All hands, brace for impact. All hands..."

A metallic screeching noise echoes through the ship. I've heard it before; the sound of a laser tearing through compartments of the ship, as if they were made of paper. There's a muffled thump too. That'll be a missile hitting the hull. "Monitor for breaches! Seal compartments as quickly as you can. I—"

Impact. When it comes, it's like being kicked in the back. All the wind goes out of me and for a moment, I can't breathe. Then the pressure on my chest eases a little and I'm taking shallow gulps of air. That means I still have air, at least in my suit.

There's a noise, like heavy rain. A part of me remembers sitting in my room and hearing the storm outside. Hale, sleet or a deluge of water, hammering against the roof and walls. That's what I can hear now, outside. Little pieces of debris, clattering into the ship, every impact another chance to wound and rend the fragile skin of our ship, our home.

The console in front of me is flashing. The two ships have collided. Le Garre is using the last of our fuel to twist our position as best she can. "Activate the cavalry!" I gasp, but my voice is no more than a hoarse whisper. I glance up, but I can't see Keiyho in his seat. Either he's unconscious and slumped forward or something else has happened.

We're locked in a deadly embrace, both ships moving and abrading each other. If things stay as they are, it will only be a matter of time before we all die in a maelstrom of rotating fragments, as everything is sliced apart by unforgiving Newtonian physics.

I key up the weapon's console controls on my own screen. The time it takes to get command of Keiyho's station feels like an eternity. Every agonising second is another moment that we have to survive.

We *have* to survive.

A new window appears. It's the weapon's system, with asset tracking in the debris field. I activate the call signal for the dormant missiles we launched hidden among our jettisoned junk. All three receivers acknowledge the signal and start moving on the tactical plot. They'll be heading this way, as fast as their limited fuel can manage, to detonate against the side of the *Gallowglass*.

Hopefully…

I glance at Le Garre. She's focused on her screen, her fingers flying across different windows and controls as she fights to control our ship in the aftermath of our collision. There are too many variables for her and the computer to track, but she's trying and we need her to do everything she can. At the moment the missiles arrive, we need to be behind the *Gallowglass*, using it as a shield.

Another window on my screen flashes. It's Sam, staring into the camera in airlock control. He looks terrified. I accept the request. "What's the problem, Sam ?"

"Airlock has been breached, Captain! They've sent over a—"

The screen goes blank.

CHAPTER FORTY-FOUR

Johansson

My world turns, rotates, spins and changes all around me.

I remember training for this. In the first few days, they'd put everyone in the gravity simulator to find out their tolerances. You never got a score, but whispers and rumours went around about who coped best. I recall lasting fifteen minutes or so, from being strapped in to being peeled out. Those fifteen minutes felt like a lifetime. They always had to wash up after, scrubbing out the cockpit with disinfectant.

When we were all lumped together as trainees, with no seniority or chain of command, how long you lasted in an endurance test like that gave you status. Apparently, fifteen minutes wasn't too bad.

I've no idea if they went easy on me back then.

Now I'm jammed inside a rocket shell, twisting and turning end over end. My stomach is churning, trying to rebel. If I throw up, it'll be in my helmet, floating around in the air I have to breathe.

In front of me is the portable screen. The exterior camera feed is a swirling mass of stars, racing around in the black. I can't see the *Gallowglass* or the *Khidr*, but they are on the tactical display beneath. I need to get this little ship under control, turn around and make my way in, but I need to be smart. I don't have to do everything alone.

I ask the screen to analyse my rotation, based on visual clues from the camera and to calculate the best burn of our limited manoeuvering jets to bring it under control.

I want to take my helmet off. I know I can't. Calm, steady breaths, that's it, *calm…*

Slowly, the little processor in the screen works everything out. Tiny little puffs of propellant from the thruster slow us down, stop us turning and redirect our trajectory. Computers have always worked out this stuff, ever since humanity first went into space. Amazing to think how exponentially more powerful the computer in this device is compared to the systems they had back in the 1960s. It's like comparing humans to plant life, I guess.

As the rotation eases, so does my heart rate and breathing. Now I can see the *Gallowglass* on the feed. She's turning slowly to the right, but I'm definitely heading toward her. There's a cloud of fresh debris all around her. Tiny fragments start to bounce off the missile casing. If I close my eyes, I can imagine rain on a summer's day.

I'm looking for a possible landing site. It's hard to make out any specific locations on the hull at this range, even though the design is similar to the ships I'm used to. It doesn't matter too much. The majority of the ship's skin will have the necessary cable feeds, buried under layers of steel and plastic, just like the *Khidr*. I'll be running a wire into the system, in the same way we did with the *Hercules*. Under normal circumstances, that kind of attack would trigger an alert, but I'm hoping the crew on board the *Gallowglass* will have too much going on to notice. The chances of me missing out and finding a 'dead plate' are pretty low − about one in fifty − but I can't work out a contingency for that. If it happens, this mission ends.

I'll have failed.

The noise from outside is worryingly loud. If a large piece of wreckage hits the torpedo, it could puncture the skin, or deflect my course. There's not much leftover propellant in the thrusters. I'll need every little bit I can save to get me back on board a ship.

Either ship, whichever one survives.

The screen is bright white, filled with shining metal, reflecting the distant light of the sun. I can see details now, the securing nuts, the lined grooves between plates. I'm aiming for that. It'll be a good place to anchor up. The mechanical arm might be able to find a weakness in the join and get through.

The next bit is tricky, a trade-off between a landing and a collision. My improvised spacecraft is designed to explode on impact. Removing the warhead and other fissile material might prevent most of that, but the shell is still designed for that purpose. Thankfully, during the eighteenth century, people learned that embedded detonations are more destructive than explosions on a surface, so the missile is designed to penetrate, crumple and explode.

Where I have a problem is the moment of impact. I'm inside here. Any damage to the casing might also be damage to me. Preserving my existence is counter to the purpose of weapon technology designed to be destroyed, so I need a carefully judged collision.

The screen counts down the distance. When I judge I have ten seconds left, I shut my eyes, tense my muscles and ball myself up as much as I can in this cramped space.

The moment we hit jams me forward into the casing. My helmet wedges against something, my left arm is twisted out at an awkward angle, and my knees slam into solid metal. That's where the pain comes from. Something has broken, and it hurts.

Oh god, that hurts!

I'm shrieking. I can't think straight. *Make the pain go away!* There's a control on my suit to release emergency medication. It's inside my helmet, requiring a specific movement to the left, so as to prevent an accidental trigger. Drugs will fog up my brain, but right now I can hardly breathe.

I turn my head inside my helmet and touch the lever with my chin. The needle jabs into my chest. Moments later, the pain settles into throbbing agony.

I can't shift my position in the casing anymore. My control screen is to the right and level with my shoulder, making it difficult to see. The metal plates Sam welded onto the housing are dented, but the atmosphere reading in my suit is okay. I'm still alive and there appears to be no leak.

I move my hand toward the screen. There's a faint feeling of awkwardness as I do so. I reckon I've cracked some ribs, but the drugs are making sure I can't feel it. I can just about see the activation control for the mechanical arm. Hopefully, it hasn't been damaged.

A little blue light reflected on my gloves confirms that the arm has successfully deployed. I can't make out the image being displayed from the camera on the arm, so it's going to be difficult to manually control it.

I need to move. That means risking more damage to myself, my suit and the metal casing around me. But if I don't try, I'm stuck here.

I reach up and try pushing myself back down. I can get one arm above my head. I grab on to a dented plate with my hand to pull as well. There's a scraping sound against my helmet that makes me wince, but the atmosphere alarm doesn't go off, and slowly, inch by inch, I lever myself back into approximately the same position I was in before impact.

Now I can see the screen. Now we can go to work.

The camera feed from the arm is in one window. The other, which was displaying the images from the front of the warhead, has gone black, with the words 'signal lost' in front of it. I should have expected that, given the impact. It'll make any effort to guide this little ship back doubly hard. I glance at the fuel indicator. There's four per cent remaining in the tank. That means any trip back to the *Khidr* will be virtually impossible without some kind of velocity assist. Something like being fired out of a launch tube would do it.

Yeah...not going to happen twice. *Who's fucking stupid idea was this little mission anyway?*

Oh...of course.

My only real chance is to be rescued, and that means I need the *Khidr* to survive all this as well. They're in the middle of a firefight, their own version of hell, better and worse than mine, I expect.

My fingers are shaking as I maneuver the robotic hand toward the seam between two deck plates. I activate the portable laser and aim at the groove between two sealing bolts. The screen confirms the weapon is working, and I can see layers of paint peeling away. Hopefully, the crew of the *Gallowglass* will be too busy to notice my work.

A tiny trail of fragments drifts away into space. I can see a dark hole growing right in the centre of the image. Now I'm in a race against time. I don't know what'll happen between the ships as they batter each other, how long it'll take until one or the other falls to pieces or all the crew are killed. I have to do my job as fast as possible and hope I've done it fast enough.

The hole looks to be of adequate size. I deactivate the laser and push the robotic fingers forward, pressing one digit into the red-hot tear. The sensor on the end pings contact with an electrical relay. A quick diagnostic on the screen indicates it's a data cable, just what I was looking for.

The fingertip clamps on. A dot of chemical burns through the cable casing, and a moment later our own feeder line is spliced into the system. I shut down both camera feeds and activate the link.

A log-on screen appears. 'Fleet authorised access – enter your username.'

Bingo.

CHAPTER FORTY-FIVE

Shann

The noise outside is deafening, like being stuck in a hurricane, but I have to focus – *we* have to focus on what we can do, what we can control.

On my instruction, the *Khidr* is jammed against the *Gallowglass*. At this range, both ships cannot deploy their most destructive weapons – their torpedoes and lasers. Instead, guns rake our hull as we do the same to them, searching for a weak point.

From this position, we can annihilate each other. There's enough fuel left in our main engines to perform one final burn. I bet the *Gallowglass* has more. A decent push from either set of engines will grind the ships together in a graceful balletic solution. We're already swirling around in a cloud of spinning debris.

We're two wounded bears, tearing each other apart.

On board, we're all strapped into our chairs, a protection against the shifting forces. The spinning and turning means continual flux in the direction my body is being pulled. The noise from outside increases. A constant hammering of wreckage against the outside of the hull. The positive is that so long as I can hear it, we're still pressurised; the bridge compartment hasn't ruptured. But it makes talking in the room almost impossible. We have to use the comms. The headphones double as ear defenders in here.

Our initial missile launches, and suicidal charge gave us a chance. The *Gallowglass* couldn't return fire accurately before we crashed into them. The turret laser can't lock on to our hull and slice us up without damaging their ship too. Duggins said most of their system worked on automated processing, so there must be some kind of safety protocol they're struggling to override, or else we'd already be dead.

We're winning, moment to moment, but I'm not sure it's enough.

I'm worried about my people. Keiyho is either unconscious or worse. Chiu is slumped in her seat too, her chair twisted at an awkward angle. Travers has taken over the weapons control. Le Garre is still flying the *Khidr*, trying to turn us away from the imminent missile impact. I've no idea what's going on in the rest of the ship.

The screen in front of me is cracked. The projectiles are still marked as flashing dots, moving toward the two ships. There's a three-dimensional model of the situation outside, a computer simulation of spinning fragments, based on all available data, a beautiful maelstrom of gathering destruction.

A green dot reaches us and the ship rocks, driving me sideways against the straps. "Impact of asset one, Captain!" Travers says. "Asset two collision imminent!"

I tense up involuntarily, despite the distance and the fact that I can see what's happening on my own screen. The simulation is moving at an angle in reaction to the first impact. The second will drive us faster toward oblivion.

This time, there's a loud booming noise as the missile hits. The screen shutters buckle and crack. A pressure loss alarm goes off, and suddenly, the noise beyond my helmet fades away into an eerie quiet. In a way, it's a relief. The world outside the bridge evaporates, and the situation in front of me becomes easier to concentrate on.

The decompression alarm is flashing in front of me. I'm grateful for the safety straps that hold me back from the pull of deep space. What was that old navy saying? A captain should go down with the ship? There are countless news articles about tragedies at sea and the dangers of abandoning your boat or face being dragged down with a sinking wreck. Out here, leaving the vessel is suicide, unless you have another to go to.

The tiny popping noise of an open comms channel grabs my attention. Travers is in my ear. "Captain, third impact is imminent."

"How's our rotation?"

"Not looking good," Le Garre says. "We're coming back around. I can't reverse our direction with the thrusters we have left."

"Do whatever you can."

"Aye, aye."

She's right; the third impact is worse than the others. It's like someone kicked me really hard in the chest and then punched me in the ribs a few times for good measure. The *Khidr* groans and twists to starboard. I feel my left shoulder pop and the straps on that side of my chair snap, sending me hurtling toward the wall. I manage to grab the frayed ends and hold on, but then the whole place shifts again, in the opposite direction and I'm slammed into the floor.

This time, I know I've broken something in my left arm. It's twisted underneath me. I can move it, but it'll be useless for doing anything.

The comms pops in my ear again; it's Le Garre. "All three impacts confirmed. We took most of the last one!"

My ribs hurt as I inhale to reply. "Can you give me a comparative damage assessment?"

"The computer is trying, Captain, but we're losing systems everywhere!"

"How long until we lose structural integrity?"

"I...I can't tell."

Structural integrity – a term that hides a multitude of problems. What it means in this context is the ship is falling apart, splitting into its various components that will probably end up drifting away in space for centuries.

A variety of coffins and tombs for those of us left alive.

The *Khidr* is a hardy vessel. Fleet builds things for space with tough and durable components. There are always redundant systems, backups, protective shells and casings; anything that can be added without compromising some other essential component is added. However, despite all the simulations, design meetings and disaster planning, no one involved in the construction of this ship had any experience of space combat.

I flinch as a whistling of radio static and shouting fills my ears. "Captain, this is Chase! They've sent over some sort of assault drone. It's in the airlock, attempting to hack into our computer system and take over the ship. I'm trying to—"

The transmission cuts off. I struggle around from my position so I can operate the screen and try to reconnect, but the system can't locate Sam on board. It's struggling to manage basic functions as different sensors and cables fail.

We're going to die out here.

Now is the time to send the transmission to Phobos Station. I key it up and select the priority distress broadcast channel. Whatever happens to us, Fleet will know what happened here. We will be remembered.

Did I do the right thing? Have I failed the people under my command? I made the judgement calls I thought were best. Would I change them? Based on the information I have now, probably, some of them, but that's second-guessing myself.

Doesn't stop me feeling guilty. The weight of the responsibility is heavy right now. People have died and will die because of what I chose. I see Jacobson's face again in the camera feed, screaming out his last breath. *That was me. I murdered him.*

I'm injured. A wounded captain, on a wounded ship, both beyond patching up by any medic.

The screen flashes. There's another communication request coming in. It's Johansson. I wonder what's happened to her. We could have used her expertise up here, but I doubt it would have made much difference.

I key up the request. The line is bad, fading in and out. "What's going on, Ensign?"

"Captain, I'm outside the ship in EVA. I've patched a data cable link into the *Gallowglass*. I'm trying to hack the environment system as we discussed—"

"Wait a minute, you're not in the medical room?"

"No, I...disobeyed a direct order.... I'm sorry."

"Not a lot I can do about that right now," I say. "You're in a race against time. Looks like we weren't the only ones who came up with computer hacking as a solution to this little war. Chase says they've landed an assault vehicle in the airlock."

"Okay. Captain, I need your help."

"What can I do?"

"There's an authorisation wall. I need a code to access their ship's system," Johansson explains. "I don't suppose you have any idea what it might be?"

I rack my brain, thinking over every encounter I had with Rocher and the people who turned out to be traitors. "Sellis and Chiu had authorisation codes to make themselves known to the *Gallowglass* crew. The transmission was recorded. I can send that to you?"

"It's worth a shot."

I key up Sellis's conversation and send the file down the line. After three tries it indicates it's gotten there. "Any use?"

"Trying it now."

CHAPTER FORTY-SIX

Sellis

I can't see.

I ache all over and there's blood in my mouth. I can feel more wetness around me as I drift in the dark.

I'm alive; there's air to breathe. While these two things are true, I have hope. I am not giving up.

The last thing I remember is Shah and the Taser. He attacked me. *Why?*

Is he a traitor? Working for the *Gallowglass*? No. I don't think so. If he was, he'd have sabotaged the ship already and killed me, or tried to recruit me with another blackmail attempt. What's his angle then? I don't know.

The world around me shifts, and I'm forced against something metallic and unresisting. Then the pressure eases and I'm pulled the other way. I raise my arms and ward off a flat wall, keeping my face from slamming into it.

My head hurts. I can't figure this shit out. Better minds than me will be trying to calculate all the variables. Better minds need to be informed.

I touch the comms bead on my collar. It's still working. "Sellis to bridge. Captain, I hope you're on the line; this is fucking urgent!"

There's static on the line, then noise as someone picks up. "We're a little busy up here right now, Specialist!"

"I'm locked in a storage compartment. Shah has gone rogue. He's headed for the airlock!"

There's an intake of breath on the other end of the line, and then it goes dead.

I'm on my own.

I raise my hand and wave it in front of my face. I can hardly see the movement. There is almost no light in here. I move my hands around, trying to find the walls and door. My knuckles catch the edge of something sharp, making me instinctively flinch away, but I've no momentum. I can't find purchase in this—

The loud and terrible sound of metal tearing echoes in from outside. There's a bang, and again I'm slammed into something as the ship surges. For a moment, light flickers on, then dies again, giving me a sense of the room I'm trapped in, one of the inventory compartments. There are three on the ship and they are huge spaces, filled with racks of shelves. The world I glimpsed was a nightmare of broken and twisted metal. The door is at the far end.

Well, fuck!

I'm pressed up against one of the surviving racks. While I've been unconscious, I've been thrown around this room as the *Khidr* has been under attack. I'm injured but not badly. Lots of nicks, slices and scratches. I don't know how I'm still alive.

If I'm going to stay that way and make a difference, I need to get out of this room.

I push off from the racks toward the door, keeping my hands out in front of me.

Twisted metal struts groan and squeal as the ship adjusts its position. I can feel every shift and alteration, dragging my body left and right, up and down. I have to compensate, sticking out an arm or a leg to touch against something and push away, keeping myself moving in the same direction.

This is the ultimate gamble. My life is at stake. At any moment, I could be crushed against torn metal. A sharp edge might slice through my suit and me. There's nothing I can do.

What a rush!

I've wanted this. It's taken all this time to realise this is what I was looking for – a moment of chance where my life is at stake in a tangible way. This is Russian roulette without the opponent – a human variable that I wouldn't want in the mix. I know now I've been searching for a way to risk my life and feel that risk. That's the ultimate high.

My heart is racing. I feel alive, connected to the here and now. I'm not sure I'll gamble again after this. I don't think I'll ever capture the same sensation.

I guess I should thank Shah for what he did. Yeah...thank him, up close and *personal*...with a fist. I may be too late. Whatever he was planning to do may have already happened. I've no way of knowing, but I have to try, to strive against the odds. That's what defines me.

The journey lasts a long time for me, an eternity of seconds or minutes, I can't tell. My fingers touch the wall, and I know I've travelled a long way physically, and spiritually. I've found myself, understood some deep urge that's always been there, but needed this moment to be confronted.

I'm not quite at the door, but my guess was pretty close. I fumble along the wall and find the release lever about a metre to my right. I grab it and one of my fingers twists. A shooting pain runs down my arm, making me gasp.

A broken finger. If I get out of here with only a broken finger, I'm lucky.

The door shivers and, with a squeal, grinds open. The corridor beyond is lit by flickering emergency lighting. It's a wasteland of torn fragments and scorched walls, but I recognise it from before. At the end, to my left, near the next hatch, there's an acceleration chair hanging off the wall with a figure slumped forward in it. I move closer. It's Bogdanovic. He's dead, his face twisted in an agonised expression. I almost feel sorry for him.

Almost, but not quite – *Fucker*.

I make my way past him and into the next passage. I'm heading for the airlock, where Shah was going. I don't know what I'm going to be able to do if I get there, but I have to confront him.

The ship is ruined. The pressure alarm is going off, and the hatch at the end of this corridor is closed. I open up the emergency compartment on the wall. There's a spare tank, helmet and suit hanging there. I strip naked and change into it. I can't take any risks with the seals on my own after being unconscious and thrown around the storeroom.

My bare arms and legs are covered in bruises and clotted lacerations. I look like I've been tortured. In a way, I have, I guess, but not like some abused prisoner, keeping special secrets. I know my place; I'm a pawn in this game.

So much for just a broken finger, eh?

I take everything I can from the emergency compartment. Now I'm a pawn armed with an axe, a short-range chemical welder and a precision zero gravity fire extinguisher.

I clip the helmet down and activate the suit's internal air supply and magnetic boots, and then I override the emergency controls on the hatch.

This time, it's like being drawn out into a tornado. I grab the edges of the door to stop myself being sucked straight through. I'm doing some sort of vertical press-up, trying to ease myself into the breached chamber.

It's the medical room. Bullet holes and scorch marks decorate the remaining structure. The flooring is damaged but intact. The dividing wall is smashed to pieces, and there's a gaping hole in the ceiling. I can see pieces of debris floating around out there. Hundreds of ration pills, painkillers, sedatives and medical tools. Even one of the beds. All of it swirling around, just like our ship. Occasionally, there's a flash as something explodes. From here, the whole sight is magnificent, awful and vomit inducing.

I get through the door and reactivate the emergency control, letting it seal behind me. Gradually, the forces on me ease. Usually, if I was going to work in a depressurised environment like this, I'd be tethered or kitting up in a full EVA suit, but I'm not here to fix stuff, just to get through.

I'm nearly where I want to be. The hatch at the other end is also sealed. It's a right-angle turn and one hundred metres from there to Arkov's control station.

But first, I need to make it to the hatch.

The magboots make walking awkward and slow, but I wouldn't try this without them. I keep my eyes on the hatch ahead of me and away from the throw-up triggers. Space walks were never my favourite thing, but you do what you have to do.

When I reach the other end, I peer through the DuraGlas plate, trying to get a look at who might be in there. Something is moving around, that's for sure. The minute I open the door, they'll get a nasty surprise, although there isn't much I can do about that, other than issue a comms warning.

"Sellis to all crew. I'm about to open the sealed hatch on corridor nine. Fair warning, people, I'm coming in."

There's no response. *Shit*. It's in moments like this that 'fair warning' takes on a new meaning. Yes, I've done all I can to let people know what I'm going to do, but that doesn't change the fact that opening the door could get someone in there killed.

The alternative is I stay out here and die.

I grab the handle and do the deed quickly. I can't hear the alarms in the vacuum, but the sudden rush of air in my face and flashing red light are both pretty clear indicators that the ship is unhappy with me. It's fucking amazing how conditioned we are to obey warnings and alerts like this. They make you feel like you've just grabbed a hot pan on the stove.

Getting into the corridor, fighting against the rush of air, is much harder than getting out of a pressurised space. As I'm forcing my way in, I'm very aware that every moment the door is open, vital atmosphere is being wasted. This is why we have airlocks, people.

The immediate danger for me is in slipping and letting go, but there's a whole heap of other problems to come. The computer sealed this door for a reason – to prevent further loss of atmosphere. When the system detects a further loss of atmosphere, it'll start to close the next hatch and stop re-pressurising this room. Anyone in here not in a suit will suffocate, and I'll have to override the controls to get breathable air restored. A bit like the last repair I did, only this time it's a lot more difficult and a lot more risky. I can't control the process; instead I have to race against it.

Of course, if I wait to let all the air out, getting in the room will be much easier, but it'll be fatal for anyone in there without a suit and oxygen supply.

I'm through the door. The effort cost me something. My hands are shaking as I reactivate the emergency close protocol. I can just hear the alerts through my helmet. That means there's still some pressure in here.

I turn toward the other door and as I do, I get a sense of the situation I just walked into.

To my left, there's a man, drifting in midair, surrounded by a spewing cloud of blood. His body spasms as it empties its contents into the thin atmosphere. I can't see his face, but he's not wearing a helmet.

To my right, there's a large mechanised vehicle blocking the passage. It has four 'grabber' arms. Three of them have torn holes in the walls to anchor the device's ovoid main body in place, right next to an access terminal. I can see the screen flickering and lights flashing on the vehicle in response. There's some kind of data transfer going on.

This machine must be what the *Gallowglass* sent over. It looks a little beat up; the surface of the ovoid is pitted and scarred. There's some kind of camera assembly on top, two optics that shift forward and backward on little runners.

I'm only a short way from the airlock, but there's no sign of Chase or Arkov.

I move toward the terminal and the machine's position shifts. The fourth arm extends toward me. There's some kind of cutter and projectile weapon attached to the end. They are both aimed at my chest.

"Hey...hey...easy there..."

After all I've been through, I don't want to die here. I reach up to the side of my helmet and flick a switch so my words are broadcast through the external speakers. The atmosphere in here is still thin, but I'm close enough so my words will carry.

"I'm Specialist Sellis. I have an authorisation code."

The arm doesn't move. Lights continue to blink from the data connection. I guess the *Gallowglass* is trying to hack our computer network and slave the ship to theirs.

I crank up the volume on the external speaker and recite the number I've memorised. "Zero, B, X, H, U, J, seven, six, nine, three, A!"

There's a moment, and then the arm retracts. The machine makes no other move toward or away from me. I'm safe, but clearly not the priority around here.

I need to restore the atmospheric pressure. Without access to the terminal, I'll need to get into the system some other way. I don't have a portable screen anymore. Shah must have taken mine away with him, or it got smashed somewhere in the storage compartment.

Shah...of course...

I make my way back to the man's corpse. He's stopped twitching, but the cloud of blood around him is still expanding. His arms and legs are twisted at awkward angles, as if the bones have snapped under extreme force.

I guess depressurisation in here and being thrown around could have done that.

I get a look at his face. Yes, it's Shah, just as I thought. Whatever his motive was in Tasering me and making for the airlock, it's died with him. I can't help but feel I'm to blame. Sure, he attacked me, but I wouldn't have chosen this as a response. I killed him, or the machine did before I got inside.

When you join the army, they give you training on taking lives. There's a whole learned psychology to protecting yourself from the aftereffects – the guilt, the shame, the anger, the self-justification. They also talk about intense situations where people rely on you and you let them down. In the military, mistakes can be fatal.

I scored badly on that test, which was why I didn't get shipped out on tour. Apparently, I don't deal well with being responsible.

Either me opening the hatch killed Shah, or the drone did. Something I said to him hit a nerve, but I don't think he was a *Gallowglass* traitor. Either he came down here to stop the drone or to make sure it succeeds.

I can't be sure, and I don't think I'll ever forgive myself either way.

If I don't survive, then maybe I don't have to. My hand strays to my hip. Unplug the oxygen canister and everything ends.

Shit, my life just got fucking dark.

CHAPTER FORTY-SEVEN

Johansson

Two passwords. Neither of them is likely.

I have a recording of Specialist Sellis's safety code that he gave to the *Gallowglass* crew. I have Captain Shann's Fleet access code and I have Ensign Chiu's code. All three are numbers I have had to memorise quickly. There were tests in early astronaut selection that required quick and accurate memorisation while performing other tasks, but they didn't involve being shot full of high-intensity painkillers. Thankfully, I also have the screen in front of me to type things onto.

Most computer systems have lockout procedures. There's an old tech tradition of 'three strikes'. That means I probably have that many tries. I can't waste them.

I try Sellis's code first. My fingers slip on the screen, but I get it entered. It doesn't work. That makes sense. While Sellis might have been a spy for them, why would they give him complete access to their ship? It fits with his story too. The captain decided to trust him and Chiu because they both claimed they'd been coerced.

The Fleet access code goes in next. My rationale is that the *Gallowglass* must have been built by the same construction yards, albeit in secret. If the same computer systems have been installed, the flag passwords would be hardwired into the memory. That's something we ensure is done on other Fleet registered ships. It means we can take control of vessels if the crew are incapacitated or dead.

Nope. Completely independent computer setup. *Shit.*

The third try could be my last. There's a whole host of default options from when I've set up profiles on different ships and stations, but if the computer on here has been configured differently from the ground up, there's no chance one of the defaults we've used will be valid.

Everything is riding on me getting into their ship. I'll die if I don't.

I close my eyes and try to think over everything I've read and been told about the *Gallowglass*, but my mind wanders. Part of me just wants to leave it. I'm warm; the darkness is nice. I could just drift away, right here. I'd sleep and run out of oxygen – die in peace, much better than all the alternatives. I know the drugs are making it like this. I can feel pain in my legs like it's far away, but it's coming back sometime if I keep going. If I just...

No!

I bite my lip, hard. I taste blood in my mouth. The hurt is a buzz, rather than the sharp stabbing sensation it should be, but it does the job. I'm not dying here without doing everything I can possibly do.

Come on, April, think!

We were given access to blueprints and specifications for the *Gallowglass* from Captain Shann's archive. I'm trying to picture them in the strategy room when she and I were talking, visualising all the different pages and drawings.

There was something...on every page...*a number.* I'm trying to remember it. There are seven digits, well-spaced across the header of each page. When I saw them, I couldn't work out why they were there. I assumed they were just copy numbers or something, but what if they were an access code for the ship's system?

Why would they put it on the plans?

There are a couple of reasons I can think of. They're both as tenuous as the ones I came up with before, but I have no other option, other than typing in some random numbers.

I type in the code – *two, eight, seven, H, B, five, five.*

The screen goes blank. That could mean anything, but I anticipate the worst. Third try would be a lockout, and that would probably be a blank screen. I mean, why display anything for someone who is trying to—

A scrolling list of code flashes up. It looks like a boot sequence of some kind. Whatever I typed in wasn't a password; it was some sort of rootkit back door. There's no graphical interface. Instead, a list of terminal commands appears. This may take longer than I'd hoped, but I'm into the system and I think with the right instructions, I can do what we planned.

All my life, I've tinkered with programming. I love languages. I remember studying Finnish at school and being fascinated by how different it looked and sounded to Swedish. Some people are hardwired into attaching specific words to objects and actions, so they have to translate all the time. I've found my mind adapts and makes room for different structures. This system might not be CNUX, but it's given me a phrase book, right above the input line, and I'm really good at breaking down phrases to construct my own.

ACC COM TREE

Command Tree Open.

INST ~CTELL [8FF] -OX _RCAL #LOC HCTRL %- BASE CUR=F TR=%+ RST -10

Confirm OX _RCAL to new parametres? Y/N

Y

Beginning Recalibration of bridge atmosphere...

I'm not sure precisely how long this will take, but it's begun. If left to work undetected, this procedure will kill anyone on the bridge of the *Gallowglass*. They may not even recognise the signs of oxygen deprivation as their brains starve. Not a good way to go. I activate my comms.

"Johansson to Shann?"

"Go ahead."

"Mission successful. The *Gallowglass* computer is starting its atmosphere calibration cycle."

"Outstanding, Ensign! What's your situation?"

I smile involuntarily and look around as much as I can. "Nowhere I can go from here, Captain. I'm going to start work on disabling the *Gallowglass*'s other systems. Hopefully, we can shut her down in time."

"We'll come and get you."

"Don't waste this chance, Captain; otherwise we all die."

"Yeah, understood." I hear her starting to move, the catch in her breath. She's in pain, probably struggling with one of the injuries she already had, or something new. I'm concerned for her, but I've never doubted her. She'll do everything she can to save me and the rest of the crew.

For some reason, even with the odds stacked against her, I can't believe she will fail.

I shut my eyes again, listening until a pop signals the closing of the link and returns me to silence. The patter of debris against the outside of the missile casing continues. There's shifting forces pulling and pushing my body as we spiral around with the *Gallowglass*. I've used the drone arm to pull me in close, but the connection is still weak and could be severed at any moment.

I open my eyes. A red light starts flashing inside my helmet. That's an oxygen alarm. The first tank must be getting low. Our EVA suits are equipped with incremental cylinders, so as to give us a clear idea of how much we have left based on calculated rates of consumption. There's also a portable Sabatier unit that tries to capture my exhalations and produce more oxygen, but it's not very efficient on this scale and needs to be able to vent methane, which can't happen in this enclosed space. If I activate the unit, I'll be releasing a dangerous gas into the compartment around me.

It'll be a while, but eventually I'll have to make a choice about that. Might be that will just prolong my long, slow death out here.

No. Captain Shann will rescue me.

I know it's all but impossible for that to happen. The *Khidr* crew will have to board the *Gallowglass* under extreme circumstances, take control of the ship, ensure that sections of it are suitable for human survival and then start trying to bring me in.

I get it. I've accepted that I'll likely die, but something within me won't let go of that unshakeable faith I have in the captain. I don't know why, but I can't believe that she'd fail at anything she chose to do.

I'm out here, alone in the dark, slowly suffocating on my own carbon dioxide, and I'm holding on to that.

I open my eyes and tap another instruction into the access window on the screen. The list of commands scrolls by again. *Time to make some changes.*

CHAPTER FORTY-EIGHT

Sellis

Get a fucking grip on yourself, Jake!

I've fought hard to live. Whatever the consequences are, there's a choice to be made right here – push on or give up.

I feel alone, but in a way I guess I'm not. Plenty of people have been in a situation like this where you fight or you don't. There's no shame in making either choice. This is where you face yourself and find out who you are.

I remember a story about a guy who was part of the Antarctic expedition who just walked off to die. He knew his whole team were on the limit, so he just "popped out" to give them a better chance. That's just as heroic as struggling on.

As for me, I'm selfish. I need to boil it all down. The oxygen supply in this suit will give up pretty soon. I've got a reserve tank from my old suit, but it could be damaged. The pressure in this corridor is too low for me to be able to breathe, but with the door shut, it is capable of being pressurised. If I can access the controls, I can get it done and extend my life by another few hours.

Then we can look at the next problem.

I can't find Shah's portable screen. He would have had it with him, but there's no sign of it. Maybe it got sucked out when the room was depressurised. I need to figure out another way to get to the computer.

I turn back to look at the *Gallowglass*'s assault drone. It's still trying to break into the computer system, with pages of data flashing up and scrolling down on the terminal every couple of seconds. Even with it distracted, I don't like my chances in taking it down. I can't see any open electronic ports that I recognise either. That means the only weak points are where the arms connect to the main body.

And my passcode.

I don't know how much of a defence that unique combination of numbers and letters will be, but there's probably a protocol hierarchy related to the drone's self-preservation and tactical programming. On the other side of it is another hatch that'll lead into the airlock control area. Right beside it is the room's emergency oxygen cylinder.

Fleet builds their spaceships with multiple redundancies. There is always a plan C and plan D for every situation. Only good old Soviet Russia tried space 'seat of the pants' style, and plenty of their missions just disappeared, or never existed. The manually operated oxygen reserve is plan C. There's a big crank handle on the side. All I have to do is pull it down and the tank will empty into the room. Sure, the balance won't be right, but that doesn't matter in the short term. You just need the pressure and enough O_2 for people to breathe.

I'm holding the axe in my right hand as I push off toward the drone. I reckon it's the best choice to fend off any attempt to grab me.

As I get close, the main body of the machine swivels in my direction, but the arms don't move or pause in their work. I'm quickly up and over. I grab a handrail and lower myself down, then reach for the emergency tank release.

There's frost around the handle, and it doesn't move when I try to pull it upward. *Fuck, I wish I'd kept the axe with me.* I brace myself and try again. This time I feel it shift a little.

Third time is the charm. I'm pulling with both hands, like some sort of gym machine where you draw your arms toward your chest. The lever grinds open, slowly, and there's a plume of white as the valve releases.

It'll take a few minutes for the room to pressurise. I glance around. The data conduit for the terminal is on this side of the room. The cables are behind the scorched wall panels. I move over to that side and jam my axe into the metal plates, levering one off. Then I take out the laser cutter and drag out the data and power cables. The laser makes short work of the connection, slicing straight through it and ending the drone's hacking attempt.

The screen goes blank. Immediately, the machine turns toward me. *Shit.*

I'm shoved forward from behind. I see the large-suited figure of a man without a suit helmet leaping toward the drone with something in his hand. One of the machine's arms slams into his ribs. He tries to grab hold of it, but he's flung away to crash into the wall. The device he was holding is left floating in midair.

I stare at it and my brain screams, *Bomb!*

I drop the laser cutter and I'm moving forward, my hands on the release points around my neck. My suit helmet comes off, and I turn it toward the floating object, catching it inside and slamming the open section of the helmet against the body of the drone.

The arms reach for me. I twist away, getting my feet braced against the side of the corridor above the empty emergency tank.

And the world turns white.

An explosion is a violent expansion of substances as they react with each other. This expansion allows the force of a reaction to dissipate as it interacts with anything, be it gas, solid objects, liquid, flesh and bone.

This room is oxygen rich and combustible. An explosion in here could ignite the air all around me. Breathing flames is not fun. People die pretty fast, particularly as the flames they don't breathe burn up the rest of their bodies.

I don't want to die.

Spacesuit helmets are designed to withstand extreme variations of pressure. Usually, all the good stuff is on the inside and the bad empty vacuum is being kept out. In this case, we want to keep the bad explosion stuff in and away from the good breathable air.

When an explosion is contained, the force can't dissipate, so it'll do more damage to the objects around it. The metal skin of the drone, the inside of the helmet, my hands.

Oh god, my fucking hands!

In a single moment, I've made a choice and placed myself in extreme danger. This time, it's all too fast for any of that delicious adrenaline-fueled tension in between risk and resolution.

My hands hurt. Everything hurts. I'm lying against the wall. I can breathe, but each time I do, my insides feel like they're on fire. I can't feel my fingers through the pain.

I can see, but everything's a blur. There's a ringing in my ears. I'm alive, though. I'm—

"Sellis, congratulations, you're a hero, now get moving!"

I recognise Quartermaster Chase's voice, but it's like listening to someone shouting at you from a long way away. The words are competing with the buzzing, making it hard to concentrate on them. Big hands are on my shoulders, pulling me away from the wall. A needle jabs into my neck. I cough, and blood fills my mouth, a bitter metallic taste to go along with everything else. I grimace and swallow it down. The retching cough helps a bit and my vision starts to clear. There are two people in front of me, Arkov and Chase. The drone is behind them and it's a wreck.

It's been destroyed and we're all still alive.

My fucking hands!

I can't look at them. If I do, I know I'll lose it. Zero gravity means that as 'walking wounded' I'm not subject to the same problems injured personnel on Earth might have with being moved. Both Arkov and Chase clearly want to get moving.

"Well done, Specialist," Arkov says. "Looks like you saved us."

"I don't... What's..."

"We're waiting on instructions from the captain. Chase is trying to get through to the bridge." Arkov's eyes flick over me. "You need to take things slowly," he says. He's holding an emergency medical kit and pulling out bandages. The injection from before was morphine and it's kicking in. The pain is settling back into the distance, helping me think about something else, anything else.

I look around. I remember the state of the corridor from before. Now it's worse. Whole storage compartments have been ripped out. There's a mixture of blood and debris, but the pressure seal appears to be holding, for now.

Arkov takes hold of my hands. That makes them hurt even more, but I steel myself to look away. "How bad?" I ask.

"If you mean the ship, I don't know," Arkov replies. "If you're talking about yourself, well...pretty bad, I'd say. We need to get you some meds and some better help."

"The medical room's gone."

"I know."

There's a calm about doctors when you talk to them. It's trained reassurance, a technique refined and passed on by practitioners for hundreds of years. Arkov has none of that experience. He's just the only person here with time to keep an eye on me.

"What happened to...Shah?" I ask.

"Came down to help us, he said," Arkov explains. "When the bot got through to the terminal, he sealed the doors, trapping it in here. We were supposed to isolate and shut down the terminal, but by the time I got into the system it had already bypassed the lockout commands. Shah tried to attack it with whatever he could find, and it killed him."

"He was...already dead?"

"Yeah. You didn't know?"

"I couldn't tell if anyone was in here."

Arkov blinks, registering that information. For the first time, I notice he's hurt too. There are tears in his suit, and his right leg is twisted at an awkward angle below the knee. "Well, we're alive," he says, trying to muster a smile.

"Shah had his own agenda," I say. "He was supposed to be watching me, but instead, he hit me with a Taser and left me locked up in the inventory section. I don't know who he was working for."

"The captain will decide what happens next," Arkov says. He's finished wrapping my hands and glances toward Chase. "Once we get through, we need to be ready to move."

Chase turns toward us both. He's focused on the comms headset he's wearing and holds a hand up to indicate he's in mid-conversation. "...it may be difficult for you to get to us, sir. Whole sections of the ship have depressurised.... Okay, will do.... Aye, aye."

Chase taps the bead at his collar and looks up. "We need to suit up for EVA," he says. "The rest of the crew are meeting us in airlock control if they can."

"What's the plan?" I ask.

Chase scowls. "Not a good one," he says. "But then, we don't have a lot of options."

CHAPTER FORTY-NINE

Shann

I've given the order. We're abandoning ship.

We don't have accurate data, but the *Khidr* has lost the battle. The *Gallowglass* is built tougher and proved more resilient. Computer projections suggest it won't be long before our ship starts to break apart.

The only hope we have is to invade theirs.

I'm holding on to the safety rail next to the bridge exit with my right hand. My left is floating in front of me. Travers is helping Chiu extricate herself from her seat. Le Garre is checking on Keiyho. They've both performed heroics fixing the atmospheric leak in the view screen and shutters with repair foam. Now they're helping their crewmates. We've all removed our helmets. Somehow, the bridge's pressure seal is intact.

Le Garre looks at me and shakes her head. I know what that means. *Keiyho's gone.*

I know that moment will be scarred in my mind. Afterward, if we survive, there will be a reckoning, an emotional and mental cost for all that has been done. I will face judgement from a board of inquiry. Above them, I will face judgement from myself.

The loss of friends, people who I cared about, will weigh heaviest on my soul.

I can't face that now. Otherwise, it will paralyse me.

The ship is a friend too. Every inch of the *Khidr* is my home, the place I live. The things I treasure and own are here. All of that, I have to let go.

We all have to let go.

"Make sure you check your suits. Your leak detectors could be faulty."

Le Garre nods. She's always been thin-faced, but now she's a hollow version of herself. Something about her is damaged or broken. I wonder if she sees the same thing in my eyes. "Ship's controls are set," she says. "We have twenty-five minutes before the *Khidr* starts to pull herself away with the tiny amount of fuel there is left in the manoeuvering thrusters. She'll then try to brake and assume a stationary position."

"We're on a countdown then," I say. "We need to be aboard the *Gallowglass* before we're too far apart to make the trip. What data do we have on getting across?"

"There's a loss of pressure in the corridor just beyond here," Le Garre says. "We'll need to check every compartment before we go inside. That's going to make this slow going."

I'm thinking about this, trying to come up with a different solution. "Do we know where the *Gallowglass* airlock is?"

"Yes, the computer identified the drone garage, service airlock and missile launch tubes as entry points to the ship," Le Garre replies. "The tubes are too small for us, but the airlock is close by. If we can find a sizeable hull breach, we might be able to EVA over to it."

"There may be a hull breach we can make use of on their ship too," Travers adds.

"Possibly," I say, "but I don't want to rely on it. Let's aim for a tethered EVA to the airlock. That way we're aiming for a known target."

"Leaping off a moving ship onto another moving ship is not going to be easy," Le Garre warns, "especially when there's debris flying around. We're more likely to die than make it. If we could get to the airlock, we'd be able to pick up some of the EVA suits."

"We don't have time."

"Chase, Arkov and Sellis are in airlock control," Travers says. "I'm in communication with them. We can ask them to make for the same place. They may be able to help us."

I look at him. "That's seven of us, with Johansson making eight. Have you heard from anyone else?"

Travers shakes his head. "I can't access the biomonitoring feeds or positional trackers. Duggins was in the reactor room. He mentioned a possible leak when he went down there."

A reactor leak would be one of the worst things that could happen. The central section of the ship holds two small nuclear reactors, advanced versions of the ones developed for submarines, and a set of RTB power units. If any of those systems have been damaged, we could already be dead and not know it. As chief engineer, Duggins is the best qualified person to assess a possible reactor breach and deal with it before it became too dangerous. Also, he cares.

"You've heard from no one else?" I ask Travers.

"No."

I hesitate. What is a captain supposed to do when there's uncertainty and imminent danger? Do we search for the people who might be alive, or save the ones who are?

Including myself.

More guilt. I know a decision has to be made, and I know what the decision has to be, but I'm responsible. These people placed their trust in me.

To be in command, to be an officer means you have to be prepared to let people die.

"We make the attempt. Gather up every emergency oxygen tube you can find. There should be at least six in this room." I look at Chiu. "Ensign, I need to know how you're doing."

Chiu doesn't raise her head or acknowledge me. Travers leans in toward her, muttering words in her ear, and suddenly she jerks up and stares wildly. "I'll make it, Captain," she says.

"Okay." I have to accept her answer. She knows staying here will mean death. If she can't cope, bringing her with us might mean the death of us all.

I take the easy choice and accept her at her word. "One tube for Chiu and one tube for me. Travers, Le Garre, you both take two."

"Captain," Le Garre says. "I'm not sure that's—"

"It's decided. Let's move on."

The emergency oxygen cylinders have approximately twenty minutes of supply in them. There's no carbon filtration, so within one or two minutes, they'll all run out at the same time. Travers and Le Garre are less injured than Chiu and myself, so they get the extra. We have to get across to the *Gallowglass* and find a compartment that's still got air, and we have to do it quickly.

I glance at each of the three in turn. "Once we leave this room, there's no going back. We have to be ready."

Le Garre and Chiu nod. "Aye, aye," says Travers. "Give the word and I'll depressurise the room."

"Tell Chase what we're doing and execute the plan, Lieutenant."

"Doing that now," he says and starts tapping on his screen. "Chase said the airlock terminal is still active, so I'm sending him trajectory plots and our expected route. They've already suited up. They're just waiting on us to give the go."

"How many EVA suits are there ready to go?" Le Garre asks.

"Five," Travers says. "Three of them have thruster packs."

"If they bring the spares, we might last longer."

Le Garre has a point. We can't transfer to the empty suits while we're trying to get to the *Gallowglass*, but they have oxygen tanks, which could be invaluable. That said, if we take all the suits, anyone else who is alive on board will have nothing.

"Ask them to bring a spare suit, but leave one behind. Keep monitoring the comms too, just in case someone else makes contact."

"What about the object we found?" Travers asks. "It's down there in the suit store. Should they bring it with them?"

"No, we leave it," I decide immediately. "I know it's a loss, but that thing's been out in deep space a long time. It'll last a bit longer in the store. Besides, we may be able to come back and retrieve it once we've taken command of the *Gallowglass*."

"That might not be easy," Le Garre warns.

"I'm hoping it will be."

Travers finishes working on his screen and looks up. "There's an arms locker a little way down from here. I might be able to make it there and pull out what's left. Could help us if we encounter resistance on their ship."

"Be quick," I tell him. "Once we're out there, we're on the clock."

"I will," he promises.

I glance at the other two. With Travers about his task, Le Garre will have to assist Chiu in getting through the corridor. I'm struggling too, but I'll cope. I have to. "Helmets on, people. Travers, tell Sam to get outside and look for us and get the computer to depressurise this room. Once that's done, we open the hatch. First sign of a breach big enough, we assess and look for the EVA."

Le Garre grimaces as she pulls down her visor. Her words come over the comms system. "An eyeballed EVA. *Merde*."

I shrug as I, too, seal myself in. "Can't be helped, Major. I doubt any cable is going to survive the comparative velocities. We'll tether together and hope Sam and Arkov can find us."

"Okay."

We wait another minute or two as the air drains from the room. I'm conscious that every moment we're breathing from our emergency supply is a moment lost. This is also a test of suit integrity. No one reports a problem. Eventually, Travers nods and I activate the hatch release.

We stumble into the corridor, struggling with the shifting forces. There is a jagged hole torn out of the wall. Beyond it I see stars and spinning ruin. I make a quick assessment of the jagged breach. It looks big enough, but we'll need to be careful. Sharp metal edges could slice through suit, skin and bone, ending any one of us. The continual alteration of the ship's motion through thruster adjustment and collisions means the reactive 'down' on us is changing constantly. You can't plan for that and it makes any movement risky.

I'm following Travers and using my right hand to do everything. My left shoulder is painful and becomes agony if I try to do anything with my arm. Behind me, Le Garre is helping Chiu.

We'll make it. We *have* to make it.

Travers turns toward me and points beyond the breach. I nod. He starts moving off to be about his task. I continue toward the breach.

The corridor reminds me of our trip to the *Hercules* a lifetime ago. Careful design and organisation have become wreckage. The spiraling movements of our ship are shaking loose more and more of its internal components, turning each compartment into rattling tins. No one ever thinks about the poor beans or coins inside those tins. Right now, that would be us.

I'm beside the breach. I activate the magnets in my suit and anchor up to the ruined wall. Le Garre brings up Chiu and helps her settle in on the other side. Immediately I start feeling the ship's movements dragging on my suit. "You go first, Major," I say. "That way you can help us both if we need it."

"Aye, aye, Captain," Le Garre replies and starts moving carefully through the gap. I switch my comms channel.

"Shann to Chase, can you hear me?"

"Yes, Captain, we're just getting outside."

"One of you needs to locate Johansson. She's in some sort of converted projectile, attached to the hull of the *Gallowglass*. If we don't reach her soon, she'll run out of air."

There's a pause before Sam replies. "We're aware of her situation, Captain."

"That your way of admitting you helped her?"

"Yes."

"We'll deal with that later. Right now, someone needs to help her before she dies."

"Understood."

"I'm ordering you to save her, Sam. Leave Arkov and Sellis to pick us up."

"Aye, aye, Captain."

Le Garre is outside. She's gesturing for us to follow. I point at Chiu, who struggles to detach herself. Le Garre reaches down a hand and Chiu grabs it, letting herself be pulled through the gap. Somehow, she makes it without being snagged on the torn layers of the ship's hull.

"You next, Captain," says Le Garre.

I deactivate the magnetic grips and let myself ease away from where I was. As if in response, a dent appears in the wall opposite and a storage unit shatters. Part of it tumbles toward me. The ship shifts, and I can almost hear her groaning. Instinctively, I push off to my right, to avoid the debris, and my left arm spasms in pain. I wish I could activate the painkiller injection built into the suit, but I can't. I need to stay clear and focused.

I'm not dying here. This captain is not going down with her ship.

I look up. Le Garre is still there, reaching out her hand. I grab it.

CHAPTER FIFTY

Sellis

Imagine living in a snow globe after it's been shaken. All those flakes falling around you, some of them bigger than your head.

Yeah, this is a bit like that, only worse.

I'm floating in a blizzard of broken and twisted metal. In all this, I could be hit by something tiny that pierces my suit, pushed off course by something large or cut open by something sharp.

Everywhere I look becomes a nightmare of fatal collisions. The lamps on my EVA suit pick out thousands of fragments, the remains of our ship and their ship, all jumbled together in a swirling mass of ruin. I feel safer without the light, more relaxed being ignorant, but it won't help.

Nothing will help me right now, except me.

I can see larger debris: A gutted corridor, spinning wildly, the remains of an engine pod, the mounting for one of the point defence machine guns and more, many more. I can't tell what parts came from what ship. It's all jumbled together, colliding and annihilating, colliding and—

"Sellis, something wrong? You need to keep up." It's Chase. He sounds worried.

"No, I'm fine, Sergeant, it's just…well…I'm worried about all the wreckage."

"We're on the clock, Sellis. We have to take risks."

I find myself smiling. "Now you're talking my language, Sergeant."

Time to focus. The computer system in my helmet is projecting a path through the chaos. Ahead of me is Arkov. He's moving through the cloud of spinning bits, dragging the spare EVA suit with him.

I need to follow and keep him in sight. I touch the propulsion control with my left hand and thumb the joystick in my right.

There's tingling pain from the burns on both hands, but not as bad as I first feared it might be. A short burst of the micro-jet and I'm away, adjusting to match the plotted pathway. The farther I lag behind, the more tempting it is to move faster. Moving faster in a debris field means more chance of death.

This is only my fourth proper EVA. The first two were orbital training runs when I worked on the station. I did a maintenance and repair mission a month or so ago. The ship looked a lot different then. Now she's taken a beating and she's bleeding out, all over the place.

We're making our way around the *Khidr*, toward the bridge section where Captain Shann and her group are. We'll pick them up and transfer everyone to the *Gallowglass*.

In old movies, pirates would board merchant ships to steal their booty. From what I've seen, they'd get from ship to ship by swinging from the rigging, or fixing a plank and charging across. Then pull out swords and pistols to fight the enemy crew. All very loud and fast, athletic stuff.

Out here, things are a bit different. Shann and the others will push off from the ship toward the *Gallowglass*, but everything is moving and changing position. They're in basic crew suits, with emergency oxygen. They don't have a means of correcting their course. That means we have to collect them.

And we have to do it quickly.

I'm coming around the side of the ship. The sun is in the distance, and my visor starts to polarise in response to the glare. I can see the *Gallowglass* now, similar but different to our ship. She's sleek, shaped like a bottle with a rounded top. She has four engine pylons extending from midsection, making her look like a cross if she was coming straight toward you. The rotational deck is a section built into the main bulk of the ship, rather than standing out, like ours. The nearest engine to me is wrecked, crumpled in upon the support struts. The cooling veins are like broken sticks or fingers, reaching out at odd angles. I can see great welts across the rest of the *Gallowglass*'s hull, but otherwise, she's pretty much intact.

I look to my right and suddenly there's a lump in my throat. The *Khidr* is a broken mess. I'm a witness to her end, an entropic death of vast beauty as she breaks apart. Fragments of her body trail into the darkness, carried away by the forces that drove them to separate from the ship. The damage is catastrophic; there is no hope of repair or resurrection. The scale of this is vast and difficult for my mind to comprehend. I'm looking at a floating cloud that stretches over miles and miles. Arkov, Chase and I are the tiny audience to a tragedy.

That was my home, you fucking bastards.

I don't know who I'm blaming. Captain Shann must have made the call to crash the ship, but the blackmailing shits on the *Gallowglass* forced her into it.

It's done. I have to adapt and move on.

The next twenty minutes will be crucial.

"Arkov, report?" It's Sam Chase on the comms.

"I'm about a third of the way around, Sergeant. Sellis is trailing. No sign of any unusual activity. If the enemy is out here, they're playing a careful game."

"We can't assume anything. Stay alert. Sellis, catch up."

"Aye, aye."

Direct orders. I've an urge to tell Chase to fuck off, but he's right. I've dawdled, and they can't afford to waste time on me. We survive by addressing the problem. Right now, that's getting everyone to the other ship. The bridge crew are relying on us, which means I'm getting a shot at redemption. If I get through this, Captain Shann won't forget my actions. She'll evaluate everything and make a judgement call. Of course, if we get taken prisoner as soon as we board the enemy ship, I've still got my code. There's no way to lose out to either side by doing my best out here.

Another push on the jets and I'm easing toward Arkov. The spare suit is trailing behind him on a tether. I ease in and grab hold. There's a heavy *thunk* against my helmet as a shard of metal the size of my hand appears out of nowhere and ricochets off and away from us. Its jagged edges gleam in the sunlight.

Close call.

I look down and note both EVA suits have accumulated a number of similar fragments. Some have lodged into the spare and torn through layers of the outer fabric and plastics. They must have done the same to my suit, but I can't look down to examine it. I have to rely on the pressure alarm and that may come too late to save me.

EVA suits are a bit like armour. There are multiple weaves,

designed to prevent a breach of the internal atmosphere. However, it's only a matter of time before something gets through. It's bad for us, but the risk for Shann and her people in emergency suits is much greater; fewer layers equals more chance of damage. They'll be sliced to pieces without warning if they try to move through all this.

"Sellis here; all caught up to the spare suit. Doing a visual check. We're accumulating a lot of debris. How's it going in front, Vasili?"

"Difficult," Arkov replies. "I'm managing a suit leak."

"Want me to lead?"

"If you can, yes."

Another touch on the jets and a careful trajectory adjustment. The pattering sound of objects colliding with my helmet increases as I accelerate. I have to force myself not to flinch every time a shard of metal or plastic smacks into the DuraGlas viewing plate. If it's going to crack, it's going to crack. There's not much I can do.

I'm alongside Arkov. He's clutching at his neck with his left hand. That must be where his suit's been cut open. The EVA propulsion unit needs both hands to manage, right for thrust and left for direction, so he's struggling. If I tether up and take the lead, he can concentrate on making a repair.

This is fucking suicide.

I activate the tether launch. The plug targets Arkov's suit and fires. The cable snakes out and magnetises to his chest. *Perfect!* If I'd snagged him anywhere else, we wouldn't have been aligned and I'd have started pulling him around in a circle. I can't claim any credit for the shot, though; the targeting system did all the work.

Carefully, while the line plays out, I maneuver myself directly in front of Arkov. My propellant tank is down to eighty per cent. After this, I'll need to conserve fuel, in case we have to make more than one run. "Okay, I have control," I announce.

"You have control," Arkov replies. The line begins to reel in. The sensor will detect when the slack has been taken up, working slowly to bring us all closer together.

We're nearly around the ship and through the worst of the debris. Ahead are three people, moving on the side of the *Khidr*'s hull. They've climbed out of a tear in the side of the corridor just outside the bridge. As I watch, a fourth figure joins them.

Last time I was on the bridge, I was part of a mutiny.

"Sellis to Shann, we have you in sight."

"Confirmed, Specialist. We see you. Pushing off now."

CHAPTER FIFTY-ONE

Shann

My back is against the broken hull of the *Khidr*, and I'm looking out into the great empty. The only thing between me and an eternity drifting away is our enemy.

The *Gallowglass*.

I'm staring at a beautiful monster. She's an attractive vessel, clearly designed to be durable, with all the extremities carefully pulled in, to make her bottle-shaped. There's damage and scarring to her hull, with some trailing wreckage, but not nearly enough to be fatal.

I hate that ship. I know the nuts, bolts, metal, plastic and DuraGlas can't really be blamed for what's been done to us, but it doesn't stop me blaming them. I'll need to reconcile that. What has hunted us to the edge of oblivion might well become our saviour.

All four of us are lined up out here, our arms linked, and our emergency tethers connected. I'm on one end, holding on to Le Garre with my right hand. We need to make the leap together, so we stay together. That way Sellis and Arkov have a better chance of saving everyone. "Travers, we all set?"

"Aye, aye, Captain."

"Together then. Three, two, one, go!"

We push off. The pain in my left shoulder makes me want to scream, but I clench my teeth and keep it in. My crew need me to be solid. We have to move together.

"Arkov, we're away."

"Confirmed, Captain, this is Sellis. We see you."

I frown. Sellis is leading. Why? I'm still struggling to trust him, but then we had to arrest and interrogate Arkov as well, before clearing him of Drake's murder, the first sign that this whole business was going bad. Ironic then that I'm relying on these two. One who I betrayed and the other who betrayed me.

I'm looking sunward, in the direction our rescuers are coming from. I can't see them, but I can see a vast field of debris. We're on the edge of it for now, but the *Khidr* is breaking apart. It's only a matter of time before this dangerous trip becomes impossible.

Hopefully, we've escaped in time.

"Sellis, you're coming in from the sun. We're not going to be able to eyeball your approach," Travers says.

"Understood, Lieutenant. I'll give you a heads-up and let you know if we need any specific alterations."

"Thank you."

Specific alterations. There's not much we can do now we're away, but Sellis means small movements, like shifting your arms to ensure you have the best chance of catching a line or a hand. Every adjustment has a cause and effect in zero gravity. That's something we have to be very careful of out here, with no walls or handholds to grab on to.

"We're six hundred metres away. Closing at three metres per second."

I'm doing the calculations; I bet all the others are too. It'll be a little over three minutes to contact. My oxygen reserve is now at twelve minutes. We'll have nine minutes to get across and get inside the *Gallowglass*. Instinctively, I want to order Sellis and Arkov to hurry, to get here faster, but that could make the situation worse. If they miss, we're screwed.

I have to trust that Sellis is happy with his interception speed. I have to have faith he'll come through. If he meant to betray us again, why would he take the risk? I don't know the answer to that.

"Captain, before we do this, I need to let you know something."

"What's that, Sellis?"

"When you left me in the corridor with Shah. After the conversation with the *Gallowglass*, I tried to convince him to let me go to the airlock and meet the boarding party. We got into an altercation and he let some things slip. I think he was working for someone else."

"You think he was another mutineer?"

"No, someone else entirely. Shah was no friend of Rocher. He died trying to stop their drone hacker. He was working for another group. Maybe all of the *Hercules* people were? A group who wants the *Gallowglass* destroyed and all this to go away, another faction?"

I remember the frozen bees and the other strange things we found on board the freighter. *Someone who was part of smuggling all that colonial stuff.* "Why are you telling me this now, Sellis?" I ask.

"I'm telling everyone because everyone needs to know, Captain. Just in case I don't make it. If Shah was working for another interest, I doubt we've heard the last of them."

"Understood." I make a mental note to sit down with all the crew and talk this all out. We've fought together and lost friends. Our bonds have been tested, and at times, they've been broken, but I need these people at least as much as they need me.

"Ten seconds to intercept, Captain," Sellis announces. "We'll be approaching from your left. We're all tethered. I'm in the lead, Arkov behind and the spare suit behind that. You all need to grab on and hold on. Once you're secure, we'll work out the adjustments to get us across to the *Gallowglass*."

"Understood." I glance toward the ship again. It doesn't seem any bigger, but judging distance and size of things in space is tricky. You don't realise how much stock your mind places in the relative positioning of other objects to determine size and range. I guess if I turned around, I'd see how far we've travelled from the *Khidr*, but I dare not shift positions now, unless I'm told to.

"Five seconds."

I grit my teeth and look left and right as much as I can. I think I can see something, a silhouette in the sun's glare. *Is that a hand reaching out?* I'm not sure, but instinctively my hand goes up in response, bringing with it another stab of pain in my shoulder. I reach out.

Something grabs hold of my wrist, pulling me forward. I scream, and the hand lets go, I feel fingers slipping away along my arm. I have to stop myself from letting go of Le Garre and trying to reach out with both hands, but I need to stay calm, wait, let Sellis and Arkov do the work.

A pull in the other direction, from Le Garre. "We're secure," she says over the comms. "I have the tether from Arkov wrapped around my ankle."

"Confirmed," Sellis replies. "Now for the hard part, sorting out this tangle and getting us across."

"Take your time," Travers says. "But not *too* much time."

Le Garre's hold on my arm loosens a little. There's different movements affecting us, dragging her forward, pulling me in behind. Something clatters against my helmet, leaving a mark on the glass. Then I feel an impact against my hip. "We're moving into the debris field," I warn.

"Can't be helped, Captain," Sellis says. "We need to get you people across as quickly as possible. I've got a plot on a possible airlock. Hopefully, we can make it."

"Ain't a lot of point if you drag in a few bags of broken flesh and bone," Travers says.

"I know that, Lieutenant. With respect, let me do my fucking job."

I'm smiling at Sellis's reply. I can't help myself. In all the time I've known him on the ship, he's been in the crowd, never one to volunteer or try too hard. I know he likes his cards and his dice. I've never once heard him bite back.

I'm pulled sharply to the right and I catch sight of the spare EVA suit to my left. It's being dragged along by Arkov, who is being dragged along by Sellis. Le Garre is behind me now, pressed against my back. Our arms are linked at the elbow. Hopefully, she's managed to keep hold of the others as well.

"Chiu, are you okay?" Travers is speaking. Out of the corner of my eye, I can see the two of them pressed together as we tumble around. The lines are becoming tangled, a problem if they constrict a limb, or worse, a neck. The forces out here can be difficult to judge at times. It's different to being inside in zero gravity. You don't realise how much walls, rails and anything else you can grab hold of stop you from losing control of your movements.

"She's unconscious. I can't get a reply." Travers's voice is professional, but there's a quiver in there. I know what he's feeling; he's the XO – second-in-command. He has the same guilt that I've pushed to the back of my mind.

"Make sure she's secure," I order, keeping my tone firm and neutral, trying to help him get a hold on himself, as well as her. "There's nothing you can do to help her right now. We'll make an assessment when we're back in atmosphere."

Travers doesn't reply, but I can see him working. Maybe he doesn't trust himself to say the words. I let that slide.

"Okay, everyone, get ready; we're moving the bus," Sellis says.

I grit my teeth and tense my arm. When the pull comes, it drags me backward. I can see the *Khidr* now, forty or so metres away. If we'd been left to drift, it would have taken hours or even days to get to the *Gallowglass*. We'd have suffocated long before we got close, even if we'd been moving in the right direction.

Now we have a chance.

CHAPTER FIFTY-TWO

Johansson

I'm getting cold and sleepy.

The painkillers I've taken are part of the problem now. I can't focus on the screen in front of me. The commands I've inputted should give Captain Shann access to the ship and all its subsystems. Now that it's done, I need to let them know.

But I'm tired and I want to close my eyes.

I reach up to reactivate the comms. It's a huge effort. I'm not sure why. Something might be wrong with my oxygen supply. In training, you'd declare an emergency, but I can't do anything about now, while I'm out here on my own.

There's chatter on the channel. I've been ignoring it, but I have the gist. Shann's led the crew outside. They're transferring to the *Gallowglass* as planned. I can only imagine how tough an EVA that will be. The terse, military instructions and reporting doesn't give much of a sense of the emotions bubbling under the surface in all of us.

There's a pause and I patch in. "Johansson to Shann."

"Good to hear from you, Ensign. Go ahead."

"I've constructed an access profile for the *Gallowglass* computer system. It should help you take control of the ship when you get on board. I'm transmitting the necessary codes."

"Good work. Any thoughts on how we can open the airlock?"

I open up the command terminal again. "I should be able to do that from here. You just need to let me know when you're in position."

"Do you have enough O_2?"

"I think so. There's some kind of circulation issue in here, but I can handle it."

"Chase is on his way to you. We'll get you out."

"Thanks, Captain, but I'll need to be here when you reach the airlock."

"There are alternative options for getting in. Don't stay out there any longer than you have to."

I don't reply to that. Acknowledgment of the order means I have to obey it. Instead, I start inputting commands into the terminal window. This time, it's hard to stay focused, but I need to try. *I need to get this done.*

ACC COM TREE

Command Tree Open.

INST ~CTELL [3AB] #LOC XLOCK OPEN

Confirm AIRLOCK open? Y/N

My finger hovers over the Y button. Once I press it, the sequence will begin. All Fleet ships have an automated safety closure procedure, which I can't override, so, if the motion sensors don't detect activity in the exterior chamber after five minutes, the outer doors will close, and the system will repressurise, meaning it won't be able to be opened again for at least fifteen more minutes. That means I need to stay awake and focused just long enough for Shann to get to the exterior hatch. Then I can trigger the procedure and give them the maximum amount of time to get inside.

I shift my elbow so it is supported. When it's quiet and I'm on my own, the sleepiness is more difficult to shake. My eyelids droop constantly and it's a fight to keep them open. I remember the feeling. It's the one you get on a long drive. They call it micro-sleeping, where your brain fights between the competing needs of your body's fatigue and paying attention to the road. Eventually it becomes a desensitised game, where you seem to lose comprehension of how dangerous it will be for you to fall asleep. Closing my eyes for just a moment won't hurt anyone, just a second of....

No! These people are relying on me. I need to stay awake.

The comms channel pops, rescuing me. "Chase to Johansson, I'm three hundred metres out. What's your situation?"

Sam's voice banishes any thought of sleep. I want to shout for joy and tell him what his voice means to me right now, but that isn't what he needs. That isn't what I need. My gaze flickers over the readouts. "Situation is tricky, but functional. Seventeen minutes of O_2 left. The torpedo took a battering on impact and so did I. I'm not sure how bad the damage is."

"Is your EVA suit compromised?"

"Don't know. There's no current pressure loss, but that could be down to how I'm wedged in. I think there might be a problem with the mixture. I'm finding it hard to stay awake and concentrate, but that could be the painkillers I took."

"Okay," Sam says. "My plan to get you out is to cut through the panels we welded on, but if the EVA system and your internal suit are abraded, you could die pretty quick. The alternative is to drag the whole casing over to the airlock as is and unpack you once we're inside. May take a little longer, but there's less risk."

"Visual surveillance from in here is limited. I can't tell if that will be easy."

"We'll know as soon as I get close then. How much thruster fuel do you have left?"

"Not much, about eight per cent or so."

"May still be useful, if we're careful."

I access the surviving camera on the drone arm. I can't turn it, so the only way to get an external view is to detach from the *Gallowglass*'s computer network. I'm not doing that until Shann and the others reach the airlock. I'll have to rely on Sam. I'm already relying on Sam way too much.

I think over my decision to do this. My illegal mission was a calculated risk that increased the chance of the *Khidr* crew, people who I care about, surviving this altercation. Back then, only the percentages mattered. Now, each moment matters. Every little effort is part of the war to live a little longer.

There's a sudden shift, and my helmet crashes against the side of the metal interior. A hole appears in the casing just above my portable screen and the torpedo starts to rotate to the left. The missile has been hit by something, probably a large piece of debris. It was only a matter of time. I've no way of knowing how long I can hold this position. I need to act fast.

I press the 'Y' on the screen keyboard. A moment later, the display goes blank and the glass cracks. Slivers and flakes peel and drift away. Without it, I've got no control over the drone thruster or the securing arm. I have to hope the command got through before—

"Johansson, can you hear me? Johansson? I'm in visual range, three minutes to intercept."

I open my mouth to reply, but everything is spinning and turning. I remember my high-g training and close my eyes, fighting to stay calm, to keep my breathing and heart rate even and regular. "Sam, I've got a problem here, some sort of collision. The controls are out."

"Yeah, I see it. You're in the middle of a cloud of wreckage. Hold on, April, I'm coming."

"Not a lot I can do," I breathe in reply. "Just got to ride it out."

"Keep talking to me, tell me what's happening."

Breathe, in...out...in...out... "The impact has started a spin. I think the drone arm's torn off. I'm no longer anchored to the ship. There are breaches in the shell too."

"Might be something we can use."

"Only if you can halt this spin." Behind the defensive wall of my eyelids, I'm thinking through the problem, mass and velocity versus the amount of thruster fuel Sam has left. Even if he can get me out, we still need to get to the airlock. "You'll need to make an assessment when you get close. If you can't reach me, then... don't try."

My voice betrays me saying that. Now I'm here, despite all the calculations and my commitment to the risk, I don't want to die.

"Thirty seconds to intercept," Sam says. "Get ready. I'm coming in fast."

I tense. There's nothing else I can do to prepare, wedged in as I am.

A moment later, the casing around me shifts again and I'm dragged in the opposite direction. I'm forced face-first into the metal plates. My helmet grinds against them and something presses against my back. The breach alarm goes off. I'm leaking atmosphere. It's what we feared; my suit has been compromised.

"Sam, I don't think I'm—"

A hand grabs my wrist. I open my eyes and see a cable snaking down to secure itself to my shoulder. A helmeted head appears in the torn gap of the torpedo casing. "Give me a minute or two to sort this," Sam says.

"I'm losing O_2!"

"Okay, I'll look for leaks as I go. Stay calm; you've done the hard bit and saved all of us. Now let me help you!"

The hand lets go and disappears. Something inside me relaxes. He's right; I need to stay calm. There's no shame in being rescued. The hard, uncompromising knot within me has built up walls of stoic resistance, while fueling a self-critical expectation to exceed. It all stems from my need for validation. The lieutenant accreditation has been right in front of me, and I'm inching closer and closer toward it. Proving myself to others has always been part of that journey, but it's made me ignore something else that will always be as important so long as I serve in Fleet.

I'm part of a team.

A line appears in the metal casing above my right eye. There's a haze around it, like you might see on a hot summer's day when you're looking into the distance. I know what it means. Sam is using thermite paste to hack through the torpedo's shell. If any of it gets on my suit, it'll burn through that and anything inside it.

Including me.

The metal peels away. The gap is a lot bigger now. I might be able to get through it, but I can't get enough leverage. I remember the casing crumpling on impact. My legs might be stuck. I can't tell.

"Sam, I need—"

"Hang on a minute longer," he says.

Something gives way around me and the spinning slows down. I can move my feet. Sam must have cut away part of the torpedo. I'm pulled to the right. "Okay, we're clear," says Sam. There's a hand on my hip and the flashing oxygen warning stops. "Okay, I've patched the leak that I can see. Give me your numbers. How long have I got to get you into the airlock?"

"About six minutes, according to the readout," I report. "I'm still venting, but it's a slow leak."

"Manageable?"

"I think so."

Sam chuckles. "We both know you've stretched the numbers before. The vents on your Sabatier system should be clear. See if you can get that working. Won't give you much more time, but a few seconds might make the difference."

I try to move my arms. My hand is trapped, and my half arm isn't dexterous enough to do what's needed without a prosthetic attachment. "I can't reach the controls," I confess.

"Okay." Suddenly, Sam is right in front of me. He smiles briefly before his face pinches in concentration. His EVA suit is a mess, full of tiny nicks and tears. He reaches around and activates the Sabatier unit. "Keep an eye on the readouts," he says. Briefly his hand touches mine again and he hands me something. I recognise the shape of a micro-laser cutter. "This'll give you something to pass the time, but be careful where you aim it. I couldn't use it too much; otherwise I might have hurt you. There's about half a charge left. You should be able to get to work on the rest of the casing."

"Will do," I reply. Sam disappears from view. There's a sharp tug and I'm moving. We're away, en route to the airlock.

At that moment, I allow myself to imagine being anywhere but out here. I remember the nice places, like my room on the *Khidr* and the small bag of possessions I brought with me. I won't see any of those again, but I might see people I care about. Some of the crew and even... Earth? Home?

There are a lot of tough times ahead, but if the *Gallowglass* is intact and we can take control of her, we might be able to get to Phobos. The station will have received our transmission by now; they might even be looking for us. *It'll be some debriefing.*

I'm working methodically on the remains of the torpedo casing. Slivers of metal drift away as I slice through each section, gradually freeing my arms. Sam's tether is attached to a band of metal around my waist. I angle the invisible beam away from it and leave it intact.

The section around my head splits apart and drifts away, along with the remainder of my portable screen, now just a shell full of frozen liquid crystal and bits of glass. I can turn my head. I glance around and catch sight of Sam, a few metres away, towing me through the debris around the *Gallowglass*. We're moving along the hull, much like I did before with the *Khidr*, during our EVA to repair the transmitter, but this time, we're using a thruster pack.

I'm facing the *Gallowglass*. Her outer skin is pitted and scarred. Hundreds of micro-impacts abrade the surface of any ship when it's been in space a while, but this damage is extensive by comparison, the sign of combat with the *Khidr*. It should be even worse than this, considering what we've thrown at her. The hull plating must be reinforced. Probably a couple of more layers on this ship compared to ours. I wonder what it looks like inside.

There's a tug on the line. The comms channel pops. Sam coughs into my ear. "April, we've got a problem."

"What is it?"

"Something's just cut my suit and I'm all out of patches."

"How far to the airlock?"

"About one hundred metres."

"Hold on, I'm coming."

I grab the tether, pull myself forward and loop the slack around my other arm. I'm a few metres behind Sam, and it's difficult to close the gap with one hand. Every move I make disturbs the straight-line velocity of our travel, meaning Sam has to use his thrusters to course correct and push against my pulling on the line.

I reach his side. I see the leak immediately – a cut under his ribs. I reach out and wrap my arms around him awkwardly, using the hug to put pressure on the wound and stop the escaping oxygen. "Better?" I ask.

"A bit," Sam replies. "Move your arm down a little.... There, that's pretty good. We'll make it."

I sigh in relief. "Good."

CHAPTER FIFTY-THREE

Sellis

Fifty metres out and I can see the airlock door opening. I almost whoop for joy; it's like someone inside rolled out the fucking red carpet.

We're going to make it!

At that moment, I feel a pull on the tether and I have to adjust, burning valuable thrust. "Hey, keep still back there!" I say down the comms channel.

"Doing our best to, Sellis," Le Garre answers. It's good to hear her voice. "Might not be us, though. I'm noting some anomalous phenomena."

"What do you mean?"

"Some of the debris appears to be moving back toward the *Khidr*."

"What?" My first instinct is to turn my head and try to look around, but, thankfully, I catch myself. The resistance is still there. Instead of constant velocity, our speed is reducing, a bit like a car back on Earth when you take your foot off the gas. Out here, there shouldn't be anything to slow us down, unless we're subject to a competing force. I can't think of anything on the smashed-up *Khidr* capable of doing that.

"Shann to Sellis."

"Yes, Captain?"

"What's your assessment of the effect of this on our chances?"

I glance at the thruster gauge. There's thirty-four per cent left in the tank, and the numbers are moving faster than I'd like. "We should be okay, provided the situation doesn't get worse."

"Understood. Best you focus on the task ahead then," Shann replies. "We'll monitor the changes as best we can."

"Aye, aye." There's some tension in her voice. I'm aware I'm being managed. Aside from the mutiny issue, there's a reversal of rank. A major and a captain relying on the ranks to get them through. They don't like it.

Ten metres to the entrance.

Five metres.

Contact.

My foot slips on the edge of the hatch. I grab a handrail for support and switch off the thrusters. I pull myself in. The airlock interior looks remarkably undamaged. I detach the thruster chair and let it drift into the room, while I stay near the door, holding another rail. I turn around to see the long, jumbled trail of people still secured to the chair by tethers. Behind them is the *Khidr*, drifting away from us. I've been dragging all these people along, but only now do I see the desperate chaos of this rescue that belies the calm, military conversation.

The *Gallowglass* is also moving, slowly rotating away from the others. The motion generates a small amount of gravity, forcing me to brace myself against the wall. I glance to my left at the airlock door control. This is a moment where I'm empowered. I could make a choice right here to detach the tethers and shut the hatch. If there's anyone left alive in this ship, I'd be demonstrating my loyalty to them by murdering my crew. Maybe that would deal with the threats and the blackmail.

No. People who try to lever you with things like that never let it go. While it might look like a way out, it isn't. It's a route to being a slave, a prisoner, forced to do what they want.

I'm under no illusions. The road back to being trusted by the people out there hanging on to me will be hard, but I want that.

I fucking want that!

I reach for the tether attachment and unclip it from the chair, wrapping the cable around one of the safety handles and looping it so it won't come undone. Amazing how you only miss something when it's gone. Le Garre aside, I didn't give a shit what these people thought of me before all this happened. Now I realise there's a bond I have with them that's stronger than any EVA cable. They are part of my life, part of the reassuring walls, even now as I watch another part – the actual walls – tear themselves apart. The people I shared rooms with, listened to briefings with, relied on to ensure things got done so I could go on living.

Yeah, all of those things.

Arkov is a metre away from the door. I reach out to him and grab his hand, pulling him toward me, then push him toward the emergency oxygen tank by the wall. There will be a suit repair kit nearby.

Lieutenant Travers is next. He's holding Ensign Chiu's wrist. I catch a glimpse of her face. I can't tell if she's alive or dead. Le Garre has a grip on her ankle, while she and Captain Shann have linked arms.

That's everyone. When they're in, I turn toward the door control.

"Chase to Sellis."

"Receiving, Sergeant."

"If you could keep that door open for a minute or two, we'd really appreciate it."

I look out through the door. I can't see Chase, but he said *we*. That means he must have Johansson with him. "Do you need assistance, Sergeant?"

"I think we'll make it. Just be ready with a hand to haul us in."

"Aye, aye."

I stand by the door, waiting for him as the others disentangle their tethers and make use of the emergency oxygen supply. They're cluttered in a pile, trying to get used to the rotation. All their conversation is on open comms. Arkov is trying to disconnect the thruster chair from his EVA suit; Le Garre is worried about Chiu as she's still unresponsive. Travers has plugged her into the oxygen supply, but the only way they can help is by taking her suit off, which can't happen until we close the door and repressurise the room.

Shann is collapsed in a heap near the wall. I wonder if she has anything left.

I still can't see Chase. He must be travelling across the hull toward us. I lean out of the doorway to get a better look and—

A change in the light makes me instinctively duck inside. A moment later, a huge piece of debris tumbles past where my head had been and crashes into the side of the ship.

Shit, that was close!

"Chase to airlock control. We're three metres out."

I take a deep breath and get a hold of myself. "Ready for you."

"Confirmed."

They appear from below me, to the left. Johansson is clinging to Chase, her arms wrapped around his waist as he guides them in at an angle. I grab their loose tethers and do my best to slow them down, but they still crash into the far wall of the chamber.

"Okay, all aboard, I'm closing it."

For a moment, the manual control resists me, but then the lever grinds its way down to the locked position and the hatch slides shut. Pressurisation begins immediately. *We made it!*

I glance at the group of survivors. Everyone in here outranks me. Does that say something about me or the priorities of people escaping a spaceship? I don't know.

Shut up, Sellis. We're alive, we lucky few. At least for now.

The red light on the wall turns green. Repressurisation is complete. I press the release levers on the sides of my helmet and pull it off. That first breath feels wonderful.

Chase is standing next to me. He's removed his helmet too. Johansson is helping unclip his thruster from his back. I stare at the dents and scars across the casing. *How the fuck did he make it?* "That thing has no right to be functional," I say.

Chase grins at me, holding his stomach, where Johansson had been hanging on to him. Thin tendrils of blood are leaking out from between his fingers. "I think we all got poked full of holes out there," he says. "Besides, you can't tell how bad the damage is when you can't look around."

Arkov joins us. He's managed to remove his thruster and his helmet. He grabs my hand firmly and shakes it. "Thank you..." he says, then struggles to find any other words before repeating himself. "Thank you, so much."

I flinch away from his gaze, feeling awkward in the face of that naked gratitude. For a moment, the three of us share something, some kind of comradeship. I guess this is what it's like for soldiers who see action. You might not like the people you end up with, but life-or-death adversity creates a bond stronger than friendship. I feel what these two are feeling.

Maybe things will turn out okay after all.

CHAPTER FIFTY-FOUR

Shann

Get up, Ellisa…

Get up!

That voice is my mother's voice. I open my eyes and look around. I'm in the airlock of a spaceship, surrounded by other people. The oxygen warning in my helmet is shrieking at me.

It sounds like my mother.

I wasn't particularly pressured as a child, but there were times when I wanted the world to go away. Getting out of bed was hard work on those days. I'd start to feel sorry for myself and make comparisons, wondering what in the divine scheme of things had singled me out to be different from everyone else.

In hindsight, I guess all teenagers go through those feelings, but mine had a physical focus every time I looked down at myself.

In those low moments, Mother learned how to deliver some tough love. She didn't want to be nagging me and pushing me, but she did. As I got older, I could see the pain in her eyes each time she felt she had to say something. She knew I could push back if I wanted and make it about having no legs, but I don't think I ever did. I understood why she was poking and prodding me.

My mother isn't really here. I know that. But I hear her voice and I feel her with me.

I reach up to the clips on my helmet and release the seals. Immediately, the alarm stops, and the voice is gone. I miss it. The link to my childhood is severed. I have to focus on the here and now.

Hands grab me. Le Garre is right in front of me, her face pinched with concern. "*Merde!* Captain, I'm sorry, we forgot you were only on one canister."

I wave my left hand dismissively, awakening a stabbing pain in my shoulder. That helps me focus. "It's okay, Major. I'm alive. How is Chiu?"

"Not good."

"How about the rest?"

"We're battered, but intact. Eight of us here. Me, you, Travers and Chiu brought in by Sellis and Arkov. Chase went back for Johansson."

Eight survivors from a crew of twenty-five. Twenty-six if you count Shah, who we rescued.

Eighteen people dead because of my choices.

I push myself up from the corner. There's gravity, not much, but a little bit that's trying to keep me down. I fight back, biting back a groan of pain. I look at my people. I can smell the damage and effort in here. Travers and Johansson are removing Chiu's emergency suit. There's blood in the air. Arkov and Sam are both injured as well. Not the perfect boarding party.

Sellis…yeah…I need to rely on him some more. I'm not entirely comfortable with that.

"Major, we need to get an idea of our situation. I don't fancy this room turning into our prison or tomb. Have you seen any activity in airlock control?"

"Not so far, Captain."

"We have to be sure before we move forward. Once we're into the ship, we have to take control and secure it quickly. Those who can't help will need to be left in a defensible place."

Le Garre nods. "We have the schematic plans for the ship. I remember some of the details. She glances around. "You want me to take a look through the door?"

"You, Sellis and Johansson." I glance over to where my communications officer is hunched over Chiu. I see her react to the sound of her name, half turning toward me, but then trying to pretend she hasn't heard me. I know what's going on. She's the best trained medic we have and feels guilty for not being around when Chiu got injured. But she's also the reason we're alive and inside this ship.

"April, we're going to need your help."

The use of her first name makes her respond. She turns to meet my gaze. She's injured, but not bad and there's an apology crafted into the expression on her face. She's wearing it like a badge of shame. Right now, I can't make that go away, or offer her the validation she craves. I need more from her before the healing can start.

"Ensign, we need your knowledge of the *Gallowglass*'s computer system and the environment controls to take over the ship."

"Chiu really shouldn't be left—"

"That's an order, Ensign."

She stiffens as if she's just taken an electric shock. "Yes, Captain, of course."

"Travers, Chase and Arkov will be staying with Ensign Chiu. You'll be coming with me, Sellis and Le Garre." I nod toward the hatch. "I need you to secure airlock control and get into the computer system. We'll leave the others in there while we head to the bridge."

"The *Gallowglass*'s medical room might be more suitable, Captain," Le Garre says.

I shake my head. "No, we need to maintain control of the airlock. Once people are settled, Travers can sort out getting supplies and equipment from there."

"Understood." Le Garre moves toward the inner door, gesturing for Sellis and Johansson to follow her. Sellis hesitates and looks like he wants to say something to me, but thinks better of it and follows the others. I turn to Arkov and Sam. Both of them are out of their EVA suits and making use of a medical kit.

"Thank you both for your efforts on this. Without you, we'd never have gotten here."

Arkov gestures to the others. "Sellis saved me and that helped us get to you."

"I'm aware of that."

"It's important you take that into consideration when—"

"I said I'm aware of that, Corporal."

"Yes, Captain."

Pushing these men and women is hard to do in these circumstances. They don't deserve being reminded of their rank and mine. They deserve medals, promotions and pampered retirements, but I have to remind them this isn't over. The crew of this ship, an enemy ship, are still out there, right outside this door.

I glance at Sam. Usually he'd be volunteering himself for the hazard, but now he's not doing that. He's let Arkov do the talking and added nothing but a mute nod. I make a mental note to talk to him later when we're through this.

"Travers, how's Chiu?"

My XO looks up. "Barely alive, Captain. We need to be careful with moving her."

"You going to be all right with her in airlock control, once we've got into the computers?"

Travers smiles. "Was going to ask if you wanted to swap. You're not in the best shape. I can see how you're favouring that shoulder."

I shake my head. "Thanks, but no. I've a burning desire to find out who has been chasing us across the solar system."

"Okay, but take your own advice. You need to make sure you can keep up. What meds have you taken?"

"None so far. I need to stay focused."

Travers looks surprised, but then he shrugs. "Okay, but when it gets too much, you need to stop and let your body rest. If you break yourself, we all lose out."

"Understood. I'll also tell Le Garre to drop me if I slow them down. What weapons do we have?"

"Six sidearms between us, plus some chemical breaching equipment and two Tasers. I've given Chiu's pistol to Johansson. You need to make a decision about whether Sellis gets anything."

"No, we use his eyes and his technical know-how; that's it for now."

"Better than being locked up, I suppose."

"Yes." I nod toward Arkov and Sam. "Once we're away, get everything set up here to defend yourselves. See if you can access the ship's external comms too. There might be more of our people left alive on the *Khidr*."

"The ships are drifting apart," Arkov says. "We were really lucky. I can't see anyone else making it."

"Doesn't mean we abandon them, though."

"Yeah, okay, Captain. I'll sort it."

I move back to see how Le Garre, Johansson and Sellis are getting on. My hopes sink when I see they have removed the panel of the locking mechanism. "What's wrong?" I ask Johansson. "I thought you set up access codes."

"I did, but they won't help with a jammed door," Johansson replies. "Someone's tampered with this lock on the other side."

"You mean someone knows we're aboard?"

"Or considered the possibility and wrecked the door to slow us down." She flashes me a humourless smile. "Could have been worse if they'd rigged it to stay open. Half the ship would have depressurised, and we'd have suffocated before we could restore a breathable atmosphere."

"They couldn't afford to do that. They need to breathe too." I'm trying to think. Either we're facing a fight or Johansson's already taken out the *Gallowglass* crew. Whether they're alive or dead remains to be seen. "How long would the crew on the bridge be unconscious if someone on board is awake?"

"Not long. If they noticed my hack into their systems, they could have reset the oxygen system and overridden the door locks from the outside of the bridge. Easy enough if you have a working user ID for the system," Johansson replies. "I did put a couple of blocks in the way in terms of changing some permissions and access codes. They would need to figure out what I've done first and undo it, but after that, getting in waking up their people and retaking control of the bridge shouldn't take long."

"That means we could be running out of time."

"Yes, I guess it does."

Sellis has pulled two wires out of the wall. "This should bridge the connection, but if their ship is anything like ours, the security system will detect what I'm doing in approximately two seconds, which triggers a deadlock. You need to get your code inputted by then." He kicks an empty box by his feet. It drifts toward me. "If it opens, might be worth wedging this in the gap, just in case."

I grab the box. "Good idea."

Johansson's fingers hover over the keypad. "Okay, I'm ready," she says.

Sellis shifts position, pressing his back to the wall. "Okay, on three. One. Two. Three!"

The wires connect in his hand. The crackle of the closed circuit seems like the loudest sound I've ever heard. Johansson taps in her code in a blur, and the door slides open.

"Nicely done," I say to them both.

Sellis smiles. "Thank you, Captain," he says.

We get everyone through the door as quickly as we can. Once we're into airlock control, Le Garre and I take up cover positions in the corridor. Johansson logs in to the terminal with her self-created account. "Crew detectors are offline," she reports. "Means we can't track whoever sealed us in."

"And also that we don't know how many people we're facing. Can you pull up a deck plan?"

"Of course." Johansson taps a few more keys, and a three-dimensional image appears in front of us. Some of the locations are flashing red. "Looks like there's been some hull breaches. Nothing like the damage to the *Khidr*, though."

"That's why we're here," I reply. "Can you plot a path to the bridge?"

A blue line appears on the screen. "There's a clear route. It'll take us about ten minutes, Captain, provided we don't run into anyone."

I study the path. "I have a feeling we'll run into someone. If you were defending this ship, where would you pick for an ambush, if you were outnumbered?"

Johansson points to the T-junction close to the bridge. "Probably there. Or I'd depressurise the passageway just before it. We'd have to work on restoring air. Being attacked while we're doing that would make life difficult."

"And it would negate a numbers advantage."

"Yes."

"Okay." I know I'm hesitating. This is an unfamiliar ship to us. Our enemy holds the advantage in having been able to plan a defence. More people will get hurt and die, but we have no option but to press ahead. "Patch this terminal into our comms frequency so we can talk to Travers. When you're done, we move."

"Yes, Captain." Johansson hesitates. She looks around, noting where everyone is, then leans in close to me. "Permission to speak freely, Captain?" she asks in a low tone.

"Go on then."

"You need to leave me here." Johansson gestures toward the terminal. "I can assist you from the terminal much better than being with you. Also, I'm the most experienced medic you have, and Chiu... she needs supervision, Captain."

I stare at Johansson. "You looking to disobey more orders, Ensign?" I ask.

Johansson flinches. "Not really," she replies. "But it's the right call. You need comms and computer access, as well as emergency aid for the injured crew. Those are my areas. Chiu might die; that'll be on my conscience if I stay or if I go. At least if I stay, I'll know I've done everything I can."

"You didn't like Chiu before."

"I don't like her now, but she deserves a chance. We all do." Johansson nods toward Arkov and Sam. "If you need four, either Vasili or Sam can make up the numbers. Arkov's leg is bothering him, and he has some cuts, but he'll be okay. Sam's taken a stomach wound, which could get serious without proper attention. He's patched up, but...he's a risk."

I gaze at Johansson, trying to measure her. All her points are pragmatic and make sense. Maybe I'm trying to keep her close because she's already gone against orders. It's not that I don't think she's capable, but by keeping her with me, I can watch her and give her a chance to win back the trust I placed in her before.

But she's right. It isn't the best use of the resources I have to hand.

"Okay, we'll make a change," I say, then raise my voice. "Change of plan. Arkov, you're with the mission team. Johansson is staying here. Make sure you've got a sidearm, Arkov."

"Aye, aye," Arkov replies.

"I found some emergency override codes in the system," Johansson says. "They might help you if you run into trouble."

I nod my thanks. "Okay, let's go," Sellis opens the door into the next passageway. Le Garre goes through, sidearm in hand as she checks in both directions.

"Clear," she announces.

Gritting my teeth, I follow her through the door.

CHAPTER FIFTY-FIVE

Johansson

I watch Shann leave. When she's through the door, I start to relax. Deciding to confront and persuade her that her orders were wrong was a harder choice to make than getting welded into a torpedo and fired at this ship. The captain's approval is something I value, a lot. I damaged our relationship when I went against orders on my first EVA to fix the transmitter and made things worse taking matters into my own hands with the second. This time, I may have broken things beyond repair.

But I know I made the right call.

I've changed. The recommendation for promotion I was focused on no longer defines who I am. The validation that would bring doesn't define me; I see that now.

A good relationship with my captain isn't about some kind of trade, with me carefully choosing when to bring my A game and when to hide in the crowd. It's about me speaking up and being honest. If someone makes a bad call, I need to let them know without worrying about the consequences to my career.

Low voices cut through my reflections. There's an acceleration chair in the airlock control room. Travers and Chase are making sure Chiu is strapped in and secure. I've examined her injuries and they are extensive. "She's lost a lot of blood," Travers says.

"And we've no idea what's happening internally," I add. "She needs a saline drip, a transfusion and blood pressure monitoring."

"Can you do that?"

"With the right equipment, yes." I turn back to the computer. "The medical room is two floors below us. I can give you a list of what's needed."

"No one should go anywhere alone," Chase says. "Wouldn't it be quicker if you went with the lieutenant?"

"Maybe, but Shann and the others need me here. It needs to be you two."

Travers fixes me with a look. "You will be technically alone," he says.

I nod. "Yes, but Chiu won't be, which is the more important priority."

Travers gives me an odd look. "Should I be worried about the chain of command, Ensign?" he asks carefully.

"No, Lieutenant," I reply.

Travers takes out his sidearm. "We've only six firearms between us all. You'll need to keep this with you," he says.

I hesitate for a moment. The right thing to do would be to refuse, but I can't fight every order I'm given. "Thanks," I say instead and slip it into a pocket.

"Okay then," Travers says. He taps Sam on the shoulder. "Come on, let's get this done."

"Aye, aye, Lieutenant," Sam says.

A moment later I'm left alone with Chiu.

I gaze at her, thinking back to the conversation I had with the captain about the fact that Chiu betrayed us. I feel ashamed of myself now. If I were to act on what I said back then, I'd be taking a knife to her throat or unwrapping those bandages.

I'm not doing either of those things.

Being stranded in that torpedo casing made me look at life differently. It was easy to input a few commands that incapacitated the *Gallowglass* crew. I didn't have to watch them choke and collapse as their bodies were starved of oxygen. The consequences of my actions were remote and distant. This isn't the same. I can't execute someone in cold blood, even though I argued for exactly that kind of treatment.

I fought hard to live while I was out there alone. I got help and got rescued. Now Chiu needs help. When Travers and Chase come back, I need to help her, and I will help her as much as I can.

The terminal flashes, and I return my attention to it. There's another depressurisation in a passageway near the engine room. Could be another collision, or could it be our enemy? The engine room would be the best place to defend if the bridge was lost. That's standard Fleet protocol. A lot of the control systems can be overridden by depriving them of power.

"Johansson to Shann."

"Go ahead, Ensign."

"I've just detected a loss of atmosphere outside the engine room. Could be a problem. I can't tell if it's sabotage or a collision."

"Understood. What's your feeling?"

The question surprises me. *My feeling?* "I err...I think it might be deliberate."

"Okay, we'll follow up when we can."

The conversation reminds me of some unfinished business. I reopen the command terminal and reset the oxygen parameters in the bridge compartment. When Shann, Le Garre and the others get in, they'll need breathable air, and by now, the *Gallowglass*'s crew will have suffocated. I'm not proud of that, but they were trying to kill me and everyone I care about.

I listen to Shann issuing orders. She's not dividing her group to investigate the engine room until they've secured the bridge. Probably the best plan, considering the limited personnel we have available. As I listen, I start to hear something in the background. Is it interference? No, I've heard that noise before. It's like...music? Strange, atonal notation that doesn't seem to repeat. There are slews, a rising and falling of pitch, some staccato, no polyphony.

I remember what I heard on the recordings from the *Hercules*. It was the same kind of sounds, only faint and indistinct. This noise is much louder, competing with the conversation between Shann and Le Garre.

What am I listening to?

I explore the *Gallowglass*'s list of programmes. To start with, I need something that will isolate and record the noise. After that, I'll want to track down where it's coming from.

There's no mention of the noise between the others. Either they're being professional and ignoring it, or they can't hear it. I'm sure someone would have said something by now. If only I'm hearing this, that makes things even stranger.

I find a programme that looks similar to the one we used on the *Khidr* and start trying to isolate the sounds. Working with one hand is frustrating when you're used to having two, but the tools are familiar, and once I have a stripped file, I start to triangulate the broadcast position.

What I discover doesn't make sense. There are two locations, as if a conversation is going on. The stronger signal is coming from the *Khidr*; the second signal is coming from just outside the *Gallowglass* engine room.

Right where the decompression just occurred.

I pull up a tracking scan of our immediate area. The laser sweeper is still working and starts plotting the debris around us. On the second pass, I notice another anomaly. The wreckage is moving away from us, toward the remains of our old ship.

I remember hearing the others mention this. Whatever's happened, the process is accelerating, but the *Gallowglass* seems relatively unaffected. The distance between the two ships is increasing.

Something is drawing all the broken parts away from us. The centre of that is in the same location as the signal.

The generator room of the *Khidr*.

I remember Duggins saying he was going to the generator room. That was the last we heard from him. I key up a long-range channel and adjust it to match our old ship's frequency.

"Johansson to Duggins, can you hear me?"

There's only static in response, but the volume of the noises seems to increase. The decibel level starts to peak into the red.

"Duggins, are you trying to communicate with me through the noise?" I separate out three distinct sounds. "If you are, repeat the low tone, three times."

Suddenly, all the noises stop.

CHAPTER FIFTY-SIX

Shann

We're outside the entrance to the bridge of the *Gallowglass*. It's taken us fifteen minutes to get here, lugging the spare EVA suit and some assorted tools. We've encountered no resistance or evidence that anyone is alive or active on this ship.

Apart from us.

I'm shaking with exhaustion. The way things are moving around as the *Gallowglass* tumbles makes everything hard, but I'm past the point where I should have been sedated and ordered to sleep. Unfortunately, no one outranks me, so it would take another little mutiny to get me to stop right now.

I need to see my enemy and look them in the eye.

There's a collection of equipment drifting around the corridor and some deep gouges in the door's metal plate. Someone was here, trying to break in.

I nod to Sellis. He moves to the door and types in the passcode Johansson gave us. The door doesn't budge. Either the attempt to cut through it has damaged the mechanism or someone has triggered the deadlock.

"Might be because of the pressure change?" Arkov suggests. "The detectors out here weren't hacked, only the ones in there. If the sensors in this room have decided there's a vacuum on the bridge, they'd automatically seal the door."

"It should respond to the override pass, though," Sellis says. "Our doors do."

"Our enemy couldn't get in, so they found a way to block us from getting in as well," Le Garre says. She looks at me, and I see a glimpse of the challenging smile she used to give me before all this started.

"You think you can break in?" I ask.

"Of course," she replies and moves forward with the chemical breaching equipment. The thermite is kept in a paste. Le Garre draws a line of it around the frame of the door. Immediately, when exposed to oxygen, it starts to smoke and give off an odour as it burns. Le Garre is covering her nose and mouth. A moment later, an alarm sounds, and the ventilation system shuts down around us. There's a light flashing over a panel on the wall that says, 'Extinguisher'.

"It'll be the doors next," Arkov says. "We need to maintain an exit." He turns around, presses the release catch on his right boot and takes it off. Then he wedges it in between the hatch and the opening we've just come through.

The smoke has subsided, but the stink remains. "I think it's done," Sellis announces. He's probably used thermite in his work more than the rest of us, so I trust his judgement on that. He drifts toward the door feetfirst and lands a boot on the centre of the metal plate, pushing off against it. The metal shifts, revealing a small gap at the edge.

Le Garre draws her pistol and mimics Sellis's maneuver, only with more force. There's a sharp screech, and the door panel falls away to reveal darkness inside.

"We'll need to restore the lighting," I say and activate my comms, but the channel doesn't connect. "Anyone getting signal problems?" I ask.

Arkov tries as well and frowns. "After Johansson resynced the system to this ship, the *Gallowglass* should pick us up."

"But it isn't."

"No, indeed, Captain. I'm getting nothing. As if we've been completely disconnected."

"You think it's deliberate?" Le Garre asks. "Should we go back and see if they're okay?"

I shake my head. "If we do, we lose any tactical advantage. Whatever has happened, we'll need to secure the bridge. We take a risk every time we make a move from one location to the other. We can be trapped in a corridor and left to rot."

"I'm not giving up like that," Sellis says.

"Me either. Arkov, you go in first. Le Garre after him, then Sellis, then me," I order. "Weapons out, be ready."

"Aye, aye, Captain," Arkov replies. He's inching forward, looking nervous. We didn't bring any torches or other portable illumination. It wasn't something anyone considered in the rush. "Could be the system's powered down owing to lack of movement?"

"Who knows? We'll find out," Le Garre says, nudging him forward.

Arkov draws his sidearm. He has a Taser in his left hand too. He drifts slowly toward the jagged gap, taking care to float straight through without touching the sides. When he's about halfway, I realise I'm holding my breath, waiting for a shout or the sound of gunfire, or…

Nothing…

Arkov is inside. Le Garre follows, with Sellis straight after. Then it's my turn.

I dive headfirst into darkness.

A hand grasps my left shoulder, sending another spasm of pain through the whole arm. I bite my lip and hold back the urge to cry out. The pitch black is all-consuming; I can't make out the shades and shadows that might at least determine what's directly in front of me.

No one speaks. The hand takes hold of mine and guides me to the wall. The touch of the metal surface is reassuring, but I'm wondering how we're going to manage to explore this place. Without any illumination or comms guidance, finding a console, activating it and logging in will take time.

My hand brushes against something. It's clothing – a person, but it doesn't move away; it just drifts. I stare in the direction of my fingers and become aware of their flickering movement against the fabric of the pressure suit. There's light coming in from somewhere…. I look around and see the change in the air. A glow, coming from outside the ship, filtered through thick DuraGlas. Sunlight through the viewing port, underneath the protective shutters. The sun moving around us fast; its rays stream through the gaps in the blind and banish the darkness to reveal our fate.

The four of us are huddled in the corner of the room by the door. There are five seats; four of them are occupied. My right hand is touching the body of the fifth crew member. His face turns into the light…. I recognise it.

It's Rocher…

How the fuck can it be Rocher?

His eyes are bulging; his expression is twisted and strained, with his left hand clutching his throat and his right arm extended outward, desperately clutching for something. I look around and notice an emergency oxygen mask and cylinder attached to the wall. Looks like a separate supply. He nearly made it, but thankfully for us, he didn't.

"The ship's still drifting," Le Garre says. "We need to get some lights on in here before the sun goes past the viewing port."

Sellis and Arkov are already moving. Arkov heads for the empty seat and starts trying to access the console. Sellis takes a more pragmatic approach and investigates the storage panels. His efforts yield results – a selection of battery-powered torches, which he passes around.

"This console is as dead as the crew," Arkov says. "Looks like they initiated some kind of localised electromagnetic pulse on the computers in here. They must have known we were coming to take the ship."

I move to one of the other occupied chairs, and my suspicions are confirmed.

"They're clones."

"What?"

"The crew, look at them. They all look like Rocher. They *are* Rocher. All of them are the same."

Le Garre is beside me. I hear her sharp intake of breath as she sees what I see. Human cloning was banned on Earth more than a century ago. The line between genetic editing and genetic engineering is clearly defined. For me, this situation just got personal. The Lopez Act, ratified by the United Nations in 2038, before it became the Earth Assembly, established the legal parameters for continued research.

"That fucking bastard," Sellis growls. He's standing over another Rocher clone sprawled in the communications chair.

"It explains a lot of things," Le Garre says. "When I was flying our ship against them, the reaction times and coordination between manoeuvering, weapons, and defence was incredibly efficient. We weren't just dealing with a computer; we were dealing with people who knew each other's minds, inside out."

I'm staring at another grotesquely stretched version of Rocher's face. "They aren't human," I mutter aloud.

"If they were alive, they might dispute that, Captain," Sellis says. "But as it happens, I agree."

"This is a tangled and sordid little web," Le Garre says. "Remember the frozen bees you found? There has to be a connection."

"A connection, but not a direct one," I reply. The mention of the bees reminds me of something else. "The *Hercules* was carrying colony building equipment. The *Gallowglass* intercepted and boarded her, but they didn't come for all that tech; they came for something else." I remember the empty egg-shaped canisters that I saw on the drone camera before the feed went down. "I saw empty boxes when we were exploring the freighter, just before the explosion. They looked like they'd been opened."

"The black object we recovered from space was sort of egg-shaped," Arkov says. "You couldn't tell with your eyes, but I did some measurements with a tape."

"You think the *Hercules* had some of them that the people here stole?" Sellis suggests.

I shrug. "Can't be a complete coincidence. There has to be some connection. It might explain why they were keen to capture our ship and not completely destroy it."

"To confirm that, we'll need to find the objects," Le Garre says.

"I've a hunch as to where they are." I turn to Sellis. "Can you repair these consoles?" I ask.

Sellis looks thoughtful. "Possibly, but it might take time."

"How much time?"

"A fair bit."

"Until we have any kind of operational control from here, the bridge is useless," I reason. "The last thing Johansson said was that there was a pressure loss in the room outside Engineering. Whoever tried to break in here, might well be down there."

"You want us all to go?" Le Garre asks.

"I think that's the best plan," I reply. "Strength in numbers, plus there's nothing we can do here until we've secured the ship."

Sellis sighs. "Well, at least this ship is more compact, so it'll be a quicker journey than it would have been on the *Khidr*."

"What about them?" Arkov asks, pointing to the floating Rocher clone.

"We leave them as they are," I decide. "We'll be back later. In the meantime, open all the lockers and search the bodies for anything that might be useful. We'll move out in five minutes."

My crew set to work while I take the opportunity to stop, rest and gather my thoughts. The whole situation is a mess, but I'm starting to see some connections.

We need the bridge controls working. Without them, piloting an unfamiliar ship is going to be very difficult. Whatever's happened to Johansson is worrying, though. If we're being picked off, then we're—

"Johansson to Shann, can you hear me?"

"Yes! Finally! We lost comms. What happened?"

"The anomalies happened, Captain. There's one or more on this ship and they're talking to the one we left on ours." Johansson's voice is wavering. She's excited and on edge. "I've tracked both signals. Whatever's over here is located near the engine room."

"We're just about to go there. The bridge has been sabotaged. We found five dead up there. Some kind of eternal EMP was triggered by the crew in all the consoles before they died."

"You may need to hurry," Johansson says. "I've been tracking the debris. It's being pulled back toward the *Khidr*. We need to get the *Gallowglass*'s engines online so we can move to a safe distance."

"What is a safe distance?"

"I don't know, but I'm running some calculations."

"We'll get moving. The depressurised corridor will slow us down, though. Can you get control of the ship from where you are?"

"I'm afraid not, Captain. Even with my rootkit access, the ship is hardwired to only receive control requests for the engines from the bridge or the engine room."

"Then we need to get in there."

"Yes, I think so."

I close the comms channel and turn to the others. They've raided the room for everything they can find that might be useful. Sellis is carrying a sidearm he must have scrounged from one of the dead clones. I open my mouth to say something about it, but then think better of it.

"Okay, people, let's go."

CHAPTER FIFTY-SEVEN

Sellis

I see the look Captain Shann gives me when she notices the gun I've found. I wait for the comment and the order, but it doesn't come. Maybe she's starting to trust me.

Or maybe she has no choice.

We're out of the bridge and making our way through the passageways to the engine room. Le Garre is leading and I'm right behind her. There's something reassuring about the major's calm efficiency. I know she's tired and pushing her limits, just like the rest of us, but she seems to be handling it, and that exuded confidence makes me suck up my doubts and push on beside her.

We reach the sealed hatch and Le Garre turns to me. "Do you think we've got enough thermite left?" she asks.

"Not sure," I reply. I press my face to the glass and try to get a look inside. The panel is corroded, and I can see damage to the inside of the corridor beyond. There's something in there too. "You mentioned egg-shaped objects?" I say. "What do they look like?"

"Like holes," Arkov explains. "They're completely black, so the eye can't determine their shape. They look like holes in the world."

"There are crates. I can see two of them," I say. The glass is vibrating against my forehead. I pull away and squint, trying to get a clearer picture. "The room's damaged. Could be I'm looking at your eggs, or a rip in the hull." I turn around. "Captain Shann, we can't take a chance on this."

Shann nods. "You're right, we can't, particularly if there's another Rocher waiting for us to make a move."

"The passcodes we have should override the seal, unless the door's been tampered with," Le Garre says. She looks around, appraising the mechanism. "I can't see any sign of that."

"Would be impossible anyway," I reply. "If our friend is in the engine room, he'd have had to have depressurised the room from the inside and sealed himself in. He couldn't have gotten out here unless he's still loose on the ship, and that would mean abandoning the engine room to us."

"All the same, eyes outward," Shann says, turning around and following her own advice. "Sellis, what do you need to do?"

"Much the same as I usually do when I'm repairing a leak, Captain." I touch the comms bead on my neck. "Sellis to Johansson. Ensign, do you have any data on the type of leak we're dealing with?"

The comms makes a strange wailing noise, like the worst kind of electro synth, before Johansson replies. Her voice is distant and far away. "The computer recorded the atmosphere evacuation rate and did some projections. Looks like a small leak, probably no more than four inches in diameter."

"We can fix that with foam," I say. "But we're screwed if the damage is more extensive."

"Yeah," Johansson agrees. "Another problem will be if someone on the other side takes an interest in your work."

"One of us should go in with you," Le Garre says.

I shake my head. "No, Major. If you did, you'd be in the way. Let me do my job. We've got one EVA suit, and we have to prep for decompression of this room. That means you all retreat into the next section and wait until I'm through and let the computer repressurise this passageway. Once I've fixed the leak, I'll open the emergency oxygen tank and then give you the all clear signal. You can follow me after that."

Le Garre is staring at me, but she doesn't say anything. Instead, she glances at the captain. Shann doesn't say anything either. She looks broken. I doubt she has much care left. She wants that living Rocher clone and she's trying to save herself for that. I get it – that slow-burning anger. I can feel it too, but for different reasons. I want a piece of that fucker.

"Okay, we follow your plan, Specialist," Le Garre says.

"Thank you, Major," I reply.

It takes the three of them a couple of minutes to evacuate the corridor. Before they go, Arkov helps me into the patched EVA suit we've been lugging around. "You sure you want to do this?" he asks.

I chuckle at him. "You see anyone else volunteering? If you do, let me know; I'll step back."

Arkov smiles in spite of himself. I can see he's still in pain, holding it together because he has to. "You be careful," he warns.

"I'll try," I say. Our eyes meet and there's an awkward moment, just like before. "We'll get through this," I add, trying to sound confident.

"Yeah." Arkov doesn't sound convinced either. He hands me the EVA suit helmet. "We'll be on comms. Check in once you're ready."

"Will do," I acknowledge. Once the helmet goes on, my worldview narrows. I'm back in the EVA suit, like before. Arkov taps on the top with his knuckles and gives me a thumbs-up. I smile and do the same back.

Then he's gone, making his way to the hatch to join the others.

I turn around and head toward the sealed door. The control panel is tricky to manage with the bulky gloves, but on the second try, I get the prepared ID typed in and select the emergency override sequence. I can hear the locks withdraw – a muffled noise through the helmet. A moment later, I brace myself and activate the magnetic contacts on my boots as the door slides back.

An air-filled corridor being opened up to a vacuum is always a violent experience. The wind pushes me forward, driving me toward the opening. Something crashes into my hand. I see what it is as it tumbles past, the lid from a storage container torn off the wall.

The wind eases and I stomp forward. At that moment, I notice a problem. The remaining oxygen in the suit tank is decreasing rapidly. I must have sprung a leak.

That means I need to work fast.

I'm through the door into the damaged section. Data from Johansson's terminal is displayed on my helmet screen. The release of air has enabled her to isolate the leak in the room, and I make my way toward it.

Two oval-shaped containers are in my way. One of them is open, and I get my first proper look at one of the anomalies inside. These are the egg-shaped things Johansson was taking about. Immediately, I'm distracted. It's like looking into a bottomless pit inside a box. Your mind knows what you're looking at can't have the depth it seems to have, but there isn't a reference point for you to use to comprehend it any other way.

I tear my eyes away and glance briefly at the rest of the container. There are extensive signs of corrosion in the metal all along the inner membrane. It's as if the object is damaging the container it's been placed in.

"Sellis, this is Johansson. How's it going?"

The words bring me back to why I'm here and what I'm supposed to be doing. "Fine, Ensign, I'm on it." I look around the room and reorientate myself. The leak is to my left and near the floor by the entrance into the engine room. Makes sense if it was sabotage. Whoever did this probably made a hole by discharging a sidearm at point-blank range or squirting thermite onto the wall and then escaping through the door. Quick and easy to do.

The foam sprayer is on my belt. I crouch down in the corner and take aim, carefully building the foam layers around in a circle and letting them solidify before I try and seal the breach completely. The hole is about three times the size of the one I fixed on the *Khidr*. It's tricky; a lot of the foam collapses and disappears into space. Ideally, I'd be waiting for the room to vent completely before I start this, but I don't have time.

As I work, I'm trying to keep my breathing even and my heart rate down. The room's emergency oxygen tank is about a metre away. I can plug into it if I need to, but I'd rather get this done as quickly as I can.

I've eight per cent of my suit O_2 left when the last bit of foam hardens across the centre of the hole. Quickly I plaster another layer over the top, then step away and activate the emergency repressurisation sequence.

I bring up a comms channel. "Leak is sealed, almost ready for you folks to join me." Then I turn toward the engine room door.

Rocher is staring at me through the DuraGlas plate.

He's fucking smiling at me.

Instinctively I'm moving. The foam sprayer is discarded. I pull out the gas-powered pistol I looted from one of the clones on the bridge. I tap in the override sequence and the door begins to open. Again, there's a powerful rush of air as the atmospheric pressure tries to equalise. Along with it comes the last Rocher, his face contorted in surprise. I make a grab for his throat and miss as he tumbles past. I turn. He's not wearing a helmet, just a dark emergency suit. I raise the gun and he raises his hands.

A shot rings out.

I didn't pull the trigger. Did the gun go off accidentally? Rocher hasn't moved. I look down. There's blood spreading out in a bubble from my chest.

I've been shot.

I blink and try to pull the trigger on my own weapon, but I can't feel my hands. Rocher is moving toward me. He takes the gun away and grabs hold of the front of my suit. That smile is there again, a wide and hungry leer. He pulls me across the room and pushes me against the door at the far end, where Shann, Le Garre and Arkov will be coming through. I look at the spiraling trail of bright red blood, expanding into the thin air. It's a beautiful cloud, all of my very own. *I made that.*

There's another gunshot. Then nothing.

CHAPTER FIFTY-EIGHT

Johansson

"You miscalculated, Ensign."

The voice is familiar, but not the one I was expecting. I look up and find myself staring at a corpse.

Rocher is standing in the doorway, aiming a gun at me. The wide leering grin of his that I remember from his meeting with Captain Shann is plastered across his face. "We've not actually met, Ensign, but I sense you think you already know me."

"You should be dead."

"Thankfully for me and unfortunately for you, I'm not."

I stare at him, and then my mind makes the connection. "You're a clone."

"Yes, I am."

A clone, out here? For a moment, I'm distracted by the ramifications of the revelation, but then I'm back in the current situation, my mind focused on what's in front of me – an enemy combatant, ready to kill me.

"Why didn't you just shoot me?" I ask.

"Perhaps I'm giving you an opportunity to prove yourself?" Rocher replies.

I remember what Sellis and Chiu said about being given passcodes. I memorised both codes when was I was in the torpedo. I could say a code, give him a reason to believe I'm one of the mutineers.... Maybe the reason he's hesitating is because he doesn't know who those traitors are.

No, I don't think I can bluff that out. One wrong move and I'd be dead. "I'm not going to betray my friends, if that's what you mean."

"Despite the fact that you're on the wrong side of humanity?" Rocher asks.

"Ironic, coming from you."

"Is it?" Rocher smiles. "You and I aren't so different. Just creatures trapped on different sides of a eugenics argument. If science were given free rein to shape humanity's physiology, you would be an abomination and I would be unremarkable. Instead, the legacy of rutting in the dirt makes you acceptable and leaves me on the outside. Don't we both have a right to live?"

"You say that while you're threatening me with a gun?" I spit out a laugh. "Why not just get it over with and get rid of me?"

"Right now, you have information I need," Rocher replies. "How many of your crew boarded this ship?"

I stare at him and don't reply.

Rocher closes the distance between us. He grabs my wrist and lowers the gun, pressing it against my stomach. "Just because I need information, doesn't mean I can't hurt you," he hisses in my ear. "You're going to die either way. Time to make a choice about how."

The wall is behind me. I brace myself against it and lash out. My booted foot connects with his crotch and the elbow of my free arm slams into the side of his face. Rocher grunts but doesn't release his grip on my arm. There's a loud roaring noise, and I'm pushed flat against the wall and Rocher is thrown across the room. A cloud of blood lies between us, and I realise it's coming from me, around the abdomen.

I've been shot.

Travers appears behind Rocher. I hear the crackling of electricity and the clone's eyes glass over. There's that burned smell you get after the discharge of a Taser.

I'm blinking my eyes, struggling to focus. Travers is moving past the twitching Rocher toward me. His hand brushes my shoulder, and suddenly, my body remembers itself. I feel pain, a stabbing, all-consuming agony that makes it hard to breathe.

"Hey, careful now. Stay with me."

I clutch at his suit, my fingers getting a handful of the collar. He's shaking me gently, trying to stop me going into shock or unconsciousness. I don't want that either, but the idea of no pain...

"Rocher, he's a clone."

"Yeah, I noticed."

"We have to warn the captain. There might be more..."

"We found some kind of cryogenic chamber next to the medical room. There are eight beds. All of them empty."

Eight? I force my mind to do the calculations. The captain found five dead on the bridge. There's a sixth person here and there was a Rocher on the *Khidr*. Did he come from this ship, or was he stowed away on the *Hercules* all along? "The engine room," I say. The words are difficult to get out.

"There has to be at least one of them down there. The captain..."

"Okay, I get it, but you need me first and so does Chiu."

I swallow, trying to get some moisture into my dry mouth. Travers glances down, staring with alarm at the growing bubble of blood between us. "Tell me what to do," he pleads.

I blink rapidly, trying to process the problem and breathe at the same time. Stomach wounds are the worst. My chest feels like there are knives in it every time I inhale. Rocher knew what he was doing.

"Which side?" I ask.

"What?"

"Which side is the wound? I can't be sure; it hurts..."

"Oh, left side. Your left side."

I nod. That's a small crumb of comfort. There's less chance of organ damage on the left side of the abdomen. Another crumb is that I'm still conscious. "To start with, painkillers, then stimulants, gauze and bandages." I'm thinking about injured people by the roadside in Sweden when we'd pull up in the ambulance. All those broken bodies, trying to make sense of their pain. "Get me a line into the oxygen tank. That'll help keep me conscious."

Travers's face is difficult to focus on. Someone else is in the room too. For a moment, I think Rocher's woken up and making another attempt to end us, but then I recognise Sam Chase. He's manhandling the unconscious clone into some improvised restraints. "Chuck him in the airlock," I suggest.

Sam shakes his head. "Can't risk him being loose, even if we can see him. He knows the ship better than we do."

The last couple of words are difficult for me to process. I'm drifting again. Must be the blood loss. Internal bleeding is a real risk right now. "You need to listen to me, before I pass out."

"Okay," Travers says. He has an oxygen mask in his hand and wraps the band around my head. I inhale deeply, and my head starts to clear. "We brought all the supplies we could find. Talk me through what we need to do."

I glance around. There are three big bags Chase and Travers brought from the medical room. "You need to gum up the gunshot wound for now and find some stims. Whatever happens, keep me conscious." I point at Chiu. "Get that done; then we work on her."

Both Sam and Travers set to work. I find myself looking down at the hole in my side. The lack of gravity makes the situation weird. Minor wounds will bleed, but the surface tension of blood has nothing to counteract it, so it 'blobs' out from your body, until some other force interacts with what's going on and detaches it as thick red bubbles. Severe wounds release fluid at a higher pressure, so we see spiraling threads, beads of blood, often exiting the body in a rhythm that matches the heartbeat of the injured person. The heart is acting as a pump and pumping blood out of the body to…

"Johansson! Stay with me!"

Sam's voice. I'm blinking rapidly, trying to clear my vision, but it's no use; everything's dark and blurry. "I need to give you instructions," I say, surprised to hear my voice so calm and even. "Firstly, you'll need to cut away the suit from around the wound. Then get the padding and a bandage. You'll need to wrap me as tight as you can. If I pass out, administer Adrenalin and wake me up."

"There's still a slug in there," Sam says.

"Can't be helped. The only way we'll get it out is with all the machines in the medical room. We'll need multiple scans to determine the extent of the damage – CT, X-ray, ultrasound, the full works. After that, we operate and remove shrapnel."

They work fast, and it hurts. It hurts a lot. I try to distract myself by talking, filling them in on everything that's happened, going through all the information from Captain Shann. "They're outside the engine room, trying to repressurise the corridor. They found five more dead Rochers on the bridge. The whole computer system up there is wrecked."

"You think there are more in Engineering?" Travers asks.

I shrug and wince at the extra pain. "Whether there are or not, the only way we're going to get the *Gallowglass* under control is to make use of the consoles down there. I can't pilot the ship from here." I gaze at the terminal. "There's something else you need to know. I think Duggins might still be alive on the *Khidr*."

"You hear from him?"

"Not exactly." I explain the signals from the anomalies and the interference with the radio comms. "I think Rocher was collecting the anomalies. I think that's one of the reasons they chased us. They couldn't risk anyone knowing about them."

"And the fact that we happened to pick one up."

"That happened after all this had already begun." I wave at the screen. "One of you needs to take over and stay on comms with the captain."

Travers nods and slips in front of me, blocking the screen from view. Sam touches my shoulder. "Tell me how to help Chiu," he says.

I glance at her strapped into the acceleration chair. Beneath her oxygen mask, her face is ashen. She's not woken up since we got here. "Hopefully, you brought an intravenous rig in your bag? You need to run a line into her and rig it to a battery pump."

"Okay." Sam starts digging into one of the bags. He pulls out a needle and syringe, rolls back Chiu's sleeve and taps her inner arm, trying to expose a vein. This procedure is something we've all trained to do. On Earth, the pump wouldn't be necessary – gravity has its uses.

"Once you're finished with her, set me up with the same," I say and shift slightly so I can see the terminal as Travers is operating it. "I set up a laser sweep to track the debris. It's all being drawn back to the remains of the *Khidr*. If we don't get the engines working, we could end up drawn back there."

"You're right and it's already begun. We're being pulled in as well." Travers expands the window and zooms in on the representation of the *Khidr*. "If Duggins is there, can we contact him and get him to turn it off?"

"The radio blackout was the only response I got. I can't be sure he's alive."

Travers stares at the screen. "You said you think the anomalies are communicating. Would that make them living beings?"

"I've no idea."

"It may explain what they want, to be reunited." Travers pulls up the schematic with the *Gallowglass*'s deck plan. I can see Shann and the others, their bio tags flashing in the corridor where I last saw them. "If we could eject that corridor, we could make that happen."

"But we can't eject that corridor while the captain and the others—"

Travers turns to look at me. "Depending how things go, we may have to."

CHAPTER FIFTY-NINE

Shann

I'm standing outside of a locked door, watching Sellis die, his face pressed into the DuraGlas window as he drowns in his own blood.

Behind him, two Rochers are in the corridor. They're working on the boxes, opening them up.

The anger within me bubbles up. I want to get in there and get my hands on the enemy. "We need to get this door open," I growl.

"Aye, aye," Arkov says. He's inputting the override access into the control panel, but Le Garre lays her hand on his arm.

"Wait a minute," she says.

"Major, we need to—"

"What are you going to do if you get in there?" Le Garre demands. She pushes her way in front, blocking us both from the door controls and the sickening view. "Sellis is dead already. Think! We need a plan!"

I take a deep breath, trying to get calm, but the rage won't go away. I remember the gun on my belt, but I don't want to use it. I want to get at these men with my hands and teeth. "Think of something," I manage to spit out.

"We need time," Le Garre says. "They've moved out of the engine room. We can seal them in." She touches the comms bead on her neck. "Le Garre to Johansson."

"This is Travers, receiving."

"What happened to Johansson?"

"She's here. We had an encounter with one of the *Gallowglass* crew. Situation is stable."

"Okay." Le Garre looks at me. "We need you to seal the doors between Engineering and the exterior corridor that had the pressure drop and lock out the manual override. Two more of the *Gallowglass* crew are in that space."

"Our sensors show Sellis is still in there."

"Sellis is dead."

There's a sharp intake of breath and some discussion on the other end before Travers replies, "Okay, yes, we should be able to do that, but it'll take time."

"Then we need to keep them in the corridor," I say and move forward to the other side of the door. The emergency two-way intercom is right in front of me. I flip the switch and activate it. "This is Captain Shann of the Fleet registered patrol ship *Khidr*. I think it's time we talked."

As soon as they hear the words, both Rochers react. They stop their work and turn toward the door. There's some soundless discussion between them before one approaches the intercom and flips the switch to answer. "What do you want, Captain?"

"To negotiate. Neither of us can survive this where we stand."

Rocher smiles. "You have misread the situation, Captain, as you appear to have misread many situations over the last few days. I assure you, our capacity for maintaining our continued existence is not yet exhausted."

I stare at the clone, looking into those mocking eyes. "You're the leader, aren't you?" I say. "You're the one who's been running this all along."

The two Rochers look at each other. The one who replied shrugs. His smile disappears. "Yes, since I have been awake throughout the voyage, I suppose you would call me leader of this crew."

"Okay, leader. If you're so sure of yourself, why have you been chasing us all this time?"

"You know why, Captain. Much like your ship, the *Khidr*, the *Gallowglass* was commissioned by Fleet to deal with problems. When you made the choice to interfere in our mission, you betrayed your crew and condemned them to death."

"I was following orders."

"Yes, you were, but then you were given specific alternative instructions, which you ignored."

I can feel Le Garre's gaze on me. Arkov's too. I remember the message we received from Admiral Langsley, ordering us to stand down. Rocher's accusation is true. This is a revelation to my people, a violation of the trust they've placed in me as their captain. I can't address them and show weakness in front of our enemy. "Our mandate remains clear. You murdered people Fleet is supposed to protect."

"We executed proven traitors, Captain." Rocher gestures to Sellis's floating corpse. "We are still executing traitors."

I'm aware that Le Garre is talking on the comms to Travers on a secure channel. Arkov has maneuvered himself into a position below the window. He has opened up the microphone panel with a small screwdriver and pulled out the leads. I can't look at him. If I do, Rocher will know something is up. "The *Hercules* is a supply freighter for the colonies. Your actions have condemned thousands to starvation and poverty. You can't say to me your attack on them was sanctioned by Fleet."

"Captain, you must realise by now you're involved in a game that is far bigger than you, your crew and your ruined ship." Rocher leans forward so his face is inches from the glass. "Millions of lives are at stake here. Those who live now and those who will live in the future."

"Clones, like you?"

"People, Captain Shann, people given the chance to live. What is coming – what you are unwittingly supporting – will break our species." Rocher smiles again, but there's a fierceness to him now that belies any humour in the expression. "History will remember that the *Hercules* had an accident in deep space. A rescue ship was dispatched and retrieved the vessel, finding its crew all dead. After some repairs, the freighter proceeded on its course. There will be no trace of the illegal goods they were smuggling to a secret base on the edge of the asteroid belt. There will be no mention of the *Gallowglass* and the *Khidr*. The status quo will be maintained."

"Sooner or later what really happened will get out."

"No, Captain, it won't." The second clone taps the first on the shoulder. I can see the boxes are open; the impossibly black shapes of the two anomalies are drifting freely in the corridor. "We're done here, Captain Shann. Whatever you hoped to gain from talking to me is irrelevant." Rocher reaches forward to the switch on the intercom.

"Now, Arkov!" Le Garre shouts.

Instinctively, I glance down. Arkov has the Taser wired into the panel. As Rocher touches the control, Arkov activates the electric charge. Instantly, the clone's face goes slack, and his body begins to spasm.

"Travers, get this door open!" Le Garre screams.

The panel slides away and all the anger within me wells up. I charge into the room, grabbing the second Rocher by the throat and slamming him backward into the wall. He struggles. There's blood coming from his forehead. I'm exhausted; my actions were fueled by rage and the last of my desperate strength. By rights, he should be able to overpower me.

But I refuse to let go.

He tries to break my hold. A fist crashes into my face, snapping my nose and sending us both tumbling through the air, toward a set of storage compartments. I manage to duck and twist, dashing his face against them while keeping a choking grip around his windpipe. The fury is a hot breath in my throat.

This ends now, in my hands!

He tries to turn me, to gouge at my eyes, to sap the strength from me. I can feel all the injuries from before, the muscles in my shoulder screaming at me to stop, the dull ache in my left arm, but I don't stop, *I can't*. I have to make everything right, do what they would do to me, execute and erase every question about my choices. Make the sacrifice of my crew right.

Die!

More hands on my shoulders, an arm around my waist, pulling at me, trying to get me to let go. I hear words, from far away. *"Captain, let go, he's had enough…"*

I'm not letting go. There's something within me, pouring all my pent-up emotions into this. I can see all the faces of my dead crew. Drake, Tomlins, Thakur, Lendowski, all of them. All of my guilt over their deaths focused into this moment, this action.

Finally, I see Jacobson again. I hear his screams as the drone murders him under my command. This time there is no confusion. This man is my enemy, the enemy of everyone I care about.

The Rocher in my hands has stopped struggling. His eyes are bulging, his expression vacant, pleading and resigned. His gaze slips away from mine toward something unseen and unknowable. His lips move, then go slack.

"Captain Shann…"

I recognise the voice. I turn and glance at the speaker. It's Major Angel Le Garre. She's staring at me. In that moment, the anger evaporates, and my hands relax.

What have I done?

Le Garre doesn't look away. Her gaze holds mine. "Captain, we need to get to the engine room," she says.

I nod and follow her, my focus on her back as she moves out of the corridor and into the space beyond. Without the rage, all I feel is shame and a strange sense of dislocation. I can't look around and accept what I've done, the act that makes me part of the problem, not part of the solution.

Arkov is here, in the operations chair, talking quietly over the comms. He doesn't look at me. For a moment, I think of Duggins, our engineer, left behind on our ruined ship. Another soul who didn't deserve…

"Captain, Ensign Johansson has given us instructions on patching the console from here through to the terminal in airlock control. We can operate the engines, but based on her calculations, it's going to take thirty per cent of our remaining fuel to execute a burn that will get us clear of the tractor effect," Le Garre explains. "The problem is the effect's strength is increasing. We've no guarantee that—"

I hold my hand up and suddenly find my voice. "Jettison the anomalies," I say. "Analyse the reaction, then power up the engines."

"Okay, but—"

"Just get it done, Major!"

"Of course, Captain."

I can feel her gaze on me. Arkov is judging me as well as he slips out of the chair and goes back to the corridor to help her. They leave me alone in here, in the beating heart of the monster.

$$\star \quad \star \quad \star$$

I look around at the walls, the control systems, the containers, ducting, lighting, atmospheric regulation, all of it. I want to get my fingers into it and start tearing the place apart. This is the enemy too. Everything that has broken me, murdered my crew, wrecked my ship, ruined my life, it all comes from here. But the only chance we have of surviving is if we make this ship work for us.

I can't get Sellis's face out of my mind. That expression of baffled hurt as he was pressed up against the DuraGlas as he died. I didn't trust him after what he did, but we were both working on it, trying to repair and rebuild the ties between us.

I see Jacobson again and taste bile. He died; they all died.

What I did to the Rocher clone did nothing to change any of that. It didn't change how I feel either.

I feel the ship moving. The acceleration is gradual, making me drift across the room to the far wall. They must have done what I said. I wonder if it worked.

"Ellisa?"

I look up. There's a shadowed figure standing by the hatch. For a moment, I think it's my father, magically transported all the way from Earth to hack at my conscience along with everything else, but then the figure moves into the light.

"Sam?"

"Yeah." Sam is in the room. He closes the hatch behind him and approaches me. "The objects are out and we're moving the ship away. Looks like we won."

"What did we win?" I blurt out the question before I've thought about the answer. Sam's always had that effect on me, dismantling my cool officer's reserve before I've realised what's going on. That's why we've always been close.

"We're alive."

"For how long?"

"I guess that depends on us."

I'm looking at him, searching for any kind of reaction, some way in which we've changed, but there isn't anything I can see. That heartens me. Same old Sam.

I push myself up and away from the wall. "We'll need to inventory this ship, get a sense of what we have, then try and plot a course to Phobos. I don't want to leave until we're sure there's no one left to rescue."

"I'll need your sidearm, Captain."

The words are spoken in the same gentle tone, but they send a shiver right through me. "Something you want to say, Sergeant?" I ask.

Sam shakes his head. "With Keiyho dead, I'm the ranking weapons specialist, Captain. We're not under immediate threat, so there's no need for the deployment of personal weapons." The words are delivered calmly and correctly. The procedures behind them are clear and accurate, but I can't help think…

No. We're not going to start mistrusting everyone.

I unclip the pistol, flip the safety switch and offer it to Sam handle first. "Here."

CHAPTER SIXTY

Johansson

"How are you feeling, Ensign?"

Slowly, I open my eyes. I'm in the medical room, strapped to one of the beds. Lieutenant Travers and Major Le Garre are nearby. It's the lieutenant who's speaking to me.

"Feeling better now," I say, forcing the words past a thick and lazy tongue. I push myself up onto my elbows. I remember what happened before. A lot of pain and intense concentration while I coached Travers through removing shrapnel from my left side.

Some of the painkillers haven't worn off and I still feel sluggish. I glance to my right. Chiu is lying in another bed, still unconscious. "How long have I been out?" I ask.

"Six hours, as you insisted," Travers replies.

"Anything happen to Chiu?"

"No."

"Then what have I missed?"

Travers looks at Le Garre. She shakes her head, and something I don't understand passes between them. He starts talking. "The external force subsided about thirty minutes after we pushed the anomalies out of the airlock. We've moved to three hundred kilometres from the remains of the *Khidr* and stopped. Arkov has rigged up some rudimentary controls in the bridge for testing, but...well...it's going to be a while until we can control the ship."

"What about the captain?" I ask.

Travers and Le Garre look at each other again. This time it's Le Garre who shares their thoughts. "That's what we need to talk to you about."

I'm trying to read their expressions and work out what's going on, but they aren't giving much away. Then I realise, aside from the captain, we're the three surviving officers from the *Khidr*.

"After they murdered Sellis, Captain Shann overpowered one of the Rocher clones that was in the engine room," Le Garre explains, her voice trembling slightly. "She...she lost it on him.... There's not much left that's recognisable."

"So, you're asking me to make a judgement on her fitness for command?"

"We need to agree what we're doing," Travers says. "There's no blame to this. Maybe she just needs a break? We've all been through the wringer."

"She won't see it that way," I say. "Where's the body?"

"Sealed in a vac bag and ready to be jettisoned," Le Garre says.

"You took pictures, though?"

"Yes, of course."

"Show me."

Travers hands me a portable screen, and I quickly scroll through a set of pictures showing the various mutilations Shann must have inflicted. "Rocher has a lot to answer for," I say.

"Determining the guilt or innocence of one clone for another's actions would be a complex judgement," Le Garre says. "It certainly wouldn't be something we'd do here. Once Rocher was immobilised, he should have been taken into custody."

"I'm not disagreeing," I reply. I pass her the screen. "I'm just saying I can understand her reaction. Doesn't mean I'm condoning it."

"Then we come back to making a decision," Le Garre says. She looks at Travers. "If we do this, the burden falls on you."

"I get that," Travers says. "But we have to be unanimous."

"Okay," I say. "In which case, I can make it easy for you both. I'm backing Captain Shann."

Le Garre's expression shifts. She's clearly not happy. "Ensign, I'm sure you're aware we wouldn't have brought our concerns to you if they weren't serious."

"Yes, Major, I understand that."

"Do you want to take a little more time before you make your decision?"

"No. I think I have a clear take on the situation."

There's an awkward silence between us. Eventually, Travers murmurs, "We should let you get a little more rest."

"If you don't mind, Lieutenant, I'll get up, check on Ensign Chiu and work on a terminal for a few hours."

"Okay, but don't tire yourself out."

After that, they both leave and I'm alone with my unconscious companion.

I touch the strap release and push off from the mattress very carefully, so as not to tear my stitches. I make my way toward Chiu. She looks peaceful, lying there with her eyes closed, an oxygen mask strapped to her nose and mouth. Her chest rises and falls regularly as her body continues doing the basic thing it has to do to keep her alive.

All the terrible things that have happened to her in the last few days haven't marked her face, but I know where her injuries are. I helped put her back together.

She lost a lot of blood. We gave her a transfusion. Like all Fleet ships, the *Gallowglass* is equipped with a full bank of universal donor blood. The fact that she's survived the last six hours without incident is good news.

She's wounded inside and out. We all are. Some of the damage will heal; other parts will leave scars and weaknesses. Mind and body, changed by what we've experienced.

But for now, she's alive and so am I.

I'm glad the captain ignored me when I urged her to execute Chiu. I'm glad she has a second chance. By the time this is over, we'll all need that kind of forgiveness in one way or another.

I'm thinking about the captain again. Strange how the situation is reversed from what it was. I've spent weeks and months on this ship desperate to get her approval for a promotion. Now, I don't care, but she needs my validation, even if she doesn't know it.

Le Garre and Travers have their doubts. Those doubts haven't gone away. I can only hope I made the right call.

I move across the room to the medical terminal. It's the same as the one in airlock control, but I haven't modified it with the rootkit yet. There wasn't time or need when I was helping Travers perform emergency surgery on me.

The system is still logged in. I start accessing the same communications programmes I was working on before, pulling down the latest sensor data on the remains of the *Khidr*. I task some of the *Gallowglass*'s remaining cameras to locate the generator room, where Duggins last went.

The system registers a whole heap of transmissions. The objects are still talking to each other. I hear the strange whistling sounds again, fainter this time. I wonder what it all means.

Once again, I activate a long-range channel and adjust the frequency to the range we used on the *Khidr*.

"Duggins, can you hear me?"

This time, the background sounds don't change, but there's a pop and a hiss on the channel.

A single word comes back. *"Johansson?"*

Did I hear that? *Did I really hear that?*

CHAPTER SIXTY-ONE

Shann

It's been seven hours since I killed Rocher and we took over the ship.

The seven of us left alive and functional have been working and resting where we can. Any last vestige of adrenaline or endorphin high has worn off, leaving us all to try to make sense of what happened and make sense of ourselves.

Chiu remains in a coma, but she's still alive.

I've tried to sleep, but I can't. I keep seeing Sellis dying with his face pressed up against the glass, or Jacobson in agony, or the messy remains of the clone I murdered. The images come back whenever they want, bringing with them a wave of paralysing guilt. It's like a spasm or a fit. When it happens, all I want to do is curl up into a ball and hide from myself.

I'm the captain. I can't do that.

An exploration of the ship gave us a better idea of the layout than just reading the schematic. There are three bunk rooms with two beds in each. Little need for privacy on a ship of clones, I guess. At this stage, two to a room, with Chiu still in medical, is a good idea. It means no one is left alone for too long to start hating themselves for what they've done, or what they've been forced to do.

Of course, that doesn't stop me wanting to be alone, to shut everyone else out and wallow in my self-loathing. My training tells me there are no answers in doing that, but it doesn't stop the urge.

I'm lying on the top bunk now, staring at the ceiling as I listen to the comms chatter between Arkov, Le Garre and Travers. They are working on rebuilding the bridge controls, pretty much from scratch. There's an awkward tension behind their conversation. People are hiding their pain, withdrawing, trying to deal with it, understand it, rationalise it. There's a part in all of us that doesn't want to share because everyone we might share with has their own problems.

Fuck this…

I'm up and moving off the bed to the hatch. I'm out into the corridor and making my way toward the bridge. The corridors are unfamiliar and my shoulder *hurts*. Turns out I dislocated it and kept going, wrecking a lot of the socket and tendons. The medical computer analysed and reset everything, but the healing will take time, and I might never regain full mobility.

If I push too hard, it'll break down again. I need to go easy and not let my fitful temper get the better of me.

Easier said than done when you're angry at the world.

I reach the damaged doorway and make my way through. They've restored lighting by rigging some new connections to the power conduit in the corridor. I see Vasili Arkov floating over an open floor panel, surrounded by cables. Sam Chase is on the other side of the bridge, sitting in one of the crew chairs. They've cleared out all the bodies, but there are still marks on the walls and a faint smell in the air. Both men are absorbed in their work. They haven't noticed me.

I take a moment to enjoy that, watching people I've come to feel bonded to work. When I was a newly promoted captain, I'd do that sometimes, just watch my crew at their jobs, taking a little pride in the way what I'd asked for got done. Now there's a different reason. Both Sam and Vasili are quietly keeping busy, getting on with what needs to be done. There's a way to healing in that, I guess, if you can find it. Sometimes, throwing yourself into some mundane tasks is just a distraction, but there's an honest lift you can get from fixing something, building something or just seeing the difference you made.

It's a moment I have to break. I almost feel guilty, just for that.

"Gentlemen," I say quietly, pitching my voice loud enough to carry. "We need to get everyone together."

Arkov turns toward me. For a moment, Sam doesn't. But then the chair swivels around. "You want everyone in here, Captain?" he asks.

"Yeah, I think so. We should make a start here. That's where we'll begin."

Sam looks at me. I don't think he quite knows what I mean, but he will in a bit, along with all of them.

I pick a chair and sit in it, letting Arkov do the comms stuff, calling the rest of the crew. One by one they file in. Travers is first, then Le Garre, and finally Johansson. I guess they were probably lying in their bunks like me, staring at the wall rather than sleeping. I can't fix that right away.

No one talks. I let them settle into comfortable spots, waiting until they're all looking in my direction.

"Okay, we're here. We've all been through worse than anyone has a right to expect, but we're alive and we're here. People died. People who we care...who didn't deserve..." I have to stop and swallow. My voice is shaking. I grip the arms of the chair. "We're here. We need to work out what happens next."

There's silence. I know issues lie under the surface. Again, I can see the bloodied mess of the Rocher clone and hear Le Garre shouting at me to let go. The haunted expression on her face from back then isn't there now, but it isn't far away. If I start into that, start into talking about my mistakes, our mistakes, all of it, we'll fall apart. This is where I have to be captain and rely on the rank to get us through.

I remember captains like that, who I suffered under. They were shadows, not really part of the crew, but existing above it, making no effort to prove themselves to their people. I swore when I got my own command, I wouldn't be that type.

Right now, though, I have to be.

"I need information. Tell me where we're at."

Le Garre glances at Travers, who nods. Then she turns to me. "Captain, we're three hundred kilometres from the remains of the *Khidr* and the battle. We executed a burn and completed braking to bring us into a static position at distance. There's no sign of the external force that was pulling us in. We have power, heat, air and food. For now, we're out of immediate danger."

"Stores will last about six weeks," Sam adds. "If we can repair the engines, we might just make Phobos Station by then, but it'll be tight."

"What's our progress on that?" I ask.

"It's been difficult," Arkov says. "The *Gallowglass* took a fair amount of damage. All the systems that were in this room are burned out. This ship doesn't have replacements, so we're trying to identify noncritical systems and completely rebuild the controls with whatever wiring we can rip out and repurpose." He shrugs and looks down at the floor. "If Sellis were alive, he'd be better at this," he adds in a low voice.

I find myself nodding in sympathy. I get the problem. The engine room controls worked to get us away from the *Khidr*, but that was moving in a straight line. The kind of careful course plotting and monitoring we need just isn't possible.

"We do have the cryogenic pods," Travers says. "They weren't built for us, but they should work. If we set a course, we can cold sleep a few or all of us so we don't have to use up all of our supplies."

"That's how this ship was designed to work," Arkov says. "Half the clone crew would sleep while the other half stayed awake."

I look around at the group and find myself facing Johansson. "What about medical?" I ask.

She flinches, as if being asked is like being slapped, but then she composes herself. "Six crew, all injured, but capable of light duties, Captain," she reports. "I've compiled individual assessments on everyone, with recommendations for diet and workload over the next few weeks. We need to be careful we don't push it. Right now, we're all on the edge."

"What about Chiu?"

"No change as yet. She's suffered head trauma and oxygen deprivation, but I'm hopeful she'll wake up. The computer is monitoring her, and if the situation changes, we'll know. A cryo pod remains an option if things get worse."

"Okay. What about our communications?"

"The system is damaged, but working," Johansson explains. "They have some advanced masking equipment, but once you deactivate that, it's pretty much the same as ours was. With the data brought over from the *Khidr*, we could send messages to Phobos or farther that should be accepted as authorised Fleet transmissions. I've also tested several of the receivers in the last hour. That's what led me back to something else."

"What's that?"

"Somehow, the objects we let go from this ship and the one left on the *Khidr* are talking to each other, and I think, in the middle of all that debris, Duggins is still alive."

The room goes quiet. We're all struggling to process Johansson's conclusion. The first thing I want to do is laugh or dismiss what she's saying, not because I don't want to believe her but because there's nothing I can draw on to rationalise this. We're all scientists and military people. We don't base any conclusions on magic, miracles or faith.

"Could you be wrong?" I ask.

Johansson nods. "Yes, absolutely, but I don't think I am."

"If he's still out there…" Sam says. I glare at him and he falls silent, but we all know the rest of the sentence – *we have to help him.*

I look around the group again. They want to act on what they've learned, to start working on the ship so we can head back and rescue Duggins. The idea makes sense on several levels. Leaving all the emotions aside, Duggins was the *Khidr*'s chief engineer. If anyone could repair this ship, it would be him.

"We have to make decisions with all the information available," Le Garre says.

"Yes, we do," I agree. "Which is why I need to tell you all something."

There's no going back now. They're all looking at me. Maybe I could have gotten through this briefing without mentioning anything, but that wouldn't be me. I can't lead without my crew's trust. When they saw what I did to Rocher, I put that in jeopardy. They need the information.

They need to know why.

I start slowly. "Travers, you remember the priority message we got from the relay point? The one you forwarded to me that had the same date stamp as the archive?"

Travers takes a moment to think about this, but then nods slowly. "Yes, I remember."

"We never discussed the message contents, Bill." I focus on him, trying to read any change of expression at my use of his first name, but there's no tell, just that same look of hurt exhaustion. "It was a priority message with orders from Admiral Langsley." My voice catches and almost fails me, but I swallow and continue. "The admiral ordered us to stand down and ignore the distress call from the *Hercules*. They didn't want us anywhere near all this."

"But we didn't receive that message until—"

"It doesn't matter. I didn't tell you, we didn't turn around and we didn't surrender to Rocher." I turn to Le Garre and Arkov. "I think that's the alternative instructions the clone was talking about in the engine room. I take full responsibility and I'll answer for it, if we get home."

Le Garre's eyes narrow as she stares at me. "I think you're reading too much into it. Whatever Admiral Langsley said, he can't have known we'd end up in this situation."

She's right. Langsley didn't mention the *Gallowglass*, but I remember the look on Rocher's face — his knowing expression. "Maybe you're right," I say. "But... I can't see it... Everything's just too much... People have died..."

They are all looking at me differently. Instead of the togetherness and purpose they found in rescuing Duggins, they're divided now, all struggling to work their way through what I've told them. The words won't come anymore. I'm crying and trying to blink away tears, but that doesn't work in zero gravity. I wipe them away with the back of my hand, letting the little tendrils of water cling to my wrist.

I find myself staring at Sam. He's the person I've known longest, the person who I've had the strongest connection with since I left Earth. It's hard to look at him, but I need to so he can see I'm not hiding anything.

He holds my gaze. Then he nods and tries to smile, but he can't. "Ellie, is this why you did that to Rocher?"

"I don't know," I sob. "I didn't think I was capable…"

A hand touches my shoulder. It's Le Garre. She's moved around the room, positioned herself beside me. "Captain Shann, under article four of the Fleet commissionary code, I need to inform you that we, the senior officers of your crew, are relieving you of your command."

The words are spoken softly, with quiet, reverent authority. I look at her and nod. "I understand."

★   ★   ★

An hour later, I'm back in the room, on the bunk, staring at the ceiling once more, counting the screws, noting the tiny abrasions along the edges of each metal panel, the patchy discolouration of the steel handrail within arm's reach. It's something to do as a distraction, I guess.

But it doesn't really work.

I feel raw, unburdened in a strange way, but all control is gone. Le Garre had to do what she did. I'd have done the same in her position. By confessing, I've hurt them, wounded them by revealing Langsley's orders.

Who am I now? So much of how I've defined myself has been through my rank and my responsibility. My journey to commanding the *Khidr* felt like the culmination of everything in my life. In being a captain, I have a purpose, an identity that separates me from the girl who grew up needing help to get out of bed.

Now who am I? Am I back to that place, where I need help?

Would that be so wrong?

I'm thinking about Mom and those last messages before she died and how she talked about me growing up – *You didn't need our pity*, she said.

When she told me that, I always felt proud, like I'd been validated as an equal. But maybe now, that's exactly what I need. What we all need. A little pity, a little sympathy and compassion spread around to soften the hard, military lines of our lives.

I had to tell them about the message from Langsley. Keeping it secret was eating me up and affecting my judgement. I see that now. Le Garre's decision to lock me up in here is so they have the time to discuss it.

That'll be what they're discussing, right now.

I think about each of them. Arkov, who we had to question after Drake's murder. Johansson, who'd been desperately seeking my approval only to find herself by disobeying my orders. Le Garre, the major, with more experience, rank and expertise than me, but who remains under my command. Travers, my number two, who doesn't want to be a number one, and Sam, my best friend out here. I can still see how he looked at me – that little nod.

And Chiu, the traitor who came back. There must have been a reason for that, a reason she regretted her choices from before.

So many others are dead. Am I to blame? *No.* Do I blame myself? *Yes.*

They were my crew. These survivors are my crew. Am I still their captain?

We're broken people on a broken ship. All I can hope is that with time, we can repair the latter and through doing so heal ourselves.

FLAME TREE PRESS
FICTION WITHOUT FRONTIERS
Award-Winning Authors & Original Voices

Flame Tree Press is the trade fiction imprint of Flame Tree Publishing, focusing on excellent writing in horror and the supernatural, crime and mystery, science fiction and fantasy. Our aim is to explore beyond the boundaries of the everyday, with tales from both award-winning authors and original voices.

•

•

Join our mailing list for free short stories, new release details, news about our authors and special promotions:

flametreepress.com